The Wolf A[

Terry Cloutier

Book 4 in the
THE WOLF OF CORWICK CASTLE
SERIES

Copyright © 2021 TERRY CLOUTIER

All rights reserved. No part of this book may be reproduced, in whole or in part, without prior written permission from the copyright holder.

For my father—the original Richard Sharpe

Character List by Order of Appearance

Lord Hadrack: The Lord of Corwick Castle

Lillia: Hadrack's granddaughter

Jebido: Hadrack's friend

Baine: Hadrack's friend

Sim: Soldier

Tyris: Archer

Son Jona: Priest

Daughter Freda: Priestess

Wiflem: Captain of the guards

Niko: Soldier

Haspeth: Soldier

Rin: Leper boy

Grindin: One of the nine

Berwin: Soldier

Nedo: Amenti warrior

Putt: Soldier

Ubeth: Gatekeeper

Daughter Tessa: Priestess

Lucenda: Daughter-In-Waiting

Parcival: Master Huntsman

Shana: Lady of Calban. Hadrack's wife.

Hesther: Court lady

Hamber: Court lady

Finol: Steward of Corwick

Margot: Former whore from Hillsfort

Osbeth: Son of Parcival

Stemper: Soldier

Saldor: Cimbrati warrior

Hanley: Finol's assistant

Gerdy: Master bowyer

Braham: Soldier

Jin: Daughter-In-Waiting

Daughter Gernet: Priestess

Son Oriell: First Son

Tyden: King of Ganderland

Bona: Soldier

Lord Porten Welis: Gander lord

Fitzery Welis: Son of Porten

Lord Falway: Gander lord

Lorgen Three-Fingers: Chieftain of the Amenti

Lord Cambil: Gander lord

Lord Vestry: Gander lord

Dack: Amenti warrior

Gafin: Amenti warrior

Kacy: Half-wit cook's assistant

Einhard: Pith. Sword of the Queen

Yaar the Windy: Blood Guard

Umar the Bleak: Blood Guard

Manek the Quiet: Blood Guard

Dace the Fearless: Blood Guard

Trula: Weaver

Malo: House Agent

Culbert: Son of a Gander lord

Lord Stegar: Gander lord

Brock: Son of Lord Stegar

Rorian: Scholar

Malakar: Pith Pathfinder

Lord Hamit: Gander lord

Fignam Ree: Commander of the king's army

Pax: Soldier

Guthris: House Agent

Pernissy Raybold: Former Lord of Corwick

Quill: Carpenter

Lord Boudin: Cardian lord

Haverty: Apothecary

Luper Nash: One of the nine

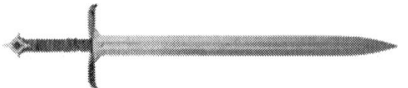

Prologue

"How much longer?" I demanded. I lay in my bed, supported by three feathered pillows propped up around me that smelled strongly of harsh soap mixed with sweat. My granddaughter, Lillia, sat at my writing desk, where she had been every day for the past week, going over my notes.

"I'm almost finished," Lillia said, not bothering to look up from the parchment in front of her.

"You told me that an hour ago," I grumbled.

I stared out the window to my left as wet snow and sleet smacked against the windowpane before melting and sliding down the narrow, glazed glasswork in long rivulets. The cold wind coming from the north whistled and shrieked in frustration as it broke against the twelve-foot thick limestone walls of the castle, searching for a way inside. I shivered, certain that I could feel the strengthening gale's icy clutches on me as I hunkered down beneath the bedclothes that covered my sparse body. Winter had come early to Corwick this year, and if this day were any indication, it would prove to be a long and hard one.

I shifted my weight beneath the coverings, which immediately brought on a series of wracking coughs that rolled up from my chest one after another like hammer blows. Each cough seemed worse than the one before, threatening to snap my frail ribs in half. I closed my eyes and waited it out, knowing that there was little point in trying to resist what was happening. Attacks like this one had occurred many times before, usually without warning. I knew one of these times it would be the end of me. Finally, the fit subsided, and I sucked in air as I dabbed weakly at the bright red blood around my lips with a handkerchief. I stared with dismay at the bloody cloth. Would I live to see another spring? You had better, I told myself, angry now as I let the handkerchief fall to the bedclothes. There was still too much left unwritten for me to die.

I turned back to Lillia, feeling spent by the coughing but also irritated by her silence. "You read too slow, child," I grunted, beginning to regret choosing her. I should have given the task ahead to Frankin, whose reading and writing skills were slightly better than Lillia's. The boy's attention span was another matter, though, so in the end, I had settled on my granddaughter. "I'm not getting any younger over here, you know," I mumbled as an afterthought.

Lillia looked over at me and she sighed in frustration. "Maybe if you would stop interrupting me all the time, my lord, I'd be able to read faster."

I glared at the girl, and she stared right back at me, clearly uncowed by my look. Few, if any, would talk to me so, but I had a soft spot for Lillia, which she knew well and used to her advantage. I could see a familiar stubborn fire burning in Lillia's blue eyes, and I felt my anger soften. It was hard for me to stay mad at her for very long. It had been the same with both her mother and her grandmother as well.

Lillia broke eye contact and looked down at the desk, the moment over as she enjoyed her victory. She read for a few more minutes while I lay in impotent silence watching her, then she gasped in surprise. "I didn't know about this, my lord," she said. I thought I could detect a note of disapproval in her voice, but perhaps it had just been an old man's faulty hearing.

"Didn't know about what?" I asked, confident that I knew what was coming next as I leaned my head on one of the pillows.

"About what happened between you and Sabina in Waldin's cave."

I shrugged. "That's because I never told anyone," I said. "Not even your grandmother. You are the first to learn of it."

I looked down at my hands where they lay clutched together in my lap. My fingers were hooked together like claws, thin and crooked, with the skin stretched tightly like a drum, all veined and spotted. I hated having the hands of an old man, thinking they looked more like something you would find on a withered corpse instead of a living, breathing person. Growing old is nothing but an affliction like any other disease, I thought, cursing the gods for what they had done to me. Why bless a man with youth, strength, and vitality, then cruelly take it away year after year until there is nothing left but a husk waiting to die? It was a question that I had been asking more and more recently, though none of the gods ever bothered to explain it to me. I thrust the thought aside and looked up at the ceiling so that I wouldn't have to acknowledge my hands and what they meant.

"So, now that you understand better, what do you think?" I finally asked as I focused back on my granddaughter. "Am I the heartless, murdering bastard that Casia accused me of being?"

"Absolutely not, my lord," Lillia said immediately. Her eyes flashed with emotion. "Sabina deserved what happened. She took advantage of you when you were at your weakest. I have no sympathy for her or any of her family either after what she did to you."

I nodded, surprised at the relief I felt at those words as I looked out the window again. My granddaughter's opinion meant a lot to me, perhaps because of how much she resembled my long-dead wife, Shana. Besides, there were many more revelations still to come, and I needed to know Lillia's feelings before we got to them. This was an excellent first step.

The snow was coming down stronger now, I saw, coating the glass like a blanket as it slapped heartily against the windowpane. I stared at the growing storm with distaste, reminded of the Pilgrimage and the treacherous ascent up Mount Halas during the Walk. I have hated snow ever since that horrible climb. I turned back to Lillia. "So, are you saying that you don't think Casia's grievance against me was valid?" I asked. "That her vow of vengeance was somehow less important than mine was, despite what I did to her family?"

"I don't know about any of that," Lillia said, looking uncertain for the first time. She gestured toward the parchment on the desk, her expression hardening. "But after what Sabina did in that cave, and who sired her, what else could you have done?"

"I have wondered that very thing many times," I admitted, as I thought about the day that I'd killed Sabina's father and brother. Their deaths had been bloody and savage, and I can still see the look of horror on Sabina's face as I stood over the bodies of her loved ones. I sighed. "She was just a child then, Lillia," I said. "Young, headstrong and foolish. She made a mistake in Waldin's cave but, even so, she was a good person at heart despite that mistake."

"Maybe," Lillia said, looking unconvinced. She folded her arms across her chest. "But it doesn't change the fact that she was tainted from birth, my lord. The gods marked her for a reason, and that reason was you."

"You can't be certain of that," I grunted in annoyance. I had thought much the same thing years ago, of course, but age and guilt had tempered my thinking somewhat since then. "You weren't even a gleam in your father's eyes when this all happened. What do you know of such things?"

Lillia smiled condescendingly. "I'm a woman, my lord. We see things that most men miss."

"Is that so?" I huffed. "So, now I'm being lectured to by a child, is that it?"

Lillia shrugged. "You asked for my opinion, my lord. Would you prefer that I just nod my head like a commoner and agree with whatever you say?" I hesitated, fidgeting in the bed as my granddaughter stared at me in challenge. "Well?" Lillia prompted, her eyes lighting up in warning.

"I'm thinking," I replied, sounding childish even to my ears. Lillia stood abruptly and started to leave. I waved her back impatiently, motioning for her to sit down again. "Enough of that now. I've half a mind to beat some respect into you."

"You have my respect and love, my lord," Lillia said, still bristling as she settled back into her chair. "You always have. But I will not still my tongue, even for you." She lifted her chin, and I was struck once again by her uncanny resemblance to Shana. "My mother taught me that, which is something, I believe, that you taught her."

I chuckled, knowing that she was right as my own anger deflated. "So I did," I said in a more conciliatory tone. "Who knew then that those lessons would someday come back to nip me in the ass?" I motioned for her to continue. "I spoke out of turn, and you have my apology. Now say your words, child, and let's be done with it."

Lillia took a deep breath, composing her thoughts. "All I was going to say, my lord, is that I believe Sabina was destined to betray you no matter what, just as she was destined to lead you to her father and brother. So, whether she was a good person or not is meaningless in that context, as I believe she was helpless to change her fate regardless of her disposition."

I pursed my lips, impressed by the maturity of thought that my granddaughter was displaying. She was old enough to be married now, yet I'd been reluctant to arrange a suitable union for her. I knew I would have to do it soon, but not until she had finished the task I required of her. "So," I said. "What you are telling me is that you think Sabina brought everything that happened down upon herself. That the gods marked her from birth, and that because of this, she had no free will to choose her own path."

"Exactly," Lillia agreed. "That is what I believe."

"You do realize that she wasn't aware of the crimes her father and brother committed in Corwick?"

"Of course I do, my lord," Lillia replied. "But that does not excuse her bloodline of responsibility for those crimes."

I shook my head at the set look on my granddaughter's face. Her mind was made up, just as mine had been at the time it had all occurred. I sighed and gestured to my writing. "Enough talk for now. I'm tired. Finish your reading, and then we will speak again." I closed my eyes. "There is still much more that you do not know," I said drowsily.

I must have slept then, for it was dark outside when I felt a hand gently shaking me.

"My lord," I heard Lillia say as she leaned over me. "Are you awake?"

"I am now," I grunted in irritation as I fought to sit up straighter. A lantern flickered on the table beside me, and long flames crackled in the fireplace across the room, working to ward off the storm's chill. Lillia helped me to sit up, fussing with the pillows. "I have to piss," I said reluctantly, not meeting her eyes.

Perhaps the hardest thing about growing old, apart from the aches and pains, is the loss of dignity that infirmity brings with it. Lillia seemed unfazed by my request, however, as this was not the first time that she had helped me. She stooped and removed a chamber pot from beneath the bed, then began to roll down the bedclothes.

I stopped her. "I can manage," I said, determined to do it on my own.

My granddaughter frowned but said nothing, watching as I fought the shake in my hands and grasped the heavy quilt that lay over me. The trembling and frequent numbness had begun two days after Frankin had killed Casia, and they hadn't stopped since. I was convinced now that they never would. I folded the coverings down past my waist, then used my feet to push them the rest of the way, revealing my withered body dressed in a nightshirt that failed to hide my purple-veined legs and misshapen left foot. Lillia placed the chamber pot between my legs, and I fumbled with it, trying to draw the brass container closer. I cursed as my unfeeling fingers slipped off the polished surface.

"My lord," Lillia said, hovering over me as she bit her bottom lip in indecision. "Let me help you."

"Just wait," I grunted in determination.

I managed to grasp the hem of my nightshirt with two fingers and drew it up, feeling sweat break out on my forehead as I concentrated on keeping my grip on the cloth. I edged the chamber pot closer with the back of my other hand, then relieved myself as Lillia looked politely away.

"There," I said when I was done, proud of myself as I let my nightshirt cover my nakedness. Lillia put the chamber pot back under the bed, and then she sat down beside me. "Did you finish your reading?" I asked her.

Lillia nodded. "I did, my lord."

"Your thoughts?"

Lillia sighed. "I don't know where to begin. It's all a little overwhelming. I'd heard the bards' tales and songs about you, of course, but I had no concept of the actual hardships you endured. The songs and stories all made it sound so easy for you, almost effortless."

I laughed at that, genuinely amused. "That misconception is why I am writing about my time in this world. Most of those stories are just lies and half-truths, anyway. I want the younger generations coming after me, like you and Frankin, to understand and appreciate how this family rose to prominence. But to do that, I'm going to need help if I hope to complete the task before I die."

"I don't understand, my lord," Lillia said.

"My hands are almost useless now," I grunted, aware of the bitterness in my voice. "Much like the rest of me, I suppose. Now that you have read what I've written so far, I want you to continue where I left off."

Lillia blinked in surprise. "Me, my lord?"

"Yes," I said. "I may not be able to hold a quill and put words to paper anymore, but my mind and mouth work just fine." I pointed a shaking finger at my granddaughter. "You are hereby tasked with spending every waking hour here with me, chronicling the rest of my life story until either I die, or it is finished."

"But, that could take months, my lord," Lillia said, looking flustered. "You're not even twenty-one years old at the end of the last manuscript."

"I know," I agreed. "I imagine you will be here all winter or longer, so you had best get comfortable."

"But, I don't know what to do, my lord. I've never done anything like this before."

"All you have to do for now is sit beside me and listen," I said. "Listen to my words and remember them. You can write those words down when I sleep."

"And when do I get to sleep, my lord?" Lillia asked, the familiar stubborn flash of resistance rising in her eyes.

I grinned at her. "You're young, child. What need you of sleep?" I pushed myself back firmly into my pillows, eager to get on with the tale. I fixated on the wooden beams above me as I let my thoughts drift back to another time—a time when I was still young and full of life.

"We'll begin with that bastard Grindin," I finally said, my voice twisting with distaste as I thought about the man.

"Not with the Piths?" Lillia asked, sounding disappointed.

I glanced at her. "Not yet," I said, shaking my head. "Patience, child." The wood in the fire across the room popped as I returned my gaze to the ceiling, seeing the wooden beams, yet not seeing them at the same time. "First, I must tell you of Grindin. Einhard, the Piths, and the war that changed everything, all begin with him."

Then I began to talk.

1: Grindin Tasker

I was on my way to kill a man—a man who had needed killing for more than thirteen years. His name was Grindin Tasker, one of the two remaining members of the nine that had yet to meet my justice. My memory of Grindin was vague—just a youthful face and dirty blond hair curling out from his coif—that was all. But it was enough for me, and I knew that I would recognize the bastard the moment that I laid eyes on him.

My men and I had just passed through a dense woodland, and we stopped on the crest of a rocky hill, looking down at a modest hamlet that lay nestled along a sluggish, meandering river below us. The houses were all small and cramped, built from dried river mud and straw, with thatched roofs made of water rushes and heather. Tendrils of white smoke rose from a circular hole in the roof of each house. A watermill stood on the river's near bank, the great wheel turning lazily with the meager tide. The land west of the river ran true and flat, with freshly-tilled fields and broad grazing meadows as far as I could see. A timber and stone manor house overlooked the village to the north, built on a mound of earth more than forty feet high.

We were in the fiefdom of Lord Wakerton, though the lord's castle lay more than ten miles to the east of this tiny hamlet and he rarely came here. I knew I should have ridden to him first to announce myself and my intent, but I had been too impatient to find Grindin to adhere to proper courtesy. I would rectify that after the deed I'd come here to do was done, I promised myself. A squat Holy House with a stone foundation and wooden frame sat at the far end of the street near the manor house's base. I could see a priest talking outside the Holy House's walls, his robed arms flailing about him as he preached to a group of children squatting at his feet in the dusty street.

"Are you sure about this?" Jebido asked from my left. He sat atop a white gelding with a narrow black ring around one eye, giving the beast an odd, comical look. My friend hocked and then spat, the green glob splattering wetly against a tree trunk.

"I'm sure," I grunted. "We didn't ride all this way to turn back now."

"I still think it's a trap," Baine said from my right, looking calm and unaffected by the notion. Nothing seemed to bother Baine these days. He was dressed in his usual black leather armor and rode a feisty brown mare that chose that moment to nip at Angry's neck. The big black shook his head in irritation and stamped one front hoof, but surprised me by not retaliating. I suspected the great stallion's unusual restraint had more to do with his obvious affection for Baine's pretty mare, rather than a softening disposition.

I gestured down toward the hamlet. "Does this place look dangerous to either of you?"

"No," Jebido grunted reluctantly. "But that doesn't mean it isn't."

"It's a trap," Baine repeated firmly. "Mark my words."

I shook my head stubbornly. "I don't think so."

"Then explain something to me, Hadrack," Jebido said in exasperation. "Why would Grindin send you that letter if it's not a trap? Do you really think the man has seen the error of his ways after so long?"

Jebido was referring to a letter that had arrived in Corwick last week. The author claimed to be Grindin, who, he'd explained, had spent the eight months since King Tyden's coronation in hiding from me. Grindin stated that he was tired of running and was ready to pay for the crimes he committed at Corwick. I admit I had been dubious, as had most everyone else I had shown it to, but even so, if there was any chance that it really was from Grindin, then I had no choice but to investigate.

"Anything is possible," I replied as I studied the hamlet.

Jebido snorted. "You are being foolish, Hadrack. That bastard knew you would never give up looking for him. Now that you have money and power, not to mention the good graces of the king himself, he realized it was only a matter of time before you found him."

"So, you think Grindin drew me here in hopes of killing me, is that it?" I asked, sounding a little more condescending than I had intended. "The man is an imbecile."

As far as I could determine these past months, Grindin had lived a wholly unremarkable life after the slaughter at Corwick. The man had soldiered for several different lords over the years and had fought for the North in the Pair War but had left far from positive impressions on all those we'd located who'd known him. With his disappearance after King Tyden's coronation, along with Luper Nash, the other remaining member of the nine, my search for them both had seemed destined to fail. That is, until the letter arrived.

"Just because the man is stupid doesn't mean he's not dangerous," Jebido warned.

I turned at the sound of hooves behind me as Sim and Tyris appeared through the trees. "I guess we are about to find out just how stupid and dangerous Grindin is," I said. I was fairly confident that there was little to fear from this place, but caution makes men live longer, so I'd sent my men to scout the area thoroughly just in case.

Sim was in the lead, and he nodded to me as he halted his horse, pausing to remove his hat to wipe at his brow. The former outlaw was dressed in mail beneath a white surcoat that bore my snarling wolf emblem on the front. But, unlike the rest of my men, Sim refused to wear anything on his head other than a black woolen hat that he had taken from a wealthy merchant during the Pair War. A ridiculous, purple-dyed feather stuck out from the side of the cap, and Sim stroked it absently. "There's no one about, my lord," he said firmly.

"You're sure?" Jebido demanded, sounding combative. "You scoured the entire woods?"

"Enough to know that there's no ambush lying in wait for us," Tyris confirmed.

"What about Wiflem?" I asked as I studied the rolling hills and sprawling trees to the east of the hamlet. Wiflem had been in charge of the men who had captured me and taken me to Gandertown months ago, and the soldier and I had developed a friendly rapport on the journey to the city. After King Tyden had made me the Lord of Corwick, I invited the older man to come and join my service. Wiflem had eagerly accepted, bringing three strapping young sons and a wife heavy with what he assured me was another son along with him. I had quickly made the experienced soldier captain of my castle guards, an arrangement that so far had worked out quite well for the both of us.

"There's been no sign of him, my lord," Sim answered, unable to hide the animosity in his voice.

Sim was usually a pleasant fellow, simple-minded at times, but genuinely likable. Except when Wiflem's name was mentioned. The big man had coveted the position of captain, and he had been quite distraught when I had given it to Wiflem instead. I pretended not to notice Sim's sullen words as I glanced up at the sun. It was well past midday, and if we waited much longer, we would lose the light. I watched as several boys herded ten or so sheep down to the riverbank north of the hamlet, where a shallow ford allowed them to cross the calm waters. The boys and sheep made it safely to the far bank, and I could hear the herders cussing as they used willow branches to force the animals toward the grazing meadows. Should I wait to hear from Wiflem, or just go down there now and be done with it?

"I know that look on your face," Jebido said, breaking into my thoughts. "You're thinking about doing something stupid, aren't you?"

I grinned. "If you already know what I'm thinking, then why ask?"

Jebido frowned. "We agreed to wait until we heard back from Wiflem. There could be fifty men in those hills over there."

I shifted my father's axe on my back impatiently, then I shrugged, making up my mind. "I've never been all that fond of waiting," I said. "Besides, my gut tells me there's no danger here."

Jebido sighed in frustration. "Then at least let Baine and me go with you."

I shook my head. "I'm going to do this my way, Jebido. If something goes wrong, you'll know soon enough and can be down there in no time to save my ass."

"Maybe that giant, stubborn ass of yours isn't worth saving this time," Jebido grumbled.

I laughed. "Maybe not," I said as I guided Angry forward. "We'll just have to wait and see."

I followed the well-traveled trail from the forest to the hill's base, where a narrow road curved toward the hamlet. A sign pounded into the ground beside the road announced in faded white paint that I had arrived in Thidswitch. Three boys no older than five or six came running in excitement when they saw me, followed closely by a pack of barking dogs. The dogs circled Angry as I entered the hamlet, nipping at his heels, while the boys held back, their initial enthusiasm at my arrival waning as they took in my armor and shield. The war had ended months ago, yet the fear brought on by an unknown armed man appearing without warning remained.

"You, boy," I said gruffly, speaking to the tallest and brightest looking of the three. The boy was dressed in a shabby brown tunic, with grey stockings and scuffed leather shoes. "I'm looking for a man named Grindin. Point the way."

"I don't know that name, lord," the boy said uncertainly.

I sighed, dismounting and kicking away one of the curs harassing Angry as I looked around the hamlet. Grindin's letter had said he lived in Thidswitch, so I knew I had the right place.

"May I be of assistance?"

I turned. The priest was walking toward me, followed by a stream of curious children.

"I'm looking for a man named Grindin," I told the Son as he paused five paces from me. The priest was young and thin, with sparse brown hair, a long nose, and sly, calculating eyes. I disliked him immediately.

"I see," the Son said thoughtfully. A girl of about four came to stand beside him, clutching at the skirt of the priest's robes as she stared up at me in fascination. The Son put his arm about the child's shoulders and drew her closer, smiling reassuringly down at her before turning back to me. "May I enquire as to what your business with this person might be?"

"That's between him and me," I growled.

A woman appeared from one of the houses, calling urgently to the little girl hugging the priest. The child looked up at the Son and he nodded, tapping the girl lightly on the backside before she ran to join her mother. "My name is Son Jona," the priest said to me, bowing as he introduced himself.

"Do you know the man or not, Son?" I asked.

"I might know who you speak of, but it is something of a delicate matter," Son Jona acknowledged. "May I ask who you are?"

"Lord Hadrack of Corwick," I grunted. "And I've ridden a long way. I'm in no mood for games." A yelp sounded behind me and I turned. A spotted bitch with a missing ear had come too close to Angry, and the big black had caught her on the haunches with a hoof. The injured dog limped away, whining, while the rest of the pack retreated a respectful distance.

"I have heard of you, of course, lord," the priest said. I noticed his voice had changed from wary politeness to frosty disapproval. I knew I wasn't a popular figure among the Sons right now, as they blamed me directly for their lowered station in life. It was a fact I lost little sleep over.

"Where is he?" I demanded.

The priest turned and shooed away the rest of the children, waiting until they were gone before answering. "The man you think of as Grindin is gone, lord."

I frowned. "Gone where?" I growled.

Son Jona spread his arms and smiled. "He has chosen to embrace the way of The Father, lord. His soul, along with his hair, has been shorn, and a new man has risen from the ashes."

"Are you telling me the bastard has taken the vows?" I said in disbelief. I cursed softly. It appeared that Grindin wasn't as stupid as I had thought.

The priest clasped his hands together in front of him, looking quite pleased. "Indeed, lord."

"Isn't he too old for that?" I asked suspiciously.

Son Jona shrugged. "No man is too old to embrace The Father, lord." He looked me up and down, then sniffed. "Or too wicked, I suppose."

I cursed again and glanced at the hill where my men waited. If Son Jona spoke the truth, then Grindin had taken the vows to become a Son-In-Waiting, which meant if I killed him, I would be ostracized from the House and my soul would burn for eternity. The bastard hadn't drawn me here to seek penance for his crimes, I now understood. He had brought me here to thumb his nose at me. It was maddening beyond belief.

"Jona, what goes on here?"

A Daughter was coming down the street with her yellow robes hitched up past her ankles as she hurried toward us. A thin, shy-looking Daughter-In-Waiting trailed behind the priestess, the child's face twisted with anxiety.

Son Jona's demeanor changed, a look of loathing crossing his features for just a moment before he turned, a fixed smile on his face. "Daughter Freda, I'm glad you have come." The priest indicated me. "This is Lord Hadrack, the famous Wolf of Corwick."

The Daughter stepped past the Son, brushing him aside dismissively as she stopped two paces in front of me. I didn't fail to notice the priest's face darken at the insult.

"I have heard much about you, lord," Daughter Freda said. She was still youthful-looking, though I guessed she had to be at least thirty or more. Her face was oval and pleasant, with a pert nose and an elegant mouth marred by a livid white scar that ran from her bottom lip to her chin.

"Most likely lies," I said, my mind working furiously. What was I to do? By law, I couldn't kill Grindin now, but I'd be damned if I would leave this place with my tail between my legs, either.

"Perhaps," Daughter Freda said, studying me. "What brings a great man such as yourself to our humble village, lord?"

"He's looking for Apprentice Cheny," Son Jona answered.

Daughter Freda's eyes flashed. "If I wished to hear you speak, Jona, I would have put the question to you, not Lord Hadrack." Son Jona pursed his lips, turning them white with anger as the priestess focused back on me. "Now, lord, may I inquire as to why you wish to see our new apprentice?"

"I came here to kill the bastard," I grunted. I couldn't stomach the idea of leaving this place with Grindin still alive, but I knew even the Daughter would defend him now that he belonged to the House.

"I see," the priestess said with a sigh, looking unsurprised. "And what did our troublesome apprentice do to deserve such a fate? Did he defile a peasant's daughter who was under your protection, perhaps? Or did he steal something from you?"

"It doesn't matter what he did!" Son Jona snapped from behind the priestess. "That is in the past. Cheny has taken the vows. He cannot be held responsible for what he did in his previous life. You know the law as well as I do."

"Does that law include letting him get away with slaughtering innocent women and children!?" I thundered in anger. Both the priest and priestess blinked at me in surprise. "How about murdering a Son and Daughter, then?" I asked into the stunned silence.

"Lies," Son Jona finally spluttered, recovering his composure as he waved away my words. "Apprentice Cheny confessed his sins to me before he took the vows. Whatever evil you think he has done, you are mistaken."

I snorted. "Mistaken, am I?" I looked away from the priest in contempt and focused on Daughter Freda. "You have heard of me, Daughter, which means you have also heard about the men that I seek and why."

"Yes, lord," Daughter Freda nodded reluctantly. "I am aware."

"Then you know that I have a vow of my own," I said, my voice low and dangerous now. "I swore to my dead family that I would hunt down the men who slaughtered my village. That bastard Grindin was one of them, which means my vow takes precedence over his, and not you, or that sniveling priest behind you, can turn me away from that task."

"Cheny cannot be—" Son Jona began.

"Shut your mouth right now!" I snapped, pointing a mailed finger at the priest. "Say another word to defend that murderous scum, and he won't be the only one to suffer my wrath this day." I shifted my eyes back to the Daughter as the priest swallowed noisily. Behind them both, the Daughter-In-Waiting was visibly shaking. I still didn't know what I was going to do, but I had to do something. "Where is he, Daughter?" I said in a flat, determined voice.

People were making their way down the dusty street now, drawn by the shouting. Some of the men held axes, mauls, or hoes, and they were grumbling threateningly. Something terrible was going to happen here, I knew, unless I got what I wanted soon.

Daughter Freda lifted her hands toward me in appeasement. "Lord Hadrack, as much as I feel empathy for what happened to you, the laws of the House are firm, and not even an oath sworn in blood like yours can change that fact."

"Where is he?" I repeated, barely listening. "I won't ask a third time."

"You will burn at The Father's feet for eternity if you touch him!" Son Jona shouted, spittle flying from his mouth.

I snarled, unable to control myself any longer. Three quick strides and I stood in front of the priest. I grabbed the Son by the front of his robe, lifting him off the ground as I shook him like a doll. "Tell me, you bastard!"

I felt a hand on my arm. "Lord, put him down this instant!" Daughter Freda demanded. "Putting your hands on a priest is sacrilege. You are jeopardizing your very soul."

"Too late for that," I said with a scowl as I flung the priest away. Son Jona landed in the dirt on his backside as I faced the Daughter. "Tell me now, or I promise you I'll tear this entire place down until I find him."

Daughter Freda regarded me in indecision. I could see a gleam of fear in her eyes, and a part of me felt shame that I had done this to her. Finally, she nodded in resignation. "Very well. Apprentice Cheny spends most of his days when not at lessons tending to the lepers in the hills." She turned, pointing to the east where I'd sent Wiflem and his men to scout. "Ride a mile that way and follow the trail until you see an ash tree stripped of bark. There you must wait. The lepers are solitary folk and suspicious of strangers. Someone will contact you before long. Tell them I sent you and they will take you to their dwelling."

I turned and swung up on Angry, pausing as the Daughter rested her hand on my leg. "Think of what you do, lord. If you murder that man, the king will have no choice but to strip you of your lands and title and hunt you down."

"I was born with neither lands nor title, Daughter, so there will be no hardship when I lose them," I said down to her. "My vow means more to me than simple wealth and possessions. As for the other, well, I've been hunted before and still live to speak of it."

I swung Angry around then, heading east between two houses as the crowd parted for me, many of them muttering angrily, though clearly wary of my armor and weapons, not to mention the promise of violence on my face. I could see a worn path leading into the hills, and I followed it, pretending not to notice the flash of mail from the trees to the south. I knew Jebido and Baine had seen me ride out of town and were following at a respectful distance. I can't say I was surprised. The only surprise, I suppose, was that Jebido had waited this long.

Ten minutes later, I reached the treeline, where I saw five men on horses emerging from the forest. I recognized Wiflem and kicked Angry toward them.

"My lord," Wiflem said, nodding in greeting. Niko was with him, along with three others who had come south with Wiflem to join my garrison. "We have swept the hills and woods, lord, but saw nothing of interest other than an abandoned longhouse."

"Show me," I grunted, thinking that must be where the lepers lived.

Wiflem studied my face. I could tell he was curious about why I was interested in the longhouse, but he just nodded. "Of course, my lord. This way."

We followed the path east, and I called a halt when we came to the ash tree Daughter Freda had mentioned. I stared up at the tree's long-dead branches and withered bark, my anger smoldering like a grass fire as I thought about Grindin. He would have walked this same path not that long ago, possibly pausing to rest against this very tree. Soon, I knew, I would have the apprentice in my grasp, and then we'd see what came of it.

"The building is a hundred yards that way, my lord," Wiflem said, pointing northeast through the forest.

I nodded, not saying anything as I looked about me. The trees to either side of the path were thick here, with twisted brambles, moss-covered logs, and mounds of leaves covering the ground. I listened but heard nothing other than the chirp of a chickadee somewhere off to my right.

"There was no one there, my lord," Wiflem added pointedly.

I glanced at him. "Are you sure of that? Did you go inside?"

"Haspeth," Wiflem called over his shoulder. "Come here." One of the men nudged his horse toward us. He was thick and wide, with a bull-like neck and heavy shoulders. Like the rest of my men, he wore my wolf emblem on his white surcoat and shield. "Tell Lord Hadrack what you saw in the longhouse."

"I saw nothing, my lord," the soldier said. He shrugged apologetically. "Nothing except dirt and rotting walls."

"You saw no signs that anyone was living there?" I prodded. "You are certain?"

Haspeth's face twisted as he thought. "Well, my lord, I can't say as to that, I suppose. I was looking for someone lying in wait for us. The place was empty, so that was good enough for me."

I grunted in acknowledgment as Jebido and the others appeared coming along the trail.

"So, this is a little unexpected," Jebido said when he reached us. He stared at me, one eyebrow raised. "Off on a foxhunt, are we then?"

"There's a complication," I grunted.

Jebido leaned forward on the pommel of his saddle wearily. "Of course there is."

"Our man Grindin is not the fool we were expecting," I said grudgingly. "The bastard has gone and taken the vows."

Jebido blinked in surprise. "Well, that's going to be a problem."

"What are you going to do?" Baine asked. "You can't kill him now, Hadrack."

I took a deep breath. "I have no idea," I said, just as a boy appeared from the trees.

The boy was around ten or so, though his face looked wrinkled and puffy like an old man's. Pale bumps that rose along his nose and cheeks disfigured his face, making his eyes look like tiny dots within a sea of swollen madness. The boy stared at us, shifting from one barefoot to the other. I noticed that similar growths on his feet had twisted them into unrecognizable lumps.

"I'm looking for Grindin," I said. "Is he nearby?" The boy just stared at me dumbly. I sighed. "I mean, Apprentice Cheny." Again, the boy said nothing. "Daughter Freda sent me," I added, hoping that might gain the boy's interest. "We are old friends of Cheny's."

"He brings us food, lord," the boy said warily.

"That sounds just like him," I replied with a forced smile. "Cheny is a kind and gentle soul." The boy looked at me oddly and I realized he had already met the bastard, so he probably knew that I was lying. "What's your name?" I inquired.

"Rin, lord," the leper boy responded.

"Can you take us to see Cheny, Rin?" I asked. "It's important that I speak with him." Rin held out a twisted hand, and I nodded to Baine, who dug a coin from his belt and flipped it through the air.

"This way," the boy said as he snatched at the coin. He shuffled away, limping as he moved off through the trees. My men and I began to edge our horses forward, and Rin paused to look back. "No, just you, lord," he said, pointing a grimy finger at me. "Just you, and no horses."

"Hadrack," Jebido started to protest.

"It's fine, Jebido," I grunted as I dismounted. I handed him Angry's reins. "There's nothing to fear here."

I pushed my way through the thick trees as Rin flitted in and out of sight ahead of me. The ground beneath me lay uneven, with branches covered in leaves and half-dried muck trying to trip me. Stands of thick dewberries lined the forest floor, clutching at my boots and tugging at my shield, making the going even more difficult. The boy ahead seemed to have no trouble traversing through it all, however, even with his bare feet and limp. Finally, growing impatient, I drew Wolf's Head and began hacking my way along, quickly breaking out in a sweat.

"This way, lord," I heard Rin call out, though I could not see him any longer through the trees.

I angled toward the boy's voice, cursing as a vine hooked my foot and I stumbled. I righted myself and pressed on, until eventually I broke through the trees into a small clearing dotted with clumps of feathered reed grass that rose almost to my waist. A long, low building sat near the treeline opposite me. The house was built of sagging timber planks and was perhaps twenty-five feet in length, with a weathered thatch roof that had collapsed in two places along the eastern end wall. Rin waited for me near the open door. I paused, searching for any signs of movement from the trees or the building itself, but heard and saw nothing.

I approached the house cautiously. "Where is he?" I asked Rin.

The boy said nothing as he turned to indicate the open doorway. I grunted, moving forward and shifting my shield in front of me. I was certain that a bunch of lepers was nothing to be concerned about, but as Jebido always told me, a wise man has to be prepared for any eventuality. I stepped through the doorway and waited as my eyes adjusted to the gloom, broken only by two patches of sunlight to my right where the roof had fallen through. Haspeth had been right, I saw. There was nothing inside the building but filthy straw and dark mounds of piled dirt here and there, just as he had claimed.

The soldier hadn't mentioned the bald man sitting cross-legged and alone against the back wall, however. That was clearly something new.

"So, you came," the man said in a triumphant voice. His eyes gleamed at me with hatred. "Wolves can be so predictable."

It was Grindin, of course. He was much older now, looking smaller in his apprentice robe than I remembered. But even with his blond locks gone and his head shaven, I knew that it was him. I growled deep in my chest and stalked forward, with only Grindin's death in my mind, regardless of the law or consequences. That's when the earth shifted beside the smug-looking bastard, and a crowd of armed men appeared, eagerly thrusting aside a crude covering of woven branches and twigs as they leaped out of a deep pit.

Men in red capes and pointed boots.

2: Cardians

    I have always held nothing but contempt for Cardians, both as men and as warriors. Yet, as I watched them swarm out from their lair like dark, hungry spiders, I realized even inferior fighters like Cardians could bring their betters down if there were enough of the bastards. The men facing me were all identical in their dirtiness, covered in sweat and black filth from the pit that they had dug. I don't know how long they had been down in that grubby hole, waiting for me to step into their trap. It hardly mattered, I suppose, as their patience had clearly paid off. The Cardians began to jeer and curse me for a fool, confident that their prey was trapped, while I stood watching them warily, thinking that maybe they were right.
    I knew the wisest course of action would be to turn around immediately and try to run back to my men. To do anything else would be foolhardy and would only confirm what the Cardians were calling me. But I can be stubborn and hard-headed at times, and I hesitated in indecision, reluctant to flee from scum such as these, despite their superior numbers.
    The last Cardian emerged from the pit, bringing the total to seven as they started to advance on me. All seven looked reasonably competent and experienced, though perhaps a little too overconfident. My pride told me that I could beat them, but my brain was whispering something else. I decided to listen to my brain and run, knowing that I could console my wounded pride another day. I crouched low and drew my shield down in front of me, snarling and tightening my grip on Wolf's Head. It was nothing but a

bluff, of course. I wanted the bastards to think that I would fight, hoping it might gain me an extra step or two on them.

The Cardians hesitated at my aggressive stance, and I started to turn toward the entrance just as the unmistakable sounds of weapons colliding and cries of battle arose from the trees south of the clearing. I heard Grindin laugh, and I cursed, understanding now just how well planned this entire affair had been. I took a deep breath and turned back to face the Cardians. There would be no help coming from my men anytime soon, I realized, so whether I liked it or not, my course was set. I crouched again, preparing to charge at the Cardians. That's when a second hatch flipped up to my left, revealing eight more red-caped soldiers crowded together in another pit. Grindin slowly stood, chuckling in amusement at the look on my face as the new men leaped out of the hole.

"Your men were lazy in their search," Grindin said with contempt in his voice. "They should have looked closer. They didn't even check their backtrail after they left here."

I straightened in resignation and shrugged. "I'll be sure to mention that oversight when I see them next," I said. I might have had a slim chance against seven men, but fifteen had just dashed my hopes. The new arrivals spread out to my left, with the initial group doing the same on my right. Grindin stood near the back wall, watching in amusement.

"Aren't you going to try to run?" Grindin asked mockingly. The bald man lifted an eyebrow. "Or is the great Wolf of Corwick too proud to turn tail and flee like a peasant girl?"

I had no idea how many more Cardians were outside assaulting my men. All I knew was if I tried to run now, I would be trapped between the two. The way back through the trees would be difficult, and one misstep would be the end of me. I didn't relish the idea of a sword thrust in my back, so really, there was only one option left. I had to fight.

The Cardians were grinning with confidence as they fingered their weapons—and why not? They had a clear advantage and were certain of what to expect from me. I decided to throw off that confidence and their expectations. I threw my shield aside, then laughed at the look of surprise on my adversaries' faces. Several of the Cardians muttered uneasily, and even Grindin appeared caught off-guard.

"You have fought before, I understand," I finally said, fixing my gaze on Grindin. "In a shield wall, shoulder to shoulder with other men, smelling the blood, the shit, and the fear."

The bald man nodded suspiciously. "I have," he said. "It's not something that I'd care to do again."

I sheathed Wolf's Head in one smooth motion, the sound of the blade ringing along the gilded scabbard loud in the silent building. "Then you know the confusion such a battle can bring. How the dust and smoke stings your eyes, blinding you and making things worse as men scream and die all around you." I slowly drew my father's axe, smiling as several of the Cardians to my right took an unconscious step backward. "Sometimes a man hesitates in a tense situation like that," I growled. "Afraid that he might take the blood of a brother by mistake." I looked around at the men facing me as I hefted the axe in my hands. "But today, I have no such concerns. I only have myself to worry about." I smiled my best wolfish grin. "And I'm more than enough to deal with the likes of you."

Then I charged.

I'd picked a tall Cardian with a droopy mustache to my right as my first target, and as I barrelled toward him, I screamed a blood-curdling challenge. The Cardian seemed stunned by my attack, frozen, with his mouth hanging open in dull-witted surprise beneath his hairy upper lip. I struck the soldier hard in the stomach with the butt-end of the axe, whirling and ducking even as the man sagged and crumpled. I swung the axe savagely as I turned, the blade hissing through the air before slicing deep into the belly of a short and stocky Cardian coming up behind me. That man clutched at himself and fell with a high-pitched cry as his companions all surged toward me, screaming for blood. I bellowed, whirling the axe in all directions like a madman while the Cardians tripped over each other in their eagerness to get to me. I sliced open one man's arm, and he screamed, dropping his sword, then cut down another man and cracked a third on the helmet, stunning him before my attackers finally began to lose their enthusiasm. They fell back in disarray and regrouped into a rough ring around me, looking shocked by my speed and ferocity while keeping a respectful distance between themselves and my crimson-stained axe.

The Cardians began cursing me then, describing in gory detail what they planned on doing to me as they boldly waved their weapons, though none seemed willing to step forward and try their luck against me a second time. I snorted in contempt as I slowly turned in a tight circle, watching the soldiers warily. I had been lucky, I knew. The Cardians had thought that I would fall quickly and had been reckless in their desire to get to me. But now that I had spilled their companions' blood on the floor and remained uninjured, they knew they were in for a fight.

The second attack would be more cautious and disciplined, I was certain, so I had to make my next move before that happened. I glanced at Grindin where he stood twenty feet away, his back pressed against the wall. Only one man stood between the apprentice and me. I grinned. So far, so good.

A Cardian in my peripheral vision took a tentative step forward, and I twisted around, my axe hissing like a striking rock snake. The soldier managed to dodge out of the way, but not before the razor-sharp blade took a hunk of beard from the man's chin. I twirled again, feinting toward the left wall of Cardians, forcing them to retreat, then I turned to face Grindin and started to run. The Cardian directly in front of me saw me coming, his eyes widening just as my shoulder took him squarely in the chest, sending him spinning sideways to the dirt floor. I kept going, barreling toward the apprentice, who only had enough time to raise his hands to protect himself before I crashed into him.

I am a big man, weighing almost two hundred and sixty pounds, even more fully armored as I was. Grindin was at most five foot six and weighed perhaps a hundred and thirty pounds soaking wet. I slammed into the apprentice like a raging bull, one hand gripping my axe, the other pinning the smaller man to my chest before I closed my eyes in anticipation of what was coming. Please let the planks be loose and weakened by cluster flies and wood-eating beetles, I prayed as we crashed into the wall. At best, I figured we would pass through easily—at worst, the planking would hold, and my weight would probably snap Grindin's neck. Either way, my plan seemed infinitely better than staying where I was and simply being slaughtered.

The Mother must have been listening to my hurried prayer, for the weathered sheathing of the longhouse snapped like dried twigs, sending the bald apprentice and me tumbling awkwardly outside to the ground. We landed in a clump of grass ten feet away from the treeline, and I rolled and jumped to my feet. I turned to look back. A Cardian had just stuck his incredulous face out through the splintered wall, and I swung, cutting through the man's helmet into bone and cartilage. Blood splattered skyward, spraying against the wood in a wide swathe as the Cardian fell without a sound. I yanked my axe free from the dead man's skull and sheathed it, then hauled a stunned-looking Grindin to his feet. I threw the apprentice over my shoulder and ran into the trees, heading north. I could hear the Cardians shouting in surprise and anger from behind me, but I didn't bother to look back.

Although Grindin was a small man and weighed next to nothing, it was still tough going as I sprinted through the forest, trying to maintain my balance over the uneven terrain. The bald apprentice did little to make it easier on me, either, as he began to pound his fists against my back and kick his legs, all the while screaming at the top of his lungs.

"Be quiet," I grunted as I crashed through the brambles, heedless of the thorns ripping at me as I ducked beneath low-hanging branches. I could hear the Cardians shouting as they gave chase, but even with Grindin's weight slowing me down, I seemed to be increasing my lead on them somehow. Perhaps Cardians were just as poor at running as they were at fighting, I thought. Then I smirked. Unless they were running away from a battle, that is.

"Let me down, you stupid ox!" Grindin shouted as he twisted and turned like a writhing snake on my shoulder while striking at my lower back and buttocks.

I barely felt the blows through my armor, with many of them landing inadvertently on the hard oak shaft of my sheathed axe, which probably hurt him more than it did me. Then the pounding stopped and I felt Grindin clutching clumsily at the hilt of my sword. I swatted the offending hand away. "Try that again," I wheezed as I leaped over a fallen log, "and I'll take a few of your fingers off and feed them to you."

"You can't touch me!" Grindin shouted, returning to his earlier strategy of striking my back again. "You'll burn if you do!"

A tall pine tree rose in front of me, and I twisted my torso sharply as I reached it, grunting with satisfaction as Grindin's head cracked solidly against the trunk. I grinned as the apprentice yelped in pain and indignation.

"You bastard!" Grindin sputtered. "I'll kill you for that!"

I reached an ash tree next, and I repeated the same maneuver, this time crunching Grindin's entire upper body into the mass of the trunk. Grindin went limp on my shoulder, moaning as I kept running. "I didn't touch you," I said to the apprentice. "The tree did. There's plenty more where those came from, too, so you might want to keep your mouth closed from now on."

I wasn't sure if Grindin was still conscious or not, but either way, he didn't say another word after that. I kept running, wondering why I was even bothering with the bastard. I knew I should just cut his throat and leave him to die, but something told me I might need him later. Besides, the man wasn't all that bright, and I found it hard to imagine him coming up with such an elaborate scheme to kill me. Someone else must have planned this, and the only way I would find out who that someone was—much as it galled me—was to keep Grindin alive.

I reached a deep gully and headed downward, fighting to stay upright as I plunged through densely-packed leaf mold and stumbled over long-dead branches. Grindin bounced and flopped on my shoulder as I descended, and I almost lost my grip on him several times before we made it safely down. A fair-sized stream awaited me on the gully floor, winding its way westward around a bend. I splashed into the eight-inch-deep water without hesitating, tripping over loose rocks and fighting the clinging muck of the streambed. Finally, after several minutes of awkward running, I came to a fallen spruce that had rolled down the embankment and now lay with half of its length submerged in the stream. The other half spanned the distance from the bank to the water, with the roots caught up in the branches of a tall birch ten feet up. A buildup of leaves, twigs, and several glistening logs were pressed tightly against the tip of the tree, creating a natural dam that forced the flow of water into a gurgling channel around it.

Was there enough space under that overhang to hide? I glanced up at the steep bank, knowing I needed time to catch my breath. I crouched down and fought my way through the outer prickly branches of the spruce into a darkened, narrow gap near the base of the earth wall. I grunted in satisfaction. It would do. The smell of oozing sap was overwhelming as I flipped Grindin roughly off my shoulder and propped him up with his back against the bank.

Grindin groaned and his eyes fluttered several times before they opened. I saw he had a nasty scrape along one side of his face. I smiled at him humorlessly. "I was hoping you were dead."

Grindin's face twisted with hatred. "Your soul will burn for this, you—"

"Enough of that!" I hissed. I grabbed the apprentice by the neck and dragged him toward me until my face was an inch from his. "I won't be lectured about burning by someone like you. I've been dreaming of killing you for a long time now, you sniveling worm, so don't tempt me." Grindin stubbornly opened his mouth to say something else, then he saw the promise in my eyes and he wisely closed it. "Now," I said, squeezing the apprentice's throat to get his attention. "Who planned this little greeting for me?" Grindin just gagged and shook his head, so I tightened my grip and rattled him around a little, then let go when his face began turning dark purple. I ignored the man's tortured breathing as he forced air into his lungs. "Who?" I demanded again.

"I can't tell you," Grindin gasped.

I snorted and slapped a palm tightly over Grindin's mouth, then gripped the little finger on the apprentice's left hand and twisted it savagely. The bone snapped with a sharp click as Grindin's body heaved, his eyes bulging in surprise, his squeal of pain muffled by my hand.

"I asked you a question," I growled. "And you have nine more fingers. Who is behind this?"

Grindin hesitated, his body shaking and his eyes tearing from the pain. I felt no pity whatsoever as I grabbed another of his fingers. "Lord Boudin!" Grindin mumbled in panic through my palm as I started to bend the digit back. I relaxed the hand clamped over his mouth, returning it around his neck.

"What name did you just say?"

"Lord Boudin," Grindin croaked. "He's the one behind this."

I frowned. I'd never heard of the man. "Who is he?"

Grindin shrugged weakly. "I don't know." I bent his finger again and the apprentice sobbed. "Please! I swear it! That's all I know! I've never even met him!"

"Then how did you set this all up?"

"Those men back there," Grindin said as he clutched his injured hand to his chest. He coughed in my face, his fetid breath washing over me. I twisted his head aside with disgust as he hacked again.

"You mean the Cardians?" I asked impatiently. Grindin nodded as he continued to cough. I probably should have been worried someone would hear him, but I was too focused on what the apprentice was telling me to care.

"Their leader is a man named Andret," Grindin explained. "He came to see me a few weeks ago with instructions from Lord Boudin to write that letter to you."

I pursed my lips as I thought about that. "How did they know where to find you?" I finally asked.

Grindin shifted his eyes away, and I could tell that he was about to lie. I dragged his injured hand from his chest and wrapped my mailed fist around his thumb. Then I waited, my expression blank, though I'm sure my eyes showed my resolve.

Grindin whimpered several times as I put pressure on his thumb before finally he slumped forward in resignation. "Lord Corwick told them where I was."

I grunted in surprise. "Pernissy?"

Grindin nodded reluctantly. "Yes."

"You're lying," I said, giving the apprentice a hearty shake. "Pernissy is locked up beneath the king's palace. He couldn't have told anyone anything."

Grindin started to shake his head before I had even finished talking. "It's not him."

I felt cold dread wash over me. "Explain," I said softly.

"Lord Corwick—"

I squeezed Grindin's throat in warning. "I am the Lord of Corwick. You would do well to remember that from now on."

"Er, Pernissy escaped the dungeons three months ago," Grindin said. "The man down there is just some stupid peasant who looks like him."

I slowly released my grip on the apprentice and he sagged, drawing in great gulps of air as he rubbed at his tortured throat. Could it be true? Could Pernissy really have been free these past few months? I shuddered as I imagined all the mischief that the man could have gotten into in that time. I knew I had to get word to Tyden as soon as possible. Pernissy hated his cousin with a passion now, and the king's life was undoubtedly in danger. I glanced with distaste at Grindin. "If what you are saying is true, how did Pernissy know you would be here? Even I couldn't find you, and believe me, I tried."

Grindin hacked and spat, looking at me with wary eyes. "He's the one that sent me here in the first place."

I gaped at the apprentice. "How?" I finally demanded.

"It was the day after the king's coronation," Grindin said. "I was told to travel to Thidswitch and take the vows, then wait for further instructions."

Nothing Grindin said was making any sense. I was beginning to wonder if the man was toying with me, despite what he knew I would do to him. If he was, I vowed, a broken finger or two would be the least of his worries. "I was there at the coronation," I said, shaking my head, "and I saw Pernissy dragged away. He couldn't have gotten word to you."

"He didn't," Grindin replied. "The First Son did. I was drowning my sorrows in some inn, about to throw myself on the mercy of the king when the priest's men found me and took me to him."

I cursed. The last I'd seen of those two, Pernissy was promising to tear Son Oriell's eyes out and piss in their sockets. I snorted in disgust. It seemed even the most treacherous of rats had a way of working out disagreements. "Why come to this town of all places?" I asked.

"Son Jona is related to the First Son," Grindin said meekly. "He's his nephew, I think. Son Jona is the one who approved my application."

"Lord," I said in annoyance. Grindin looked at me strangely. "You call me lord from now on and show me the respect I deserve, you bastard, or so help me, I'll snap the rest of those fingers and start working on some toes."

Grindin lowered his eyes. "Yes, lord."

I looked away from the apprentice, thinking. Why go to such elaborate lengths to kill me? I knew Pernissy hated me and wished me dead, but did he hate me enough to risk his escape being exposed if the plot failed? And who was Lord Boudin, for that matter? And what was his stake in all of this? I shook my head, unable to fit the pieces together just as muffled voices reached me, coming from the ridge of the gully directly above us. The voices grew stronger, at least three, while I could also hear the sounds of booted feet splashing through the water to the south. I cursed myself for a fool, knowing that I had spent too much time questioning Grindin. The Cardians had used that time to catch up to us. I glanced at the apprentice, who I could tell was sorely tempted to call out to our pursuers. I drew my sword and placed it against his thin chest.

"One word," I whispered, "and it will be your last in this world."

Grindin glared at me, but he nodded and said nothing.

"Do you see anything?" I heard a man call out from the gully ridge. I glanced up, but the spruce boughs were still thick and green with sap, with only the tips on the outer branches beginning to show signs of browning. I couldn't see the men up top from where I crouched, which meant they couldn't see us either.

"Nothing," came back the gruff reply from the south. "We're wasting our time out here. The bastard must have turned and headed west."

I peered through a gap in the boughs, just able to see three men cautiously making their way along the stream. Had they missed seeing where I'd climbed down the gulley, or did they know we were here and were trying to catch me off-guard? It seemed hard to imagine that anyone could miss the trail that I had gouged into the soil on the way down, but perhaps these men weren't very competent trackers. The Cardians were getting closer to the felled tree with every step, and I felt sudden hope that maybe they really didn't know we had come this way. If that were true, then there was a chance they also wouldn't realize that there was enough space beneath the spruce for two men to hide. That hope was dashed with my next thought, however, as I realized even the poorest of trackers wouldn't fail to see the prints that I'd left in the mud by the tree. I put my finger to my lips as Grindin shifted his weight, and I pressed the tip of Wolf's Head tighter to his chest.

"We're going to double back," the man above called down. "Follow the stream as far as you can. They probably didn't get this far, but we need to be sure."

I heard one of the men in the water grunt in response, then the rustle of leaves as the soldiers up top walked away. I grinned. So, they really had missed my trail, it seemed, and now I only had three men standing in the way of my freedom. I glanced at Grindin as he stared back at me sullenly. I knew dealing with the approaching Cardians would be difficult with the little bastard just waiting for an opportunity to sound the alarm. I still wasn't ready to kill the apprentice, much as I dearly wanted to, so only one solution was left for me.

"I'm going to take care of those men out there," I said in a low voice. "You stay here and keep your mouth shut."

I saw Grindin's eyes light up. "Of course, lord. You have my word. Not a peep from me, I swear."

I smiled. "Good, then we understand each other perfectly," I said as I lifted Wolf's Head and crashed the golden hilt down on Grindin's skull.

The apprentice gasped in surprise and slumped sideways, his face pressed into the muck. I sighed, thinking for a moment that I should just leave him that way before I reluctantly grabbed the back of his robe and dragged him up so that he could breathe. Grindin was unconscious as far as I could tell, but just to be sure, I covered his mouth again and bent his broken finger back, watching his face closely. There was no reaction. Satisfied, I propped the apprentice against the wall, then turned, using my sword to part several branches in front of me so that I could see what was happening. The Cardians were only twenty yards away now, with a big, bearded man in the lead as he made his way down the center of the stream. His companions were following along either shore, searching the banks for any signs of footprints.

The big Cardian's eyes were focused on the spruce, and I heard him whistle softly to the other two before he motioned with his sword toward the fallen tree. I knew he had seen the tracks. I dropped to my belly and dragged myself closer, trying not to make any noise. What would they do? I paused behind a drooping branch to watch their progress through the long needles. If it were me out there, I decided, I would have my men encircle the spruce on all sides, with one coming from the north, the other the east, while the third man stayed where he was as a distraction.

The Cardian leader whistled a second time, gesturing for his companions to move east out of my line of sight. I had guessed right.

"We know you're in there," the big Cardian said loudly once his men had disappeared. "Come out and we'll let you live." He glanced to his right and I saw him nod imperceptibly. I knew I didn't have much time.

"How do I know I can trust you?" I called out before I scurried back to Grindin.

The apprentice was still sitting slumped over where I had left him. I sheathed my sword, then fought to withdraw my axe, cursing under my breath as it became entangled in the branches around me. I finally managed to free the weapon, then slammed my helmet on Grindin's bald head before I pulled off my mailed gloves and slipped them onto his limp hands. The gloves were much too large for the little man, of course, but they would have to do. I dragged Grindin back the way that I'd come.

"You don't," the big Cardian shouted. He was thirty feet away, crouched over as he tried to peer through the branches at me. "But if you make us come in there, you'll regret it."

"All right," I said. "I give up."

"Throw your weapons out here," the Cardian demanded. "Then crawl out on your belly. No tricks!"

I slid the axe along the ground, pushing the head out through the boughs before I flung it as far as I could.

"Now the sword," the Cardian ordered.

"I lost it in the woods," I called back as I maneuvered Grindin onto his belly and thrust him forward through the mud. The crest of my helmet finally broke through the branches into daylight. I stopped pushing, certain the Cardian had seen it. I moved the apprentice's hands over his head so that the gloves could be seen from outside as well. "Please don't hurt me," I added, making sure to put a tremor in my voice.

"Well, well," I heard the big Cardian say with a chuckle. "The mighty Wolf of Corwick lying down like a beaten dog." I heard him snort in contempt. "All right then, you pathetic bastard, crawl out of there like a good boy, and maybe I'll let you lick my boots."

I paid the man's words no mind, scurrying over to the north side of the tree while awkwardly drawing my sword as I slithered through the muck. I could see a flash of mail through the branches, then a man's bearded face as he parted the boughs to peer curiously inside. I lifted Wolf's Head and stabbed upward without hesitating, taking out the Cardian's right eye. The soldier squealed and fell back as I burst through the remaining branches between us. I knocked the man to his knees with a vicious backhanded blow, then slapped his sword away as he tried to lift it. I stabbed with Wolf's Head again, this time in the Cardian's other eye. I felt the tip of my sword punch through the tough cartilage and soft brain matter there before bursting out the back of the Cardian's skull with a meaty pop. I let the dead man fall as I jerked my bloodied sword from him, growling with battle rage as I turned east.

The second Cardian stood in the water near the piled debris, parting the spruce branches with his sword. His mouth hung open in shock as I bore down on him, and he barely had time to lift his blade or shield before I reached him. I slashed once, then a second time for good measure, ignoring the spurting blood as the soldier gagged and dropped his weapon, trying to staunch the flow of blood from his neck. I knew it was pointless. The man was already dead. I splashed through the water around the tree, heading for the last Cardian, who was waiting for me and looking surprisingly calm.

"A good ploy," the big man said grudgingly. He glanced at Grindin, who was moaning now as he lifted his head. My helmet slipped off the apprentice, and I could see him staring in befuddlement at it where it lay in the muck.

I nodded, taking a moment to catch my breath. "I'll make this as quick and painless as possible," I said as I began to stalk toward the man. "I promise."

The big Cardian laughed. "We'll just see about that."

I was true to my word, despite the Cardian's bravado, and the struggle was brief and quick, though not before he managed to cut through the mail along my right side with a lucky strike. The gash was small and didn't hurt at all, though I could feel a persistent wetness trickling down my side from the wound. I ignored it as I plodded through the water to the spruce and dragged Grindin out by his filthy robe. The apprentice protested feebly and tried to flee, so I slapped him across the face several times until he fell, then kicked him in the stomach as he lay in the mud. I crouched down and took back my gloves, ignoring his hiss of pain as the mail hooked his broken finger. Then I picked up my muddy helmet and washed it clean in the stream before putting it back on my head.

"Come on, you ugly bastard," I grunted as I lifted Grindin and threw him over my shoulder once again. "I'm tired of this damn place. Let's go find my men and get out of here."

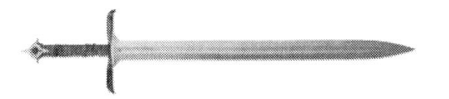

3: Pernissy

I decided to head east after my run-in with the three Cardians, then circle back to the south and try to either locate the hamlet or find the trail that would lead me to the dead ash tree where I'd last seen my men. I had no idea where I was or how many of the enemy were spread out through the trees looking for us, or, for that matter, what had become of Jebido, Wiflem, and the others. The men I had brought with me to Thidswitch were all experienced fighters, and I was confident that they had survived the surprise attack and had struck back with the kind of fury and tenacity that had made them feared across the kingdom. The trick for me now would be trying to locate them in the sprawling forestland before the Cardians found us first. Tramping through the woods was not a task I relished at the best of times, even less so with a foul-smelling apprentice draped over my shoulder. I decided I had carried Grindin's sorry ass far enough, so I set him down to walk on his own.

"Try to run or cry out," I warned, "and I'll cut that withered excuse of a sack from you and feed it to the village hounds."

Grindin visibly paled at my threat, and he kept his mouth closed and his feet moving as I prodded him ahead of me with my sword.

I kept a watchful eye out for Cardians as we progressed, but heard and saw nothing that indicated they might be anywhere close. Had they given up the search? It seemed hard to believe after all the trouble they had gone through to draw me here. We walked east through rough forestland for over an hour, with the sun finally beginning to set in the west behind us. The deep shadows cast by the trees twisted and danced like the fabled forest folk my father had told me about as a child. Soon it would be pitch dark out, which would help hide us from our pursuers, but would also make locating the trail or the village that much more difficult. Without the light, I knew it would be very easy to become lost in woodlands of this size.

"Why couldn't you just leave things well enough alone?" I heard Grindin whisper in a surly voice. The bald apprentice looked over his shoulder at me while clutching his injured hand to his chest. I could see he expected me to strike him for his insolence, which I was sorely tempted to do.

"Leave what alone?" I growled instead as we skirted a small peat bog. The pungent aroma of decaying peat, dead animals, and bog scum tickled my nose, reminding me strongly of Patter's Bog.

"What happened at Corwick," Grindin said with a slight whine in his voice now. He watched me warily for any signs of violence, then, when I showed none, he returned his attention to the way ahead. "I mean, it was so long ago, and it wasn't personal. Surely you know that? We were just doing what we were told like any good soldier would."

I stared at the back of Grindin's bald head with loathing. Every one of these bastards fell back on the same, tired excuse when faced with their crimes. It was never their fault. Wolf's Head was bare in my hand, held by my side. It would take less than the blink of an eye to lift the blade and plunge it into the apprentice's back. I had to force myself not to do it, determined to keep the man alive until I fully understood everything that had happened here today. "It was personal to me," I said, trying to keep my voice even. "You murdered my family and my friends."

"On Lord Corwick's orders," Grindin protested. I growled low in my chest, and he hurried to say, "I mean, on Pernissy's orders, lord. What else could we have done?"

"You could have said no," I spat, feeling the need to kill the man welling up inside me again. I pushed it back down, determined to control my urges. I knew Grindin's death wasn't that far in the future. I just needed to be patient until the time was right. I toyed with different images of my blade cutting and slicing into the Son-In-Waiting's vulnerable flesh instead, which made me feel somewhat better.

Grindin snorted, clearly gaining courage from my unexpectedly calm reaction to his words. "Said no, lord?" he asked sarcastically. "Have you met Pernissy?" He paused to look back at me again. "I once saw him thrash his falconer to death because his favorite bird lost several tail feathers." Grindin shook his head. "The man does not react well to disobedience, lord. In any form. We had little choice."

Grindin started to head west around an alder thicket, and I thumped him in the ass with my boot, indicating he take the eastern route around it instead. "You forget that I was there and saw everything," I grunted. "Pernissy left. You could have ridden away once he was gone and let those people live."

"And go where?" Grindin demanded. "He would have hunted us down."

"Jebido left his employ when he found out what happened," I pointed out. "That's what an honorable man does."

Grindin sighed. "The Captain was always a better man than me back then, lord."

"He still is," I replied gruffly.

We walked on in silence for a time, until finally, Grindin asked, "Is it so hard for you to believe that maybe I have become a better person since Corwick, lord?"

"Yes," I said bluntly. "But even if by some miracle it's true, I don't care." I paused, then grabbed the bald man by the back of his robe, stopping him in his tracks. Had I just heard something from the trees in front of us? I turned my head at an angle to listen. There was nothing now but the faint rustling of leaves and the birds singing. Finally, I motioned for Grindin to continue onward. "Do you actually think that by taking the vows, it somehow absolves you of what you did?" I asked, amazed at the audacity of the man. "That the crimes of murder and rape can just be wiped clean by putting on a flea-infested robe?"

"Of course they can," Grindin responded immediately. "I belong to The Father now, and He has cleansed my soul of all my past sins."

I rolled my eyes. "The only thing He cleansed on you is your ability to think," I retorted. "Assuming, of course, you had any to begin with."

Grindin started to reply, and I hissed at him to be quiet, certain this time that I had heard something. We paused in the deep shadows of a gnarled oak, where I put my hand on the back of the apprentice's neck and squeezed, my message clear. We waited in silence, listening. A twig snapped a hundred yards to my right, breaking the forest's stillness, then a second cracked loudly from the same direction. Someone was coming our way.

I pressed my lips to Grindin's ear. "If you move from this spot or make a sound, I promise I'll find you. And when I do, I will slit the skin off of you strip by strip. Am I clear?"

Grindin swallowed and nodded. I squeezed his neck one last time, then slipped away, my sword ready as I cautiously made my way toward where I'd heard the sounds. I made it perhaps fifteen paces before terrified screams arose from behind me. I cursed and turned back, running for the oak as Grindin's cries grew louder and shriller. I could see the apprentice on the ground by the base of the tree, his shadowy form surrounded by dark, distorted figures. I shouted and raced toward the fallen man, a part of my brain wondering at the irony of me trying to save someone who I had sworn to kill. I raised my sword to strike at the closest assailant, then hesitated as I got a good look at the man's face. He was old and shrivelled, his white hair long and wild, with gruesome bumps and sores twisting his features into a nightmare of ugliness. Lepers, I realized.

"Wait!" Grindin shouted, lifting a hand to me. "Hold your sword, lord! They are my friends!"

I stepped back as the lepers around Grindin grunted and mumbled like crazed beasts as they struggled to lift the diminutive Son-In-Waiting. Finally, they got the bald man to his feet, and they began to talk all at once in a strange lisp that I could barely understand.

"It's all right," Grindin said, reassuring the lepers. "I'm fine. No harm done." He glanced at me with a sheepish look. "I thought they were forest ghouls at first, lord. They scared the wits out of me when they appeared from the shadows like that."

I snorted and sheathed my sword as the lepers faded back into the trees. The shrivelled old man with the long hair remained where he was next to Grindin, and I could see a boy that I recognized standing in the shadows of the oak. It was Rin.

I grabbed Rin by his filthy, greasy hair and dragged him forward. "Come here, you," I growled. The boy trembled as I shook him roughly. "You led me into a trap!"

"I didn't know," Rin protested.

"Do you expect me to believe that?" The boy twisted in my grip and I let him go, booting him roughly in the behind with the toe of my boot. He fell awkwardly and lay staring up at me in fear, his swollen face looking harsh and unnatural in the waning light. I wiped my glove off on my mail with distaste, then drew my sword and put the blade to the old leper's mottled throat.

"What happened to my men?"

The leper tried to speak, but nothing came out but incomprehensible mumbles.

"They search the land around our dwelling, lord," Rin said tentatively. "Looking for you."

I nodded in relief, my sword arm unwavering. "And the Cardians? Where are they?"

Rin stood painfully. I could see a gash seeping blood across the back of his swollen hand from the fall. "Most are dead, lord. The others ran west toward the great river. Your men chased after them." Rin shuddered. "I could hear their screams through the trees as your men slew them."

"How far are we from the longhouse?" I demanded.

"Not far, lord," Rin said, his eyes on the ground. "An hour, maybe."

"Good," I grunted. "Take me there, and no tricks from you, understand? Do what I ask and there will be another coin for you." I lowered my sword and glared at the older leper. "If your people try anything, I swear by The Mother that I will hunt every one of you down and kill you myself."

The old man grunted in acknowledgment, one eye barely discernable through his deformity. His swollen and cracked lips twitched as he mumbled something unintelligible. I glanced at Rin.

"He says Cheny is a good man," Rin explained. "He's begging you not to hurt him."

"I won't hurt him," I promised the old leper, lying. I grabbed Grindin and spun him around as I motioned for Rin to lead the way. "He's a Son-In-Waiting, after all," I added over my shoulder as the leper stood watching us. "It would be a sin."

We set out early the next morning, having lost only two men to the Cardian ambush. Both Haspeth, and a hulking man named Dell, who had been another of Wiflem's recruits, would be sorely missed, but I knew we had gotten off lucky. Had we been attacked by more competent warriors, things could have been far worse. Jebido rode to my right, with Baine on my left, and Grindin stumbling along behind Angry with a rope attached to my saddle tied around his neck. Wiflem, Tyris, Niko, and a razor-thin youth named Berwin brought up the rear, with Sim scouting half a mile ahead.

"He'll die before we get him anywhere near Corwick at this rate," Jebido said as we headed back to Thidswitch. He glanced at the apprentice, who was lurching back and forth over the uneven, rocky path like a drunkard and begging for mercy in a whining voice.

I shrugged. "So what?" The morning had begun foggy and cool, with a light drizzle falling that left a sheen of wetness on everything it touched. "He told me all he knows anyway. If he's fated to die out here, then so be it."

I had spent the previous night sitting by a crackling fire, with Grindin tied spreadeagled on the ground beside me as I questioned him. If I didn't like the answers to my questions or thought that he was lying or being evasive, I would draw Wolf's Head from the flames and give the Son-In-Waiting a taste. Grindin's answers quickly became very forthcoming after the first few times he felt hot steel, though he didn't have much more to add to what I already knew.

Jebido sighed, fighting to keep his gelding in line with me as we talked. Angry didn't like the white horse one little bit, and he delighted in putting his muscular shoulder into the smaller beast whenever he could. "Have you thought this through, Hadrack?" Jebido asked.

I could feel my eyes gleaming as I looked at my friend. "Oh, I've thought it through," I said. "The murdering bastard is lucky that I didn't just kill him last night and be done with it."

"Why didn't you?"

I shrugged. "Because I decided the spirits of Corwick's dead deserve to witness his final moments, just like they did Hervi Desh's."

"He's a Son-In-Waiting, Hadrack," Jebido said with a weary sigh. "It's not the same as with Desh. You need to get it through that thick skull of yours that you can't kill him."

I shook my head. "No, he's not a Son-in-Waiting, Jebido. He's just a slimy rat turd walking around in a filthy robe. Nothing more, and nothing less." I leaned forward. "And mark my words, I will kill him."

"The House will be furious when they hear about it, and the full weight of their power will fall on you," Jebido warned.

"What does that matter when weighted against my vow?"

Jebido glanced across at Baine, where he rode his mare silently beside me. "I could use a little help here," he muttered sourly.

I turned and focused on Baine. "You as well?" I demanded. I looked back at Jebido, a challenge in my eyes. "What would you two have me do? Give the bastard lodging in Corwick Castle and shower him with delicacies, fine wine, and eager whores?" I blew hot air from my nose, furious at my friends' lack of loyalty. "That bastard helped murder my family!" I finally shouted in exasperation as they remained silent.

"I had no choice, lord!" Grindin sobbed from behind me. "I had no choice!"

I turned. Green snot was running down the apprentice's nose like twin rivers of slime. I pointed. "You shut your mouth!" I snarled. "Or I'll cut your damn tongue out."

I caught Wiflem's eyes where he rode behind Grindin, and he just stared at me stone-faced as I whirled back around, my angry gaze on Baine now. "Well, go ahead, then," I said sarcastically. "Why don't you explain to me why I should turn my back on my vow and let that murdering scum live?"

Baine's helmet hung on his saddle, and he hesitated as he ran his fingers through his long black hair. I waited impatiently as my friend thought about what he wanted to say. "What happens if you kill him?" Baine finally asked.

"When I kill him," I corrected.

Baine inclined his head. "When you kill him, Hadrack. What happens then?"

I shrugged in annoyance, not anxious to think about it. "What does it matter?" I asked evasively.

"Humor me."

I sighed as Baine's calm demeanor helped to cool my anger. "The House will most likely cast me out," I said simply, sounding less worried than I actually was. Truth be told, I was terrified, but I couldn't let my friends know that. Banishment from the House was a rare occurrence, and I knew if it happened, it would mean my soul would be lost forever, exiled to the shadowy world of oblivion where it could never be reborn. I had a sudden memory of Ania telling me her greatest fear was to spend all eternity looking for the right path to the Master. I now understood her fear, but even the threat of banishment and the consequences wasn't enough to dissuade me from fulfilling my vow.

"What else?" Baine prompted.

"Isn't that enough?" I grunted.

"What about Tyden?" Jebido asked. "What will he do when the First Son and First Daughter go to him with their ruling?"

I thought of Son Oriell and how much he hated me. I wouldn't have a friend there, I knew, and even the First Daughter would be reluctant to speak up for someone who would kill a member of the

Holy House. "He will come for me," I said, knowing that despite what I had done to gain him his throne, King Tyden could not let my act go unpunished.

"Yes," Baine agreed. "He'll take Corwick away from you too, and your name."

"There is no other choice," I said stubbornly, though a part of me felt sorrow at the prospect of losing something so precious. "I'll kill Grindin and then find Luper Nash and finish this. After that, I'll go see the king and beg for leniency."

"You are being selfish, Hadrack," Jebido said, his voice hard and judgmental. He shook his head. "And stupid as well. I expected better from you."

I stared at him in amazement. How was killing Grindin being selfish? I was willing to sacrifice everything that I had earned to fulfill my vow. Jebido should be praising me, not criticizing me. "What do you know about it?" I grunted, hurt more than I cared to admit by his words and lack of support. "Nobody slaughtered your family."

Jebido pursed his lips, and I could see anger burning along his cheeks. "So, what of Lady Shana, then?" he finally asked, his voice cold now. "Have you given any thought to what will become of your pregnant wife once you turn outlaw?" I stared at Jebido, startled. "That's right," Jebido said, his eyes frosty with judgment. "Now you're starting to see, though I daresay it shouldn't take us to point out what should have been obvious."

I looked away, feeling shame creeping along the back of my neck. I had been so focused on Grindin that I hadn't even considered what would happen to my wife and babe once I killed the apprentice. Shana was only three months pregnant, but she had already assured me it would be a boy, even though I knew there was no way to be certain. I would miss the birth and so much more, I realized bitterly, sick with sudden indecision. I glanced back at Grindin, letting the hostility I felt for the man twist and writhe in my gut. Finally, I nodded, my weakening resolve buttressed by pillars of pure hatred. I looked at Jebido, feeling determination rise in me. "Shana will return to Calban after I turn outlaw," I said firmly. "If the king decides to hang me, then I pray she will find happiness with another man and that he will raise my son as his own."

Baine snorted. "What nonsense is that?" He shook his head in amazement. "Your willful blindness is astounding, Hadrack. The law is clear whether you want to acknowledge it or not. The union that brought you two together also merged Calban and Corwick under one banner—yours. If you go outlaw, the king will have to strip you of land and title, which means Calban will be lost along with Corwick, regardless of Lady Shana's claim to it. She will lose her title and be destitute, with a new baby and no husband to care for them. Is that what you want?"

I gaped at him, understanding now what my friends had been trying to tell me. They were right. It wouldn't just be me who would pay for Grindin's death. It would be those that I loved as well. I dropped my eyes, staring at Angry's twitching ears as I tried to come up with a solution that would satisfy my vow, as well as my duty to my family. Maybe I could have one of my men kill him, I thought, discarding that notion almost immediately. Grindin's life belonged to me and the dead of Corwick and no one else. Besides, Son Oriell was the First Son now, and I knew such a ploy wouldn't fool him. Finally, I sighed, out of ideas, knowing that even for my vow, I couldn't sentence my wife and unborn child to the fate Jebido had described. As much as it pained me, I realized I had no choice but to let Grindin live.

"I'm sorry," I said to my friends, my voice thick with bitterness. "You were both right all along. I should have listened to you sooner." I closed my eyes, letting the crushing disappointment wash over me.

"There is something else, Hadrack," Jebido said, breaking into my thoughts.

"What now?" I asked, suddenly weary and feeling weighted down.

"We still need to talk about the Cardians."

I opened my eyes and looked at him. "Who cares about them?" I said glumly. "They tried to kill me and failed. They don't matter now."

"Did they?" Jebido said in a thoughtful voice.

"Did they what?"

"Did they fail?" I started to respond angrily, and Jebido held up a hand, stopping me. "Just hear me out, Hadrack. You told me the Cardians were sent here to kill you by someone named Lord Boudin. We don't know who he is or why he wants you dead, but we do know who helped him."

"Pernissy," I breathed out noisily, glad to have a new target to aim my hatred.

"Yes," Jebido nodded. "We don't know what Lord Boudin is capable of, but we certainly know what Pernissy can do. He's ruthless and cruel, but he's also smart, as we have learned all too often."

"So, you think Pernissy sent the Cardians here, expecting them to fail?" Baine asked, his voice rising with interest.

I just stared at him in surprise as Jebido shrugged. "Maybe. I'm sure the man wouldn't have shed any tears if they had succeeded in killing Hadrack. But Pernissy knows our stubborn friend enough by now to recognize it would take more than a handful of bumbling Cardians to kill him."

I glanced between my two friends as they continued to talk, my presence apparently forgotten in their enthusiasm to piece together what had happened.

"And he used Grindin as the bait, knowing the man was stupid and Hadrack wouldn't be able to resist coming after him," Baine said.

"Exactly," Jebido nodded. "By drawing Hadrack to Thidswitch, Pernissy knew one of two things was going to happen." Jebido lifted a finger. "One, the Cardians kill Hadrack." He flicked up another finger. "Or two, the Cardians fail in the attempt, and Hadrack kills Grindin, setting off the inevitable House judgment against him, which would force the king's hand."

"So, either way, Pernissy was guaranteed to win," Baine said as he shook his head in wonder. "It's diabolically clever."

"Only if one of those two options actually happened," Jebido replied, looking at me meaningfully. "He probably didn't even consider that you might let Grindin live, which means he doesn't know his plan failed, and we now have the advantage."

I turned and looked back at Grindin, who was listening with an expression of wild hope plastered across his ugly face. "Wiflem," I grunted with distaste.

"Yes, my lord?"

"Cut that bastard's rope and let him ride Haspeth's horse."

"Yes, my lord."

"And Wiflem?"

"My lord?"

"If he says even one word during the ride back to Corwick, feel free to bash in whatever teeth he has left."

"Gladly, my lord," Wiflem growled with enthusiasm.

I glanced at Jebido. "You don't need teeth to stay alive," I explained. Jebido laughed as I leaned sideways and patted his arm affectionately. "I'm a fool," I said under my breath. "I should have listened to you sooner."

"That's true," Jebido agreed. He winked. "But as long as you keep on listening to me, then there's always hope for you."

I chuckled and nodded. "I'll try to remember that."

"So, what do we do now?" Baine asked.

I glanced behind me at the apprentice, trying not to let the hatred that I felt for the man cloud my thinking. The plan to ensnare me had been carefully conceived, and as Jebido had said, now that it had failed, we had the advantage. But how was I to make use of that advantage? Grindin's robe hung on his thin body, covered in blood and filth. A section had torn along the hem and was dangling and flicking in the wind. "I need to go to the village alone," I finally answered.

"Why?" Jebido asked.

I didn't answer him. "Wiflem," I said instead.

"Yes, my lord?"

"Bring me the Son-In-Waiting's robe."

"His robe, my lord?"

"That's what I said." I turned to Jebido. "They wanted me to kill the little bastard, and that is just what I'm going to let them think that I did."

4: The Piths

    We were less than three miles from Corwick Castle, and I was already picturing the enthusiastic greeting I knew Shana would give me when I saw the smoke over the hills to the southeast. My men and I paused on a ridge, and I felt a thud of dread in my stomach as we sat in silence, watching the ominous black tendrils rising high in the cloudless sky. I knew nothing ever good came from smoke like that in open country.
    "A grass fire?" Baine finally asked hopefully.
    I shook my head. The dark smoke was twisting and rolling upward in great plumes from at least seven or eight different locations at once. Burning grass and light brush gave off white smoke and burned in a line or ring. Trees and timber burned darker, but the southern hills in that direction seemed to have few woodlands. This was something else. "Whatever that is," I said grimly, pointing. "It's on my land and can't be ignored." I had lived in the village of Corwick until I was eight, but other than a trip to Bloomwood once, I had rarely left the town's borders, so had little knowledge of the surrounding countryside. I had planned to change that when I became the Lord of Corwick, but a lord's life is a busy one, I'd found out, and I had yet to make the time. I glanced at Jebido. "You know the land here better than anyone else. What lies to the south of those hills?"
    Jebido grimaced. "It's been a long time, Hadrack, but if I'm not mistaken, there is a village called Lestwick somewhere in that direction."
    I nodded, having been afraid of that answer. I had heard of Lestwick, of course, though I had never been there. I remembered the Widow Meade's husband had come from Lestwick and that he had been a cheerful man, with an odd, high-pitched laugh that

always ended in a snort. A bear mauled the poor bastard when I was four.

    I urged Angry down the ridge, giving the big black his head as we reached flat ground and headed southeast, away from Shana and Corwick Castle. My men streamed out behind me as we galloped across the lowlands, with me fretting with worry the entire way. Finally, we reached the rock-strewn hills, where we were forced to slow as we began the ascent. Angry was the first to reach the top, and I paused on a circular, windswept plateau, waiting for the rest of my men to join me. Trees rose in a solid wall of green to the west, with a gurgling river gushing southward along its boundary. I was looking at the Little Run, I knew, one of the many offshoots from the mighty White Rock. Smoke swirled toward the plateau suddenly as the wind shifted, sending a voluminous, acrid black cloud my way. I coughed and waved at the clogging smoke as it descended on me, then signaled for my men to move forward.

    We crossed the rocky plateau at a canter and paused along the southern crest, staring down at an open plain dotted with grass-covered hills. The Little Run twisted and turned in sweeping curves around those hills before heading south, the cheerful, sparkling water tainted by sheets of heavy smoke that drifted from one grassy bank to the other. A village sat below us, close to a wide bend in the river dominated by a craggy bluff. The smoke was coming from the village, just as I had feared.

    I could smell the unmistakable scent of death on the wind as I kicked Angry down the steep grade while my grim-faced men followed. I glanced once at Grindin, who now wore only a grubby tunic, surprised to see a strange look on the Son-In-Waiting's face. If I hadn't known better, I would have sworn it was concern and empathy. We reached the valley floor and thundered toward the village, spreading out in a line, our weapons drawn. If whoever had committed this act was still here, I vowed, they would pay dearly for what they had done.

    "Wiflem!" I shouted when we were less than a hundred yards from the nearest burning buildings. I gestured to my right.

Wiflem nodded in understanding, and he whistled for Tyris, Sim, and Berwin to follow him as they cut away at an angle, sweeping around to flank the settlement. The Little Run guarded our left, so Jebido, Baine, Niko, and I headed directly for the village square, with both Grindin and the extra horse tied to Niko's saddle helpless to do anything but follow. Every house and outbuilding was ablaze, with many having already collapsed as the flames fed hungrily on the skeletal remains. The heat was gaining in intensity as we approached, and the sound of the wood snapping and the roaring flames was deafening as the wind helped to stoke the fires even further. I could see bodies strewn about everywhere, even several goats and a mule, and I started to curse over and over again as we entered the village. This was my fault, I knew. The people here had depended on their lord to protect them, and I had failed in that trust.

I paused Angry in the village square as I looked around, the fury I felt inside threatening to unhinge me. Wind-driven black smoke swirled and twisted around the shells of the burning buildings like wraiths, making visibility difficult. I had seen this very thing before as a boy, and it was something that I'd hoped never to see again.

Wiflem and my men appeared through the haze, all with identically grim faces. "They're gone, my lord," Wiflem told me. His eyes gleamed with anger, along with a promise of retribution. "They burned the Holy House."

"The Son and Daughter?"

He shook his head. "No sign of them, my lord, but there's a blood trail leading from the building."

I closed my eyes as Baine muttered angrily beside me. "How many were there?" I finally grunted.

"At least forty, my lord," Wiflem answered. He pointed behind him. "They rode from the south and went back that way when they were finished. It looks like they took some cattle and sheep with them, too."

"How long have they been gone?" Jebido asked.

Wiflem shrugged. "Hard to say. Perhaps an hour or two, maybe more than that."

I glanced at the sky as I considered what to do. I had eight men, nine if you counted Grindin, which I didn't. Chasing after the raiders with my tiny force would be risky, I knew, yet doing nothing rubbed me the wrong way. I could send for more men from Corwick, but that would take many hours, and, by then, the raiders would be too far away to catch. I knew men like these moved fast after a raid, expecting pursuit.

I sat in indecision as Jebido sighed beside me and wearily dismounted, moving to stand over the body of an older woman lying on her stomach. He crouched and gently rolled her over, then cursed. The woman's dress had been slashed open down the front, revealing pendulous white breasts crisscrossed by livid red lash marks. She had been brutally raped, I saw. I closed my eyes as the heat from the fires worked at searing my brain from the inside. It was happening again, just like Corwick.

Jebido stood and slowly retraced his steps, pausing to look up at me. "We both know who did this, Hadrack," he said, his voice low and dangerous. "No Ganderman would slaughter all these people like this and burn the House. This was the work of Piths."

"We don't know that," I said. Nothing had been heard from the Piths since their defeat at Victory Pass years ago. I didn't want to think about what it might mean if he was right. I glared down at Jebido. "That's what everyone said about Corwick, too," I reminded him. My friend looked as though he was about to protest, and I added, "Even you." I thought of the ploy Pernissy had used to blame the slaughter at Corwick on the Piths. Was it a coincidence that the bastard was free and the same thing had happened again? I didn't know, but I was determined to find out. I turned to Wiflem. "Search the entire village. Someone might still be alive."

"Yes, my lord," Wiflem said, pulling his horse around.

"And Wiflem?" The soldier paused. "I want the Son and Daughter found."

"I understand, my lord," Wiflem responded gravely.

I flicked my eyes to Grindin, who I was surprised to see had tears rolling down his filthy cheeks. I snorted, not believing it for a moment. "Baine," I said. I gestured to the apprentice. "Take this bastard back to the castle and lock him up in the White Tower. I don't want to see his ugly face again until I decide what to do with him."

"You can't be thinking of going after them," Baine said.

"Why not?" I growled, intent on doing just that.

Then I heard the scream. The sound had come from the west near the river, though it had been very faint and brief. Had I imagined it? With the stubborn wind and raging fires, it was hard to be certain. I held my hand up for silence and listened, trying to hear past the crackling wood and roar of the flames as the wind swirled harsh smoke in my eyes. I had just about decided that I'd imagined the scream when I heard it again, this time lasting longer, with a higher pitch.

I kicked Angry into a gallop, swerving around a burning barn as I headed for the marshy shoreline of the Little Run. The river looped in a wide bend before me and then straightened out, heading south. It was maybe fifty feet wide, with a dense forest along the opposite bank. I glanced to the trees across the water just in time to see a brief flash of bright yellow before it was gone, then the unmistakable sounds of men shouting in pursuit. I knew I had just found the missing Daughter.

I reached the marshy shoreline and paused there. I had no idea how deep the river was, but there wasn't time to go looking for a ford. I guided Angry down the muddy bank, fighting to keep from being unseated as the big horse plunged into the water without hesitation. The current was surprisingly strong, and the water quickly reached the stallion's haunches before we were even a quarter of the way across. I could hear my men splashing into the river behind me, but I kept my focus squarely on the opposite bank as Angry fought against the stubborn current. The water was much colder than I had expected, and it swirled and gurgled all around me as we forged deeper into the river. Eventually, the big stallion was forced to swim until only Angry's head and my upper torso were all that showed above the waterline.

I could feel the big black's enthusiasm for the swim starting to lag just as we made it to the halfway point, and I breathed a welcome sigh of relief when Angry's hooves found firm footing again. We reached the far bank and the big stallion powered out of the river, both of us shedding water like a rooftop in a rainstorm. I halted along the treeline, listening. The forest was still, broken only by the metallic jingle of bits, the clang of weapons, and the creaking of leather behind me as my men fought to get their horses across the river.

I leaned down and patted Angry on the neck in gratitude for his effort. "Now," I said, sitting up. "Let's go find that Daughter."

Angry snorted, which I took for agreement, and we set off through the trees as my men climbed from the Little Run one by one and followed. I quickly located the area where I believed I'd sighted the Daughter earlier, and Sim dismounted, searching for tracks. The former outlaw wasn't nearly as accomplished a woodsman as Sabina, but he was far from incompetent, and it was only moments before he located her trail.

"The Daughter's feet are bare and bleeding, my lord," the big man said, standing to look west. "She went that way but won't get far on those feet." He gestured to the south. "Riders came from that direction, hunting her."

"How many?" I grunted.

Sim grinned. "Only three, my lord. This will be easy."

"Wipe that stupid look off your face, soldier," Wiflem commanded gruffly. "Take nothing for granted here."

Sim gave Wiflem a dark look. "Yes, Captain," he said softly.

The big man began to walk away, his body stiff as he studied the ground. I could see the back of his neck was blood-red with anger. I knew Wiflem was highly intelligent and could be thoughtful, almost philosophical at times, and that he was comfortable in any conversation, be it with a peasant or a king. But when it came to his men, Wiflem was all business, with no time for humor or dissent. So far, the men seemed accepting of it, but I knew I would have to watch things closely and step in if needed. High morale made men fight better, but many a lord had lost a battle because his men despised their captain. I had offered the position to Jebido first, of course, but my friend had declined, saying it was a job that he'd done before and had no interest in doing again.

Sim paused, crouching less than a hundred yards from where we had first seen the Daughter's blood-stained tracks. "Look here, my lord," he said, motioning to the scattered leaves and scuff marks that marred the forest floor. "They caught up to her here. There was a struggle, and then it looks like she broke free again." He stood and looked north. "She ran that way."

"Did she get away?" Grindin asked, sounding anxious.

I glanced at the bald apprentice in annoyance, then shifted my look to Baine. "I thought I told you to take him back to Corwick?"

Baine shrugged. "And miss all the fun?"

"There's something else, my lord," Sim said.

I glared at Baine, then shifted my eyes to Sim. "What?"

"There are two sets of tracks now, running together."

"Two?" I said in surprise.

"Stop it! Stop it!" suddenly rang out from the trees ahead of us. "You're hurting her!"

"That's no, Daughter!" I growled, jumping from Angry's back.

I drew my sword and plunged through the trees and scrub brush, heedless of the noise I was making. The voice I'd heard was that of a child, not a woman. Jebido caught up to me, and we both ducked under a low branch and continued, pushing our way through the trees.

"That has to be the Daughter-In-Waiting, Hadrack," Jebido said, panting. I nodded, conserving my breath for what I knew was coming. "I swear," he added, knocking aside a hanging branch with his shield, "if they've hurt her—"

My friend didn't have time to finish as we burst out of the trees to find three horses tied along the rim of a deep basin in front of us. I moved to the edge and looked down. The Daughter lay naked at the hollow's base, her bare feet facing me and covered in blood, while a man stood with his boots on her wrists, drinking from a flask. Another man lay on top of her, his trousers off. He moaned as he thrust into her enthusiastically while he forced his mouth over hers. A third man stood off to one side, holding a young Daughter-

In-Waiting with one hand as he fondled her barely-formed breasts through her grey robe with the other. All three raiders were big and dirty, with wild blond beards and long hair knotted down their backs. The men below me were Piths, just as Jebido had warned me they would be. I cursed under my breath and pointed downward with Wolf's Head.

"Kill the bastards!" I screamed.

I plunged over the rim of the hollow with my men taking up the cry as they followed. The soil beneath my boots was loose and gave way in large clumps, and I was doing more sliding than running as I descended. I heard Niko curse to my right as he lost his balance and fell, rolling end over end before becoming entangled in some bushes. His helmet flew off from the impact and kept going down the hill in front of me, bouncing and twisting crazily. I followed the tumbling helmet's path, leaving Jebido struggling to keep up as I reached the basin floor and aimed for the man holding the child.

The Pith saw me coming and he flung the girl aside, his sword out and waiting for me. I lowered my shield and kept going, roaring as I crashed into him. I heard my opponent's blade scrape loudly across the metal boss of the shield, and he staggered backward three paces, somehow managing to stay on his feet. I snarled, visions of the dead at Lestwick stoking my fury as I whirled and swung Wolf's Head. The Pith warrior brought his sword around incredibly fast, blocking me, but that left him off-balance and vulnerable. I hooked the man's leg out from under him with my foot and swung for his head as he fell. The Pith anticipated me and twisted sideways and all I hit was dirt and leaves. He rolled safely away and then bounded to his feet. I growled low in my chest as the Pith crouched with his sword held two-handed in front of him, watching me warily.

I heard the familiar thrum of bowstrings from the rim of the basin, and I glanced toward the prostrate Daughter. One of the Piths lay thrashing on the ground beside the sobbing priestess with two arrows in his stomach. The second man stood over the naked woman with a sword in his hand. His legs were bare and dirty and his long chainmail hung almost to his scuffed knees. The raider screamed a challenge just as an arrow sliced through the mail high on his right breast, staggering him. He took a step forward, grunting, then fell back as a second arrow caught him low in the stomach, just above his groin. The warrior sagged to one knee, supporting himself with his sword as my men surrounded him. He snarled, spitting blood and wobbling as he tried unsuccessfully to stand. Wiflem snorted with contempt, then stepped forward and took his head with a vengeful slash of his sword.

I focused back on my opponent. The man was tall, almost six feet, though he was thinner and less muscular than most Piths that I had known. His nose was long and narrow, and his eyes brown, which was an unusual trait for Piths. My men moved to flank me on either side, and I caught a glimpse of Baine's black leather armor moving through the trees above me to my right. I knew without having to look that Tyris had taken up a similar position to my left. There was nowhere for the Pith to run.

I could hear Grindin and the girl consoling the hysterical Daughter behind me, and I felt the haze of the killing-blood starting to fade. I slowly relaxed, lowering Wolf's Head to my side. There was no hurry now, and I needed to get some answers first before the Pith died.

"Who are you?" I demanded.

The Pith stared at me, his eyes surly, his expression filled with contempt. "My name is too good to waste on a Ganderman," he finally spat.

I smiled coldly. It was just the kind of answer that I would have expected from someone like him. The Pith was young, no more than sixteen or seventeen, with an aura of arrogance and cockiness about him that I remembered well from my days among his people. The Pith's hair was shaggy and tall on top, then twisted into a long pleat behind. His scalp was shaven on the sides, revealing hundreds of thin ridges of black scar tissue formed into identical, dragon-like beasts on each side. I knew the scars had been made using intricate cuts that were then filled with fine charcoal dye. It was a painstaking procedure usually reserved only for Piths of special stature, so whoever this boy was, I realized that he must be important.

A silver torc hung around the Pith's neck and I studied it with interest. I'd seen similar torcs before and guessed that the Pith was either one of the Amenti, Tutanti, or Cimbrati tribes that dwelled along the southeastern coast of the Pith homeland. I could see what appeared to be bears carved onto the surface of the torc, and knowing that Amenti meant 'bear people' in the Piths ancient language, I assumed he was one of these. I had met only a few Amenti in my time with the Piths, and quite truthfully, had liked none of them. Einhard had not hidden his dislike for the Amenti from me, either, describing them as too blood-thirsty, perverted, and quarrelsome to trust. I remember I had found the description amusing, coming from him, but had wisely chosen not to point out the obvious irony.

"You have come a long way," I said. "Are the Amenti so desperate and weak now that they have to travel this far north to prey on innocent women and children?"

The Pith's eyebrows rose in surprise. "You know of the Amenti?"

"Enough to know you are all shit-eating cowards," I grunted. The Pith's eyes gleamed with anger, which made me smile. I casually wiped specks of dirt from the blade of my sword. "I am the Lord of Corwick," I continued. "And you have come to my lands and killed my people. I want to know why? Surely there is easier prey closer to home for vultures such as you?"

The Pith just snorted in contempt. "When the lands of your cursed kingdom run red with blood from coast to coast, then you will understand why we have come." He laughed. "But by then, it will be too late."

I felt a momentary uneasiness at the Amenti's words. "What have you done to the Son and his apprentice?" I demanded, hiding my concern from the Pith.

The boy's lips twitched in amusement. "We have done nothing to them, Ganderman. They live to serve a higher purpose now. What would have been wasted lives prostrating themselves before your false gods will now bring strength to the Piths instead."

I frowned. "What does that mean?" The warrior just smiled. "Tell me what I want to know, Amenti," I finally said when he added nothing further, "and I promise your death will be quick and painless."

The Pith just shrugged. "All men die, Ganderman. If this is my time, then so be it. I am not afraid."

"You're right," I agreed. "All men do die. But some die old in their beds, while others die in horrible pain screaming for their mother." I grinned. "Which death do you see coming for you?"

The Pith looked unaffected by my threat as he glanced at the twisted corpses of his companions. "You have killed my brothers, Gander, and soon you will kill me. But hear my words before my tongue is silenced. My people will return for me, and when they see what you have done, they will burn your mighty castle to the ground and slaughter your people. They will rape your woman and whatever foul children you have sired while you are forced to watch, then they will geld you and drag you home behind the slowest ox. You will spend your last miserable days being tortured by Pith children, begging for the sweet release of death."

I turned and shared a look with Jebido, knowing that the young Amenti wasn't just talking bravado. What he said was the truth. The savage Piths had been known to travel for weeks to retrieve a fallen brother and take them back to the Ascension Grounds. They would ride back to Corwick looking for these men, just as the warrior said. Once the Piths found the bodies, or even if we got rid of them, I knew they would turn vengeful eyes on my people and strike back the only way they knew how—with death and destruction. I couldn't allow that to happen.

"What do you think, Jebido?" I asked, moving closer to him and lowering my voice so that the Pith couldn't hear.

Jebido shrugged. "They will come back. No question about it."

"That might not be a bad thing," I said thoughtfully. I had seventy soldiers garrisoned at Corwick, with twenty more stationed at Knoxly Manor, a small holding of mine forty miles to the north. "If we can choose the time and place to meet them," I added. "We can wipe the lot of them out and get the Son and boy back at the same time."

"That's risky, Hadrack," Jebido said. "We don't even know for sure how many Piths are out there. And even if they go where you want them to, most of your troops are still young and raw. They can't even grow a proper beard yet, let alone go up against warriors like the Piths."

Jebido was right, of course. I had dismissed most of Pernissy's men when I'd become lord, unable to stomach the idea of anyone working for me who had sworn an oath to that bastard. The garrison's replacements were mostly strong village lads from my lands I had hired to serve alongside the more seasoned men that Wiflem had brought with him. We were training the youths, and some showed great promise, but it would still be some time before they were ready.

I glanced at the Amenti. It would be useful to know what the Piths' actual strength was, but I knew the boy wasn't going to tell me. I could try torturing the information from him, of course, but even though the Amenti was young, he was still a Pith, and I knew I would get nothing. The raiders would come back, that was certain, and when they did, I needed their full hatred focused on me and not the villages of Corwick. The only way I saw to do that was to send them a message through the boy—one that couldn't be ignored.

I turned, my mind made up. "Wiflem."

"My lord?"

I pointed to the dead men. "Take the heads of those two raping bastards and put them on poles right there. Make sure you take out the eyes. Then strip the bodies of their mail and throw the stinking carcasses in the river." The Amenti was staring at me in confusion. I smiled as I took several steps closer to him. "You can't Ascend a soul if you can't find the body," I explained cheerfully. "And a head without eyes isn't enough to find the Path."

The Pith's features twisted ugly with hatred, and his sword wavered and then dropped as he spat angry curses at me. The boy's reaction was exactly what I had been hoping for as I launched myself forward. I crashed the hilt of my sword into the young warrior's face even as I rammed the edge of my shield down on his foot. The Pith yelped in surprise and pain, yet still had the presence of mind to bring his sword back up. I slashed the weapon out of his hand, then kicked him in the chest, sending him reeling backward to the ground. I tossed my shield and sword aside and dropped my full weight onto the Amenti's chest, then began pummeling him with my fists until he stopped struggling. I stood, forcing myself not to take his life right there. He wasn't getting off that easy. One of the Pith's eyes was swollen closed and seeping dark blood from the side, but the other glared up at me with naked hate.

"I am Nedo," the Amenti finally managed to say through cracked and broken teeth. "A better man than you can ever hope to be. I am not afraid to die."

"Oh, I know you're not," I growled as I stood over him. "But the real question is, are you afraid to live?" I held out a hand to my men. "I need a knife." Wiflem stepped forward and wordlessly slapped the worn hilt of his blade into my palm. "Make a fire," I told him. "A small one."

Wiflem paused for a heartbeat, then he nodded. "Yes, my lord."

"Jebido," I said, glancing at my friend. "Get the Daughter and the girl away from here. This isn't for their eyes."

"Hadrack, are you sure about this?"

I just glared without saying anything until Jebido finally shrugged and walked away. Nedo was trying to sit up, and I placed a boot on his chest and shoved him back down. "Hold him tightly," I grunted to my men. Then I knelt, and with several quick slashes, cut open his trousers. The Pith struggled ferociously in the arms of Sim and Berwin, spitting and cursing me, but he was helpless in their strong grips. I locked eyes with the young warrior as I grabbed his ball-sack and pulled the sweat-slicked flesh toward me. "I am the Lord of Corwick," I growled, "and this is what happens to raping bastards on my lands." Nedo's eyes were wide with fright as he pleaded with me for mercy. But after what I'd seen in Lestwick, I had none to give. The knife flashed, and the boy screamed as I took that which made him a man. His body contorted as dark red blood splattered over the both of us before it began to pool in a black puddle at my feet. I stood, ignoring the Pith's pitiful whimpering as I held the dripping mass of flesh up for him to see.

"Consider this an offering to your Master," I said as I threw the boy's severed balls into the hungry flames, where the juices, blood, and flesh immediately began to sizzle. "Maybe someday the both of you can be reunited with your precious Master." I stooped and set the knife down with the red-stained blade lying directly in the fire. "Now you have a choice, Amenti," I said as I stood over him again. "You can lie there and whimper like a dog as your lifeblood spills on the ground, or you can drag yourself over to that knife and staunch the flow and live." I shrugged. "I don't really care which choice you make."

I turned away from him then, motioning for my men to follow me as I headed up the incline of the basin. No one said anything, and other than the agonized sobbing coming from the Pith below, the woods were silent. Finally, we reached the rim where Jebido waited with Grindin, the Daughter, and the girl.

"You're a monster," Grindin said in a horrified whisper as I stalked past him.

I paused, then came back to tower over the apprentice as he shrunk from me. "Count yourself lucky if that's all I do to you when the time comes," I said. The apprentice began to tremble, his lips twitching as white sticky mucus formed at the corners of his mouth. I turned away in contempt. "Niko!"

"My lord?"

"Stay here and watch that bastard down there. If he dies, put his head with the others and dump the body in the river. If he survives and gets on his horse, follow him until his stench no longer stains my lands, then let him go."

"Yes, my lord."

"And Niko."

"My lord?"

"If he does die, make sure you take his eyes."

"Yes, my lord."

I nodded in satisfaction. That should do it, I thought, regardless of whether the boy lives or dies. Jebido fell into step beside me, his expression filled with worry. "What?" I grunted at him.

"Nothing."

I snorted. "I know that look on your face, Jebido. Do you think what I did was wrong?"

"Not at all," Jebido responded. "I'm just afraid you might have kicked a hornet's nest, that's all."

I nodded, feeling suddenly weary and homesick. "I expect you might be right about that."

And he was.

5: Corwick Castle

We live in a ruthless world filled with cruelty, indifference, and pain. There are good men and women among us, to be sure—people like Jebido, Baine, Wiflem, and my dear wife, Shana. But for every one like them, there are ten more like Pernissy, Hervi Desh, and First Son Oriell. For men like that, mercy and pity are considered weaknesses—fatal character flaws that make a man feeble and easy prey. Woe to the lord who shows timidness and vulnerability around any of those baying wolves. You either show your teeth early and fight, or get pulled down by the pack as they feast on your still-warm flesh.

I was not yet twenty-two years old the day the Piths raided Lestwick, and because of the king's generosity, as well as my marriage to Shana, I had become one of the richest and most powerful men in Ganderland. I now controlled not only Corwick, but Calban as well. It was a fact that never failed to astonish me. I had three main responsibilities as the Lord of Corwick and Calban. First, I was to serve and obey my king at all times. Second, ensure that my holdings remained profitable, enabling me to pay the yearly fees due to the royal house. The third, and to me the most important, was to protect the vassals of my two fiefdoms. I had failed miserably in that last duty here in Corwick, and that failure was a heavy weight for me to bear.

I knew I couldn't change the past and save the people of Lestwick, nor raise the dead, but I could still avenge them. Grindin had called me a monster for what I had done, and perhaps he was right about that. But, offering any form of leniency to Nedo—while maybe the wiser choice—was unthinkable to me after what he and his fellow Piths had done. A message had needed to be sent. Not just to the Piths and any others that would dare try to pillage my lands. But to the people who looked to me for their welfare and protection as well.

I sent Sim and Tyris to warn the other villages about the Piths after we left the hollow, with instructions for my people to flee to the hills or take refuge in the castle until I had dealt with the threat. I wasn't sure how many of my vassals would come or, for that matter, how long they would need to stay behind my walls. I just knew that the next day or two would be very unsettling for a great many people until this was over. A part of me was starting to regret not going after the remaining Piths after we had located the Daughter. I had chosen not to in the end because I knew I would lose some of my men if I did—maybe even all of them. These were Piths we were dealing with, after all, not cowardly Cardians. The hurried plan that I had devised while talking to Nedo had seemed a far safer bet. But, now that I'd had more time to think it over, I realized that I would need a great deal of luck, not to mention The Mother's support for it to work at all.

There were still many miles left to go before we reached Corwick Castle, and I could feel the mischievous fingers of self-doubt working on me as we rode. What if the Piths didn't do what I expected? What if there were more of them than I thought? I knew the Piths as well as any man in Ganderland possibly could, but even I couldn't always anticipate what they would do. I frowned, hunching down in my saddle as I mulled over the different possible outcomes to the message that I'd left. I sighed, feeling my stomach start to twist and turn with unease, knowing there was a good chance that it wouldn't be what I wanted. Perhaps instead of finding a solution to the Pith problem, my actions had just made it infinitely worse.

My men must have sensed my troubles, for they chose to leave me alone with my thoughts for the duration of the journey. I was in a bleak mood by the time we finally sighted Corwick Castle, and not even seeing the stout walls and elegant spires flying my snarling wolf banner was enough to break me out of that mood. It hadn't helped that the Daughter had cried most of the way home either, with Grindin riding beside her, his gentle, hugely annoying voice offering endless false words of sympathy. I'd strongly considered striking the apprentice to keep him quiet, but figured the last thing the distraught Daughter needed right now was more male violence. Besides, there was always the slim chance that the little bastard's words were helping her in some way. The Daughter-In-Waiting rode with Jebido, perched in front of him on his saddle, even though we had extra horses. She never said a word the entire trip and just stared with sad eyes at the ground in front of her while Jebido kept his arms wrapped protectively around her slight body.

Corwick Castle was built on a towering promontory that dominated the midday skyline, with the bustling market town of Camwick sprawling out along an open plain a quarter-mile from the hill's base. Why the town was named Camwick, and the village I grew up in was called Corwick, was a riddle that I had never been able to solve, even to this day. The castle's history was a long one, and it had begun life as a simple wooden hillfort, built almost four hundred years ago by the famed Flin king, Banon of the Hand. It had been called Tinagru then, which roughly translated, meant—*the place where eagles sleep.*

We joined the busy road that led toward the town as traders, woodsmen, grain merchants, and all manner of travelers moved aside for us, many of them calling out my name. I nodded to a few I knew but pressed on, clattering over an arched stone bridge that spanned a canal that King Banon had dug long ago. The channel had been just a rough ditch to begin with, designed to ferry water from the Muddy Dip River that lay miles to the west. The canal's course ran along the southern edge of the town's outer limits and then swept north to feed the thirty-foot wide moat that circled the hill's base where Corwick Castle sat. Banon's original ditch had been less than six-feet wide and four-feet deep, but it had been widened and deepened over the years to almost triple that in places.

Now, the canal not only fed the moat, but allowed merchants from Camwick to transport goods by barges to the larger towns that lay to the north. Long swaying horsetail weed grass choked the waters on either side of the bridge as we passed over it, reminding me that Finol had mentioned that we would need to dredge the waterway soon before it became impassable. I had forgotten all about it when I received the letter from Grindin.

I led my men through the open gates of Camwick at a canter, having to immediately skirt Angry around a small cart laden with milk, eggs, and cheese that had lost a wheel. An older man with a long white beard and red face stood beside the cart, shouting at a crestfallen-looking youth. Neither man nor boy noticed us as we rode deeper into the town. We reached a street lined with rich merchants' houses, most with their shops open, selling everything from Afrenian silk to fine jewels and rare Parnuthian wine. Today was market day, I realized with a curse, which meant the town's population had probably tripled. The knowledge that I would have even more bodies crammed into the castle now did nothing to improve my mood.

Merchants were calling out their wares in shrill voices, competing with each other for the attention of well-to-do ladies and their servants who browsed the traders' merchandise. Half-wild packs of barking dogs and equally wild grubby children roamed the streets while wary food sellers eyed them suspiciously. I could hear bells ringing from the Holy House to the west, and then the sounds of deep chanting arose as a group of newly ordained Sons-In-Waiting in crisp brown robes marched smartly down a side street, their freshly shaven heads gleaming in the sunlight.

A man haggling with a merchant over a stick of hot sheep's feet waved as we thundered past, shouting, "Hail to Lord Hadrack! Hero of the Pair War!"

I glanced back over my shoulder, bristling at being called a hero. Will he still call me that when he learns of Lestwick? I knew the news couldn't have reached Camwick yet, but soon, once the castle bell began to ring, they would learn of the slaughter. Would my name be cheered then, or cursed?

We reached the town center, where more traders' shops and stalls lined the market square. These were the smaller, less affluent merchants who catered to the common folk—the ones with only the odd coin to spare. The shops were all narrow and packed together in a jumble, many of them less than ten-feet wide. Painted signs above each place of business depicted the trader's occupation, since few if any of their intended customers could read. I saw scissors for a hair-cutter, a fine brush for an artist, a loaf of bread for a baker, and even an oversized shoe perched on a pole for a shoemaker. That last one made me think of Emand, the savage cordwainer that I had killed in Oasis. I thrust the little man from my mind as we left the crowded market square behind, heading toward Camwick's outer limits.

We left the town and followed the road north as it sloped up toward Corwick Castle. Our horses' gait began to increase despite the grade as they sensed they were almost home, with the reward of a few handfuls of grain, some water, and a thorough rubdown awaiting them. The terrain around the castle for a quarter-mile in all directions was littered with chipped stones of all shapes and sizes, forcing any attacker—or traveler for that matter—to stay directly on the road. Castis Corwick, the original Lord of Corwick, had brought in the stones after he'd laid siege and captured the castle three hundred years ago.

The dark, sludge-filled moat sat motionless to my right as we rode, the stillness of the water broken on occasion by the brilliant colors of yellow-legged dragonflies skimming the surface. I glanced up as someone hailed me, while unconsciously wrinkling my nose at the smells coming from the moat. Men in armor watched from the ramparts high above our heads, and I could hear their faint cheers. I gave them a perfunctory wave despite my mood as we climbed the ramp and clattered across the open drawbridge. Putt was waiting for us on the other side of the barbican with Ubeth the gatekeeper, a bear of a man with a bushy beard, bald head, and looped silver rings in his ears.

You had best hope a Pith doesn't see all that silver, I thought to myself sourly as I dismounted.

"You're back early, my lord," Putt said with a welcoming grin. He reached out to stroke Angry's neck. The big black snorted in warning and Putt hesitated before he carefully drew his hand away. "Did you find the bastard, my lord?"

"Where is Lady Shana?" I snapped.

Putt's grin faltered at the look on my face. "Uh, at the academy, I believe, my lord."

I nodded, not surprised. I handed Angry's reins to one of the many grooms waiting nearby. Shana had become fascinated with the science and theories behind Haverty's healing methods and had enticed the strange apothecary to come to Corwick and begin a school of learning here. "Tell her I have returned and wish to see her right away."

"Is something wrong, my lord?"

"Piths have laid waste to Lestwick. Everyone is dead."

Putt gasped in surprise, and I could hear men muttering angrily around me at the news. "Wiflem," I grunted, turning to my captain as he dismounted. "Assemble the men. Pick thirty that can shoot a bow competently, then meet me in my solar."

Wiflem bowed his head. "I'll see to it, my lord. What of Knoxly?"

I had twenty of my soldiers stationed at the manor. Those men were my rawest and least promising, watched over by a rarely-sober old veteran with one eye named Daminco. I dearly hoped that I wouldn't need any of them. If I did, then the lands of Corwick were truly in trouble. "Send a rider with the news, but tell Daminco they are to keep the gates closed and to stay put until he hears from me."

"Very good, my lord," Wiflem said with a curt nod.

"Ubeth."

"My lord?"

"Ring the bell. Keep the gates open and the drawbridge down until I say otherwise. We are about to get very crowded in here."

"Right away, my lord."

I watched as Grindin dismounted stiffly and then hurried to help the still-shaken Daughter from her horse. I was relieved to see that she had finally stopped crying. The Daughter's name was Tessa, I'd learned, and her apprentice was called Lucenda. Jebido gently lowered Lucenda to the ground before she ran to the Daughter and hugged her tightly.

"Is that bald bastard who I think he is?" Putt asked, gesturing to Grindin.

"Yes," I grunted with distaste. "I want him locked up in the White Tower. Give him food and water, but keep a guard on him at all times." I looked around. "Where is Parcival?"

"Here, lord," came the reply as a very short, thin man dressed in dark green leather appeared from the shadows of one of the storehouses.

Parcival was my master huntsman and almost as good a tracker as Sabina. I'd seen him disappear within the trees like magic on many an occasion. Parcival had three sons nearly as accomplished on the trail as he was, and even Piths wouldn't know they were there if they didn't want to be seen. "The enemy fled south after sacking Lestwick," I told the hunter. "But I have every reason to believe they are coming back this way soon. Take your sons and find them and report back to me. I want to know everything about their movements and strength. Whatever you do, don't let them see you, and be careful."

Parcival nodded. "Consider it done, my lord."

"Lord Hadrack, may I have a word?"

I paused as Daughter Tessa strode toward me with the child apprentice still clutching possessively at her tattered yellow robes. "Yes, Daughter?" I said as I tapped Parcival on the shoulder, indicating he could go. The bell began to ring from the watchtower, the deep, resonating sound a clear message that couldn't be ignored. I vowed it would keep ringing until every last soul on my lands was safe.

"I know you have much to do, my lord, but I wanted to thank you once again for coming to our aid."

I glanced at the girl apprentice, who just stared back at me with a blank expression on her face. I guessed she was no more than ten, which was young for a Daughter-In-Waiting. "I only wish I had found you sooner," I said, meaning it.

Daughter Tessa lowered her eyes, then turned and glanced through the open gates to the southwest. She shuddered before turning back to me. "Are you certain the heathens are coming back, my lord?"

"Positive," I said firmly. "But this time, we'll be ready for them." I motioned to a servant girl. "Take the Daughter and her charge to the Holy House and see to their needs." I turned back to the priestess. "I imagine Daughter Verica will be along shortly and will wish to speak with you."

The priestess bowed. "Thank you, lord, I know her well." She hesitated. "I want to apologize for my lack of restraint earlier. I should have composed myself better after—" She paused and looked away, tears on her cheeks. She smiled down at Lucenda and hugged her closer, ignoring the tears as she regarded me again. "It's just that I vowed when the time came for me to join The Mother in the world Above, that my body would still be pure and unsullied by the hands of men."

"There was nothing you could do, Daughter," I said, uncomfortable now. "I'm sure the Mother will not judge you for the sins of others."

"Perhaps," Daughter Tessa said, looking unconvinced. "There is one other thing," she added as I turned to go. I waited. "I don't know what the disagreement between you and apprentice Grindin might be, my lord, but I just want you to know that he is a good man. His compassion and kind words during the journey helped me immensely."

I felt instant anger well up. "Did he ask you to say that?"

Daughter Tessa blinked at me in surprise. "Well, he did wonder if I might consider interceding in the dispute on his behalf. But—"

I snorted and pointed at the apprentice's back as Putt and one of my soldiers led him away. "Don't be fooled by that bastard, Daughter. He's as evil as they come. That man makes the Piths who raped you look like harmless children."

I turned and strode away before she could say anything more, my back stiff with anger. Everywhere I went, people kept telling me what a good man Grindin was. It was maddening how easily he had fooled them. Jebido and Baine fell into step beside me, both wisely staying silent as we walked past the smithy, the stables, then the barracks before heading up the ramp that led toward the inner bailey. Soldiers bearing shields and spears stood at attention as we passed through the gates, their obvious unease with the weapons marking them as recent peasants. I shuddered as I thought of men like these facing Piths in open combat. If only I'd had another year with them, I thought.

We skirted the fish pond, which was stocked this time of year with trout and pike, then headed for the keep. Servants tended the garden near the kitchens, with fruit trees and vines growing neatly at one end and vegetables, flowers, and herbs at the other. The kitchens were already busy, I saw, with even more servants bustling about preparing a welcoming meal in celebration of my return. I could hear Hanley's raised voice over the clang of the bell as he scolded one of the servants inside. I smiled despite my bleak mood. The boy had the power of my steward, Finol, behind him, and the servants lived in terror of Hanley's unyielding need for perfection in all things.

"My lord?"

I turned as Shana hurried toward me, holding up the hem of her blue dress as she half-ran and half-walked. She was attended by twin girls of seventeen, Hesther and Hamber, who were the daughters of Lord Lamburtin of Nothlington. The girls were exceedingly ugly, and Lord Lamburtin had all but given up hope of arranging marriages for them since they were not only equally undesirable but inseparable from each other. The very nature of their closeness and dependence on one another meant the unlucky man who married one would be obligated to take both. So far, no lord had risen to the challenge, even with the promise of a hefty retainer and lands dangled before them. Shana had graciously agreed to take the girls on as her court ladies, with the idea that perhaps she could work on their dancing, etiquette, and command of languages, not to mention their appearances.

"Is it true?" Shana asked, her eyes wide with concern. "The entire town?"

I nodded. "All but the Daughter and her charge as far as I know." I gestured toward Camwick. "And any that were lucky enough to come to market today, I suppose."

Shana studied me, the grief on her face switching to anxiety when she saw the dried blood splattered across my legs and mail. "You're hurt, my lord!"

"It's not mine," I said, reassuring her as we headed for the keep. "We caught up to three of the Piths," I explained. "The blood belongs to one of them." Shana and I walked side by side, with her hand on my arm, unconsciously squeezing it. Baine and Jebido walked behind us, with the twin girls following them, their red-pimpled faces lowered in sorrow.

"Putt tells me you returned with that horrible man who wrote the letter," Shana said after a moment.

"I did," I replied, frowning.

"Why?" Shana asked. "I thought you were going to kill him."

I patted my wife's hand. "That, my love, is a question that deserves a long answer. One which will have to wait until later, I'm afraid. We have bigger problems right now."

"What are you going to do about the Piths?" Shana asked. I could hear the worry in her voice.

I shrugged, feeling my bleak mood start to slip away now that I was with my wife. "I'm going to kill every one of the bastards," I promised as we climbed the ramp to the keep. "Then I'll deal with Grindin."

Finol was waiting for us inside the keep, his usual neutral expression fixed with sadness. "Greetings, my lord," he said. "A great tragedy, to be sure."

"Yes," I said with a nod. "We are about to receive a great many guests, so you had best get to your preparations."

Finol's forehead creased down the middle, which I knew from experience over the last several years meant that he was annoyed. "I am aware of the significance of the bell, my lord," he said with a sniff. "Arrangements for the care of those coming have already been seen to. We will have temporary lodgings, food, and drink prepared for at least four hundred people within the hour."

"Good," I grunted over my shoulder as I climbed the winding wooden stairs that led up to the second floor.

Most of the castles in the realm had their great halls on the ground floor, but Castis Corwick had rebuilt the castle after he'd sacked it and had added a second floor with a much bigger hall—called Corwick Hall. The original hall on the ground floor—called the Lesser Hall—was now being used as sleeping quarters for the servants and as an extended buttery and pantry.

A hundred years after Castis Corwick's death, his grandson, Brimal Corwick, added a third floor, where the lord and lady now had their bedchambers. The castle remained unchanged after that until King Jorquin granted Pernissy the lands of Corwick after the Border War. The new Lord of Corwick added a masonry arcade at the back of the dais in Corwick Hall and built a series of small chambers above it overlooking the moat on the eastern side, accessed by wooden stairs. One of the chambers was used as a communal privy, while many others were simple stockrooms and guest rooms. I'd taken over the largest chamber and now used it as my solar and meeting room, just as I had back at Witbridge Manor.

"Will you be ready to dine soon, my lord?" Finol asked me.

I just shook my head as I entered Corwick Hall. "Have some pork pie and beer brought to my solar. Enough for all my counsel. There will be no feast this night for any of us." I paused, watching as three servant girls finished sweeping and cleaning the hall's timber floor while men came behind them, spreading fresh rushes mixed with herbs such as basil, balm, and cowslip. The floor had been covered with many years' worth of rushes when I arrived, with servants just removing the top layer and replacing it occasionally. I had changed that, having it all replaced once every two weeks. The walls of the great hall were paneled with fir boards and painted white and gold, with wall hangings of painted wool or linen at the back of the dais and to either side. Oil lamps fixed to the walls with metal brackets lit the interior.

"I'll see to it right away, my lord," Finol said.

"One more thing," I said as the old steward turned to go. "I need maps of my lands. Have you seen any?"

Finol paused, thinking. "I believe I heard Son Chester mention something about maps, my lord. I can go speak with him if you like?"

"Please do that," I said. "Also, have you seen Margot?"

Finol shook his head. "Not since this morning, my lord."

"Send a boy to find her then," I grunted. "I wish her advice."

I had begun discussing all my plans with my men and the whores that I'd brought with me from Hillsfort when I masqueraded as the lord of Witbridge Manor. It was a habit that I had grown used to, and I saw no reason why that needed to change now that I was an actual lord. Margot was the last of the three whores still alive, with Aenor dying in the attack on Calban and Flora to the blade of an outlaw assassin. Margot's opinions were not as sharp-witted as Flora's had been, nor as thoughtful as Aenor's, but she was quite intelligent, and when she chose to speak, we all listened to her with great respect.

I sent Hesther and Hamber away, then waited with Baine, Jebido, and my wife in the solar, resisting Shana's queries about what was happening until the others arrived. I didn't want to have to repeat myself each time. Finally, Shana gave up her questions with a snort and started exchanging pleasantries with my two friends instead. I ignored their conversation, turning my thoughts inward as I began to pace impatiently in front of a single arched window that faced the eastern plains. Putt eventually joined us, then Sim, Wiflem, and Tyris, all of them sitting along the low wooden benches that lined the walls.

Margot came in next, looking slightly embarrassed, I thought, then servants carrying steaming pork pies, mugs of foaming beer, and oil lamps to light the chamber now that dusk was approaching. The servants put the food and drink on the long table in the center of the room, then quickly left. Niko was the only one missing now, but I didn't want to begin until I had heard from him and knew Nebo's fate, so we continued to wait. My men started to eat, talking in subdued voices, but I felt no desire to join them. I would eat, I decided, when the Pith threat was over and my people were safe.

I stared out the window as long shadows cast by the castle's towers stretched like seeking fingers across the open plain. The wind had strengthened, and I could feel the coolness of the breeze teasing at my beard as it whistled through the opening. I thought about closing the shutters, then decided it could wait until darkness fell. I'd heard the Lumarians had perfected a new way of making glass last year—something called crown glass—that sealed a window yet still allowed you to look outside. It seemed an impossible concept to me, yet I made a mental note to talk with Finol about looking into it at some point.

"My lord."

I turned as Niko finally entered the solar. "Ah," I said. "There you are. What happed with Nedo?"

"He's alive, my lord," Niko said as he sat on a bench beside Putt. He eyed the beer on the table and unconsciously licked his lips. "May I, my lord?" he asked, indicating the mugs. I nodded, my arms crossed over my chest as I waited. Niko took a deep gulp of beer, burped, and then wiped his mouth with the back of his hand. "Thank you, my lord. I needed that. Trying to get through that mob down by the gates gave me an awful thirst."

"You said the boy lives," I grunted. "Did he use the knife, then?"

"He did," Niko said with a shudder. "A horrible thing to watch, my lord. He lay there for a long time afterward, then dragged himself to his horse and rode south. I wasn't sure if he would make it, but he's a tough bastard, that one. The last I saw of him, he was still in the saddle."

"Very well," I said, impressed at the Amenti's strength of character. Most men would have just laid there and died in his situation. "Any sign of the rest of them?"

"Nothing, my lord," Niko said with a quick shake of his head before he took another gulp of beer.

I took a moment then to finally explain to Putt, Margot and Shana what had happened that morning with the Piths, finishing just as Finol appeared with a long roll of parchment in his hand.

"The map?" I asked hopefully.

"Indeed, my lord," Finol said. He unrolled the map and spread it on the table, using empty mugs to hold it open. "This was drawn for Lord Corwick not long before his death in the war," Finol explained. Everyone crowded around the table to see as Finol pointed to a crude depiction of a castle. "Here, you see Corwick Castle. And this blue area over here is Lake Castis. These wiggly lines are rivers and streams, and these open areas are pastures, farmland, and such. The rest is mostly forested areas and small woodlands, with the iron ore and coal mines here and here."

"What is this?" Putt asked, pointing to a tiny black square near one of the woodlands.

"That is the village of Oakwick," Finol answered.

Putt whistled. There were a lot of black squares on the map. I knew I had fourteen villages on my lands, which I had learned amounted to almost five thousand acres. It was a staggering number, and though I understood that all the lords in Ganderland only held their lands in trust for the king himself, it was still humbling to see everything laid out so plainly in front of me like this.

"Which one of these is Lestwick?" I asked.

"Here, my lord," Finol said, tapping a tiny square far from Corwick Castle.

"So, this is the Little Run," I said, understanding now as I pointed to the river near the town. "And this would be the forest where we found the Piths."

"Yes, my lord," Finol agreed. "I would expect that is correct."

I drew my sword, surprising everyone, then used the blade to mark a line from Corwick Castle, out at an angle to the east of Lestwick. I turned to Wiflem, who stood beside me. "Your weapon, please." Wiflem wordlessly handed his sword to me, hilt first. I did the same thing with his blade, this time angling it to the west of Lestwick.

"The Piths will be coming back from the south this way," I said, sweeping a finger down to where the two swords crossed each other. "It won't be today, I imagine, but most likely tomorrow. They will be moving fast and looking for blood." I glanced up at the faces around me. "So, where will they go first?" No one answered. Four black squares were lying between the two blades, and I tapped the southern-most one. "This is Lestwick." I slid my hand north. "And this is Camwick." I gestured to the remaining squares. "But what about the other two?"

Finol leaned over, squinting at the barely seen writing below each square. "Leedswick and Ashwick, my lord."

"And what happens when the Piths reach those villages?" I asked.

"They'll burn them to the ground, my lord," Putt said without hesitation.

I nodded in agreement. "Yes, they will. But the villages will be empty by then, and our people will be safe. Villages can be rebuilt."

"Which means the Piths will become very frustrated and keep pushing north," Jebido said, staring at the map as he pulled at his beard. "Until they find somebody to kill."

"Exactly," I agreed. "And even if there are twice as many as we think, they would need a thousand men to be any serious threat to Corwick Castle." I grinned. "Which only leaves them Camwick to vent their hatred on when they get here." I looked around at the serious faces. "And that, my friends, is where we are going to trap the bastards and kill them all."

6: The Battle of Camwick

The Piths didn't come the next day like I thought they would. Nor the following day or the day after that, either, which left me feeling confused and uneasy about their plans. Why were they waiting? Parcival and his sons had located the Pith camp ten miles from Corwick's borders on the first night of the attack on Lestwick. The hunter had counted thirty-two warriors, a Pathfinder, and five women in the camp, which surprised me. While female Piths joining their men on raids wasn't that unusual, the Amenti tended to leave their women behind. Parcival had seen no sign of Nedo, nor the missing Son and his apprentice, though the hunter did mention a single tent stood in the center of the camp, guarded by two Piths. I knew the savage warriors rarely bothered with tents when raiding, preferring to sleep outside, so the tent was of great interest to me. Could Nedo be inside receiving treatment for his wound? It would certainly explain why they hadn't moved yet.

The Piths were vulnerable where they had chosen their camp, which rarely happened. It left a bad taste in my mouth to know that we were helpless to take advantage of that vulnerability because of me. If I'd kept Pernissy's experienced soldiers in my garrison as Jebido had suggested months ago instead of dismissing them, I could have surrounded the Piths and wiped out the entire band. But, as usual, I had been too stubborn to listen to my friend's advice. Most of my men were plucked from the villages and were nothing at the moment but well-meaning, untrained farm boys. Of course, we'd been working with them, but molding a man used to wielding a hoe all his life into a soldier that could swing a sword effectively takes time. I remembered all too well what had happened when the Piths had faced Pernissy's peasants at

Gasterny, and I knew any assault I tried to make with men similar to those would end in disaster.

My tenure as a lord, I had come to realize with some bitterness, had so far been marred by nothing but bad choices and stupidity. I was determined not to make any more mistakes, but as each day went by with no movement from the Piths, my resolve to stay put was weakening. Was that what they wanted? The Piths couldn't get to me behind my stout walls, so were they playing a waiting game, hoping I would lose patience and come out to be slaughtered? Or did they have some other plan in mind?

"Just what exactly are you up to?" I muttered to myself as I stood on the ramparts, staring south over the deserted town. My preparations in Camwick were completed the first night, with my hidden men now growing bored and undoubtedly less alert by the hour as they awaited the Pith attack.

"I would guess they're holding back until reinforcements arrive," Baine answered, thinking that I had spoken to him. He stood beside me with his back against the battlements as he cut a thick wedge from an apple. Baine paused, then offered the slice to me on the blade of his knife. I shook my head and he popped the fruit in his mouth. "I'm surprised they are showing such restraint," Baine added as he chewed. "It's not like Piths to wait for anything."

"I know," I grunted. "Assuming it's actually restraint."

Below me, I could hear the continuous drone of voices rising from both baileys, mixing with the sounds of yelping dogs, braying mules, bleating goats, and the piercing, shrill cries of hungry babies. Three hundred and six displaced people were crammed into Corwick Castle, and after three long days of waiting, the tension inside the walls seemed thick enough to cut with a knife. I sighed, thinking for the hundredth time that maybe I had made a mistake by bringing them all here. I'd had to hang a man for killing his own brother over a whore yesterday, and arguments and fights inside my walls were increasing by the hour. Putt had told me that he'd heard rumblings the people were far from satisfied with how I had handled things so far. I couldn't blame them for that, I suppose, since neither was I.

I glanced to the hills south of the castle and frowned. If the Piths didn't come sniffing at the trap I'd laid for them soon, then I feared the villagers hiding in the hills would eventually become impatient and return to their homes. The moment that happened, all my careful preparations would fall apart. We would then be left sitting on our thumbs and helpless as vengeful Piths rode with impunity across my lands, raping and pillaging. Trying to chase after highly mobile, expert riders like the Piths on foot would be pointless. And, assuming I could even come up with enough horses for all of my men, I was sure more than half of them couldn't ride anyway. If something didn't change soon, the ploy that I had thought so clever three days ago would end up ensnaring me instead.

"Don't fret, Hadrack," Baine said, looking unworried. "The troops from Calban will be here in a week or so. We'll deal with the bastards then."

I snorted. "We don't have a week. Another day or two of this, and the people inside our own walls will start to revolt. The Piths won't even need to lift a sword against us."

I'd sent Jebido and Sim to Calban, requesting as many troops as they could spare to ride for Corwick. Calban had a garrison of eighty-eight men, most of whom were grizzled veterans of the Pair War. My original plan hadn't included using those extra troops to deal with the Piths who had sacked Lestwick, but more as a deterrent against the next wave of southern warriors that I knew would be coming. But as each day passed without an attack, I was starting to think that Baine might be right.

Once Jebido and Sim had met with Kylan—the steward of Calban—they were instructed to ride on to Gandertown and warn the king about Pernissy. I hadn't forgotten about that bastard and Grindin. I just had bigger problems at the moment than them. I knew it would be at least a month or more before I saw Jebido again, and I was very much regretting sending him on the journey. I could have sorely used my friend's experience and advice right about now, but he'd been the logical choice to go since Kylan knew and trusted him, as did King Tyden and those at his court.

Baine yawned and tossed the stripped apple core over the ramparts. "Why don't we just go in tonight and end this, Hadrack? We have, what, maybe fifteen or so experienced fighters? If we put bows in all those farm boys' hands and surround the encampment, we can catch them by surprise in their beds. They won't even know what hit them."

I rolled my eyes. "You're as likely to get a free hump from one of Klester Beck's whores in Camwick as catch Piths by surprise in the open."

Baine gave me a lopsided grin. "A fair point," he conceded.

"Besides," I added. "I've already considered doing just that more than once."

"Yet, here we sit three days later, no better off than we were the first day," Baine said. "It's a good plan, Hadrack, with a decent chance of success. So, why are we waiting?"

I sighed, rubbing my hand along the weathered stone of the battlements as I stared through the embrasure in the parapet wall. "Remember that first battle after we escaped Father's Arse?" I finally asked.

"The one where you killed that little weasel, Calen?"

"That's the one," I said with a nod. "We were outnumbered four to one, and by rights should have been easy prey."

"The Ganders were too eager," Baine responded.

"Yes," I agreed. "But they were also overconfident because of their numbers. That overconfidence made them forget who they were up against." I gestured over the wall to the south. "Those are Piths out there, Baine. The most savage, well-trained warriors that exist in this world. I've got a handful of capable men and a bunch of fresh-faced farm boys with their mothers' milk still wet on their lips. In time, some of those boys will become good soldiers, maybe even great soldiers. But if I take those poor bastards into those hills now, most of them are going to die before they ever get the chance."

"Men die all the time, Hadrack," Baine said, looking unimpressed. "That's just the way of things."

"I know," I grunted. "But I'm hoping it doesn't have to be that way this time."

Baine scratched his beard as he thought. Finally, he said, "You didn't ask the Piths to raid that village, Hadrack. And the men who signed on to join this garrison all understood the risks involved when they swore their oath to you. I've spoken with many of them. They want to avenge Lestwick just as much as you or I do."

"But at what cost?" I asked.

"I don't know," Baine responded with a shrug. "But what's the cost of doing nothing?"

I pursed my lips, not having an answer to that. I knew Baine had a good point, but I'm a stubborn man, and I was loath to give up on the plan that I had so carefully worked out. Besides Baine and Jebido, no one else in Corwick knew the Piths like I did, nor understood how they thought. If we marched now, good men would die, but at least we would be seen as doing something. If we waited much longer, unrest would fester inside the castle and would choke the morale within my walls, just like the horsetail grass was doing to the water in Banon's canal. A single hawk started to circle high over the castle, and I watched its flight for a time, trying to come up with a solution.

"Maybe the decision has been made for us," Baine finally said. He pointed over the wall. "There, near the bridge."

A lone rider was thundering down the road, his cloak billowing out behind him. He reached the bridge and galloped across, not slowing as he passed through the open gates of Camwick.

The man disappeared into the jumble of buildings and I lost sight of him. I glanced at Baine. "Did you recognize him?"

"Young Osbeth," I think," Baine answered.

I grunted. Osbeth was one of Parcival's sons. "Then let's go see what young Osbeth has to say."

The Master Hunter's son was already dismounted when Baine and I reached the outer bailey. Wiflem was standing over him, steadying the winded boy.

Wiflem turned to me, his face hard and serious. "The Piths have broken camp, my lord."

I felt my heart skip a beat. "Which way did they go?"

Wiflem allowed a small grin. "North, my lord. They have already sacked Leedswick, just as you predicted."

I nodded, my own face set and serious, though inside, I was smiling with relief. "Alert the men in town," I told Wiflem. I glanced up at the sun. It was not even midday yet. There would be plenty of time to see this thing through if the Piths did as I expected. I turned to Osbeth. "Did you see who was in that tent?"

Osbeth shook his head. "No, my lord. It was struck before dawn. But my father believes three men rode away to the south."

"Three men," I said thoughtfully. I wondered if Nedo was one of them, then I shrugged. It hardly mattered now. They were leaving, and what mattered was the Piths were still on my lands. "Did you see the Pathfinder among the men who sacked Leedswick?" I asked Osbeth.

"My lord?"

"The Pith in the purple cloak. Did you see him among them?"

"No, my lord," Osbeth answered.

"Very well," I said. "How long did the Piths take at the village?"

"A while, my lord," the boy said. His voice was shaking with either excitement or exhaustion—I wasn't sure which. "They dug up some of the floors in the houses looking for anything of value, but found nothing, so they fired the buildings and rode away."

"Heading where?" Wiflem asked.

"North again, Captain," Osbeth said.

"Which means they are heading for Ashwick next," I growled. "And when they finish there, they're coming here." I looked around at my men. "And we'll be ready for the bastards when they get here."

"Beggin' your pardon, my lord, but are you quite sure this is a good idea?"

I glanced at my companion. We sat together on the bench of a small cart, waiting near the south side of the bridge that spanned

Banon's canal. We had been lingering in the same spot for two hours already, sweating in our heavy robes beneath the hot sun. A scrawny mule in a worn leather harness stood attached to the cart, the beast only moving occasionally to stamp its hooves or snap at a fly with yellowed teeth. The disinterested mule seemed more than content to remain there all day, but I was not, and I cursed the Piths for their tardiness.

The man beside me was named Stemper, one of my many untrained men. He wasn't much of a soldier, but he understood carpentry well enough, which was a skill that I had needed. We sat pressed together on the narrow bench so tightly that I could feel the sweat soaking through his cloak where his thigh touched against mine. I glanced over my shoulder, but the road and plains to the south remained empty.

"You assured me the wheel will come off well ahead of time," I said, turning back to Stemper. "So there's nothing to worry about as long as we get a good enough head start before it does."

"It will come off, my lord," the man said, bobbing his head. His hair was shorn close to his scalp, revealing a stark white scar across his crown. "I just can't guarantee when."

I looked ahead at the quiet town of Camwick, calculating the distance with my eyes. I guessed it had to be at least two hundred yards to the open gate, so we would need to be well over the bridge before the wheel came off. Huts stood along the walls to either side of that gate, the thatch and timber structures having been hastily constructed by my men days ago. I knew a wagon lay hidden behind those huts to either side, with soldiers waiting inside, staying out of sight beneath canvas cloths.

"It smells like shit under here," I heard a muted voice grumble from the covered bed of the cart behind me.

"That's because it's a dung cart," I said, not turning around.

Camwick had been filthy when I had arrived as the new lord, and one of the first things that I'd done was hire men to clean the dung and refuse from the streets. The plan had been successful to a degree, and the town smelled and looked cleaner. But all that shit had to go somewhere, which I hadn't given a lot of consideration.

Not knowing what to do with all the waste, the dung-farmers, as they were jokingly called, eventually dumped it into Banon's canal. It was a logical solution to the problem from their perspective, I suppose. But unfortunately, that choice had unintended consequences, since the canal water flowed into Corwick Castle's moat. I had put a stop to the dumping as soon as I'd realized the problem, and the dung-farmers now spread the shit in the fields. But that did little to help the smell that still hung over Corwick Castle. All we could do was wait until the filth floating in the water disappeared, but even when it did, I feared the new name for the moat—Turd Lake—was here to stay.

"You told me this cart was used for eggs and milk," Baine said accusingly from his hiding place beneath the worn canvas covering.

"No," I replied. "What I said was I saw a cart hauling eggs and milk with a broken wheel. That's what gave me the idea."

"Now you tell me," Baine muttered.

Stemper nudged my arm. "Uh, lord, we've got company."

I peered over my shoulder. Riders were coming down the road, moving fast and bunched tightly together as plumes of dust rose behind them. They were still at least half a mile away, but already I could hear their war cries. Piths!

I grinned and glanced down at Baine as he peered out at me from his concealment. "Remember what I told you. Wait until they're all past before you come out."

"Yes, yes," Baine said in irritation. "And take the archers first. I know, my memory hasn't gotten worse since you told me the same thing half an hour ago."

I nodded, then picked up the reins and snapped them as I whistled for the mule to move. Nothing happened. I cracked the reins again, and the mule turned to look back at me with blank eyes. I cursed, shouting every insult I could think of at the ugly beast, but the animal just stared dumbly back.

"Here," Baine said urgently as his hand jutted out from beneath the covering. He dropped three dried horse turds into my palm. "Try reasoning with it with these."

I grunted and flung one of the missiles at the mule, catching the beast squarely on the ass to the right of the leather crupper around its tail. The mule snorted in annoyance, and I threw the second turd, followed by the third, all the while screaming at the cursed animal to move. Finally, with a shake of its ears, the mule started a half-hearted trot. I snapped the reins harder, and the stubborn mule reluctantly began to pick up speed, while behind me, I could hear the Piths' cries growing louder. I stood as we crossed the bridge, fighting to keep my balance on the unsteady cart as I worked the reins frantically, urging more speed from the mule. I took a glance over my shoulder as the Piths swept ever closer, then down at the right wheel.

"Come on, you bastard!" I grunted under my breath just as the wheel started to wobble. I glanced at Stemper. "Get ready," I warned him.

I heard something crack beneath me, and then the wheel twisted off and went careening away. The right axle dropped instantly and plowed into the road, sending up a spray of dirt as Stemper and I jumped free. I landed on my feet, but Stemper fell heavily to the ground. I hauled the man upright, dragging him after me as we started to run while the Piths behind us roared with delight. No mounted Pith warrior could resist an enemy on foot fleeing for his life. I glanced over my shoulder. The nearest rider was two hundred yards behind the one-wheeled cart as the terrified mule fought to drag it along the road. I rolled my eyes. Now the damn beast shows some heart!

"We're not going to make it, lord!" Stemper cried less than twenty yards from the gate.

"We'll make it!" I shouted back. "Now run faster, damn you! Run if you want to live!"

I peered over my shoulder again. The mule had finally stopped its wild flight, standing exhausted in the middle of the road with its head down as Piths swept around each side of the cart. A big, grinning warrior with silver rings in his nose slashed with his sword as he galloped past, tearing a gaping wound in the side of the animal's neck. Blood sprayed and the mule shrieked and then collapsed in a heap. I looked away, focusing on the open gate. That's when Stemper staggered and crumpled to the ground.

I turned back to help him, then saw his staring eyes and the arrow sticking out of his neck. I instinctively twisted aside just as several more spinning shafts flicked past me. Then I started running again. I knew the Piths always attacked the same way, with the female archers bringing up the rear in support of their men. That's why I had left Baine behind in the cart with his bow. I just prayed his aim would be true and quick.

I was less than ten feet from the gates when an arrow struck my back, and I stumbled as it lodged in the shield slung over my shoulder beneath my cloak. I regained my balance and kept running, streaking past the huts as I tried not to look at the wagons where I knew my men crouched in hiding. My instructions to those men were clear, and I knew they wouldn't reveal themselves until all the Piths had entered the town.

I sprinted through the gates, making sure to run along the narrow white line painted in the dirt. Three more wagons waited on the road fifty yards ahead of me and I raced toward them, my lungs on fire. A helmeted head suddenly popped up from behind one of the wagons and I cursed as I waved the man down. I needed the Piths focused on catching me and nothing else. If they realized that this was a trap, they would break off the attack and all my careful planning would be for nothing.

The first of the Piths burst through the gates just as I made it to the wagons. I spun about, snapping the arrow from my back as I tore off my cloak, revealing my armor underneath. I drew Wolf's Head and unhooked my shield, shouting to get the Piths' attention. A howl of eagerness arose from the riders when they saw me. Nothing gets the blood boiling in a Pith more than the sight of an arrogant Gander lord dressed in rich armor. The tightly bunched warriors spurred on their horses, aiming right for me as they swung swords, axes, and war hammers eagerly over their heads. I smiled, urging them on with insults as more Piths entered the town.

The closest rider to me—the man who had cut down the mule— leaned over his horse, his sword held low, clearly intending to skewer me. I waited, while behind him, the last of the Piths came pounding through the gates. The moment they were through, my men pushed the wagons into place just as I'd ordered, blocking the way out. I turned my gaze back to the lead Pith as he bore down on me, his eyes gleaming with triumph, his looped nose rings bouncing and flopping against his cheeks. The nose rings reminded me of the gatekeeper's earrings back in Corwick Castle, and I decided I would make a gift of them to the bald man once the current owner had no further use for them.

The Pith warrior started to laugh, probably already envisioning how good he would look in my armor. I remained where I was as he rushed toward me, my sword at my side, my shield held casually. The Pith was less than twenty feet away from me when the road beneath his mount's front hooves collapsed, pitching the animal chest-deep into a hole. The horse shrieked in surprise, sending the shocked Pith sailing through the air to land in the dust at my feet. The fallen man started to rise, his helmet gone, and I slashed Wolf's Head down his face, taking his left eye, part of his nose, and one of the glittering silver rings attached to it. The Pith howled in agony and I slashed again, silencing him for good. I looked up from the still-twitching corpse. More and more of the Piths' horses were falling prey to the traps that we'd dug, the animals screaming and twisting as they sent their riders tumbling to the ground.

The pits were called wolf holes, which seemed fitting, I suppose. Each hole was roughly conical in shape, dug six-feet deep and three-feet wide, with a sharpened stake pounded into the soil at the pit's base. Wicker covers topped with a light layer of dirt concealed the traps from the enemy. We had staggered the holes all across the road for twenty feet, making it next to impossible for mounted riders moving at speed to avoid them. Jebido had told me about wolf holes once, explaining how they had stopped a cavalry charge dead in its tracks when he was still a fresh-faced soldier of seventeen. I couldn't imagine Jebido ever being that young, but I'd had no trouble understanding the value of what he was telling me. Of course, the key to the wolf holes was ensuring that the enemy rode where you wanted them to go. That's why I had needed the

Piths to come to Camwick. The town's tightly-packed buildings were ideal, and with both ends of the road blocked off, the mounted warriors were trapped, at least for the moment. I knew that wouldn't last for long, though, and now was the time to strike before the Piths overcame their confusion and regrouped.

I lifted my sword. "Now!" I cried, sweeping Wolf's Head down.

The canvas coverings on the wagons blocking the road at the gate tore away, and vengeful farm boys appeared holding ash, elder, or yew bows in their strong hands.

"Nock! Draw! Loose!" I heard Baine call from the wagons at the gate.

"Nock! Draw! Loose!" Tyris shouted from the wagons behind me as more of my men appeared there.

A swarm of barbed arrows fletched with triangular white goose feathers smacked into the struggling Piths from behind and in front. Some of the Piths had barely gotten to their feet after being thrown from their horses, still looking stunned before they were struck down again by well-aimed missiles. My untrained farm boys might not be that familiar with swords and shields yet, but most of them had been shooting bows all of their lives.

Six mounted Piths who had been the last to enter Camwick whirled and tried a desperate charge toward the wagons blocking the gate, with the clear intent to leap over them. For a moment, I thought the gamble was going to work, but Baine and my farm boys held their ground, replying with a withering barrage that dropped three men and forced the others to retreat. I'd never been prouder of those boys. The three survivors swung about and tried to get to me instead, but were snatched from their saddles before they could get close. I didn't feel even the slightest amount of pity or remorse as I watched them die.

Finally, with only five bloodied and battered warriors still on their feet in the dusty street, I waved Wolf's Head in the air. "That's enough!" I shouted.

My men reluctantly lowered their bows. Dead Pith warriors lay strewn all across the road, with many of the fallen horses writhing and squealing in the dirt. Jebido had explained that even if the stakes in the wolf holes didn't impale the mounts, many times the sudden drop would be enough to snap a leg, which was just as effective. Riderless horses wandered among the dead and dying, trailing their reins and looking confused.

The five surviving Pith warriors stood bunched together, their backs pressed against each other. I could hear them whispering, and I knew they were preparing to charge me in hopes of cutting me down before they died. I strode around the bloody carnage and stopped ten feet away from the Piths, letting them see that I was unafraid.

"I am the Lord of Corwick," I said. "Who will speak for you?"

One of the warriors hesitated, glancing at his companions before he tapped his chest. "I will speak."

"Very well," I said. I pointed with Wolf's Head at a light brown mare lying on her side nearby. The horse's eyes were wide with pain as she wheezed bloody pink froth from her nostrils. "You have five minutes to put your horses out of their misery, then you die."

The Pith looked surprised, then he nodded. He gestured to the other men, who quickly and efficiently moved to slit the throats of the injured horses. I knew Piths valued their mounts above most other things, and it was the one kindness that I was willing to offer them.

"Wiflem," I called. Men in armor appeared from the buildings on either side of the road holding heavy rectangular shields. These were my experienced fighters that I had kept in reserve in case something went wrong. "As soon as they're finished dealing with the horses," I said. "Give these men a proper warrior's death." I paused and pointed toward the Pith who had spoken. "All but that one. I want him alive."

"Yes, my lord," Wiflem said with a grim nod.

I turned and headed wearily back to the wagons, leaving the remaining warriors for Wiflem and his men to handle. I had gambled and won, at least for the moment. But I knew Piths, and unless I came up with a way to be rid of them once and for all, I feared the battle we'd just fought was only the beginning of something worse.

Those fears were soon to be proven right.

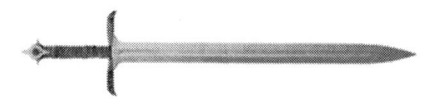

7: Saldor

The last surviving Pith's name was Saldor. The warrior was determined not to be taken alive by my men, and he made his stand among the corpses of his fallen brothers, daring us to kill him. I was greatly impressed by his spirit and tried to make the man understand that I had no wish to see him dead. But, the Pith either didn't believe me or just didn't care. First Wiflem, then Putt, and then Niko tried to disarm Saldor, but the Pith was quick as a rock snake and just as deadly. I finally had enough when Niko suffered a nasty cut to his cheek after the Pith slipped past his guard, which clearly infuriated the young man to no end. I could tell by the baleful glare on Niko's face as he circled Saldor that he intended to kill him now, regardless of my orders. That's when I stepped in and drew the wounded youth aside to take his place. I probably should have done it sooner, but my men had been insistent, wanting to test themselves against the Pith. Fighting men have pride that needs to be stoked at times, and this had seemed a good moment for it. Now, it no longer seemed that way.

The battle didn't last long. Though I can't take too much credit for it, I suppose, since the Pith was bleeding from a half dozen wounds and could barely lift his sword by the time I faced him. Crossed blades rang out in the silence of the street, then a quick flick of my wrist and Saldor's sword went flying, followed by an armored elbow to the face, and that was that. Now, I sat near a merchant's warehouse on a piece of firewood as I studied the bound and glowering Pith who sat cross-legged on the ground before me. Saldor was my age, I guessed, with blond, shaggy hair swept back to the nape of his neck. His eyes were a blueish-green, and his beard was long and thick, twisted at his chin and held in place by a silver beard ring. The torc around the Pith's neck was different from Nedo's, I was surprised to see, which meant he wasn't one of the disagreeable Amenti. I hoped that fact might allow me to reason with him.

"You should cut that off," I grunted, getting the conversation started as I pointed at the rope-like beard. "An opponent could latch onto that thing and drag you out of a shield wall and gut you." The Pith just spat on the ground close to my boot. I smiled and shrugged. "I'm here to offer you a deal. One you would be wise to accept."

"I don't make deals with Gandermen," Saldor said.

"So, you really would prefer we kill you, then?" I asked.

"I don't care what you do," the Pith responded defiantly.

I took off my gauntlets, placed them on the ground beside me, and then blew into my hands. The sun was touching the western hills now, and the wind had risen, bringing a chill along with it that hadn't been there earlier. "You're not of the Amenti, are you?"

Saldor hesitated, then he shook his head. "I am Cimbrati."

I nodded, pleased to hear it. I had met Cimbrati before and knew they were a tough but fair people. Some of the Piths in Gasterny, like Gadest and young Peren, had been Cimbrati. Hopefully, I could use that fact to my advantage. "I assume you know what happened to the three Amenti we caught?" I said.

"I know," Saldor replied evenly. I had seen a brief flicker in his eyes as he spoke. The Pith was afraid and was doing his best not to show it.

"Good," I said cheerfully. I glanced past the warrior. My men were dragging the corpses of the dead to an open wagon pulled by a set of oxen. The wagon was the biggest that I could find in Camwick, and I was hopeful that all the bodies would fit inside. "There are certain things that I wish to know," I continued. "And I would be grateful if you would tell me." Saldor just blinked, then he deliberately looked away. "For instance," I said, unfazed. "Why did you come here? Why my lands?" Saldor watched my men loading the nearly naked, red-streaked bodies onto the wagon, his expression blank. We'd stripped the dead of their armor and weapons, which would add greatly to my armory. "One of two things is going to happen here today," I said, my voice harder now. "Either you tell me what I want to know, or all of you will end up as food for the fish in the Western Sea."

Saldor turned back to me. "And if I answer these questions?"

I nodded toward the wagon. "Then you will be allowed to go home with your dead, where they can be given a proper Ascension."

Saldor studied me in surprise. "Why?" he finally asked.

"Consider it an offer of peace," I said. "Your people destroyed a village of mine, and I took the lives of those who did it. So, the scales are now even enough for me to accept that justice has been served. I am offering the souls of your dead in exchange for information from you as well as a promise that the Piths will never return here."

Saldor looked thoughtful as he watched my men struggling to lift the body of a big warrior onto the wagon. Finally, he turned back to me. "It is a fair deal, Ganderman. One which I know the Pathfinders would approve, but even so, I cannot accept it."

I stared at the Pith in surprise. "Why not?" I asked. "You know what will happen to all those souls if you don't."

"I do, Ganderman," Saldor said. "But it would be a bargain struck in bad faith, so I must decline."

I stared at the Pith, incredulous. "Since when do Piths worry about such things?"

Saldor shrugged. "Some do. Some do not. I am one that does."

I frowned, thinking as I stroked my beard. "You are afraid of what I might ask. Is that why you won't agree? Because of the secrets you would have to tell me?"

"No," Saldor said. "I would gladly speak to save the souls of my brothers and sisters. There is nothing you would learn from me that will change what is coming for Ganderland, anyway."

"Then why not talk if that's true?" I asked.

"Because the Amenti chieftain will never accept our bargain," Saldor said. "So, knowing this, I cannot agree to your terms. He will come for your head, no matter what I promise you."

I frowned. "And who is this chieftain?"

"His name is Lorgen Three-Fingers," Saldor replied. "Nedo is his son." The Pith gave me a hard stare. "His only son, Ganderman."

I groaned inwardly, understanding the tattoos on the boy's head now. "Then, when you see this chieftain," I said gruffly, hiding my unease from the Pith. "Tell him the Lord of Corwick said that he should stay home near a warm fire and make more sons. We don't need to start a war over a pair of hairless balls."

Saldor chuckled. "You do not know him, Ganderman. Besides, it is much too late for that. Even if Lorgen were so inclined, which I promise you he will not be, war is coming. There is nothing that you can do to stop it."

I pursed my lips, thinking. There had to be a way to stop this from going any further. "What of Einhard, then?" I finally asked, seeing a possible way out of the mess that I had made. There had been no word about what had happened to Einhard after the Pith defeat at Victory Pass. I knew he had survived the battle, but that was all. He could have been long dead these past few years without me ever knowing. I prayed that he wasn't. "Does the Sword of the King still live?"

The Pith looked at me curiously. "How do you know this name?"

"Everyone has heard of Einhard the Unforgiving," I said with a sweep of my arm. "Even Gandermen. So tell me, is he your king now?" I waited, not daring to breathe. If my friend had become king after Clendon the Peacemaker died, then I knew with only a single word from him that my Amenti problem would end.

Saldor paused, his eyes calculating as he thought. "He is not," he finally said grudgingly.

I nodded in disappointment. "Then who is?"

"There is no king," Saldor said. "Queen Alesia claims the right to lead the Piths now."

I sat back in surprise. "Alesia? Do you mean Einhard's wife?" Saldor nodded. I glanced over at Baine, where he leaned against the warehouse wall behind me with his arms crossed, listening. Baine just shrugged, his expression neutral. Alesia made sense, now that I thought about it, since she was Clendon's daughter. Still, I was surprised, trying to imagine the fiery, mischievous woman that I'd known leading the quarrelsome tribes. Alesia's father had managed to bring those tribes together, but it hadn't been easy. If anyone were to lead the Piths now, I would have expected it to be Einhard, not his unpredictable wife. I turned back to Saldor. "What do you mean by, she claims the right?" I asked. "Are the tribes not united?"

Saldor didn't respond, and he looked up at the sky instead, his expression neutral.

I knew I would get nothing more out of the Pith about that, so I decided to change my approach. "Did Alesia's child live?" I asked. "After she left Gasterny?"

Saldor regarded me in surprise. "Yes," he said cautiously.

I grinned, happy to hear it. "Was it a boy or a girl?"

"A boy," Saldor responded. The Pith allowed himself a small smile. "He's already as strong as an ox."

I laughed and slapped my knee. "A boy! Einhard has a son!"

"How is it that you know these things?" Saldor asked, unable to hide his curiosity.

I took a deep breath, still chuckling as I imagined Einhard bouncing a wailing baby on his knee. "I know these things," I said, "because Einhard and Alesia are friends of mine."

Saldor snorted. "You lie. Piths do not befriend Ganders."

I had begun to suspect that the raiders didn't know who I was and that their attack had been nothing more than a random coincidence. Saldor's reaction was confirming that for me. "You say Piths and Ganders can't be friends, yet there were three Ganders allied to the Piths at Gasterny. What of them?"

The Pith's face darkened. "Those three were traitors."

I frowned. "What do you mean, traitors?"

"They betrayed Einhard," the warrior responded. "They were sworn to him, yet it was they who opened the gates of Gasterny and organized the ambush in the pass that killed our king."

I sat back, stunned. "Is that what all Piths believe? Even Alesia and Einhard?"

"Of course," Saldor said. "Because it is the truth."

I clenched my jaw in dismay, imagining what my friend must have thought of me these past few years. "Do you know who I am?" I demanded.

"You are Lord Corwick," Saldor responded.

"No," I replied. "I am the Lord of Corwick. There is a difference. My name is Hadrack, and I was one of those Ganders with Einhard at Gasterny. I fought by the Sword of the King's side and would have given my life for him. When the garrison was captured, my friends and I were taken prisoner. We did not betray anyone!" I said that last bit forcefully as I leaned forward, glaring at the Pith. "Now, look me in the eyes and try to claim that I am lying."

Saldor's forehead furrowed as he studied me. "This is truth?" he finally asked.

"I swear it," I said. "On The Mother, The Father, and the Master." I paused, glancing past the bound Cimbrati. Two of my farm boys had dragged one of the dead female Piths to the wagon and had stripped her naked. One was fondling her breasts, while the other kicked open her legs and started to prod her mound with his boot. I stood, feeling an instant explosion of anger inside me. "Wiflem!" I roared. I pointed. "Stop those men!"

"Yes, my lord," Wiflem said. He strode toward the soldiers and cuffed the nearest man. "Get away from there, you worthless turds!" He grabbed each by the scruff of the neck and marched them toward me. "What would you have me do with them, my lord?"

I glared at my men. "What you were doing was despicable and will not be tolerated," I said. Both men dropped their gazes to the ground, and one was visibly shaking. I glanced at my captain. "Ten lashes each, then a day in the stocks." I shifted my stern look back to the men. "Be glad you get to keep your heads and your cocks."

"Yes, my lord," one of the soldiers mumbled. "Thank you, my lord."

I sat back down, still muttering angrily to myself as Wiflem prodded the offending men away.

"You have honor," Saldor said, sounding surprised. "It is unexpected, coming from a Gander."

I glared at him, still hot with outrage. "Don't speak to me of honor. You came to my lands and murdered and raped innocent people. Where is the honor there? You are no better than they."

Saldor shrugged. "If you are who you claim, Ganderman, then you know the Master placed those people in this world for our amusement. Their lives are ours, to do with as we see fit."

Baine snorted in disgust behind me, but I kept my eyes squarely on the warrior. The Pith's attitude was nothing out of the ordinary. All Piths—even Einhard—believed that other people living in this world belonged to them. "I propose a new deal," I said, regaining my composure. "You answer all of my questions right now. Do that, and I will let you go with your sisters and brothers with no further obligations from you."

"And Lorgen Three-Fingers?" Saldor asked. "What of him?"

"He's not your concern," I grunted. "Those souls over there are. If Lorgen Three-Fingers dares to come to my lands, then I'll take whatever fingers he has left and shove them up his arse. Now, do we have a deal?"

Saldor nodded, and I thought I could see a look of respect in his eyes. "We have a deal, Ganderman."

Saldor did answer my questions as promised, though I have never met a man who could say so much without actually telling me anything at all. The townspeople were already streaming back into Camwick now that the threat was over, and Saldor was justifiably viewed with suspicion and hatred when they saw him. After many insults and several barrages of rotten vegetables were thrown at the bound and helpless warrior, I finally moved us into the nearby warehouse where we could talk undisturbed.

Hours went by as I questioned the Pith, who danced nimbly around my queries like a sharp-tailed grouse in mating season. Saldor was a highly intelligent man, I quickly learned, and I began to suspect that he was enjoying himself immensely in our battle of wits. Finally, exhausted and frustrated with answers that sometimes rambled on for long minutes with no satisfactory conclusion, I realized that I would get nothing of further use from the Pith. I had been able to piece together enough information to know we were in trouble, but not enough to understand everything that was going on. I left the warrior in the care of Wiflem and his men for what remained of the night, then headed back to the castle with Baine. As agreed upon, Saldor would leave at first light with his wagon of dead, though I suspected by the way he looked at me when we parted that the Pith believed he and I would meet again, probably over swords. I had no reason to think after what he had told me that he was wrong.

"We have to get word to the king," Baine said.

I glanced at him as we rode side by side, his face a knot of twisted shadows in the darkness. "I'll send a messenger with extra horses in the morning," I said, feeling tired and depressed. "But even riding day and night, it will take at least a week to reach Gandertown."

"How long do you think we have before they attack?"

I shrugged. "There's no way to know."

"Do you think there really are as many Piths as he claims?" Baine asked into the silence.

"The Mother help us if there are," I muttered as we reached the castle. I'd asked Saldor repeatedly how many men Lorgen Three-Fingers had, but the Cimbrati only answered with the same question. "How many blades of grass are there on the western plains?" I could only hope and pray that the Pith had either been lying or exaggerating.

We crossed the drawbridge and paused our horses in the outer bailey, and I sighed with relief at the quiet inside the walls. Gone now were the constant sounds of crying babies, arguing spouses, and drunken brawls that had filled the castle day and night. "Ubeth!" I barked into the silence.

The bald gatekeeper appeared like a wraith from the gloom, looking impossibly awake and alert. If the man ever slept, I wasn't aware of it. "Yes, my lord?"

I tossed him the bloody nose rings. "A present for you from the Piths."

"Thank you, my lord," Ubeth said gratefully, holding up the silver rings. "I'll wear them with pride, my lord." The bald man turned, cursing at several sleepy-looking grooms as he ordered them to attend to our horses.

"Will you join me for a drink?" I asked Baine as we dismounted.

My friend shook his head, heading for the servants' quarters. "It's been a long day, Hadrack. I'm going to get some sleep."

Baine had a gleam in his eye that I recognized—one that contradicted his words. "Don't hump whoever she is for too long," I called out to his back. "All my servant girls are looking exhausted lately."

"Only the pretty ones!" Baine's voice rang out from the darkness.

I laughed and headed for the keep. Few people were about as I climbed the stairs that led to the third floor, though I could see Hanley standing in front of the entrance to Corwick Hall with a stern look on his face. He was peering down at a snoring servant propped against the doors with an empty bottle of wine lying in his lap. The boy saw me, and he started to head my way, but I just waved him off and kept climbing. I had sent word to Shana hours ago about our victory and that I would be quite late returning to the castle. But as I passed her door, I felt a sudden restlessness rise in me. I realized I wasn't ready for sleep just yet and needed to hear her voice. I turned and walked back to the door and listened, but heard nothing. I knocked softly, and after a moment, I heard mumbled voices coming from inside. The door opened a crack, grating loudly on its hinges before revealing either Hesther or Hamber—I could never tell which—peering out at me.

"My lord!" the girl said with a surprised squeak.

"Is the lady awake and decent?" I asked.

The girl hesitated, looking uncertain.

"Who is it, Hesther?" I heard Shana ask sleepily.

The girl turned. "It's Lord Hadrack, my lady."

"Well, don't just stand there, gawking. Let him in."

Hesther colored, lowering her eyes as she swung the door open. For some reason, both girls were terrified of me, even though I had been nothing but polite and considerate towards them. I couldn't understand why they feared me so.

"Thank you, Hesther," I said with a tired smile as I stepped inside.

The room was cool, lit faintly by glowing embers from a small fireplace that sat along the eastern wall. Central hearths had originally heated the castle until Pernissy became the Lord of Corwick. The bastard had spent a lot of money to have fireplaces built into the lord's and lady's chambers, as well as both halls. The additions had been a good move on Pernissy's part, and the castle was infinitely warmer because of his foresight. It was the only thing the man had ever done that I agreed with, much as I hated to admit it.

The other girl, Hamber, scurried out from a bundle of thick furs that lay on the floor at the foot of my wife's bed. She and her sister lit several candles and then waited against the back wall, both staring nervously at their feet. The girls were dressed in light shifts and had linen veils wrapped around their heads, each tied with a bow. Shana was sitting up in bed, her long black hair pinned and tucked under a silk headdress accented with gold edging.

I glanced at the two girls. "Please leave us," I said. "You can sleep in the Lesser Hall for the rest of the night."

"Yes, my lord," both girls said at once.

They curtsied, then turned and hurried from the room as I took off my cloak and tossed it across a chair. I had sent most of my armor up to the castle by packhorse after the battle, and I started to struggle with my mail coat.

"So, my lord," Shana said as she came to help me. "I understand your plans were a success and that the Pith threat is over."

I sighed, sitting on the edge of the bed. "If only that were true," I said bleakly.

Shana paused, and I could see sudden worry creasing her face. "I don't understand. Did some get away?"

I shook my head. "No, we killed them all," I answered. "All but one, that is. I let that one live. I'm sending him home in the morning with the bodies of his brothers and sisters."

"As a peace offering so that they can Ascend," Shana said, nodding her head thoughtfully. "That's very smart, my lord."

I smiled, taking her hand in mine and squeezing it. I was always surprised at how quickly Shana understood things, though I probably shouldn't have been. My wife was not only a compassionate and caring woman, but a highly intelligent one as well. Shana paused, her face suddenly tense as she leaned over and clutched at her belly.

I stood up in alarm. "Is everything all right?"

Shana nodded, her eyes closed. "I'm fine, lord." She straightened carefully, forcing a smile. "It's just the baby letting me know that he's not happy we are awake."

I put my hand on Shana's belly, marveling at the slight roundness of her flesh beneath my hand. I knew somewhere inside that roundness my child grew, gaining strength by the day. It was a humbling realization. "Let's get you back into bed," I finally said, guiding Shana around the bed and helping her under the covers. I stroked her cheek as she looked up at me. "I'm going to go now so that you can rest. We can talk again in the morning."

"No, my lord, please stay," Shana said. "Tell me what's going on. I know something is wrong."

"Are you sure you are all right?" I asked, reluctant to leave despite my words.

Shana smiled and tapped the bed beside her. "Of course, my lord. There's nothing to worry about. Now sit and tell me what is happening."

I did as she asked, holding her hand as I told her about the battle, the capture of Saldor, and then what I had managed to learn about the Piths' plans. Shana listened attentively, asking pointed, well-thought-out questions until finally, I finished. We sat in silence for a time, both of us content to just be together as we thought about what the next few days and months might bring.

"What will you do now?" Shana finally asked as she rubbed her belly beneath the bedclothes.

I shrugged. "Prepare for war, of course. What else is there?"

"Can Ganderland withstand that many Piths?"

"Saldor wasn't serious about that," I said.

"But what if he was? Can we defeat them?"

I breathed out loudly. "I honestly don't know, Shana. We have barely recovered from the Pair War, with thousands of dead on both sides. Many of the southern and northern lords don't trust each other, and our king is young and untested. If ever there was a good time for the Piths to attack, this would be it. All I can do is wait to hear back from the king and prepare as best I can." I chose not to tell my wife that she would be on her way to Calban in the morning, knowing I'd have an argument on my hands when I did. With a possible Pith invasion only days or weeks away, I wanted my wife and unborn child as far from it as possible.

"What about Einhard and Alesia?" Shana asked. "Can't you go see them and ask for a truce? Surely they will listen to you."

I frowned. "They think that I betrayed them."

Shana snorted. "Einhard knows you better than that, my lord."

I shrugged. "Maybe, but even if I convince him of what really happened, I'm not sure he can do anything to stop this, even if he wanted to. It sounds to me like this Lorgen Three-Fingers has plans of his own that don't include Einhard and Alesia."

"Oh," Shana said, the hope in her eyes dying. "What about the priests and priestesses, my lord? Why did the Piths take them?"

I rubbed at my itchy eyes, then dropped my hand wearily into my lap. "I don't know for certain, and I hope I'm wrong, but I think they might be going to sacrifice them to the Master."

Shana gasped. "You can't be serious."

I stood, wobbling on my feet in exhaustion. "I'm going to let you sleep now. Tomorrow is going to be a long day."

"Hadrack," Shana said, holding her hand out to me. "Stay with me tonight, please. I don't want to be alone."

"I can bring Hesther and Hamber back," I said, hovering uncertainly above the bed.

"No," Shana said, shaking her head. "I want you."

I looked down at myself. "But I'm covered in filth and blood."

"I don't care, my lord," Shana said, drawing me down onto the bed. "Just stay tonight and hold me. That's all I ask."

How could I say no?

8: The Trial

Shana wasn't happy about leaving Corwick, just as I had predicted, and the argument between us the next morning turned out to be loud and drawn-out. It was our first heated disagreement since our marriage, and Hamber and Hesther sat through it all, looking like a pair of frightened puppies after a beating while we shouted back and forth at each other. In the end, common sense prevailed, and Shana agreed to leave—though not before she had made me promise not to do anything stupid and get myself killed. It was a promise that I made easily, though I knew I might not be able to hold up my end of the bargain.

"That's the lot of them, my lord," Wiflem said, coming to stand beside me on the southern parapet.

A line of covered wagons moved through the gates below me, rolling over the drawbridge and onto the road that curved northward. I knew Shana was in the lead wagon, accompanied by her young court ladies. The rest of the wagons were filled with priests and priestesses from Camwick and the other villages, including Daughter Tessa and Daughter Verica. Brown-robed boys and girls in grey marched behind the wagons, followed by ten armed men on horseback led by Putt. All the riders were experienced fighters and were men that I could ill afford to lose right now, yet I'd had no choice but to send them. To leave those wagons defended only by farm boys with Piths about was unthinkable.

"And the messengers?" I asked, focusing on my captain. I had decided to withdraw all the priests and priestesses from Corwick, sending them north far from the raiding Piths. If Lorgen Three-Fingers' men really were targeting the Sons and Daughters as I suspected, then I wanted them as far away as possible. I'd also sent messengers to the garrisons guarding the border and all the southern lords, alerting them to what had happened in Corwick and explaining my suspicions about the priests and priestesses. I wasn't sure what the reaction to those warnings might be, but either way, I wasn't counting on any help arriving from any of them.

"They were all gone at first light, my lord," Wiflem replied.

"But will anybody listen?" I wondered out loud.

"Why wouldn't they, my lord?"

I sighed. "Because most are stubborn, arrogant men, Wiflem," I said. "Men used to power and authority who have little if any love for a commoner like me."

"They just need to get to know you better, my lord," Wiflem said with a tight smile.

I laughed. "Indeed," I agreed. I glanced up at the midday sun as a large cloud slid across its face, casting us in shadows. More clouds were rolling in from the south. "You've armed the villages?"

"Yes, my lord," Wiflem nodded. "As best we could. Mainly spears and clubs, but it will be better than nothing."

"Let's hope it doesn't come to that," I muttered. I noticed a small man dressed in a faded brown tunic waiting uncomfortably near the wooden stairs that led down into the bailey. "Is that him?" I grunted.

"It is, my lord. His name is Gerdy."

"Did you tell him what I need?"

"I did not, my lord," Wiflem replied. "I thought it best that he hear it from you."

"Very well," I grunted as I strode toward the little man. "Good day to you, Gerdy," I said, pausing in front of him.

"My lord," Gerdy responded, staring up at me nervously as he played with his hands. I noticed those hands looked strong for such a small man, with thick, hairy wrists.

"You are a master bowyer, I understand?"

"I am, my lord," Gerdy said. He shifted on his feet and looked at the ground. "Been so for almost ten years now. I was apprenticed to Master Wadley, and when a fever took him, his wife sold the business to me."

"And how is business these days, Gerdy?"

The little man grinned. "It has been quite good lately, my lord. Much better since you came to Corwick."

"I am pleased to hear that," I said. All merchants in the kingdom paid a tax to their lord, which in most cases was thirty percent. But Pernissy, in his never-ending greed, had levied a crushing fifty percent on all goods produced and sold in Camwick, which had done nothing in my view but help to stifle business. I had reduced the taxation to twenty-five, and the town was now not only expanding, but booming. I found it hugely amusing that my coffers were pulling in far more now at twenty-five percent than Pernissy's ever had at fifty, simply because of the rise in commerce.

"Will you be needing more bows, my lord?" Gerdy asked. "I'm contracted to provide forty per year to the castle right now, but I can certainly look into increasing that if you wish."

"I'll need a hundred," I said bluntly.

Gerdy gaped at me. "A hundred, my lord?"

"At least that, for now at any rate," I said. "How long will it take you?"

Gerdy blinked rapidly, clearly thinking. "Perhaps a month, maybe more, my lord. I have enough dried bowstaves to cover the order, but I will need to speak with Farben and see what his schedule is like before I can give you a firm date."

"And who is Farben?" I asked.

"The stringer, my lord."

"I'll need the bows in a week," I said.

Gerdy's eyes went round in surprise. "A week, my lord?" He mopped at his brow with the sleeve of his tunic. "I...I don't know, my lord. I suppose it could be done, but I would need to hire other tradesmen to do the dressing and horning, as well as the smoothing and sealing of the bows for me. I normally do everything with my apprentice, but we couldn't possibly have a hundred ready in a week." He looked at me with warning in his eyes. "An order of this magnitude in such a short time will be very expensive, my lord."

I waved off his words. "We are on the verge of war, Gerdy. Now is not the time to worry about costs."

"War, my lord? I thought the Pith threat was over?"

"You thought wrong," I grunted. "Can you guarantee delivery of the bows in a week with the extra help?"

Gerdy paused, then he nodded firmly. "I can, my lord. As long as you understand the costs and the complexity involved, then I will be happy to service the order."

"Good," I said. "These bowstaves of yours. The dry ones. How long are they?"

"Long, my lord?" Gerdy tipped back his felt hat and scratched his bald head. "It varies, but I usually cut them around seven feet tall and perhaps a foot wide. May I ask why, my lord?"

"You have heard of the Cardian longbow, I take it?"

Gerdy looked surprised. "I have heard mention of them, yes my lord."

"Could you make similar bows?"

Gerdy pursed his lips. "Undoubtedly, my lord, but I wouldn't recommend it."

I frowned. "Why not?"

"The draw on a bow of that size will be twice the normal draw, my lord. Most men couldn't pull it even halfway."

"Are you saying that Cardians are stronger than Gandermen?" I challenged.

Gerdy shook his head. "No, of course not, my lord. But Cardian archers have been trained their entire lives to pull those bows. The muscles in their backs, arms, and shoulders will have developed to handle the draw. Men unused to that weight would struggle greatly, my lord, and would undoubtedly miss more than they hit."

"Well, this is unexpected," I muttered to Wiflem. I turned back to Gerdy. "What's the draw weight on a Pith bow?"

Gerdy looked up at the cloudy sky, thinking. "Horsebows are usually no more than sixty pounds, my lord," he said after a moment. "They are designed for quickness and rapid shooting, not distance. Most Pith archers are women, and they're not as strong as men, so it's possible the draw might be even less than that." The little man nodded, coming to a decision. "More like a fifty-pound draw on a Pith bow would be my guess, my lord."

"And the longbows of the Cardians?"

"I'm not sure, my lord," Gerdy said. "I've never seen one, but I would say at least double that."

"Well, I've seen plenty," I said. "And the arrows from those bows went at least fifty yards farther than the best Pith arrow could." I put my hand on Gerdy's shoulder and squeezed. "Nobody can shoot like Piths. That's undisputed. But if I can keep my archers out of range of their arrows, yet still be able to strike within their ranks, then we might stand a chance. I need you to give us that chance."

Gerdy looked up at me and I could see a gleam of interest in his eyes. I could tell this was a man who lived for his craft as well as a challenge.

"I'll make your longbows for you, my lord," Gerdy said with determination. "They might not be as formidable as the Cardian ones, but they will be close."

I patted the little man on the shoulder and grinned. "That's all I can ask for."

One week later, I stood watching as Baine and Tyris each held one of the new longbows, both men examining them with little enthusiasm. Tyris was a tall man, and his bow was almost the same height as he was, while Baine's bow towered over his head.

"You can't be serious about this," Baine said, turning to look back at me. "How do you expect me to use this thing?"

I shrugged my shoulders with my arms crossed over my chest. We stood on the high grassy plains north of the castle, with straw targets sitting at a hundred yards, then fifty yards farther, then another fifty yards beyond that. Every able-bodied man in my fiefdom between the ages of fifteen and fifty was gathered behind me, watching. "What's the matter? Are you afraid of being embarrassed?" I asked Baine with a chuckle.

"Damn right, I am," my friend grumbled. He plucked at the bowstring, testing it. "What is this, flax? I prefer hemp strings."

Tyris nodded his agreement. "Hemp is stronger, my lord."

"Can we get on with this?" I grunted, trying not to show my nervousness. I knew both Tyris and Baine were perfectionists when it came to their craft, but I didn't have the time nor the patience for an argument right now.

Baine nodded reluctantly and he took a step forward, studying the first target. I'd had five hundred arrows made, each one long enough to fit the new bows, with hundreds more being made day and night in Camwick. Baine drew one of those arrows from his sheath, nocked it, then carefully lifted his bow and pulled back the string. My friend's left arm began to shake before the nock was even a quarter of the way to his ear, then his right started to shake as well when he made it halfway. Finally, with a grunt of disappointment, Baine let fly. The arrow traveled less than fifty yards before arcing downward into the tall grasses and disappearing. I heard snickers and laughter coming from the crowd and I turned and looked back.

"Silence!" I shouted. I glared at the suddenly anxious faces. "Do you think you can do any better?" Nobody answered me. "That's what I thought," I said with a snort as I motioned to Tyris. "Go ahead. Let's see what you can do."

Tyris strode forward purposefully as Baine moved back, a flush of shame evident on his face. I felt bad for my friend, but I'd needed to know where we stood with the bows, and he and Tyris were the best archers in Corwick. If they couldn't use them effectively, then I knew I had probably just wasted a lot of money and a week of Gerdy's time.

Tyris drew an arrow and knocked it, then pulled back on the string in one smooth motion. The blond archer was tall and lanky, but he had enormous shoulders and arms from a lifetime with the bow. He started to shake slightly at the three-quarter mark, the bow wandering off target before, with a determined grunt, he brought it back in line. Tyris' right thumb finally touched his chin, and cheers erupted from the crowd as the blond archer released, which grew even louder as the arrow slapped with force into the first straw target. Tyris seemed unaffected by the cheers, and he drew another arrow, this time pulling the nock to his ear before sending the shaft spinning through the air into the second bundle of straw. Another chorus of cheers rang out as Tyris shot a third time, with the arrow landing in the grass ten feet to the right of the farthest target.

"A fine bow, my lord," Tyris said, turning to me. "One I would be proud to use."

"Then it's yours," I said. I patted a dejected-looking Baine on the shoulder. "Don't fret, my friend. Everyone knows you have the heart of a lion."

"Maybe," Baine grumbled. "But it's surrounded by the body of a fourteen-year-old boy."

I laughed and turned to the tall blond archer. "I'm putting you in charge of training, Tyris." I glanced behind me. "Test every one of these men. I need forty or fifty that can use the bows with some skill."

Tyris studied the crowd critically. "That might be a difficult task, my lord."

"One you are more than capable of completing," I replied. "So you had best get to it."

In the end, Tyris found forty-eight men who could use the longbows to some degree. All were similar in body type—big and strong, with mighty shoulders and arms. Most of the archers came from my garrison of farm boys, with a few woodsmen, tanners, masons, and one apprentice blacksmith thrown in as well. I wasn't willing to give up any of my experienced fighters to train with the longbows, so those men were exempt from the trial.

Tyris worked with the selected men for six hours a day, honing their skills, and by the end of the first week, the newly formed archers—who had been given the nickname, the Wolf's Teeth—were hitting targets standing a hundred and fifty yards away two times out of four. Anything past a hundred and fifty yards, Tyris had explained to me, and the iron arrowheads would become mostly ineffective against armor. While that was undoubtedly true about mail and plated armor, female Piths usually wore light leather, so once I explained that to Tyris, he agreed that it made sense to push the targets back to two hundred yards. Even if the barrage from my men failed to kill their archers from that distance, I figured the threat alone would be enough to cause concern and uncertainty among the Piths' ranks, just like it had at Gasterny.

Seventy men had arrived mid-week from Calban and seemed to be settling in well, though I could tell they viewed my Wolf's Teeth boys and their longbows with a certain amount of disdain. That would change, I hoped, when my new archers saw action and proved what they could do. I sent riders to patrol my lands, setting up a network of signal fires so that if Piths were spotted anywhere within my borders, we would have some warning. As expected, I had heard nothing back from the southern lords or the garrisons. All I could do was hope that they had taken my words seriously.

Three weeks after the battle of Camwick, a rider arrived flying the king's banner. I met him in Corwick Hall with Wiflem, Baine, and Niko. Pernissy had set an elegant Lord's Chair carved in mahogany and draped in furs on the dais overlooking the hall, but I always preferred to stand on the rush-covered floor below, feeling out of place in the chair.

"My lord," the man said, bowing. His name was Braham, and he was richly dressed with an air of importance and arrogance about him that I immediately found annoying. He held a fine helmet with an elegant black plume on the crest under one arm and toyed with the cloth of his red, fur-lined cape with the other. The cape reminded me of Cardians, which made me like the man even less. "The king wishes to see you, lord." He said my title with what sounded to me like disdain.

I just gaped at him, then shook my head in anger. "This is not the time to go riding to Gandertown. I could have thousands of Piths rampaging across my lands at any moment."

Braham blinked, looking surprised. "Piths, lord?"

My men began muttering where they sat together on a bench, and I held up a hand to silence them. I felt a coldness settling in my gut like a knife. Braham didn't seem to know anything about the Piths recent actions, which, if true, meant my messenger hadn't made it to Gandertown. "I sent a man weeks ago to warn the king that the Piths are planning an attack. Are you telling me that man never arrived?"

Braham shifted his feet, looking troubled now. "He may have indeed, lord. I don't know because the king is not in Gandertown."

"Well then, where is he?" I demanded.

"Less than a day's ride from here, lord."

Now it was my turn to blink in surprise. "The king is here? In the south?"

"He is, lord, and he has sent me to fetch you to his camp immediately."

I glanced at Wiflem's stony face, then at Baine before turning back to Braham. "At least tell me he's brought an army with him."

Braham shook his head. "No army, lord. He has three hundred of his personal bodyguard along, that is all."

I groaned. "The Piths sacked one of my villages, and more are coming. Are you telling me that the king is unaware of that?"

"The king is not aware of any trouble with the Piths, lord," Braham said. He lifted his chin and stared at me with cold disapproval. "But I'm sure it was nothing more than a simple summer raid not worthy of his attention. That's why he made you the Lord of Corwick, after all, to handle minor details like this."

"Minor detail?" I said, incredulous. "Do you think that's what this is?"

"What I think has no bearing, lord. It's what the king thinks that matters." He turned, gesturing with his helmet. "If it pleases you, lord, we had best be going. King Tyden and the First Son are expecting you before dark."

I paused in surprise. "Son Oriell is with the king?"

Braham nodded. "As is Daughter Gernet. They all await you, so please, lord, if you will come with me."

I shared a look with Baine. The fact that the First Son had come, as well as Daughter Gernet—who was effectively the First Daughter in all but name now—meant this truly had nothing to do with the Piths at all. This was something else entirely. "Wiflem, Baine," I grunted. "Come with me." I started to follow Braham, then, after a few steps, I turned back, leaning over Niko to whisper in his ear. The youth listened attentively, and then he nodded when I was done.

"What was that all about?" Baine asked as we left Corwick Hall.

"Just a hunch," I answered. "We'll see soon enough."

Baine pursed his lips and nodded. "What about Jebido and Sim?" he asked. "Do you think they talked to the king about Pernissy before he left Gandertown?"

"I guess we'll have to wait to find that out," I replied, wondering the same thing.

The king had chosen his campgrounds well, setting up his tents along the edge of a bluff overlooking a deep valley. Other than a few low hills and sparse woodlands, the plains were viewable to the eye for miles. Braham and I had spoken little on the journey, which seemed to suit him just as much as it did me. I wasn't quite sure what role Braham had in service to the king, but by his attitude and demeanor, it was clear to me that Tyden favored the man.

We reached the camp and dismounted as several men-at-arms came to take our horses.

"Please stay here, lord," Braham said curtly, not waiting for an answer as he strode toward a large tent in the center of the encampment.

"Is it just me," Baine said under his breath, "or does that bastard say lord the way that I say turd?"

"Hadrack!"

I turned, my face breaking out into a welcoming smile as I recognized Jin running toward me. The Daughter-In-Waiting flung herself into my arms, staggering me.

"It's so good to see you!" Jin said loudly. She pressed her lips to my ear and whispered, "Be careful, Hadrack. Whatever you do, keep your temper in check."

I lowered Jin to the ground, surprised but unable to ask anything further as Daughter Gernet appeared, trailed by several stern-faced priestesses and a House Agent that I didn't recognize.

"Jin, come away now, dear," Daughter Gernet said. Her features were cold and unwelcoming as she looked at me. "This is not the place nor the time."

"It's good to see you, Daughter," I said cautiously. All the priestesses were glaring at me with clear reproof in their eyes. "How have you been?"

"There! That's him! That's the murderer!" A flock of black-robed priests appeared, bustling their way between the tents toward me. I grunted with distaste when I saw that Son Oriell led them. The First Son had grown fatter since I had last seen him, and he pointed his finger at me, his ugly face twisted in rage. "That is the man who killed my apprentice!"

"What nonsense is this?" I said to Daughter Gernet, ignoring the First Son. "I've killed no one."

"Liar!" Son Oriell hissed. He stopped in front of me and thrust his nose an inch from mine. "You murdered Apprentice Cheny in cold blood, you heathen!"

"I did no such thing," I said. I noticed Braham exiting the king's tent, and he gestured for all of us to come inside.

"We'll soon see about that!" Son Oriell crowed, his eyes gleaming with triumph as he stormed toward the tent with the troop of angry priests close on his heels.

Daughter Gernet paused as she and her entourage moved to follow the priests. "Why couldn't you have used your brain for once and not your sword, Hadrack?" she said frostily. She sighed, moving away. "I can't save you from this, even if I wanted to."

"Your men can wait out here," Braham told me gruffly as I approached the tent. Both Baine and Wiflem started to protest, but I just gave them a quick nod of reassurance, then bent and stepped inside.

"That's him, Your Highness!" Son Oriell said shrilly the moment I entered the interior. "That's the man that slaughtered poor, innocent Cheny!"

King Tyden sat perched on an ornate stool at the back of the tent with his bare feet splayed out on an elegant, furred rug. A servant girl was working oil into his left foot, while a second girl trimmed the toenails on his right. The king waved the servants away as I knelt in front of him.

"Highness," I said. "It is good to see you well."

"You know what amazes me, Lord Hadrack?" Tyden asked as he absently motioned for me to stand.

"I can't imagine, Highness," I said, rising.

"How few people bother with proper foot care." The king lifted one foot, admiring it as his white skin gleamed in the candlelight. I had to admit, it was a fine-looking foot. "I mean, we spend hours tending to our horses' feet, yet give little or no consideration to our own." Tyden stood, scrunching his toes into the fur. He sighed in pleasure as he faced me. "Our feet are the foundation on which we live, Hadrack, and just like that of a house, if you let your foundation rot, then everything above will eventually crumble as well."

"Your Highness!" Son Oriell huffed, stepping forward impatiently. "How can you speak of feet when we have a murderer among us?"

Tyden fixed his light blue eyes on Son Oriell. I could see no love in them for the ugly priest. Finally, the king sighed and looked away. "Very well, First Son, now that Lord Hadrack is here, you may speak your grievance."

"This man," Son Oriell spat, waving a finger inches away from my face. I had to stop myself from grabbing his wrist and snapping it. "This...this...heathen, rode to Thidswitch earlier this month for the sole purpose of murdering one of my order."

"Yes, so you have told me," Tyden said dryly as he began to pace on the rug. "Yet, you have so far declined to give me a reason for why he would do that."

"Who can say what goes on in a heartless savage's mind, Highness," Son Oriell said. He lowered his head in sorrow. "Not only did he murder a valued and promising apprentice, he killed an entire colony of lepers that poor apprentice was tending."

I gaped at Son Oriell. "That's a lie!" I said, finally finding my tongue. I glanced at Daughter Gernet and Jin. The young girl had her hands pressed over her mouth, her eyes wide with dread, while her grandmother stood beside her, the priestess's expression, if anything, even more dour than before.

King Tyden stroked his finely-trimmed beard as he thought. "Lord Hadrack," he finally said. "Were you in Thidswitch at the time the First Son claims?"

I'd managed to get my surprise and anger under control by now, and I nodded. "I was, Highness."

"Why did you go there?" Tyden asked.

"I went to see Grindin, just as the First Son says," I answered. Tyden's brow furrowed. "Apprentice Cheny, Highness," I explained. "Grindin was his name before he took the vows."

"Ah," the king said, understanding now. "Did you announce yourself to Lord Wakerton when you arrived?"

I shook my head. "I did not, Highness. I meant to, but it slipped my mind."

"Because you were too busy killing my apprentice!" the First Son hissed.

King Tyden lifted his hands as all the priests began hurling accusations at me at once. "We will have order here," the king said calmly. He gestured to me. "This is not some ruffian plucked from Beggar's Row. This man is a lord, and he will be treated as such."

"This is what you get when you raise scum beyond their station," I heard one of the priests mutter.

If the king heard it, he chose not to react. "Lord Hadrack, can you please explain what it was that you were doing in Thidswitch."

I glanced at Son Oriell, whose eyes were burning with anticipation. "I went there to kill Grindin, Highness," I said truthfully.

"I told you!" Son Oriell howled, joy on his face. He jabbed his finger at me over and over. "That man is a murderer! He's admitted to killing one of our order! There can be nothing left now but banishment from the House and execution as soon as possible!"

"May I speak, Highness?" I said, ignoring the clamoring priests, my calm reflecting that of the king's. Tyden nodded, though I could see by his expression that he was now convinced of my guilt. "I fully admit to going to Thidswitch to kill Grindin."

"Why?" the king asked.

I sought out Jin with my eyes, sharing this with her. "I went to kill Grindin because he was one of the nine men who destroyed Corwick."

Jin's eyes went round, and gasps arose in the tent. I saw Daughter Gernet's steely gaze thaw a little, her features turning thoughtful as she studied me.

"A filthy lie from a desperate man, Your Highness!" Son Oriell snapped. He sniffed, composing himself. "But even if it were true, it does not excuse this man's actions. Apprentice Cheny was a representative of The Father Himself. There can be no leniency for such a vile act. This man must die!"

I turned to face the ugly priest. "And what if I didn't kill him?" I asked. "What if he is still alive?"

Son Oriell hesitated, and I saw a shadow of doubt cloud his eyes. Then the priest shook off my words and his doubt, facing the king. "We have a witness, lord."

Tyden sighed, looking suddenly weary. He waved a hand. "Bring in your witness, then, and let's be done with this."

Son Oriell turned, pushing the priests crowded together behind him aside until he drew one into the open. I hadn't noticed the man before, but it was Son Jona. The thin priest stepped forward self-consciously and bowed to the king.

"You claim to have witnessed this murder?" Tyden said, his arms crossed over his chest now.

"I did, Highness," Son Jona responded in a soft voice. He glanced sideways at me, and I thought I could see a faint smile playing about his lips. "I blame myself, Highness. I did not fully appreciate Lord Hadrack's intent when I directed him to the hills where Apprentice Cheny was selflessly caring for the unfortunate lepers. What occurred in Thidswitch was a terrible tragedy, Highness, and the crushing weight that I bear from witnessing the murders will stay with me until my last day in this world."

The thin priest sniffed, wiping at his eyes. I had to stop myself from snorting in disbelief. Son Jona wasn't much of an actor, in my opinion.

"What say you to this?" the king asked, focusing on me.

"Have him swear it, Highness," I said calmly. I pointed to the Rock of Life hanging from around the priest's neck. "Have him swear before The Father that what he is saying is the truth."

"Do you so swear?" Tyden asked Son Jona.

The thin priest clasped the dark stone in both of his hands, his face set in comical earnestness. "I do so swear, Highness. Lord Hadrack murdered Apprentice Cheny and the lepers before my very eyes."

"Very well," King Tyden said reluctantly. "I see no reason why—"

"Excuse me, Highness," I said, cutting off the king in mid-sentence. "Before you pass judgment on me, I have a witness of my own. If it pleases you, I ask that he be allowed to speak."

Tyden frowned, looking surprised, then he bowed his head. "The witness may speak."

"What is this nonsense?" Son Oriell sputtered as I put two fingers in my mouth and whistled.

Niko appeared almost immediately in the entrance, holding Grindin firmly by the arm.

I gestured to the new arrivals. "Highness, I would like to present Grindin, who is also known as Apprentice Cheny."

9: Invasion

"I haven't laughed that hard in years!" Tyden gasped, wiping tears of mirth from his eyes. He took a long drink of ale, then slammed his mug down on a small chest beside the stool he sat on. Night had fallen, and tallow candles standing in deep wooden bowls were placed around the tent, lighting the interior. "Did you see that fat bastard's face when you dragged the apprentice in here?" The king stood, his face still red from laughing as he removed his crown and tossed it casually on the stool. "I thought he was going to piss himself!"

"It was a great surprise to us all, Highness," Daughter Gernet said, her voice neutral. Jin stood beside her, the apprentice's eyes brimming with happiness. The four of us were alone now, everyone else having been cleared out after Grindin's long and reluctant testimony. "But despite this Cheny person being alive," the priestess added gravely. "Some of Son Oriell's accusations still bear weight. He has a case against Hadrack that can't be easily ignored."

Jin blinked in surprise, her face falling as Tyden waved a dismissive hand. "Nonsense. Hadrack might have been a little rough with the apprentice, I'll grant you that, but it was hardly without cause."

"I do not believe using a heated blade on naked flesh can be termed a little rough, Your Highness," Daughter Gernet said.

The king's grin faltered and he glanced at me. "Well, that may be true enough, but under the circumstances, I think that it is justifiable." Jebido and Sim had missed the king when he'd left Gandertown to come south for my trial, so Tyden had known nothing about Pernissy's escape or the clever plot that the bastard had hatched. However, he had heard of Lord Boudin, who he'd never met, but knew was a very rich and powerful Cardian lord. Why that lord was in league with Pernissy was a mystery none of us could understand. Tyden studied Daughter Gernet thoughtfully. "Are you saying that you will cast your vote with the First Son, despite what he has been up to?"

The priestess snorted. "Certainly not, Highness. I enjoyed watching that fool get humiliated and, if it were possible, I would gladly see the First Son removed from his office. But since he has denied everything and we have no actual proof of his guilt, there is little within the law that can make that removal happen, which leaves us obligated to acknowledge his current complaint. One that isn't without some merit."

"But certainly not worthy of banishment or execution?" Tyden said.

Daughter Gernet glanced at me appraisingly, and then she shook her head. "No, it is not. Not yet, anyway. But I think all of us here understand the singular path that Hadrack has always taken regarding those who destroyed his village. That apprentice was one of them, which means I guarantee you Hadrack intends to kill him, probably sooner rather than later. When that happens, I will have little choice but to side with Son Oriell."

Tyden turned to me. "Is that true? Do you still intend to kill this man, Hadrack, even though you know what the consequences will be?"

I briefly considered lying as I toyed with my mug of ale, then I shrugged. "Of course I'm going to kill him, Highness."

The king sighed in resignation, drumming his fingers idly on his chin as he studied me. "I had forgotten how direct and honest you can be, Lord Hadrack. It's a refreshing change after being surrounded by two-faced vipers and fawning arse-lickers with liquid-honey tongues." He started to pace, then stopped and turned to me. "What if I say I forbid you to kill this man?"

"I have no wish to anger you, Highness," I said, meaning it. I turned and nodded to the priestess. "Nor bring down the wrath of the House upon my head, Daughter. But not even the power of a king or the word of The Mother will stop me from killing Grindin when the time is right." I took a deep breath. "But you have my word that he won't die by my hand anytime soon. There are, unfortunately, greater problems that must be dealt with first."

"You mean Pernissy?" Tyden asked.

"No, Highness," I replied with a shake of my head. "I mean the Piths."

"What do those heathens have to do with anything?" Daughter Gernet said.

"They attacked one of my villages last month," I explained. "Slaughtering everyone but the Son, the Daughter, and the apprentices."

"That is terrible news," the king said. I thought I detected a brief flash of outrage rise in his eyes, but it faded quickly. "You have my full support to deal with this unfortunate incident in any way that you see fit. It's been years since the Piths raided us, and I had hoped never to hear their cursed name spoken again. Beaten people should accept their fate and lie down and die."

"I have already dealt with it, Highness," I said. "The Piths who sacked Lestwick have all been killed." King Tyden's eyebrows rose in surprise. I explained then about how I had rescued Daughter Tessa and Apprentice Lucenda and about sending Nedo back to the Piths as a message—though I didn't go into any detail about what I had done to the boy. That could wait. Then I told them of the battle in Camwick and my letting Saldor go home with the Pith dead.

"Mother help her," Daughter Gernet whispered when I was through, looking stunned. "Have those heathens no decency? She wears the yellow robe!"

"Piths care nothing for that, Daughter," I said. "They view our beliefs as backward and strange."

"Then what do these people care about?" Daughter Gernet challenged.

I shrugged. "Gambling, horses, drinking." I glanced at Jin, then shifted my eyes away. "Rape and plunder."

"You said you let a Pith take his dead and return home," Tyden cut in. "Why would you do that?"

"I needed information, Highness, so I made a deal with him. The souls of his brothers and sisters in exchange for what I wanted to know."

"And did you get what you needed?" Tyden asked.

"Yes, and no, Highness. The Pith was no fool, and he answered most of my questions with riddles, lies, and half-truths."

"Yet, he told you enough to cause concern," Tyden said, his face tightening.

I nodded. "He did. There is a Pith chieftain named Lorgen Three-Fingers." I paused as Daughter Gernet snorted in contempt at the name. "This Pith has raised a sizable army, and according to the man I spoke to, he plans on invading us."

Tyden pursed his lips. "Are you certain of this?"

"Yes, Highness," I said. I hesitated as I collected my thoughts, knowing now was the time to tell Tyden everything. "There is more, Highness. Nedo was Lorgen Three-Fingers only son, and I gelded the bastard and sent him back to his father like that."

I heard both Daughter Gernet and Jin gasp, but I kept my gaze focused squarely on the king.

Tyden's eyes narrowed. "You're telling me that because you, in your judgment, felt the need to disfigure a man's son, that my kingdom might now be facing a war?"

"It is possible that my actions might have made things worse, Highness," I conceded. "But I needed to draw the Piths to where I could kill them, and the only way that I could see to do that was to enrage them. I had no idea at the time who Nedo was, but even if I had, I would have done the same. Those men killed people under my protection, and I could not let that stand."

Tyden turned his back to me, scrunching his still-bare toes aggressively in the soft fur as he thought. I waited, sharing a glance with Jin, who smiled weakly at me in reassurance.

Tyden finally turned to face me after several long minutes, his expression and eyes calmer. "Very well, Lord Hadrack. I accept your explanation. I agree with you that you could not have known who this boy was. It is unfortunate, but what is done is done. You did what you thought was best for the people of your fiefdom and the realm."

"Thank you, Highness," I said. I paused, reluctant to bring up my fears with Jin and Daughter Gernet listening, though I knew they needed to hear it. "There is something else." The king frowned, but he remained silent as he motioned with a hand that I should go on. "The Pith I spoke to said Lorgen Three-Fingers had gathered as many men as there are blades of grass, and that war was coming for Ganderland and couldn't be avoided. At the time, I'd thought that he meant because of what I had done to the man's son. But I no longer believe that is the only reason. I believe the raid on Lestwick was just one of many and that this coming attack has been planned for some time."

"Then why raid at all if that's true?" Tyden asked. "Why not attack in force and be done with it?"

I shifted my gaze briefly to Daughter Gernet. "Because I believe there might be a purpose to the raids, Highness. I pray that I am wrong, but from what I could get from the Pith I questioned, it's possible that they may have come north to capture Sons and Daughters."

"What!" Daughter Gernet said loudly. "That's preposterous. Why would they do that?"

"Yes, why would they do that, Hadrack?" Tyden asked. "You said yourself that the Piths care nothing for our people, so why take them as prisoners?"

"Because I think the Piths intend to sacrifice them to the Master, Highness."

"Dear Mother, preserve me!" Daughter Gernet gasped. She wobbled on her feet and Jin had to move fast to steady her. Tyden hurried to help, and together, the girl and king supported the priestess as they gently sat her down on the stool. Daughter Gernet clutched at the king. "This can't be true, Highness! Hadrack must be mistaken."

The king patted her hand, and then he stood to face me. "I too pray to the gods that you are wrong about this, Hadrack," he said.

Tyden brushed his blond hair from his eyes, looking suddenly young and vulnerable as he stood in indecision.

"Highness," I said to break the sudden silence. "I sent riders to warn the southern lords and garrisons about the Piths several weeks ago, so they are aware of the danger. I also sent all the Sons and Daughters on my lands north, away from the Piths, and suggested that they do likewise." I shrugged. "I have heard nothing back from any of them, so I can't say whether or not my warnings were heeded."

"That was very wise of you, Hadrack," Tyden said, biting at his lower lip. He took a deep breath. "We'll have to—"

Braham abruptly appeared, pushing his way without announcement into the tent. "Forgive me, Highness, but a rider has just arrived with an urgent message."

The king and I shared a look, then he nodded. "Show him in," he said.

I moved to stand beside Jin as Braham slipped aside the tent flap and gestured outside. A moment later, a thin man wearing nothing but a tunic and trousers and looking worn, tired, and dusty appeared. Jin slid her small hand into mine and squeezed it anxiously. I pressed back, knowing whatever this was about, it was going to be bad news.

The man knelt, bowing his head. "Highness," he said.

"You have a message for me?" Tyden stated, motioning impatiently for the man to rise.

"I do, Your Highness," the rider answered. He briefly shifted his eyes to me—eyes filled with apprehension, I thought—before focusing back on the king. "I have just come from Gasterny, Highness. An army of Piths have laid siege to the garrison."

King Tyden blinked, and his already strained white face drained of whatever color was left. "How many?" he managed to say in a strangled voice.

"Many, Highness?"

"How many men do they have!?" Tyden snapped.

The rider flushed, looking at the rest of us helplessly. "Forgive me, Your Highness," he said. "I am very tired, and I'm not good with numbers. There were a lot of them."

"That tells me nothing useful," Tyden growled. "There are lots of whores in Gandertown, too, but I don't actually know how many."

The rider looked crestfallen. "My pardon, Highness."

The king sighed. "What is your name?"

"Bona, Highness."

"Very well, Bona, give me your best guess. How many Piths do you think there are?"

The messenger looked down at his feet as he thought. "Seven hundred perhaps, Your Highness," he finally mumbled. "No more than that, I would say."

"Seven hundred?" the king repeated, looking thoughtful. "You're certain?"

"Yes, Highness," Bona nodded. "I believe so, yes."

"When did this happen?" I asked.

"Four days ago, lord."

"Highness," Braham said urgently. "If we issue a call to arms now, we can raise double that in a matter of days and crush these heathens."

"I agree," Tyden replied. He nodded to Braham. "See to it."

"Just a moment," I said, raising a hand. I turned to the messenger. "Were you in Gasterny when the Piths arrived?"

Bona nodded. "Yes, lord, I was. Captain Destin had me slip over the walls the first night." He shrugged his shoulders. "I'm a really good swimmer, lord. The Piths had blocked the bridge, so he needed me to cross the White Rock."

"You swam the White Rock?" I asked, impressed, remembering how treacherous the waters near Gasterny were.

"I did, lord," Bona said. "I thought I was dead for sure. Three Piths saw me jump in the river, but all they did was stand on the bank and watch me. I figured they expected me to drown and didn't want to waste an arrow, but when I made it to the other side, they didn't do anything, either. I eventually found a mule in a village and rode here as fast as I could."

I nodded absently. "What were the Piths doing before you left?"

"Lord?"

"You said they blocked the bridge, which I find curious. Didn't they attack the gatehouses?"

Bona shook his head. "No, lord. They just blocked the southern end of the bridge, that's all."

"And after that?" I asked. "What did they do then?"

"Why, they made camp, lord."

"Did you see them attack the garrison or gatehouses before you left?"

"No, lord, but I'm sure they were about to."

I nodded, convinced now as I turned to the king. "They don't want Gasterny, Highness," I said firmly. "They just want you to think that they do."

"That's ludicrous!" Braham snapped. "Of course they want Gasterny. Why wouldn't they?" He faced the king. "Highness, if we don't attack now, we could lose that fortress and with it control over the entire southeastern corridor. We must take the fight to them as soon as possible."

I frowned as Tyden glanced at me. "You don't agree, Lord Hadrack?"

"Piths don't care much about sieges, Highness," I replied, uneasy with Bona's description of the army outside Gasterny's walls. I knew Saldor might have lied to me about the strength of Lorgen Three-Fingers men, but my gut told me that he hadn't. The Cimbrati had described that army with a certain amount of pride, almost bragging about it, but his words had a ring of truth about them. As many men as blades of grass, he'd said. Seven hundred men didn't seem to fit that description. "Piths prefer to move fast, grabbing what they can and burning and destroying everything else in their path," I added. "Nothing this man has told us makes sense. I think this is a trap, Highness."

Braham snorted. "The Piths already took Gasterny once," he said, not hiding his contempt as he glared at me. "With your help, Lord Hadrack, as I recall. It's obvious they want it back."

I ignored the man's jibe. "I know Piths, Highness. They prefer fighting in the open, man against man, and blade against blade. Gasterny has been greatly reinforced since it fell, and the walls are much stouter now and are well defended. The Piths don't have siege engines, nor do they understand them. Taking that fortress will be no easy task with that small a force."

"Lord Corwick managed," Braham responded with a sneer.

I stared at the other man coldly. "That's because the garrison was weak then, and he had no qualms about sacrificing as many lives as he needed to. Piths don't think that way. They always fight to win, but will never needlessly lose men to do it." I turned to the king. "We need to be cautious, Highness. Something isn't right about this."

Braham strode forward, stopping in front of me. "Cautious!" he spat into my face. "So says the man who thought of the Piths as brothers not that long ago. A man who was loyal to a bunch of heathens and one who gladly shed the blood of Ganders for them! Now we're supposed to listen to your advice? You could still be allied with these Piths right now for all we know!"

"That will do, Braham," King Tyden said. "Lord Hadrack's loyalty is not in question here."

"Well, maybe it should be," Braham grunted.

"I said that will do, Braham!" Tyden snapped. He closed his eyes and rubbed them with his thumb and index finger. Finally, he sighed. "Very well," he grunted, focusing on Braham. "Issue the call to arms. We march on the Piths as soon as possible."

Braham's face broke out in delight and he bowed. "Yes, Highness," he said, giving me a look of triumph before he took Bona's arm and guided him outside.

"You disapprove of my choice, Lord Hadrack?" Tyden asked when they were gone.

I felt Jin gripping my hand tighter in warning, and I glanced down at her before turning back to the king. "My place is not to question your orders, Highness," I said dutifully. I could feel my insides roiling with apprehension, but I made sure my features showed none of it.

"Good," Tyden said. "Then we understand each other. Once the levy has been raised, we will smash these heathens once and for all, and then you and I can deal with Pernissy together."

"I look forward to it, Highness," I said, knowing that the king had made up his mind. I squeezed Jin's hand one last time before letting her go. "With your permission, I would like to return to Corwick Castle to prepare."

"By all means," the king agreed.

I turned to Daughter Gernet. "Daughter."

The priestess inclined her head slightly. "Lord Hadrack."

Jin and I shared a look, and then I stepped outside, where Baine, Niko, and Wiflem were waiting for me. Torches lit the campground, flickering in the cool breeze as I led my men toward our horses.

"What was that all about?" Baine asked. "Braham ran out of there as if the husband of the woman he's been humping just came home."

"We're going to war," I grunted. "The Piths have laid siege to Gasterny."

Baine frowned. "Our Gasterny?"

"Is there any other?" I asked as I swung up on Angry's saddle.

"But Piths don't lay siege to anything, Hadrack," Baine said as he climbed nimbly onto his mare's back.

I swung Angry's head around. "Tell that to him," I said, hooking a thumb at the king's tent.

I paused, my eyes narrowing with suspicion. Son Oriell and Grindin—now once again wearing the brown robes of an apprentice—stood together beside a lone tree that grew at the edge of the bluff. Grindin held up an oil lamp, illuminating a wooden cage tied with rope hung from a branch over the precipice. A pale, naked figure huddled inside the cage, shivering against the evening chill. The First Son stood bent over, his hands on his knees as he talked with the cage's occupant.

"Wait here," I grunted to my men. I urged Angry closer to the priest and apprentice, who seemed oblivious of me.

"But you promised, Uncle!" I heard the prisoner say in a high-pitched whine. It was Jona, now stripped of his robes and station.

"I promised nothing!" the First Son hissed back. "It's only going to be for a day or two. Show some backbone, boy!"

Grindin glanced over his shoulder, and even in the lantern light, I could see his face turning white as he saw me approaching. He plucked at the First Son's robe urgently.

"Not now!" Son Oriell snapped, waving him off.

"It's Lord Hadrack, First Son," Grindin whispered. I could hear the fear in his voice, which gladdened my heart.

I halted Angry ten feet from the two men as Son Oriell turned, a forced smile upon his lips. "Ah, Lord Hadrack, there you are. I was just offering the prisoner one last chance to explain why he felt the need to lie before his king and god."

"Is that so?" I said. I shifted my gaze to Grindin, who had suddenly found something on the ground to keep his interest. "And what did your nephew tell you, First Son?"

Son Oriell sighed. "Sadly, the stubborn fool refuses to answer, lord. I can't for the life of me understand why."

"Oh, I think we both have a pretty good idea why," I said with a sarcastic chuckle. Son Oriell's features turned hard as I regarded Jona. The former Son clutched the cage's wooden slats with both hands as he glared at me. "You should unburden yourself, Jona," I told him. "Carrying the full weight of crimes committed by others must be exhausting. Tell me the truth, and I promise I'll go to the king on your behalf and have your sentence repealed immediately."

Jona blinked in surprise as Son Oriell cleared his throat nervously. "Now, now, Lord Hadrack," the priest said, glancing sideways at his nephew. "Let's not be too hasty about offering absolution and false hope. The Holy Law is clear on matters as grave as this, and even the king himself cannot overturn it. Jona may still breathe for the moment, but he is already dead as far as the House is concerned. All any of us can do now is pray that The Father can cleanse the evil from my nephew's poor, misguided soul."

I stroked my beard, thinking as Jona shifted his gaze from me to his uncle, the hope fading from his eyes. "You are right, First Son," I said. "Forgive me. I just feel the sentence of death might be a little harsh, especially since he is of your blood."

The priest nodded, his features twisted in sorrow. "Your generosity and empathy towards my family is staggering, lord. I cannot thank you enough for your kind words. But Jona must suffer the fate required by the House, regardless of my affection for him. To do otherwise would send a message of inequality amongst us in the eyes of the people that I am honored to serve."

"That is truly admirable and selfless of you, First Son," I said, trying not to let the disdain I felt for the man show. "I applaud your dedication to the people." I hesitated, looking back over my shoulder at the tents. "The king plans on breaking camp in the morning, but I'll have one of my men sit with Jona until the end. It's the least that I can do for blood kin of yours, since you tried so hard to get to the bottom of this for me."

Son Oriell's eyes widened and I heard Jona gasp. "That won't be necessary, lord," the priest protested. "While your kind offer truly humbles me, Jona was once of my order. I couldn't ask a stranger to sit with him." He gestured to Grindin. "I will leave Apprentice Cheny behind to stay with my nephew until he passes into the next world."

"Ah," I said. "That is a fine idea, First Son." I casually guided Angry closer to the edge of the bluff. The big horse snorted in warning at Grindin, pushing him easily out of the way with his shoulder as Son Oriell scurried from the stallion's path. "My apologies," I said. "This horse of mine has a mind of its own at times."

"He is a magnificent creature, lord," Son Oriell muttered, watching me cautiously.

"He is," I agreed. I halted Angry between the two men and the hanging cage, then leaned on the pommel of my saddle. "There is one thing you said that I find most interesting, Son."

"Oh, and what would that be, lord?"

"You mentioned that in the eyes of the House, your nephew is already dead. What did you mean by that, exactly?"

Son Oriell smiled condescendingly. "The Holy Law on this is quite explicit, lord. Once a Son is convicted of lying under oath to The Father, no one can help him. The moment he enters that cage, the accused ceases to exist in our world and must wait until his soul departs his body, however long that might take. So, even though Jona yet breaths and speaks, he is nothing more than a shadow to us now."

"I see," I said as I glanced briefly at the doomed man before turning back to the priest. "That is a miserable way to die, First Son."

"I agree," Son Oriell said sadly. "Yet, there is nothing we can do but wait and pray that the end comes quickly for him."

"That's not entirely true," I said. Son Oriell's eyebrows rose, but before he could say anything more, I drew my father's axe and lashed out at the rope holding the cage. The axe blade cleaved the cable effortlessly, and Jona had only a moment to register what was happening before, with a high-pitched wail, he plunged downward into the darkness. A moment later, I heard the satisfying sounds of the cage striking the rocks in the valley far below. I turned Angry away from the rim as Son Oriell and Grindin stared up at me in horror. "You told me he was a dead man anyway," I said in explanation as I sheathed my axe. "So why make the poor wretch suffer?" I smiled down at the two men as Angry trotted past them. "No need to thank me, First Son," I called out over my shoulder. "I'll gladly do the same for either one of you, should the opportunity ever arise."

10: The Battle of the Bridge: Part Two

One of the first things Tyden did when he became king was establish a standing army that answered to him and to no one else. Before that, wars were mainly fought by conscripts—those from the lowest feudal ranks—as well as mercenaries and whatever professional soldiers each lord had under his employ. It was a shrewd move on Tyden's part, I thought, since a king is only as strong as the men who support and protect him. A great deal of unrest remained after the civil war, and many of the northern lords who had originally sworn fealty to King Jorquin and then Prince Tyrale openly distrusted their new king. If not for the unswerving loyalty and affection that this fledgling army had for Tyden—due mainly, I suspected, to the generous pay he gave them—I have little doubt that the king's reign would have been very short-lived.

The king's new army numbered almost ten thousand men, but unfortunately for us in the south, most of those forces were too far away to be of much help. There were troops stationed in the garrisons along the border, of course, but Tyden didn't want to weaken those fortresses by drawing men away, fearing that might be what the Piths ultimately wanted. The majority of the king's forces remained around his power base of Gandertown, a clear deterrent against any of the ambitious northern lords who might try to seize the crown for themselves. Tyden had not listened to my concerns about Gasterny, but he had compromised somewhat by summoning a thousand of his men south in case the Pith threat was bigger than expected. For now, though, we would have to deal with the siege of the garrison on our own.

A call to arms, known as a levy, had been issued the morning after I met with Tyden, with messengers sent to every southern lord within a three-day ride. From there, more messengers working in relays went to every village, town, and hamlet, throwing a garland of straw in the town centers, which signified every able man must report to their lords to fight.

The king had shifted his camp to the plains that lay to the west of Camwick, which he had decided would be our rallying point. I'd offered him the use of Corwick Castle, but he had declined, saying that he preferred to be with his men. Tyden believed his presence would help with morale and inspire the commoners when they saw him living as they did, which once again I considered a wise move on his part. The king had initially hoped to march to Gasterny's aid in less than a week, but by the seventh day, some of the southern lords still had not arrived with their men, so we continued to wait. Camwick was doing a brisk business supplying food, drink, and whores to the growing army, though all of it at a greatly reduced price imposed by the king himself. Tyden might be generous with his soldiers at home, but with the royal treasury greatly depleted in the wake of the Pair War, the merchants of Camwick were getting little from their new king other than flowery words and the miserly grip of his hand.

With each successive lord who arrived in camp came confirmation of Pith raids on their lands, with many of the village Sons and Daughters being abducted, just as I had foreseen. The king railed against those lords, furious that they had ignored my warnings, though there was little that could be done about it now. Finally, on the morning of the eighth day, King Tyden decided that he'd waited long enough, and his army that had swelled to several thousand strong began to move out, trudging southward. Moving an army of that size is a slow and complicated process, with infantry, cavalry, pack animals, and supply wagons all adding to a long line that stretched for more than a mile along the road that would lead us to Gasterny.

I rode in the rear of that army, eating dust thrown up by the wagons as I led fifty of my men-at-arms on horseback while my

Wolf's Teeth marched behind us on foot. I didn't trust the scant information we had about the Piths movements, so I'd left Wiflem in command of Corwick Castle with the remainder of my men. If Lorgen Three-Fingers planned on trying to seize the castle in my absence, then he would learn that the fiefdom of Corwick still had sharp teeth even if the wolf wasn't home.

As usual, Baine rode beside me, and it was he who first noticed the two horsemen far to our rear. My friend plucked at my arm. "Unless my eyes are deceiving me, that white horse back there looks like Jebido's."

I turned, watching as two figures on horseback drew closer. "I think you're right," I said as a smile of pleasure broke out on my face. I pulled Angry out of line, motioning for my men to continue onward as Baine swung his mare around to join me. Then we waited.

Five minutes later, with the backs of the Wolf's Teeth fading in the distance around a bend in the road, Sim and Jebido paused their winded mounts in front of us.

"I should have known you two wouldn't miss a good fight," I said.

Jebido grinned. "Somebody has to watch out for you."

"You spoke with Wiflem?"

My friend's face turned serious as Sim nodded beside him. "We did," Jebido said. "Piths laying siege to a well-defended fortress like Gasterny? This has a smell to it, Hadrack."

"I know," I grunted. "I tried telling the king that, but he didn't want to hear it."

Jebido and Sim rode beside Baine and me as I filled the two in on everything that had happened since they'd left Corwick over a month ago.

"So, what do you think the Piths are up to?" Jebido asked when I was done.

I shrugged. I had been mulling that very question over for the last few days, always coming back to the same answer. "The attack on Gasterny has to be a ploy," I said.

Jebido nodded. "That's what I think, too. They want the king's eyes focused there, but why?"

"A bigger target?" Baine suggested.

"Like what?" I asked.

Baine sighed. "I only wish I knew."

Five days later, our army lay encamped across the White Rock from Gasterny. Pith scouts had dogged us most of the way, watching our movements from afar, so it was a great surprise when word came that the gatehouses on either side of the bridge were lying open and undefended. The Piths had set up a camp in the fields a mile east of the garrison, but they seemed unconcerned at our appearance, which made me even more uneasy. I could see Gander soldiers patrolling the fortress's ramparts, but as far as I could tell, the garrison appeared undamaged. The wooden walls that I remembered from my time in Gasterny were gone now, replaced with formidable stone ones. I knew if we'd had those walls years ago, Pernissy's men would never have gotten to us, and my life would have turned out very differently.

"All of this seems just a little too familiar," Jebido grunted as he followed me toward the king's tent. My friend was dressed in heavy mail, with a conical helmet and dented nose guard that struggled to cover his hooked nose entirely.

I grunted my agreement as we stepped inside.

"Highness, this doesn't make any sense," were the first words that I heard. The man who had spoken was tall, with closely-cropped grey hair and bushy black eyebrows that always made him look angry. His name was Lord Porten Welis, an experienced warrior who had brought almost three hundred men with him, half of them archers. His son, Fitzery Welis, stood beside him, also with the same bushy eyebrows, though they were light brown, as was his hair. "Why remove the gates and leave the gatehouses undefended like this?" Lord Porten added with a frown.

"Because the Piths know they can't stop us from taking them, lord," Braham said. I noticed he said lord with a great deal more respect than he did when he talked to me.

"It does make a certain kind of sense," Lord Falway agreed. The speaker was short, with enormous shoulders and legs offset by a bulging gut under his mail. He moved to a small table that sat in the center of the crowded tent as men stepped aside for him. The lord ran his finger across a map that lay on the table's surface. "They know that any men they place in those gatehouses will be lost when we attack. But if they forget about the buildings and set up a shield wall to box us in right here, our men will be hemmed in by the gatehouse walls to either side. Removing the gates ensures we can't use the buildings for defense."

"With perhaps what?" Tyden asked as he toyed with his beard. "Ten or fifteen men that we can send against them at a time?"

"Exactly, Highness," Lord Falway said. "The Piths could hold that position all day long, rotating tired men out for fresh, while our men are jammed into that building with nowhere to go."

"But by ceding us this gatehouse," Lord Porten said, tapping a finger on the map. "They have effectively given us the high ground."

"Exactly," another lord agreed. "Get archers up on the ramparts and they can make quick work of the Pith shield wall."

"Not necessarily," I said, remembering the assault that I had been involved in on the same gatehouse years ago. "Your men will have to lean over the battlements and aim down, which would leave them vulnerable to Pith arrows."

"Then my boys will deal with their archers first," Lord Porten said in a confident voice. I just shook my head as the tall lord snorted. "What? Do you think a bunch of Pith girls can outshoot us?"

"Yes," I said bluntly. "If you try to go bow against bow with them, I promise you will lose."

Lord Falway nodded his head in agreement. "As much as I hate to admit it, Lord Hadrack is right. To start, we will have to match the Piths shield for shield and push them back with sheer brute strength. Their archers will be limited in their targets that way, at least for a while. If we can flank the Piths and get behind their wall, it will fold, and then we can slaughter them all."

"And if it doesn't fold?" Lord Porten asked.

No one answered that question, and finally, King Tyden cleared his throat. "Very well. I appreciate the advice given here today. We will attack in one hour, but not with our best in the first wave. We will throw the levy against the Piths to wear them down first, then hit them with pikes and swords."

"That's a bad idea, Highness," I said.

Tyden crossed his arms over his chest, a frown on his face. "How so, Lord Hadrack?"

I stepped forward. "Sending men with little to no armor up against Piths in that confined space would be madness. They'll get slaughtered."

"That's what they're here for," one of the lords said, raising a chuckle from the other men.

"Really?" I snapped. "Because I thought we came here to win. Wasting lives like that is just stupid. It will do nothing but bolster the Piths' morale and tear ours down. How do you think the men waiting on the bridge are going to feel watching their brothers getting hacked down and ripped apart in front of them?"

"Do you have another option, Lord Hadrack?" Tyden asked.

"Yes, I do, Highness," I said. "But I'll need more than an hour to get ready. Probably two." I glanced at Lord Porten. "I would also need some of your archers, lord."

The tall man shrugged. "If the king agrees to this plan, then you can have them."

I nodded to him in gratitude. "Good," I said. "Then this is what I propose we do."

Just over two hours later, I stood with Jebido and Baine and my fifty men-at-arms in the center of the bridge. Six carts pulled by mules waited behind my men, with sixty archers and two hundred heavily armored mounted lancers led by Sim lined up behind the carts. The Piths had formed a shield wall outside the southern gatehouse when they saw us move onto the bridge, positioning themselves exactly where Lord Falway had predicted they would. More warriors waited behind the wall, with hundreds of female archers making a cordon behind them. The Pith archers were shooting over the gatehouse at us, but I had been careful to stop well out of their range. The shafts cracked harmlessly against the stone in front of me, and finally, the Piths gave up wasting arrows and just watched us.

Lord Porten's borrowed archers were lined up along the riverbank east of the bridge, looking confused as to what their purpose might be. A grizzled soldier in heavy mail stood off to one side of the line, watching me closely. Finally, I nodded to him that I was ready.

"Archers, nock your arrows!" the man shouted at the top of his lungs. I had selected him specifically for his booming voice.

I turned to see what effect the man's words were having, praying that the Piths would be able to hear over the roar of the White Rock. Some of the warriors waiting behind the shield wall shifted over to the riverbank, peering across the water at us. I grinned. Piths were notoriously curious.

"Archers, draw!" the soldier commanded.

Thirty-five bowmen drew nocks to their ears while I could hear the Piths laughing and jeering from across the river. Even more of the warriors were moving closer to see what we were doing, including many of the female archers. "Come on," I grunted under my breath. "Come and join the fun."

"Archers, loose!" the man cried.

A dark flight of spinning shafts hurtled upward, arcing toward the watching Piths before plunging into the swirling water well away from the opposite bank. The river was roughly five hundred feet wide where we stood, which was more than I would have liked, but still feasible for what I had in mind. I just prayed the steady breeze blowing at our backs would remain.

"Again!" I shouted, ignoring the mockery coming from the opposite bank.

"Archers, nock your arrows!"

"Look at that fool," Jebido said, nudging my arm and pointing.

A Pith warrior had run down the steep grade and was dancing on the rocky shoreline. He turned and dropped his trousers, pointing at his stark white ass and wiggling it.

"Archers, draw!"

"Get ready," I grunted. I glanced at Baine. "Wait until we hit their line, then up you go with your archers, and keep your head down."

Baine just nodded, his eyes dark and dangerous as he focused on the massed Pith shields bristling on the far side of the gatehouse.

"Archers, loose!"

Dark shafts rose in the air for a second time, only to fall short of the southern side again. More Pith warriors were plunging down the opposite bank to join their naked comrade, forming a line and dropping their trousers. One was a woman with a shapely behind, which was causing quite a stir of appreciation among my men.

"I think I've seen enough stinking arseholes for one day, Hadrack," Jebido growled as he clutched his sword. "Excluding the girl's, of course. Can we get on with this, please?"

I chuckled and nodded. I turned and started to curse loudly at Lord Porten's archers, ridiculing them for their lack of skill as the Piths hooted with delight. I paced back and forth across the bridge, kicking the stone and screaming, promising each man that they would be mucking stables for the rest of their lives after this. I wasn't sure how much of the tirade the Piths could hear, but they seemed to be enjoying my performance just the same, crowding along the riverbank in their eagerness to watch. Lord Porten's archers finally turned and shuffled away in dejection as I hurled even more curses at their backs.

"Is there anyone here that can shoot a damn bow!" I screamed in mock outrage.

My Wolf's Teeth appeared in answer all along the riverbank, led by Tyris. "We will try, lord!" the blond archer's voice boomed out.

I pointed at the jeering Piths with Wolf's Head. "Wipe the smiles off those bastards' faces," I shouted at the top of my lungs. "Or I'll roast your balls over a fire and feed them to my hogs!"

I turned, gripping my sword and shield tighter as I waited.

"Nock!" I heard Tyris's command ring out. "Draw!" Forty-eight bows drew back and aimed at the laughing Piths. "Loose!"

I could feel Baine and Jebido tensing beside me as the flight of arrows left the longbows. "Wait," I called to my men. The arrows were halfway over the river, still arcing upward. I held my breath until the shafts began to angle downward. "Now!" I screamed, waving Wolf's Head. "Kill the bastards! Kill them!"

We barreled forward across the stone bridge as the arrows fell amongst the massed Piths along the bank. More shafts were already on the way as the first flight ripped into the astonished Piths. Warriors dropped all along the bank's ridge, tumbling down its length into the White Rock, where the foaming water swept them away. I glanced down as I ran, noticing the first warrior who had bared his ass now lay dead on the stones, his trousers still around his ankles. I grinned as we reached the gatehouse and plunged into the coolness of the building.

"Kill them! I screamed, lowering my shield as my men and I sprinted through the building toward the rear gate where the Piths awaited us. "No mercy! Kill every last one of the bastards!" We crashed into the line of Piths, forcing them to stay under cover as my men hacked and stabbed wildly at their shields. I knew Baine and his archers were following closely behind us, but he would need time to get all the contents of the carts up to the ramparts. "Form a wall!" I shouted, slamming my shield against the gatehouse's stone floor and locking it over Jebido's beside me. Berwin was on my left, grinning like a fool as he overlapped shields with me, with more men joining us, matching the line of Piths until we were four ranks deep. The last two ranks of my men held long poleaxes, which they used to try and hook the Pith shields while we searched for openings. "We hold here!" I cried, cursing as a sword blade snuck through a gap and clanged off my helmet. "Tighten up, damn you!" I roared as something heavy pounded against my shield.

I glanced over my shoulder, but there was nothing to see other than a wall of stinking, sweating men. I faced forward again, stabbing through a gap in the shields and laughing as I heard a yelp of pain. That's when the horn sounded from the ramparts.

"Get ready!" I shouted, bracing myself as I put my shoulder to my shield just as the first of the rocks started to fall from above. I could hear the surprised grunts of pain from the Piths as stones bounced and clanged off their armor. I grinned. The Pith archers waiting behind the shield wall could only target what they could see, and Baine and his men didn't have to show themselves at all to lob the rocks we had collected from the riverbank over the battlements. Berwin started to press forward impatiently and I glared at him. "Wait for the second horn!" I growled.

That horn came moments later, signaling Baine's job was done and it was safe to advance. "Now! I shouted. Our wall surged forward in a wedge formation, pushing the stunned and broken line of Piths back from the gatehouse entrance. "Make a hole!" I cried, aiming for the Pith center while slashing at the head of a screaming warrior in front of me. The man defected my blade with his shield, but the iron head of a poleaxe appeared over my shoulder, the spiked end cutting open my opponent's vulnerable throat. The Pith fell, trampled beneath heavy boots as we pressed onward. I could hear my men chanting, "Wolf! Wolf! Wolf!" as foot by foot, we pushed the disorganized Piths backward.

Bodies were dropping all around me, with hardly enough room to swing a blade effectively. A Pith warrior broke out into the open with Jebido, forcing him back with vicious slashes of his sword. I lunged toward the Pith and ran him through, then ducked under a wild swing of a war hammer from another warrior. I smashed the top of my shield against my opponent's wrist, and he dropped his hammer, then I kicked his legs out from under him and put my boot on his neck as I stamped down hard. I heard something snap, then the warrior shuddered and lay still. I moved on. "Kill them!" I cried as my men screamed my name. "Kill the bastards!"

"Hadrack!" Jebido called out from beside me. My friend dodged as a Pith swung his shield at his head, then he grabbed the off-balance warrior by the beard and dragged him onto his blade. "There's too many. We need the horses, now!"

We had made it through the Piths onto relatively open ground, but more of their warriors were joining the fray now, encircling us and shoring up the shield wall behind my men. We were effectively cut off from our forces in the gatehouse, with enraged Piths battling us on all sides. I knew Jebido was right, and in another moment we would be overwhelmed. I lifted my sword. "Sim, now!" I shouted, hoping the big man would hear me over the sounds of battle.

I heard Sim's faint answering call, then a shrill horn before the lancers appeared, clattering through the gatehouse at a gallop. Pith warriors screamed and died as the horsemen rolled over them in a relentless wave, shattering the hastily reforming shield wall before it could be fully locked. Cheering men-at-arms on foot came rushing behind the lancers with poleaxes, hacking and stabbing at any Pith that had somehow managed to survive that unstoppable charge. The untrained levy followed the men-at-arms, pouring through the breaches of the collapsing Pith shield wall as they screamed for blood.

The female archers were in full retreat behind the Piths, trying to gain higher ground where they could shoot effectively without striking any of their brothers. But they had forgotten all about Baine and his men on the battlements. Waves of Gander arrows hissed toward the lightly-armored Pith archers from the ramparts above our heads, dropping more than a dozen women on the first volley.

"Kill the bastards!" I screamed as my men took up the call.

There is no feeling quite like the mixture of fear and ecstasy a battle can bring, and I reveled in it, taking on all challengers with cold-blooded joy. I fought with a mindless fury, heedless of my wounds as first a sword nicked my cheek, and then a thrown spear tore a gash through my mail. I moved forward, bellowing like a man possessed as my men paced me, driving the Piths back. I slashed, blocked, stabbed, kicked, and gouged my adversaries, doing whatever was needed to beat the man opposing me before I moved on, hungry for more.

A huge Pith with tattooed arms appeared in front of me, growling as he swung a one-handed battle-axe for my head. I dropped to one knee beneath it and slashed upward with my sword, cutting across the man's right thigh and groin. The warrior screamed, dropping his weapon as he stumbled away, clutching at himself. I released Wolf's Head, picked up the fallen axe, and then flung it, catching the man between the shoulder blades. I didn't see the warrior fall, as his body was suddenly hidden by the press of swirling bodies that blocked my view. I took up my sword again and stood just in time to see Niko drop to the ground with a Pith towering over him. The youth looked panicked as the warrior smashed his shield apart with two mighty swings of his war hammer. Then he drew the hammer back to strike again. I bounded forward and grabbed the Pith's fur-lined cloak before he could swing, dragging him away from Niko as I cut open the warrior's throat with a quick slash of Wolf's Head.

After that, the battle became a blur of hacking, slashing, cursing, and killing as we continued to force the Piths backward along the road that led to the garrison. Men-at-arms fought side by side with farm boys, merchants, and traders who wielded hammers, cleavers, mauls, or whatever else they had brought with them for weapons. We outnumbered the enemy almost three to one, and though the levy were not trained fighting men, they swarmed over each Pith like rabid wolves, piling onto the armored warriors and holding them down while one of them plunged a knife into their eyes. It was a slaughter like I have rarely seen—a beautiful, glorious, bloody slaughter.

Finally, I paused, with no more Piths in front of me to kill. I looked around, confused. Gandermen were shouting and waving their weapons all around me, and it took me a moment to realize that they were cheering. Incredibly, the Piths were running away, streaming up the road to the south as they fled from our fury. I sagged in relief, leaning on my sword as I watched our lancers skewering the backs of the fleeing Piths. I saw the drawbridge to the garrison begin to lower, with eager horses massed at the gates. There were only fifty or so men stationed at Gasterny, and they would have mattered little at the beginning of the battle. But now that we had won, those men who had been trapped for days behind the walls clearly wanted to share in the victory and bloodshed. A horn sounded behind me as more mounted horsemen streamed around my exhausted men, led by King Tyden himself.

"It's a great day for killing Piths!" Tyden yelled at me, grinning broadly as he swept past, waving his sword. Lord Porten rode on the king's right, his eyes alight with excitement, while Braham rode on his left carrying Tyden's red and gold eagle banner.

I just waved, too tired to bother replying as the men of the levy cheered their king, following in his wake up the road.

"He fought well," Jebido said as he came to stand beside me, motioning toward the king.

My friend had lost his helmet and his silver hair was streaked with blood, but he seemed unaware of it. "I hadn't noticed," I said. I shrugged as I watched the king smash his sword on top of a fleeing Pith's metal helm. "Somebody should tell Tyden that he needs to strike a running man across the back, not the helmet," I grunted. "Swords break on helmets."

Jebido laughed, then his face drained of blood. "Mother's tit!" he whispered in disbelief.

I felt a jolt of cold dread wash over me. A mass of horses were barrelling out of Gasterny, but they weren't Gandermen like I had thought.

The riders streaming out of the garrison were Piths!

11: The White Rock

One of my biggest regrets in life—now that I am old and near the end of that life—is that I didn't protest enough to the king about what I believed the Piths were up to at Gasterny. Had I done so with greater conviction, it's possible that many good men who died that day might have gone on to live much longer lives. Now, in my dotage, I understand why I didn't. But at the time, if someone had told me that I was secretly intimidated by the king and his lords, I would have reacted with both outrage and fury. All of those men were born into their titles, wearing them just as comfortably as they would a warm cloak on a cold winter's day. Yet I had not been. In my mind, my cloak was torn and grubby, reminding me constantly that I had no right to stand among them as an equal. The king and those lords were all part of an elite class that had always seemed unattainable and, down deep, I knew I was just a commoner in their eyes who had only been raised by chance and a strong sword arm.

The Piths, I learned later, had sent two of their women dressed as Gander peasants into Gasterny a week before they arrived in force. The girls were young and pretty, and they became an instant sensation within the fortress, where even one attractive girl was a rarity, let alone two. The Pith women, being Piths, quickly began to flirt and rut with anyone who showed even the slightest interest, including the garrison commander and his officers. In my opinion, that alone should have been a warning sign to them. But garrison duty on the border is a lonely affair, and the Ganders had clearly been blinded by lust. On the second night of the siege, the girls slipped from their beds and killed the guards at the gates before lowering the drawbridge, allowing the waiting Pith warriors inside, where they proceeded to slaughter the inhabitants. After that, they simply waited for our army to arrive, keeping the fortress sealed and walking the walls to complete the illusion it remained in Gander hands.

Now, those Piths thundered out of Gasterny and over the drawbridge, screaming their war cries while Jebido and I watched helplessly, too far away to stop what was about to happen. All I could do was hope that the king would understand his danger before it was too late and flee. More Piths appeared along the road to the south, with some breaking out of the forest behind the garrison. There were hundreds of them, I realized with dismay as they converged on the king. We had stepped into a carefully planned trap, I now understood, designed to draw our entire army over the bridge before it was sprung. The Piths had initially been caught off-guard by our unexpected tactics at the gatehouse. But despite our early success, it seemed the gods had now abandoned us, snatching what had seemed like a sure victory away and turning it into what would soon prove to be a rout.

The lead Gander lancers—perhaps eighty strong at best—saw the mounted Piths descending on the king, and they swerved to block them, the heavy iron points of their spears leveled in a bristling wall of death. The Piths came on, heedless of the lances, snarling as the two forces met. Gander spearpoints hardened in forges across the kingdom impacted steel-rimmed willow Pith shields, shattering many of them. Yet the Piths didn't waver as they hacked and smashed their way through the riders blocking them. I saw Sim in the midst of the battle, his great axe flailing about him, emptying first one, then a second enemy saddle before a Pith brought his war hammer down on Sim's unprotected head from behind. The big man arched his back and his fine hat fell off, then he tumbled from his horse before disappearing from my view.

The mismatched battle didn't last long after that, as hundreds of Piths swarmed over the remaining lancers like locusts. Tyden had his men bunched together in a defensive knot fifty yards away from the wild melee, and both Jebido and I were shouting at him to turn and run. But the king didn't flee like any sane man would. Instead, he launched his men forward into the eye of the storm. I cursed, though my words were salted with grudging respect. Whatever else you could say about the man, Tyden was no coward. The two forces crashed together in a collision that sounded to me like the end of the world itself. I saw Braham and his horse go down immediately with the king's banner still clutched in his hand. Then Lord Falway and Lord Porten fell as they desperately tried to protect the king from the howling Piths hammering away at them from all sides.

The remaining Ganders of the king's guard put up a valiant defense around him, but they were overmatched and died quickly until Tyden was left to stand alone as the Piths boxed him in from all sides. The king slashed and hacked at the Piths in desperation, trying to break free, but the warriors just used their shields to deflect his sword thrusts as they laughed. Finally, one warrior using a dead lancer's spear cracked the butt end across Tyden's chest, knocking him from his saddle. Two Piths immediately leaped to the ground and grabbed the king by the arms before throwing him face down over his horse. Then they headed south over the ridge with their prize, waving their weapons in triumph.

Meanwhile, the levy of more than a thousand strong continued to stream up the hill a quarter-mile ahead of me, so overwhelmed by killing and bloodlust that they still hadn't realized what had happened. That changed the moment the vengeful Piths were in amongst them, cutting and hacking men down savagely. The Gander army that had seemed so unstoppable only moments before now turned in fear, running back the way they had come in a mindless panic. I could hear more than one voice taking up the call, "The king has fallen! Run for your lives! The king has fallen!"

I started to move forward with a growl just as Jebido grabbed my arm. "Where do you think you're going?"

"I'm not running, Jebido," I grunted. Men on foot and horseback were streaming around and past us, racing to the safety of the bridge as shrieking Piths slaughtered men in droves. Behind me, Berwin, Niko, and the rest of my men who had survived the attack on the shield wall fingered their weapons nervously, waiting to see what I would do.

Jebido put his hand on my shoulder. "The battle is lost, Hadrack," he said. "Accept that and move on. Throwing your life away won't change what happened here." He smiled, looking old and tired. "There is no shame in running. The shame will be if you are too stupid and proud not to see that."

I hesitated, wobbling back and forth in indecision. Finally, I nodded. "We fall back across the river to the northern gatehouse." I glared at Jebido. "And then we hold it! I'm not done with these bastards yet!"

Jebido laughed as he patted my shoulder. "That's the spirit, lad."

My men and I formed a shield wall twenty feet in front of the southern gatehouse entrance, allowing the remnants of our panic-stricken army to swarm around both sides. More men-at-arms bolstered us when they saw what we were doing until we numbered close to a hundred bone-weary, determined men. Baine and his archers remained on the battlements, shooting at any Pith that came close, though the savage warriors seemed more than content now to stay clear and hack apart any of our forces too far away to reach us in time. Finally, the flow of panicked Ganders was reduced to a trickle, and I had my men retreat until we were safely back inside the confines of the gatehouse. I looked up to where the giant portcullis once hung, wishing we could lower it now, but the Piths had destroyed it when they had torn apart the gates.

The Piths began to mass out of bowshot range. I guessed there were easily two thousand of the cheering warriors as I braced for the inevitable charge. But long minutes went by, and still that charge did not come. I glanced behind me at the confusion of men and horses pushing and shoving at each other in panic as they tried to flee across the bridge. Soon my shield wall could start to make a cautious retreat, but that time hadn't come yet. I prayed the Piths would stay their charge a few minutes longer.

"What are the bastards waiting for?" I heard someone mumble.

I was beginning to wonder the same thing until I heard the Piths start to chant a name, and then I understood. Lorgen Three-Fingers. I felt my mouth go dry as four men on horseback appeared through the Piths' ranks and trotted toward us. The lead rider trailed the reins of a black pony behind him, and on that pony rode a naked man, his hands and feet tied with rope. The naked man wore a crown of thorns and rode backward, facing the pony's ass. It was Tyden. I cursed under my breath as men around me muttered angrily.

"Hadrack?" Baine shouted down at me from one of the murder holes in the ceiling. I glanced up. "Should I drop the bastards?"

I shook my head. "No, let's hear what they have to say first."

The riders paused forty feet away. "Is there a cornered wolf cowering inside there?" The man who had spoken was big, wearing a fur-lined cloak over blood-splattered mail. His hair was black with streaks of grey throughout, and it hung down well past his shoulders. His beard was black as well, with thick patches of white on either side of his chin. The Pith held the reins of Tyden's pony in his left hand, which I saw was missing the last two fingers. I was looking at Lorgen Three-Fingers.

The warrior chieftain urged his horse forward another ten feet, dragging the smaller animal along and looking unconcerned about our archers on the battlements. Dusk was beginning to set in, and Lorgen squinted as he peered into the gloom of the gatehouse. "I say again, is there a wolf hiding in amongst all those terrified sheep?"

I lowered my shield and sheathed Wolf's Head, then pushed my men aside as I strode forward into the waning sunlight. "What do you want, Pith?" I said.

Lorgen Three-Fingers stared at me with hard eyes. "So, you would be the whelp that I've heard so much about."

I glanced at the men waiting behind the Pith. One was Saldor, and he nodded to me in greeting, his face etched in stone. The other was Nedo, looking pale and unwell, though his eyes burned pure hatred at me. "Have you come here to crawl on your knees and surrender?" I asked Lorgen in a steady voice.

The Pith chieftain stared at me in astonishment for a moment, and then he surprised me by slapping his leg and laughing. "For a man who likes to cut off balls, you certainly have a weighty pair of your own."

I shrugged. "I'm only going to make the offer once, Amenti, so stop wasting my time."

Lorgen Three-Fingers' smile fell away. He sighed, picking at his nose as he regarded me. "You have lost, whelp." He gestured behind him at Tyden. "We have your runt of a king and have crushed your pathetic army. Surrender now, and I might be merciful with some of your men."

Now it was my turn to laugh. "Mercy from a Pith is like love from a whore. Neither one exists."

Lorgen Three-Fingers' eyes narrowed. "I can destroy you right now if I choose."

I spread my arms, remembering years ago when Einhard stood where I was now with an overwhelming army of Ganders surrounding him. We had faced impossible odds on that day too, but had managed to survive. "You can try," I said. "But it won't be easy, and many of your brothers will die in the attempt."

Lorgen brushed something off his cloak, looking unconcerned. "What if I say no more blood needs to be spilled this day and that both sides can go away happy?"

"Go on," I said, not believing him for a moment.

Lorgen leaned forward. "I propose a deal. I will return your king to you, and your men can go in peace."

I grinned before he could say anything else. "I accept your terms."

Lorgen chuckled, raising a finger and waggling it back and forth. "You are much too quick, whelp, as I have no doubt every woman who has ever bedded you can attest." He lifted his head, looking up at the archers on the battlements. "Listen to me, Gandermen," he shouted. "No more of you need to die here today. I will give you back your king and let you go." Lorgen pointed at me. "In exchange for him!"

"Hadrack!" I heard Jebido shout from behind me. "Don't do it!"

Lorgen grinned. "So, what do you say? Your worthless life for that of your king and all these men. There has never been a fairer bargain than that."

I paused as I glanced at Nedo. The boy was leaning forward eagerly, licking his lips as he waited for my answer. I could see an almost feral madness swirling in his eyes, and I had to stop myself from shuddering as I focused back on Lorgen. "If I agree," I said as more shouts of objection arose from my men. I turned and glared behind me, silencing most of the voices, though I could hear both Baine and Jebido still protesting. "If I agree to your deal," I repeated. "How do I know you will honor it?"

Lorgen shrugged. "All life is a game, whelp." He grinned again. "Care to play?"

"Don't listen to him!" Tyden suddenly called out, turning awkwardly to look at me. "You hear me, Lord Hadrack. Shove your sword up this bastard's ass and make him eat his own shit off of it."

"Shut your mouth, you!" Nedo shouted, drawing his blade and slapping the flat end of it across Tyden's back. The king cried out as red welts instantly appeared on his flesh, while behind me, I could feel my men tensing, getting ready to charge.

I turned and raised a hand. "Stay where you are," I ordered. I glared at my men until they reluctantly relaxed, then faced Lorgen Three-Fingers again. "I will need time to consider it," I said.

"Very well," Lorgen said, amusement on his face. "I'm hungry anyway, and it's getting dark." He pulled his horse around, then paused to look back at me. "You have until tomorrow morning to accept my generous offer, whelp. Come to me on your hands and knees when the sun clears the trees. If you do that, then I will free your king." He pointed at me in warning. "But if you choose to flee during the night like a coward instead, then I will flay the skin from your runt king and wear it for a hat as I hunt every one of you down like the dogs that you are."

Lorgen Three-Fingers rode off then, hauling the tiny pony and naked king behind him as he headed for his camp in the eastern fields. The Pith warriors roared as they parted for their leader, many of them spitting on the humiliated king and slapping his bare skin with their open palms. I watched the Piths go, then turned and headed back to my men. Jebido and Baine flanked me as soon as I entered the gatehouse.

"You can't go through with this," Jebido said before I could even open my mouth. I could see the worry lying heavy on his face. "I won't let you."

I gave him a tired smile. "And how exactly are you going to stop me?" I asked.

"Do you have any idea what those bastards will do to you?" Jebido demanded.

I grimaced. "Of course I do. But we need to get Tyden back. If this is the only way to do that, then I have to consider it."

"He's just one man, Hadrack," Baine said. "There will be other kings."

I shook my head, realizing that they didn't understand yet. "Don't you two see what will happen if Tyden dies?" My friends just looked at me with blank expressions. I sighed. "Without him, someone else will have a clear path to the throne again."

Jebido groaned. "Pernissy," he said, spitting the name out like rotten meat. "The sniveling bastard."

"Exactly," I said. "The man may have lost his lands and title, but he still has royal blood in his veins. With Son Oriell backing him, it's guaranteed Pernissy would succeed Tyden if he dies. There's no way I'm going to allow that to happen, even if the price is my life." I put my arms around both my friends' shoulders as I guided them across the bridge. "Don't look so glum. I'm not dead yet, and we still have all night to come up with a better plan."

We returned to our camp on the northern side of the river, using whatever we could find to blockade the gatehouse doors in case Lorgen Three-Fingers tried to attack us during the night. Many of the senior lords had fallen in the battle, and strangely enough, the remaining four still alive were looking to me for leadership as we met in the king's tent. The consensus among those lords was that we should flee, leaving the Piths with nothing but frustration to eat in the morning when they saw us gone. I let the lords speak their piece without saying anything, each man advocating for flight before I finally stood.

I began to pace as I thought, knowing that without the support of the men around me, whatever chance there might be to get Tyden back alive, slim as it was, would be gone.

"You don't agree with us, Lord Hadrack?"

I turned. The man who had spoken was Lord Porten's son, Fitzery, now Lord Fitzery after his father's death. "It makes sense to leave under cover of darkness," I said. "We are vastly outnumbered, and if Lorgen lied about letting us go, then everyone will be slaughtered in the morning." I shrugged. "But if we leave, then what?"

"Then we go home," Lord Cambil answered. He was short and bald, with a nervous habit of licking his lips after every sentence he spoke.

"To do what?" I asked, one eyebrow raised. "Hide in our castles while the Piths ravage our lands? Is that what you suggest?" Lord Cambil looked at his hands, not meeting my eyes. I glanced at Jebido, who I'd asked to assess the strength of our battered army. "How many men do we have left?"

"Three hundred horse," Jebido responded. "A hundred and fifty archers, and perhaps six hundred foot soldiers."

"And the wounded?" I asked.

"Too many to count," Jebido stated flatly.

I looked around at the lords. "So, what happens to those men if we leave? We won't be able to move fast with that many wounded, which means Lorgen will catch up to us eventually."

"Then we leave the wounded behind." This from Lord Vestry, a timid man of sixty or so who was always quick to side with the majority opinion.

I frowned. "That's not an option," I said, not hiding my disgust.

Lord Fitzery turned to Jebido. "How many of those foot soldiers that you mentioned are from the levy?" he asked.

Jebido grimaced. "Almost three-quarters, lord," he said. "And that number will probably be halved by morning unless we watch them closely."

Many of the lords groaned at Jebido's words as I held up my hands. "I understand how difficult a decision this is for all of you.

But we can't just skulk away from here like beaten dogs while Tyden still lives. We have all night to come up with a plan to get him back. All I'm asking is that you keep your men here until the morning and help me think of something."

"And then what?" Lord Cambil asked as he licked his lips. "If we fail to come up with this plan, are you really going to sacrifice yourself to that bastard to save the king?"

"If I have to," I said firmly. "But I'm hoping it won't come to that."

Lord Fitzery came to me, offering his hand. "You are a brave and dedicated man, Lord Hadrack," he said as we locked forearms. "I will stay the night and will spend it praying to The Mother for inspiration."

"Thank you," I said gratefully as, one by one, the other lords pledged their support. Now all I needed to do was find a way to rescue the king from close to two thousand savage Pith warriors before the sun rose—warriors who would undoubtedly be on guard for just such a ploy.

Two hours later, I sat along the riverbank half a mile east of the bridge, staring across the White Rock at the sprawling Pith camp. I could hear the faint sounds of laughter and music drifting over the water, carried along by a steady breeze. A quarter moon hung high in the sky, brushing the roiling water beneath me with sparkling threads of white and silver as the river foamed over hidden rocks. I threw a pebble into the depths as I glanced to the southwest toward a thick stand of trees that blocked my view of the gatehouse on the southern bank. I didn't need to see it to know what was waiting for us there. Lorgen Three-Fingers was no fool, and he had posted a strong force of Piths to guard the bridge in case we tried to cross it during the night.

I heard footsteps behind me but didn't bother to turn around as I threw another rock into the river. I knew who it was going to be.

"So," Jebido said as he crouched down beside me. Both his knees cracked loudly, and he groaned as he lowered himself to the ground. "By that look on your face, I would guess you haven't come up with a plan yet."

I shook my head and threw another rock. "It's impossible," I grunted. I gestured toward the gatehouse beyond the trees. "Those bastards over there will know the moment we try to move on them."

I had sent scouts east to Victory Pass in hopes that it had been left unguarded, but the Piths were taking no chances and had men blocking it, so going around was not an option.

Jebido tossed a smooth stone in the air, caught it, and then flicked it down into the churning river. "What about rafts? We could float men across."

"Across that?" I said, pointing at the rapids. "We'll never make it. We'd just get swept downriver."

"It's better than swimming," Jebido grunted. "The Mother knows there's no other way across this damn thing other than the bridge."

I thought about the messenger from Gasterny, Bona, who had somehow managed to swim the White Rock. It seemed incredible to imagine, yet the man had done it somehow—though the river wasn't nearly as wild to the east where he had crossed. But he had been just one man, and I knew I would need hundreds, all of them wearing heavy armor and carrying weapons. It would be impossible. I shook the notion aside as movement across the river caught my eye. Shadowy figures were flitting in and out of the moonlight along the forest that bordered the Pith campsite. I could hear the faint ringing of axe heads striking tree trunks, then shouts as men called loudly back and forth to each other.

"What are those bastards up to now?" Jebido wondered out loud.

We stood together, trying to make out what the Piths were doing until a weak flame appeared, quickly gaining in strength as men fed wood to a massive bonfire. The growing light revealed warriors wielding axes in the trees, along with even more of the Piths digging in the field. Suddenly I understood their purpose and I started to laugh.

Jebido looked at me as though my mind had suddenly fled. "What's so funny?"

I grinned at him. "The Master might have just shown me the way, my friend."

12: The Rescue

The messenger, Bona, had managed to survive the battle, and he stood naked and shivering on the rocks near the raging river. We had moved much further east from where Jebido and I had sat an hour ago, using the thick cover of the trees across the water to shield us from the Pith camp. The place that I had selected twisted north in a sharp bend for fifty feet, then curled to the east again. It was a good spot that would help hide us from the Piths' eyes at the bridge. Lorgen Three-Fingers had made a mistake by failing to post men to watch the White Rock here, clearly confident that we were beaten and that there was no way to cross other than the bridge. I intended to make him pay for that mistake.

A thick rope lay twisted around Bona's waist, with three burly men braced along the rock-covered slope behind us, holding the other end. We'd had to tie four ropes together to ensure that it would be long enough, and the extra lengths lay coiled in piles along the riverbank's ridge. I had more men there making sure the cable didn't get tangled as it unwound.

"Remember," I told the shivering man. "Find the stoutest tree that you can and tie that rope securely to it."

"Yes, lord," Bona said, his teeth chattering. The skinny messenger looked at the seething water nervously. "It's much worse here than it was on the other side of the bridge, lord."

I grinned and patted his bony shoulder. "That's true. But we would be seen if we tried this there. Besides, you didn't have that rope to save you then, now did you?"

"No, lord," Bona agreed in a meek voice.

I turned at the sound of small rocks tumbling down the slope as Baine carefully descended in the weak moonlight. "The wounded are all away with the rest of the levy, Hadrack," he said when he reached us.

I nodded. I had chosen only my most capable men for the attempted rescue of the king. The rest would guard the wounded as they headed back to Corwick, where I knew Haverty would do what he could for them. "And Jebido and the lords?"

"In the woods to the north, waiting for the signal to move."

"Good," I said. I looked to the south, where I could hear exultant cries echoing over the treetops despite the sound of the White Rock's churning waters. An orange glow lit the sky unnaturally and I grunted in satisfaction, picturing the wild scene that I knew would be unfolding on the other side of the trees. "And the Piths at the gatehouse?"

"No change as far as I can tell," Baine said. "But I'm sure someone must have ridden to tell Lorgen what's happening."

"I expect you're right," I agreed. We had made no secret of our intentions as we struck camp, wanting to be noticed by the men guarding the bridge. I had hoped the Piths there would relax when they saw us withdrawing and that maybe some would even abandon their posts to go join in on the ceremony. Apparently, that wasn't happening, which, while unfortunate, would not affect my plans.

"You're sure Lorgen won't come after us right away?" Baine asked, looking worried.

I snorted. "In the middle of an Ascension Ceremony?" I shook my head. "Not a chance. He'll wait until the morning."

"If you're wrong, we're lost," Baine warned.

"I'm not wrong," I promised. "What about Lord Vestry? Is he ready?"

Baine grimaced. "He was still crying for more men, but Jebido set him straight."

I chuckled, imagining the look on my friend's face as he scolded the timid lord. Lord Vestry's job was to secure Gasterny with thirty men, and despite my insisting that the fortress would have few if any Piths inside it, the older lord had pleaded for more men—men I could not afford to give him. "Then we're ready?" I asked Baine. My friend nodded and I turned to Bona. "All right, off you go."

Bona cautiously waded into the river, stumbling over the rocks until he was knee-deep in the surging water. The White Rock foamed and sprayed all around the messenger's skinny legs, threatening to tear the man's feet out from under him. But Bona pressed onward in determination anyway as the men on the bank played out the rope above him. Finally, the water reached his waist and the skinny man dove into the surge, disappearing for a moment beneath the foaming waves before his head broke the surface. Bona started to swim then, fighting the current as it worked to drag him eastward. I could see the rope around his waist snapping taut as the men holding it fought to keep him in place, and I prayed Bona was as good a swimmer as he claimed.

Agonizing minutes went by as the messenger gallantly fought the current, and more than once, the waters dragged him under, only to have him reappear moments later, flailing his arms like a giant, hooked fish. Finally, Bona reached the far bank fifty feet downriver from us and he stumbled from the waters. I expected the skinny man to drop to the ground to catch his breath—I know I would have—but he surprised me by striking out along the shore until he stood opposite us. Bona untied the thick cord around his waist, then he turned and dragged it up the bank, disappearing beneath a shadowy aspen. The messenger finally reappeared, returning to the shore and waving weakly to us in the moonlight before flopping to the ground. The rope now hung suspended four feet over the river, arcing upward to the men on our side holding the free end. At a signal from me, the men clambered down to the water's edge, where they each looped the rope twice around their waists, then leaned backward, pulling the entire length spanning the river taught.

"That was the easy part," I grunted to Baine as we headed up the riverbank.

Niko was waiting for us as instructed, wearing another length of rope around his waist that trailed behind him the same as Bona's had. I nodded and the youth hurried down the slope and started across the river, dragging himself hand over hand along the stretched cable. The hostile water from before that had so resisted Bona was now an asset as it helped buoy Niko's weight, though that didn't stop the White Rock from trying to sweep the youth away. I knew any man who lost his grip during the crossing would be as good as dead.

I watched Niko's progress until he made it safely to the other side, then turned to the next man waiting with more rope. "Your turn."

Half an hour later, we had a total of five cables stretched across the White Rock, with burly men from the levy anchoring each one. I would have preferred trees to tie the ropes to, of course, but the banks on our side of the river were barren of anything useful, so muscle power would have to do.

"All right," I said, keeping my voice low. I had fifty men-at-arms and a hundred archers—including my Wolf's Teeth—organized into five lines that disappeared into the darkness. The lead man in each line turned and passed my words on to the next. "Make sure your arrows and strings stay dry. We go one at a time across the rope. Once you get to the other side, you wait in the forest on the ridge for instructions. No one is to talk. If the Piths suspect anything, then we are all dead." I moved to order the men down the slope, then I paused. "One more thing," I said, pointing to the glowing sky. "You are probably going to see things over there that you've never even dreamed of." I waited until those words had been passed along, then I continued, "Pith men and women will be humping like beasts and doing all manner of things to each other. Do not let that sway you. We have one objective, and that is to rescue the king. If you stand there ogling the tits on one of those Pith archers, then I guarantee you those tits will be the last ones you ever see." I stepped out of the way and swept my hand forward. "Now, let's move."

I had allotted each man five minutes to get across the White Rock, so by my calculations, with five men crossing every five minutes, it would take several hours to get them all to the other bank. Would the ceremony still be going on by then? A lot of Piths had died in the battle earlier, and I could only hope and pray that it would take all night to Ascend them. Otherwise, we were going to be in big trouble.

Baine and I stood along the bank's ridge, watching as our men began to cross the moonlit water. Half an hour went by with no major incidents, and finally, I turned to my friend. "I think it's time."

Baine nodded and I held out my hand. He snorted, then drew me into an embrace. "Be careful," he whispered into my ear.

I grinned and patted his helmet. "I always am."

I turned and made my way down the slope again, motioning one of the archers about to step into the water aside. I took his place, steadying myself on the rope before taking a cautious step forward. The White Rock welcomed my approach with eagerness, foaming around my boots and sending up sheets of spray that quickly drenched my face and armor. I shook the wetness from my eyes and moved deeper into the river, surprised at how cold the water was. I could feel the power of the surge tugging at me as it rose over my hips, and I tightened my grip on the line just as a rock rolled out from beneath my feet. My legs instantly shot out from under me as the river howled in triumph and tried to rip the rope from my hands.

"No, you don't, you bastard," I said through clenched teeth. The cable was flexing back and forth like an angry snake in my hands as I moved forward one arm length at a time, drawing myself along with sheer willpower as the frothing water raged against me. Finally, I made it to the southern bank as eager hands reached out to drag me to the shore.

"You had me worried there for a moment, lord."

I looked up at Berwin's grinning face. "You and me both," I said, panting.

I took a few minutes to regain my breath, then climbed through the trees up to the ridge where Tyris and my men who had already crossed were waiting. Most of those men looked nervous as they waited in the shadows beneath tall oaks and spindly white birch. I couldn't blame them for that, I suppose, considering two thousand blood-thirsty warriors bent on their destruction were massed only a few hundred yards away. I could hear the cries of the rutting Piths better now, echoing through the forest, and could even make out the ancient words coming from a Pathfinder chanting to the Master.

"I'll meet you in the trees near the center of the camp once everyone is across," I told Tyris in a low voice. I glanced at the men, who were clearly entranced by the sounds coming from the west. "Keep them quiet and focused, Tyris, and whatever you do, don't let them get anywhere near the treeline until you have to."

"Yes, lord," Tyris said with a grim nod. "No need to worry about that, lord."

Despite my words of warning to my men, I still didn't trust them to look upon the humping Piths without reacting with desire. But, I had seen it before and knew what to expect, so I made my way west through the underbrush to see how far along the ceremony was. I reached the edge of the forest and crouched on my hands and knees, pushing my way forward through the leaves and bracken until I could see. Then I gaped in surprise at the sight that awaited me.

I had been involved in two Ascension Ceremonies—one after the escape from Father's Arse, and the other in Gasterny for a warrior who had been kicked in the head by a horse. But this, this was something beyond even my imagination. Piths of all shapes and sizes lay within the Rutting Rings, their naked skin gleaming red from the flames as the bodies of the dead burned and smoked above them. A purple-robed Pathfinder stood in the center of the circles, chanting with his hands held to the sky while hundreds of naked Piths stood in groups, laughing and talking as they awaited their turn. Many of the circles were filled by a man and woman, but I could also see three or four women together, or sometimes one man with two women or more, as well as groups of men with men. Some of the Piths were lashing each other with horsehair whips while they humped, or using knives to slice open skin, or even dripping hot candle wax on each others' flesh. I felt my stomach twist with disgust, thankful that my farm boys and men-at-arms wouldn't have to bear witness to this kind of depravity. I'd thought after having lived with the Piths' perversions for over a year that I had seen everything there was to see, but now I knew better.

"Amenti," I spat with distaste as I pulled back from the forest's edge and turned south, trying to shake away the images of what I had just seen from my head.

I pushed my way through the trees until I thought that I had gone far enough, then made my way to the treeline again, staring through the branches as glowing flames from metal braziers lit up the campgrounds. Several rows of round canvas tents with sharply slanted walls stood in front of me, many of them decked out in brightly colored reds, yellows, blues, or greens. Beyond those tents were open campfires, some with Piths around them drinking and roasting meat over the flames. I kept moving along the treeline as more tents arose, until finally I saw what I wanted. I crouched behind the trunk of a twisted cedar surrounded by low bushes to wait for my men as I studied our target.

I was looking at a large red and yellow pavilion tent, surrounded by four smaller ones that I knew housed the men sworn to protect the chieftain. Lorgen Three-Fingers' bear banner fluttered from a mast at the top of the bigger tent, with two Amenti guarding the entrance covered by a bright blue canvas overhang supported by poles and strengthened with guy-lines. I dearly hoped the guards meant that Tyden was being held inside. More of the round tents rose to the south, then a vast open field where the Piths had picketed their horses with ropes for the night.

I could see Pith warriors sitting around a fire in the open fifty yards away from Lorgen's tent. The men were laughing and appeared quite drunk as two of them began to wrestle good-naturedly over a bottle. Somewhere along the camp's western perimeter would be sentries, I knew, but they were invisible to my eyes in the darkness beyond the fires. We would deal with them when the time came. A shadowy trench sat ten feet back from the forest line a hundred yards to my right. I wrinkled my nose at the smell as a Pith with his trousers around his ankles squatted over the hole.

I waited, glancing up occasionally at the faint quarter moon as it slowly traversed the sky, until finally dark forms began to appear through the trees like wraiths behind me. I bird-whistled low and quick, knowing that it would be impossible for my men to see me where I was. I heard an answering whistle, then Tyris pushed his way through the bushes to crouch down beside me.

"Everyone is across, my lord," the blond archer said.

"Any losses?"

"Just one, lord. One of Lord Fitzery's archers. He lost his grip and was swept away."

I nodded, having expected worse. "I'll handle the two guards at the tent," I said. I gestured to the drunken Piths around the fire. "As soon as you see me move, you drop them. Keep your eyes open for the sentries."

"It will be done, lord," Tyris promised as Berwin crouched down beside us.

"The men are in position, lord," Berwin said.

I knew there would be Pith youths who were on their first raid tending to the horses, and twenty of my men-at-arms were tasked with eliminating them once the attack started. The other thirty would set up a protective cordon around Tyden once I located and freed him.

"Then let's do this," I grunted.

I stood, removing the yellow and red Pith shield from my back. One of my men had lost his shield during the fighting earlier that day, and he'd picked up the garishly painted Pith one to replace it. Now, I hoped the warriors would see me with it and believe that they were looking at a brother. I'd also braided my beard and hair in the Pith way and rubbed dirt on my face to add to the disguise. I was fairly confident that no one would recognize me from earlier in the day when I had spoken with Lorgen Three-Fingers. I waited until I was sure none of the Piths were looking my way or using the latrine, then I stepped out from the protection of the trees. I started to angle my way toward Lorgen's tent as I stumbled along, humming to myself.

"Brother!" one of the Piths around the fire cried when he saw me. He stood and made his way unsteadily toward me, pressing a bottle into my hand. "You look thirsty!"

"I'm always thirsty, brother," I said with a laugh. I raised the bottle to my lips and drank, surprised it contained a thick, honey-sweetened mead. Piths usually preferred ale or wine. I handed the bottle back, swaying as I nodded in gratitude. "My thanks to you, brother."

The Pith stared at me, his face clouding. "I don't know you."

I chuckled. "Maybe not, but your sister and mother know me well. I'm Garles. Surely they have spoken about my prowess in bed?"

The Pith's eyes narrowed as he debated whether I was serious or not, then his face broke out into a wide grin. "I've heard them speak of a Garles. But all they said was he had a shriveled maggot hanging between his legs. Would that be you?"

I laughed and shook my head. "That must be a different Garles, brother. Your mother and sister spread their legs for so many men that they probably got us mixed up."

The Pith chuckled. "You bastard," he said. "I would knock you on your ass for that, except everything you just said is the truth!"

I grinned, glancing casually over my shoulder toward Lorgen's tent. Then I stiffened, my hand dropping to my sword.

"What is it, brother?"

"That man there," I growled. "He owes me two fingers of silver."

The drunken Pith peered at the tent in confusion. "Which one? Dack, or Gafin?"

"Dack," I grunted as I started to walk away. "And I'm going to collect it."

I could hear the Pith protesting behind me, but I ignored him as I strode toward the tent.

I was less than twenty feet away when one of the guards spoke. "Turn around, brother," he said, his voice sounding calm, almost bored. "You don't want Three-Fingers seeing you so close to his pet king."

I paused, wobbling as I peered at the man who had spoken. "Is that you, Dack?" I slurred. The man didn't deny it, and I waved the shield on my arm, stumbling and almost falling. "You bastard! You still owe me for last night's game." I moved several steps closer. "You said I couldn't hit three out of four, you whore's whelp!" I laughed as I took another step. "And you were right! I didn't. I hit four out of four, you worthless turd! Remember? Now pay me what you owe me!"

"Brother," the second guard said, raising a hand to stop me. "You know you can't be here. Turn around and walk away before you get hurt."

"You piece of weasel shit!" I spat at Dack. I drew my sword and waved it wildly about me. "You're trying to rob me!" I could hear the drunk warriors around the fire laughing and encouraging me as I pointed Wolf's Head at the other man. "And you, Gafin, are no brother to me. You're in league with a liar and a cheat. I'll rip both of your foul hearts out from your stinking arseholes, you greedy bastards!"

"Enough of this foolishness," Dack said. He strode forward until he was facing me. "I played no game with you last night. I don't even know you, so get away from here before I shove my boot up your ass."

Dack reached out and gave my shoulder a push, which was what I had hoped he would do. "Don't touch me, you turd-sucking bastard!" I shouted as I slashed Wolf's Head upward. The Pith stared at me in surprise as dark blood started to spray from his neck, drenching me, then he sagged and fell at my feet.

"What have you done, you fool?" Gafin cried. He rushed forward right onto the point of my sword, while behind me, arrows hissed out from the forest line, striking down the men around the fire.

My men-at-arms came crashing through the trees next, and they silenced any of the Piths that the arrows hadn't, while behind them came my archers.

"Form a shield wall here," I ordered Berwin as I wiped blood from my eyes, then I plunged into the tent. The first thing I saw inside was a sleeping man wearing a filth-stained tunic lying awkwardly on the fur-lined floor. It was the king, and his hands were manacled and chained around the center post that supported the tent. I knelt and shook him roughly awake.

"Huh? What?" Tyden muttered. He blinked up at me, his mouth hanging open in surprise. "Hadrack, is that really you?" The king glanced in confusion toward the entrance. "But how?"

"That's a long story, Highness," I muttered as I examined the manacles and chains. Both were made from heavy iron and would be difficult to break apart. "Where are the keys?"

"Uh, that bastard Lorgen has them," Tyden answered. I could see he was shaking off the drowsiness of sleep. "What's going on?"

"Turn your head away, Highness," I said, not answering as I stood and drew my axe. The king saw my intent and he nodded before twisting his face away. The tent pole was a thick, young poplar, freshly cut and buried deep into the ground. It took four tries for me to chop through the wet, green wood, with the tent shuddering and shaking around me with every blow. The moment the pole snapped in two, the roof canvas sagged inward, enveloping the king and me. I had expected it, of course, but I cursed anyway, lifting Tyden to his feet as we fought our way outside.

Things had changed dramatically by the time we extricated ourselves, with my men-at-arms under siege by a group of snarling Piths hurling themselves against their shield wall. Baine and Tyris had formed their archers to the rear of the shield wall on either side of the now partially collapsed tent. My men were shooting into the Piths, dropping many of them, but more were streaming half-naked from the north as the celebrating warriors slowly became aware that the enemy was in amongst them.

Baine stood off to one side of his archers, shooting with calm precision. "Baine!" I shouted. My friend paused to glance my way. "I have the king! Fire the tents!"

Baine nodded as he turned to five archers standing behind him who had been waiting for this very purpose. The archers dipped their arrowheads into a well-stoked brazier burning beside them, igniting the resin-soaked tows tied below the iron barbs. Then they began to target the lines of tents, and within minutes the camp was alight with flame. That was the signal Jebido would be watching for from across the river, and I knew the moment he saw it that he and his three hundred men would be galloping toward the bridge. Each of those men would be carrying a sharpened lance, as well as a deep grudge against the Piths who had humiliated their king. Would the force guarding that bridge have done what I expected and rushed back to help when they saw their camp under attack? I couldn't imagine that they wouldn't, as they had to believe this was a new threat and that we were long gone. That should present Jebido and his men with tempting targets as they caught the warriors from behind.

"Hadrack!" Baine called. "There are an awful lot of angry Piths coming this way!"

I nodded. I could see hordes of Piths running from the Ascension field toward the burning tents, many of them stark naked and clutching only a sword or bow. We had mere minutes before they were on us. It was time to go. "Fall back!" I cried as I drew Tyden further south, away from the flames and the light.

My men gave ground, retreating around Lorgen's fallen tent in a disciplined unit, though the center of the wall was wavering as a huge, naked Pith swung an axe like a man possessed, bellowing and crashing it against the heavy Gander shields. Other Piths were emboldened by the crazed warrior, joining him as they threw themselves at our wall.

"Berwin!" I cried over my shoulder. The tall soldier appeared from the gloom as I pushed Tyden into his arms. "Get the king to safety. The moment he's clear, blow the horn and send the horses."

"Yes, lord."

My archers began to shift to the west as planned, still shooting with both Tyris and Baine screaming orders at them to hurry. The Piths came on like rabid dogs, heedless of the arrows decimating their ranks as they focused with single-minded hatred on our shields. I could hear more screams and the clang of weapons from the fields to the north, where I knew Jebido would by now be creating havoc. "Hold the wall, you bastards!" I shouted at my men as I ran to join them. "We're almost there!"

The naked Pith warrior roared at the sound of my voice, and his enraged gaze fixated on me. Then he swung his great axe. The Pith shield on my arm shuddered as he struck, and a great hole appeared in the wood, with the gleaming axe blade narrowly missing my arm. The warrior tore his weapon free and I peered through the jagged rent as he reared back to strike again. That's when I lunged forward with Wolf's Head, catching the man under his left armpit. My blade went in deep, and the warrior bellowed, dropping his axe as he fell just as a horn sounded from the west.

"Run!" I shouted. "Run for your lives!"

My men needed no urging, having been warned by Tyris earlier that this would happen. We turned and fled west, while behind us, the ground began to shake like an earthquake. The lead Piths started to chase after us, then the first of the running horses appeared, bursting from the darkness with terrified eyes glowing like red-hot embers. The savage warriors hesitated in surprise, which was their undoing as more and more of the panicked horses appeared, trampling everything in their path as they stampeded through the burning camp. The naked Pith warriors coming from the north had no chance to dodge aside, and they fell in droves beneath the hooves of the charging animals. I could see the torches of my men waving to the south and hear their shouts as they drove even more of the vast herd north. I called out to them that it was enough, but with the horrific sounds of screaming coming from both the terrified horses and dying Piths, I wasn't sure that they could hear me.

I caught up to Berwin and the king, and together, we half carried Tyden in our arms as we raced west across the long grasses.

"Where are we going?" the king gasped.

I pointed ahead toward the dark mass of Gasterny that rose in the distance. "There, Highness."

Then we ran, saving our breath as a dispassionate moon stared down at us while the night burned and men died. Jebido and his lancers appeared from the gloom halfway to the garrison, their horses blowing hard, then more riders with extra horses and packhorses. I helped Tyden into the saddle of a white mare, then gratefully swung up onto Angry's back. We didn't have enough horses for all the archers, so Jebido's lancers guarded their backs as they ran, though by now, the Piths were offering up only the occasional futile assault in small bands. The main body of warriors was desperately trying to contain the thousands of terror-stricken horses and had, at least for the moment, forgotten about us.

We finally reached Gasterny, where Lord Vestry waited on his horse on the open drawbridge, his usually timid face broken by an enormous grin. "Thank The Mother, you're alive, Highness," he said with relief as the king rode up to him.

"No, Lord Vestry," Tyden said as he glanced back at me. "We have Lord Hadrack to thank for that."

I waited with Jebido for Baine and Tyris to arrive with the rest of our archers and lancers, then sent them all inside Gasterny to safety.

"I can't believe that worked," Jebido finally grunted as we sat alone together studying the Piths burning camp. I said nothing, lost in my thoughts, and finally, Jebido turned his horse and clattered across the drawbridge. He paused at the barbican to look back at me. "Are you coming, Hadrack, or do you love Piths so much that you want to stay out here and see what they do?"

"I'm coming," I said with a tired chuckle. I glanced once more toward the destroyed encampment, wondering where Lorgen Three-Fingers was in all that confusion, knowing instinctively that the Amenti chieftain had survived. "Your move, you bastard," I whispered as I guided Angry into the darkened fortress. "Your move."

13: Return to Gasterny

Gasterny. Once again, I found myself, however reluctantly, under siege within her walls. The memories that the cold stone and cheerless buildings evoked in me as Angry trotted into the outer bailey threatened to overwhelm my senses. The drawbridge clanked and rattled as it rose behind me, then finally closed with an ominous crash that made me jump. I paused the big horse to look back, wondering if the gods had returned me to this place on purpose just so that I could add my ghost to those of my long-dead brothers and sisters. Torches were being lit one by one along the walls, filling the bailey with growing light. Soldiers shouted to each other in a bustle of activity, working to unload the milling packhorses laden with provisions for the men, grain for the horses, extra lances, and hundreds of sheaves of arrows. I hadn't known what resources, if any, we would find inside Gasterny, nor how long we would be forced to stay here, so I had prepared for the worst.

Despite Lord Vestry's fears, he had found the garrison empty and devoid of life, with no one to witness his entrance other than a few half-starved goats and some festering corpses left behind by the Piths. Long, flickering shadows cast by the torches caressed the stone of the walls, buildings, and watchtowers as the fortress slowly returned to life. Men were leading horses to the stables, while others were busy removing the stinking bodies and cleaning out the barracks as archers climbed to the ramparts and took up positions in the watchtowers. I doubted the Piths would attack us in the darkness, but I knew Lorgen Three-Fingers would be enraged and humiliated by his defeat, so it was best not to make any assumptions.

More of our men were heading toward the inner bailey to begin preparing the keep for the king's arrival. All of this was being organized by an energetic Lord Fitzery, who though young, had an air of confidence and command about him that I could only envy. Only Lord Vestry, Lord Fitzery, and myself of all the lords who had come south with the king had survived the long day and night to make it to relative safety in Gasterny.

I guided Angry across the cobblestones, certain that I could feel the eyes of Gasterny's dead watching me as I paused the big black by the steps to the Holy House. I dismounted and stared at those cold-looking stone steps, remembering sitting on them many times. Almost four years had passed since I had seen them last. Those four years had transformed me from an impatient, headstrong boy into a veteran warrior, husband, and privileged lord. Still, a part of me longed for the carefree days that I'd spent gambling and playing dice with the Piths or talking on these same steps with Ania, Einhard, Betania, and Eriz. I had hated being here at the time, desperate to be free so that I could fulfill my vow to my family. But an oath of service to Einhard that honor would not let me break had hampered that vow. But now, as I looked back, I felt nothing except fondness for my time here and the people that I had known and loved.

"I imagine you're thinking about Ania." I turned as Baine walked over to me. He was smiling, though it was a sad smile tinged with melancholy. I could tell he felt the presence of the ghosts the same as I did.

"Yes," I said. "About her and Betania and Eriz, and everyone else who died in this cursed place."

Baine climbed the steps and sat on the landing, looking up at the walls. "It's hard to believe we're back here again. It's like a bad dream." A soldier came to take Angry away, and I moved to sit beside my friend. "I try not to think about what happened here," Baine continued. "Whenever I do, I see Padrea bent over that barrel being raped and I want to kill someone."

I nodded, understanding. "I like to believe they all found the Path to the Master on their own," I said. "It helps me sleep better."

Baine looked at me oddly. "You don't actually believe all of that, do you, Hadrack?" he asked. "About the Master and the Path?"

I shrugged. "Piths believe it, and we believe something else. One of us has to be wrong."

Baine snorted. "You're starting to sound just like Jebido."

I laughed and stood wearily, putting a hand on my friend's shoulder. "There's nothing wrong with that, Baine. Nothing wrong with that at all."

"Lord," one of the archers called down from the watchtower. "We've got riders approaching."

I sighed and looked up. I had hoped to have more time for my men to rest and recoup from the long day. "How many?"

"Five or six, lord, no more than that."

"Well, thank The Mother for that," I muttered as Baine rose to his feet with a tired groan and followed me to the ramparts. Lord Fitzery and Jebido were already waiting for us when we got there.

"Where's the king?" I asked.

"Lying down in the keep," Jebido answered. "Should I go wake him?"

I shook my head. "Let's see what this is about first."

"Looks to me like they just want to talk," Lord Fitzery said. He grinned at me. "I don't imagine they have ridden all this way just to say nice things about you, though, so try not to get offended, Lord Hadrack."

I laughed, finding myself liking the young lord immensely. "I'll do my best."

I studied the six riders as they approached. Lorgen Three-Fingers rode in the center, with his son riding to his right. The rider on each end carried a flickering torch, which a brisk wind coming in from the north was working hard at extinguishing. I didn't recognize any of the other men with Lorgen and his son, but I didn't need to—I knew who they were. The Ear, the Eye, the Sword, and the Shield. They were the Blood Guard, the four men sworn to protect the leader of the tribe.

The riders stopped their horses just out of bowshot range, and I smiled to myself when I realized they had forgotten about my Wolf's Teeth. We could pick all six off easily with the longbows, I knew, if it weren't for the glowering hulk of a man to Lorgen's right who carried a wilted parlay branch in his right hand. Honor dictated that we could not harm the six men while carrying that branch, though I was sorely tempted to give the order just the same.

Lorgen Three-Fingers took one of the torches in his bad hand, and then he kicked his horse forward. He lifted the torch so I could see his face as he peered up at the ramparts where I stood in the shadows. "Do you see me, Wolf?" he called.

"Get me a torch," I told Baine. My friend was gone for just a moment, returning with a flaming brand. I leaped to the top of the battlements with it in my hands, staring down at Lorgen Three-Fingers. "I see you, Pith," I growled back.

We just stared at each other for a time, neither saying anything. I could feel a malevolent hatred emanating from the Amenti chieftain that would have taken my breath away had I not been prepared for it.

"Do you think you have won, whelp?" Lorgen finally demanded in a husky voice. "Hiding up there behind those walls like a coward."

I laughed. "If you don't like these walls, old man, then why don't you crawl over them so that I can kill you?"

"I was going to give you to my son after what you did to him," Lorgen said, ignoring my taunt. His horse fidgeted, and it took a moment for the Pith to settle the beast down. "But now," he continued once the animal had quieted, "I'm going to keep you all to myself. Your death will take days, whelp, with so much pain that you will beg me to slit your throat and end your suffering."

"You must have a lot of time on your hands," I said down to him. "Most old men usually do. But I don't, so when I kill you, I promise it will be quick."

"You bastard!" Nedo shouted from behind his father. He pointed at me. "Fight me, you coward. Just you and me, man to man."

I laughed and spat over the wall into the moat. "Don't waste my time, boy. I've already taken your balls, so you're no man now. Don't be in such a hurry to lose your head along with those balls."

Nedo started to curse me in a long string of foul words. I turned to glance down at my friends in mock astonishment, impressed despite myself at the boy's command of language. Finally, the youth ran out of words to say, and he just sat his horse, breathing heavily while his father studied me with hooded eyes.

"We will come for you, whelp," Lorgen finally said, his voice even now, yet filled with malice. "When the sun rises, we will come. So be ready to die." The chieftain dismounted and tossed the torch aside, then he drew a knife and cut a gash across the top of his good hand. Nedo dropped to the ground beside him and used the same knife to slash open his palm and the top of his hand. Then the glowering Pith came next, doing the same, followed by the rest of the Piths until they all stood together, one hand over the other, sharing blood as they stared up at me. "In the name of the Master, we six make a blood-oath of vengeance against Lord Hadrack of Corwick and the Gandermen in this garrison," Lorgen said loudly. "Nothing will stand in our way of your complete destruction. Be it one day or ten years from now, we will not sway from our purpose while we still breathe. That is our oath and pledge to each other and to you, Hadrack of Corwick. So hear our words and know that you are doomed."

"Doomed," the five Piths repeated. Then they turned without another word, mounted their horses and rode back to their camp.

Half an hour later, we sat in the keep, explaining to the king everything that had occurred.

"But you told me Piths don't like sieges, Lord Hadrack," Tyden said. We were sitting around one of the long tables in the hall, eating a meager meal of bread and ale.

"I said they prefer to strike fast and hard, Highness," I responded. "Not that they won't attack a fortress if they have enough motivation." I tore off a piece of the stale bread and popped it in my mouth, talking around it. "Unfortunately, I would have to say that the Piths are very motivated now."

"Yes," Tyden agreed dryly. "I would say you're right about that." The king toyed with his mug. "Can we hold them off until reinforcements arrive?"

I shrugged. "We'll have a better idea about that in the morning, Highness. But I don't see why not. Our walls are stout, and we have plenty of men and arrows. Without siege engines, there's not much Lorgen can do but shake his fist at us and rattle his sword."

"The armory in the garrison is well-stocked, Highness," Lord Fitzery added. "I'm not sure why, but the Piths left it untouched for the most part."

"They prefer to use their own weapons," Baine explained. "And I imagine they never expected we would end up in here."

"What about food?" Tyden asked. "Do we have enough for a long siege if it comes to that?"

"We can last for months if we are careful, Highness," Lord Fitzery said. He smiled as he tore off a hunk of bread. "Though I don't promise the fare will be up to your usual standards, Highness."

The king waved away his words. "I'll eat grubs and dog shit if that's what it takes to beat that bastard out there."

"Well, I'm not partial to dog shit, Highness," Lord Fitzery said with a laugh. "But I've roasted my fair share of mealworms over a fire, so I could live with that if we must."

The next morning began cool and cloudy, with a hint of rain in the air. I had risen early from my straw bed in the great hall, wanting to lay eyes on the Pith camp the moment the light allowed for it. Now I stood alone on the eastern parapet in the darkness, clutching my cloak against the wind and wondering what the day would bring. Jebido and Baine came to join me, both still looking half asleep as we stood together, waiting for the sun to rise.

"This has a very familiar feel to it," Baine said with a yawn. The Pith camp still lay in shadows, with only a few weak fires burning that we could barely see through a thick mist drifting south from the river.

"Let's hope not too familiar," Jebido replied sourly. He looked up as a light rain started to fall. "Wonderful," he grunted with a frown.

Lord Fitzery appeared from the keep, and after he had relieved himself, he climbed to join us, blowing on his hands and stamping his feet. The lord was dressed in a rich mail coat etched with a golden hem and a hanging coif that was much too big for him. He had to pull it back from his eyes constantly. A sword with a serpent head hilt was sheathed across his back, and a matching short sword lay on his hip. "A good day for a battle, I would say," the lord said with a laugh.

Jebido turned away and said nothing, though I saw his features had darkened considerably. My friend was usually in a foul mood first thing in the morning from all his aches and pains, and this day appeared to be no different. Cheery people before the sun had risen tended to get a strong rebuke from him, even a young lord, and I was glad that he'd chosen to hold his tongue.

"You're right, Lord Fitzery," I responded with a smile. "The rain will make the ground slick, which will be in our favor."

Lord Fitzery waved a hand. "All this stuffy lord nonsense between us has to stop. How about I call you Hadrack, and you call me Fitz? All my friends do. Is it a bargain?"

I chuckled as we locked forearms. "It's a deal."

"Good," Fitz said as he looked east. "Now that we have that settled, what have our heathen friends been up to this morning?"

"Not a damn thing as far as I can tell," I said. "But it's early yet."

Fitz and I talked for a time about our theories on war and tactics as we waited, while Jebido and Baine listened, offering an occasional opinion. Fitz was only seventeen years old, but even though he was young, he had a keen mind that missed very little. Fitz knew nothing of our time in Gasterny other than vague rumors, and he was curious to know what had actually happened here. I told him how, by clever misdirection, Pernissy had managed to take the fortress by sending men on rafts down the river to climb the walls behind our forces.

"That was smart," Fitz said with admiration when I was done. He grinned. "Let's hope the Piths don't decide to use the same ploy."

"They can't this time, lord," Jebido responded. The clouds above us were clearing now as the sky brightened, taking with them my friend's bad mood. "The walls back then were made of wood and easily scaled," Jebido said. He slapped the battlements beside him. "Now they are twice as high, twice as thick, and made of solid stone. No one is coming over them from that side."

"Hadrack," Baine warned, nudging my arm.

The mist was quickly lifting as the wind shifted, sending it back toward the river. I could see the Pith camp now, with many of the collapsed tents still smoldering and sending up tendrils of weak smoke. A long line of horses with bodies draped over them were moving slowly toward the bridge, with purple-robed Pathfinders guiding them along.

"What are they doing?" Fitz asked.

"Taking their dead back to the Ascension Grounds would be my guess," I said. "After last night, I doubt they're willing to chance Ascending them here again."

"That's too bad," Fitz said with a chuckle. "I rather enjoyed all those bouncing tits and round bums."

Another half an hour went by before the line of horses disappeared across the bridge, heading east toward Victory Pass. The moment they were out of sight, drums began to pound as the remaining Piths mounted their horses.

"Here we go," Jebido muttered.

I signaled the archer in the watchtower above us to ring the bell as the Piths massed along the western side of the ruined campsite. It was hard to tell with all the milling horses, but I guessed they still had at least a thousand men, maybe more. My face fell in disappointment as I shared a look with Jebido. I had been hoping a lot more of the warriors had been killed or injured during the night's attack. I thought I saw Lorgen Three-Fingers amongst the riders, and perhaps his son as well, but from so far away, it was hard to be certain. I wondered if Saldor had survived the battle and destruction of the camp. A part of me hoped that he had. I'd actually liked the man and wished him no ill.

We had close to two hundred and fifty men-at-arms left and nearly a hundred archers, with thirty-seven of them my own Wolf's Teeth boys. Those men were lined along the parapet to my left under Tyris' command, waiting with their great warbows. Whatever Lorgen Three-Fingers planned for us this day, he was about to find out that getting over these walls would be very frustrating and costly, despite his bold words from last night.

The Piths came on as the ground shook beneath the hooves of their horses. Each warrior held a bow and had several sheaves of arrows hooked to their saddles, but none were on foot carrying scaling ladders or ramps for the moat, which I found strange. What did they expect to do? I glanced at Jebido and he just shrugged, having seen the question on my face.

"Wolf's Teeth!" I heard Tyris shout as the Piths drew closer. "Nock!" The Piths came on in a solid wall of horseflesh, the colorful banners of the Amenti sub-tribes fluttering on lances all along the front line, with Lorgen Three-Fingers' giant bear banner dominating the center. "Draw!" Tyris commanded as the Piths came within range. "Now, loose!"

I watched the flight of shafts fill the sky, anticipating seeing Pith riders in the first rank start to crumble and fall as the rest of our archers began to shoot. But then something incredible happened. The Piths broke apart before the lead arrows fell in amongst them, sweeping both left and right in a breathtaking exhibition of horsemanship and coordination. Then they started to curl like flocks of birds, breaking up into bands of twenty or thirty riders all moving in the same, practiced rhythm as they galloped past our walls. How they didn't collide into one another was a mystery to me. The Piths were remarkable riders, and they guided their well-trained horses with leg pressure alone as they stood in the stirrups, shooting arrows up at our battlements and towers. I looked up as a man screamed above me, then his body plunged to the ground from the watchtower as dark spinning shafts hissed like hundreds of buzzing flies over the battlements or cracked against hard stone.

"Everyone, get down!" I shouted as I dropped to my knees. An arrow cracked into the wall above me as several men who had been too slow to take cover twisted and fell.

"This really does seem familiar," Jebido grunted from beside me.

I could hear the triumphant cries of the Piths, and I took a chance and stood, taking a peek over the wall. The mounted warriors had turned and were retreating out of our range, bows raised over their heads. As far as I could tell, we hadn't gotten even one of the bastards.

"Well," Fitz said as he came to stand beside me. "That didn't go so well."

"No," I muttered, staring at the celebrating Piths as they laughed and jeered on the way back to their camp. "No, it did not."

And so began Lorgen Three-Fingers' patient plan to wear the men of Gasterny down. Days went by, then weeks, with multiple attacks occurring at all hours of the day, even at night. Sometimes the Piths would come with only a few hundred men, sometimes with many more, but come they did in endless waves at least ten times per day. And every day or two, we would lose a man, despite repeated warnings to stay down and not attempt to go bow to bow against them. Sometimes the Piths would throw grappling hooks across the moat to the walls, drawing men from cover only to have them skewered with multiple arrows by the waiting Pith archers. Several times a day, they would send fire-arrows into the garrison, then wait as we hurried to beat out the flames before sending another volley of barbed shafts unerringly to the same area, striking down the men fighting the blaze. The attacks were endless, varied, and coldly determined, requiring an iron will and discipline that I hadn't believed the Piths possessed as they sought to wear us down. And it was working.

I'd always had a healthy respect for Pith archers, both male and female, but the astounding skill of the Amenti day after day had surprised even me. Except for Tyris and Baine, our men were horribly outclassed with the bow, even with our longer, more powerful ones, and the mood inside Gasterny had turned bleak and dark by the end of the second week. Our supply of arrows, which had seemed limitless at first, was slowly being depleted, despite our determination not to waste them. And though the Piths had taken losses, there were so many of them that it hardly seemed to matter. But for us, every man we lost was one less we could put on the walls, never knowing for certain if the next attack would be the one where they tried to breach us.

"It really is quite clever," Fitz was saying, a theme that he had been hammering away at to anyone who would listen. We were sitting on the Holy House steps—which had once again become my preferred place to think and talk. "I mean, look at you two," the young lord said, motioning to Baine and me. "You both look like a horse dragged you a mile over sharp rocks."

"As if you look any better," Baine snorted. Fitz gave my friend a dark look. "Lord," Baine added reluctantly.

Fitz's face broke out in a smile, his anger nothing but a sham. I knew the young lord didn't care much about his title, but for some reason, he seemed to take great pleasure in teasing Baine about it. "Perhaps on the outside, I look no better than you miserable bastards do, but inside I am as fresh as a morning breeze. My constitution is stronger than most men, you see, and while my toilet may not be up to its usual high standard, the current events have done little to discourage me that we will ultimately prevail."

"Of course we will prevail," King Tyden boomed as he strode toward us, his hands behind his back. A tall, gangly youth with an odd overbite and slow way about him trailed the king. The boy's name was Kacy, and he had become Tyden's unofficial assistant in Gasterny, running his errands and seeing to his everyday needs. Kacy was clearly a halfwit, but one who was just smart enough to be an assistant to one of our army's many cooks on the march to free Gasterny. The boy had misunderstood his orders to return to Corwick with his master and had somehow been left behind. Jebido hadn't had the heart to leave him, fearing he'd get lost or worse, so he'd given him a horse before the charge on the Pith camp and had hoped for the best. Miraculously, the boy had survived and had even acquitted himself quite well according to several men-at-arms that had seen him down a Pith with his horse.

Baine and I both stood, bowing to the king, while Fitz half-stood and nodded his head before dropping back to his previous position.

"Any sign of our friends yet, Lord Hadrack?" Tyden asked.

I shook my head. "Nothing since this morning, Highness. This is the longest that I can remember them going between attacks since we got here."

"Maybe they're getting tired," Fitz said with a smile.

"Were that only true," the king said as he paused in front of us. He pursed his lips as he regarded me. "Do you think the man drowned? Should we send another?"

The king was referring to Bona, who I had sent over the wall a week ago to swim the White Rock yet again and try to locate Tyden's men. We had expected the King's Army to have arrived by now, and I knew the king was becoming concerned. We all were.

I shook my head. "No, Highness. Bona made it. We just need to be patient."

Tyden nodded, though I could tell he didn't fully agree with me. "Very well, Lord Hadrack, we'll wait." He paused as he tugged at his growing beard. "But only for two more days. If they haven't come by then, we send another man."

I opened my mouth to respond, but was cut off by the watchtower bell ringing. I sighed as I glanced over at Fitz. "So much for them being tired."

Fitz nodded in resignation as one of the men in the watchtower leaned over, his hands cupped around his mouth. "Riders approaching!"

"I would say that's rather obvious, you imbecile!" Fitz shouted back as he stood.

"No, lord," the archer called down. "I mean from the north. Riders are coming from the north! Many of them!"

The king's eyes lit up at the news, and he ran to the ramparts with the rest of us following. Tyden was the first to reach the northern wall, and he gasped loudly. A vast army on horseback was approaching from the north and along the riverbank, while I could hear wild cheering coming from the rebuilt Pith camp.

"Oh shit," Jebido said under his breath.

We weren't looking at the King's Army coming to save us as we had hoped, but instead, the force riding toward the bridge were Piths—and they were led by Einhard the Unforgiving.

14: Einhard the Unforgiving

"It's not him," Jebido said with conviction.

"It is," Baine insisted.

"It is not," Jebido responded heatedly. "It can't be."

"You're wrong, Jebido," I said as I watched the lead riders making their way across the bridge. "It's him." The Piths were still too far away to make out faces or banners, but I knew instinctively that I was right.

"Him who?" Fitz asked. If the young lord was dismayed by the sight of so many Piths, he hid it well.

"Einhard," I said in a low voice.

"Oh," Fitz said as he peered curiously to the north. "That him."

A sobering silence had descended on the fortress at the appearance of the Pith army. I could see by the haunted looks on the faces around me that whatever flame of hope we'd had of surviving had effectively just been extinguished.

"Mother help us," Tyden muttered, looking shaken. "There has to be five thousand of the bastards." He turned away, his eyes bitter. "I thought we would win. I really did."

I moved to stand beside the king. "We aren't dead yet, Highness," I said, trying to sound confident, though inside, I was reeling just as much as he was. Einhard and I might have been friends years ago, but I knew his hatred of Ganderland far outweighed whatever he might have felt for me once. There would be no rescue for any of the men inside Gasterny now, whether the King's Army arrived soon or not.

The lead Pith riders passed through the southern gatehouse, breaking back out into the sunshine. I could see the colors of their banners now, confirming my suspicions of who it was that led them. It was Einhard, just as I had known it would be. Einhard stopped his horse, shielding his eyes as he looked toward the garrison and the parapet where I stood. I remembered watching him leaving Gasterny years ago to return to the land of the Piths. We had both waved to each other then, a silent message of friendship shared between us before he had ridden out of my life. Now, we were together again in the same place, but this time on opposing sides.

On impulse, I grabbed a lance with my wolf banner tied to it. I jumped to the battlements, staring down at the man who had meant so much to me once. Einhard's helm was shining like a brilliant golden beacon in the sun, impossible to ignore. What was going through his mind as he looked my way? Was he feeling hatred for a man he believed to be a traitor, or was it sadness and regret, knowing that he would soon have to kill a friend?

The White Rock rushed and gurgled below me, sweeping along the western wall before curving north in a loop and then flowing east beneath the bridge. Einhard was almost half a mile away, and I could see nothing of his features, but even so, I sensed somehow that he was smiling up at me. I lifted my free hand in the air with my fingers splayed wide, then I waited with the banner twisting and snapping in the breeze over my head.

Einhard seemed frozen on his horse, locked in that moment in time, until finally, almost reluctantly, he raised a hand to me. Then, the moment broken, he kicked his heels against his horse's flanks and rode at a gallop with his men toward Lorgen Three-Fingers' camp.

"I always prayed we would never have to cross swords with that bastard," Jebido said as I jumped down to the walkway. "I guess The Mother wasn't listening."

I shrugged, looking away to hide my face. Seeing Einhard had greatly affected me, and I didn't want those around me to know just how much. "He bleeds like any other man," I grunted as I moved away to an unoccupied part of the parapet. I stared east, alone with my thoughts. I felt a lump rising in my throat, and I put my hands on the solidness of the wall and leaned on it, feeling the coarseness of the stone beneath my fingers. Einhard might be coming over this very wall soon, I knew, and if he did, I swore that I would do everything in my power to stop him, even if it meant killing him.

An hour went by as the Pith army that stretched like a winding snake along the river crossed the bridge three abreast. The eastern fields were alive with noise as newly arriving warriors joined those already encamped. Finally, the last of the Pith supply wagons bringing up the rear rattled over the bridge, followed by a rearguard of two hundred Piths.

"Care for some company?" Fitz asked as he wandered over to me. I shrugged as the young lord rested his shoulder against the wall beside me and crossed his arms. "I take it this Einhard fellow means a lot to you?"

"He did once," I said, not taking my eyes off the Pith camp. Lorgen had erected a wooden palisade around his encampment weeks ago in case we tried a sortie, but it was much too small to house all the new arrivals. Einhard's men were busily setting up a second, bigger camp near the river where the Ascension Ceremony had taken place. I could see Einhard's tent sitting back near the forest as warriors chopped more trees for a second palisade. Fitz gestured behind him. "Baine and Jebido think he'll let you go."

I turned in surprise. "Do they, now?" I said. "And why would Einhard do that?"

Fitz shrugged. "How should I know? He's your friend, not mine."

"He was my friend," I corrected. "A lot has changed since those days."

"Maybe they have, and maybe they haven't," Fitz replied. He nodded toward the east. "Either way, I guess we are about to find out."

Einhard was approaching on a shimmering black horse with a parlay branch held in his hand. Another group of mounted Piths followed fifty yards behind him. I could see Lorgen Three-Fingers and his son amongst them, as well as the chieftain's four Blood Guards.

Several overeager archers on the walls started to draw back their bows. "Don't shoot!" I shouted, raising my hands. "Put your bows down."

I watched as Einhard slowly made his way toward us, finally pausing his horse on the ramp before the moat. Lorgen Three-Fingers and his men stayed well back as Einhard removed his helmet and balanced it on his saddle horn before grinning up at me. Despite the situation, I found myself grinning back. The Sword's hair was still long and blond, though I thought I could see grey tinges here and there, with more grey showing in his beard. He wore a brown leather patch over his right eye. A thick scar ran from his hairline, disappearing beneath the patch before continuing along his nose and down the side of his mouth.

"You're not nearly as handsome as you used to be," I called down to him.

Einhard laughed—a deep, genuine sound of pleasure that erupted from somewhere in his belly. "That's rich coming from you, puppy."

I smiled, both of us silent as we stared at each other, enjoying the moment. Finally, Einhard sighed as he examined the solid walls of the garrison. "Things have changed since the last time I saw this place." I nodded, not saying anything. Einhard gestured with a thumb over his shoulder at Lorgen Three-Fingers. "You certainly have a way of bringing out the worst in people, Hadrack."

"I learned that from you," I replied with a laugh.

Einhard chuckled and nodded. "That you did. That you did indeed." He shifted in his saddle. "So, it seems we have a problem."

"And what would that be?" I asked in mock surprise.

Einhard's smile faded. "I warned you years ago that we were going to destroy Ganderland and your false gods. Do you remember that, Hadrack?"

"I do," I called down. "But you failed. Do you remember that?"

Einhard's face tightened as Jebido gave me a warning look. I ignored him.

"Did you open the gates and betray my brothers and sisters?" Einhard asked me bluntly. His voice was hard and dangerous now, with a hint of tension in his words.

"If you need to ask that, brother, then you don't know me at all."

Einhard stroked his beard as he looked up at me. "I want to believe you didn't do it," he finally said. "You once told me honor defines a man, Hadrack, and that it makes you stronger, not weaker. So swear to me now, on that same honor of which you are so proud, that you did not betray my people."

"I swear I did not," I said firmly. "They were my people too, Einhard, and I would have slit my own throat rather than cause any of them harm."

Einhard took a deep breath, and I saw his shoulders relax. "Very well," he said, his voice losing some of its edge. "I believe you, Hadrack."

The king came to stand beside me then, and before I could stop him, he pointed a mailed finger down at Einhard through the embrasure. "Get off my lands, you heathen!" he shouted. "Take your rabble and ride back to the cesspool you crawled out of, or I swear by The Mother Herself, every last one of you will die in these fields."

"Highness, please," I said urgently. "This is not a man who reacts well to threats."

"And who would this talking turd be then, Hadrack?" Einhard asked, a smile on his lips. I groaned. I recognized that dangerous-looking smile, having seen it many times before.

"I am the King of Ganderland, you filthy heathen!" Tyden spat back, anger on his face now. "So watch what you say to me."

"Or what?" Einhard asked, looking amused. "Will you climb down from your walls to defend your wounded pride if I call you turd-sucker next, or arse-licker, or maybe even goat-humper?"

Tyden's eyes went dark with rage, and he opened his mouth to answer as I put my hand on his arm. "Please, Highness," I implored him. "Say nothing more."

"I'm not afraid of that bastard," Tyden hissed, glaring at me. "Is that what you think? That I am afraid?"

"No one doubts your bravery, Highness," I said. "But that man down there is no ordinary warrior. I promise you, if you try to fight him, you will die."

"You think me so easily beaten, Lord Hadrack?" Tyden demanded, bristling with indignation.

"No, Highness," I said, shaking my head. "Not against most men. But Einhard is not most men." Tyden stared at me defiantly, stubbornness burning in his eyes. I had to change his mind now, I knew, before it was too late and he challenged Einhard to a duel. "Look around you, Highness," I said, sweeping my hand around the battlements where our men waited and listened. "Every one of these men here risked everything to rescue you from the Piths. They could have run to save their own lives, Highness, but they chose to save yours instead. And now, after all that, you want to sacrifice that life over a few stupid words that mean nothing?" I snorted and shook my head. "That's not what true leaders do, Highness," I said. "That is what selfish people do who care only for themselves."

"You go too far, Lord Hadrack," Tyden growled.

I shrugged. "When you made me the Lord of Corwick, Highness, I gave you my oath of fealty, which included protecting you with my life. That is what I am doing right now and what I will continue to do until my last breath. I should have been more vocal about my doubts when we first learned the Piths were here, but instead, I held my tongue. I won't do that again, Highness. So, you can punish me for my words if you must, even have me killed, but I am not sorry for telling you the truth."

Tyden pressed his lips together as he studied me. I could see the anger slowly fading from his eyes, and finally, he took a deep breath. "You are an insolent man, Lord Hadrack," he said, clamping me on the shoulder. "But sometimes even a king needs to hear honest words that he'd rather not acknowledge." Tyden motioned to the wall. "Continue your talk with the heathen. I will do my best to contain myself, should the bastard choose to insult me again."

I nodded, relieved as I looked over the wall again.

"Ah," Einhard said when he saw me. "There you are, Hadrack. Did your foppish king faint away, or has he gone and hidden himself in the keep under his bedclothes?"

I glanced at Tyden, but other than twin circles of red burning high along his cheeks, he seemed in control of himself. "What do you want, Einhard?" I demanded.

"Why, isn't it obvious?" Einhard asked, spreading his arms. "I want you to surrender."

"You know we won't do that," I said. "So why bother asking?"

"Of course you won't," Einhard replied in an agreeable tone. "I would have been disappointed in you if you had. I should mention though, since we are both being so honest with each other, that I ran into a sizable force of Ganders less than a day's march from here." He shrugged apologetically. "I'm sorry to say there will be no rescue coming from them, in case that's what you were counting on." I just stared down at Einhard, not letting him see the dismay on my face. The Sword waited, then when I said nothing, he looked behind him at Lorgen Three-Fingers before focusing back on me. "This is not what I want, you know, old friend," he said in a lower voice.

I nodded—I did know. "I hear Alesia is queen now," I said, still reeling from the news that our reinforcements had been destroyed.

Einhard sat back in surprise, then he grinned. "She is, and she has been a fine queen. Alesia wanted to come and join in the fun, but she is heavy with child."

"Again?" I said, remembering the last time that I had seen Alesia. She had been pregnant then, too, and had seemed to grow even more beautiful every day of her pregnancy. "I understand you already have a son," I added. "And that he is strong and fit."

Einhard beamed at the mention of his son. "He is all that and more, Hadrack. His name is Einrack, and the seers have promised me that he will grow up to be a great and mighty king." I paused, not trusting my voice to speak, overwhelmed by the name that Einhard and Alesia had given to their first-born son. Finally, I cleared my throat. "You are the Sword of the Queen and her husband," I said. "Which means you can speak with her voice." I waved a hand toward the Pith camp. "One word from you and this all goes away."

"It is not that simple, Hadrack," Einhard said. "Lorgen Three-Fingers has sworn a blood-oath against you, and not even the word of the queen can reverse it."

"Then ride away with your men and let us deal with the Amenti on our own," I suggested.

Einhard shook his head. "I can't do that, Hadrack. The Pathfinders have read the blood-message of your people, and that message says that Gasterny must be returned to us."

I grimaced, certain that he was speaking of the captured Sons and Daughters. "So, you intend to help that bastard, then," I said, motioning to Lorgen Three-Fingers.

Einhard nodded as he swung his horse around. "A blood-oath like theirs is no small thing, Hadrack, as you of all people must know. It cannot be taken lightly. As long it remains, I must support them. Tomorrow morning we will come in force, and I promise you we will take Gasterny back." He paused his horse to look at me, his one eye seeming to glow as it bored into mine. "Unless, of course, the blood-oath has somehow been fulfilled by then." Einhard held my eyes for a moment longer, then he turned and joined Lorgen Three-Fingers, leaving me to stand in puzzlement as I watched them ride away. There had been a message in the Sword's words, I was certain of it, but for the life of me, I couldn't understand what it had been. How could the Amenti blood-oath be fulfilled if that oath meant the death of every man in Gasterny?

That night, I lay in my bed in the great hall, unable to sleep, listening to the men around me snoring as I tried to understand the riddle that Einhard had given me. Finally, I couldn't take it any longer, and I thrust my furs aside and stepped outside. The night air was cool for the time of year. I clutched my cloak tighter about me as my breath fogged around my head like a cloud while I climbed to the eastern ramparts. An archer greeted me, and I mumbled something to him as I passed by, lost in my thoughts.

"Couldn't sleep?" someone said in a soft voice as I reached the eastern watchtower. I paused in surprise. Fitz sat propped up against the stones where the tower and walls met, hidden within the shadows. He had a battered tin mug in his hand, which he held out to me. "Here, something to help take away your troubles, my friend."

I took the tin gratefully, sipping the flat beer before I handed it back and slid down the wall beside the young lord. "I can't stop thinking about Einhard's last words," I said. "I know he was trying to tell me something."

Fitz shrugged. "Maybe you're reading too much into those words. Maybe he just threw them away and they meant nothing at all."

I shook my head. "No, I could tell by the way he looked at me when he spoke. He just couldn't be any clearer about what he wanted to say with that bastard Lorgen listening."

"Tell it to me one more time then," Fitz said with a sigh, leaning his head back against the stone.

I had repeated Einhard's words multiple times to the king and the rest of my men, with none of them able to interpret the Sword's meaning any better than I could. I looked to the star-filled sky, picturing Einhard and the expression on his face. "Unless, of course, the blood-oath has somehow been fulfilled by then," I said, speaking each word slowly and carefully.

Fitz took a sip of beer when I was done, burping softly as we both sat in silence, thinking. "Maybe he misunderstood the scope of the Amenti oath," the young lord suggested after a time. "Maybe he thinks it's just against you and was saying that if you sacrifice yourself, then the oath would be fulfilled, and then he wouldn't have to support Lorgen."

"Einhard's no fool," I said. "He would have questioned Three-Fingers thoroughly." I shook my head. "No, there's no mistake."

"Then I have no idea what he meant," Fitz said, sounding tired now. He stood, pressing the almost empty tin into my hands. "What I do know is my bladder hurts, and so I must piss or perish. After that, I'm going to try to get some sleep." He patted me on the shoulder. I could see his thin face twisted into a wry smile in the starlight. "I suggest you do the same, my friend, for tomorrow will be our last day in this world. I would rather not have you nodding off beside me just as the Piths come over our walls, if you don't mind."

Fitz moved unsteadily to the edge of the walkway. He fumbled with his trousers, hopping up and down in frustration before he finally sent a steaming stream of urine down into the bailey. He sighed with relief when he was done, then waved to me as he headed for the ladder. I watched the young lord go, absently twirling the tin mug in my lap as I went over again what Einhard had said. Finally, no closer to understanding than I'd been hours before, and with my brain aching from the frustration, I put my head back against the cold stone and closed my eyes. I slept then, dreaming of the many ghosts of Gasterny, until suddenly I jumped awake, the memory of a conversation that I'd had with Ania not long before the garrison fell coming back to me in vivid detail.

We were sitting on the steps of the Holy House together. Ania was weaving a conical fruit basket she planned to use to collect the tiny apples that grew in abundance in the forest behind the fortress. I was set to go on patrol in that very forest soon and was spending the time before I left with Ania as I enjoyed the morning sunshine. The patrol I was about to go on would eventually lead Baine and me to Shana's tortured servant, and ultimately Shana herself, which would soon set off a chain of events that would be the undoing of Gasterny. But of course, I had no idea of that at the time.

"You have deft hands," I said to Ania in admiration as I watched her work quickly and efficiently.

"Well, you would know," Ania replied with a coy chuckle. She winked. "Especially after last night. I'm surprised you can even walk this morning."

I laughed, no longer caught off-guard by the Piths' boldness the way that I had once been. Ania and I had spent much of the night in lovemaking but, despite that, I could feel myself stirring with desire again as I studied her fine features and healthy, glowing skin. I had a sudden vision of her lying naked and splayed out on the steps as we humped in front of everyone, and I grinned, keeping it to myself. Knowing Ania, she would want to do it if I said anything.

"What's so funny?" Ania asked, one eyebrow raised.

"Nothing," I said as I looked away, still chuckling to myself. Baine had just come from the stables leading his horse, and he began checking the cinches and going over every loop and belt with studious attention. Young Peren came out next, leading his horse and Angry. Today would be the Pith youth's first patrol, and I knew he was greatly looking forward to it. I stood and stretched my back, pausing as I saw Einhard walking with Eriz. The Sword glanced my way and his expression turned frosty. We had argued the night before, and the words we'd said to each other still hung heavily between us. I returned the look—frost for frost—until the men disappeared through the gates into the inner bailey.

Seeing Einhard made me think of the Pith king he served, and I turned back to Ania. "You were going to tell me a story about Clendon the Peacemaker last night," I said.

"I was?" Ania replied, distracted now as one of the hazel branches she was weaving broke and she had to draw it free and start over.

"Yes," I nodded. "Before we found something else to do. You wanted to tell me how the king won the tribes over, remember? You said I would enjoy it."

"Oh," Ania said, pausing to look up at me. "That's right." She glanced at Baine and Peren. "Maybe it should wait until you get back?"

I waved a hand. "Baine is going to take another ten minutes, knowing him. We've got time."

"All right," Ania nodded. She set the basket down, playing with the broken branch as she talked. "Clendon was known as Clendon the Thinker then. He was a Peshwin."

"Like you and Einhard, Alesia, and Eriz," I said, knowing that they all came from the same tribe.

"Yes," Ania agreed. "But this was long before any of us were born. Clendon fell in love with the daughter of Obed the Knife, the chieftain of the Hadrees tribe. And even though Obed refused their union, they married secretly anyway. Obed was furious, and he, along with his Blood Guard, swore a blood-oath against the Peshwin for allowing the marriage. Obed disowned his daughter and sent his warriors to destroy the Peshwin. He couldn't actually do that of course because the Peshwin were just as strong as the Hadrees, so what followed were years of bloodshed, murder, and betrayal. Finally, Clendon went to Obed on his knees, offering up his life in exchange for an end to the war. But Obed spat on Clendon." Ania's face turned hard and dangerous as she relived the insult. "He told Clendon that there could be no peace until every last Peshwin was dead, including his disowned daughter and the child that she had borne. Angry and bitter at the stupidity of Obed, Clendon was so enraged that he called for a Tribal Challenge of the Hadrees."

"So, he fought Obed and killed him," I said, nodding my head in understanding.

"Not exactly," Ania replied. "Any Pith can challenge the chieftain of a tribe to a Tribal Challenge, even those not of that tribe. But to earn the right to fight the chieftain, that challenger must first go through his protectors."

"You mean the Blood Guard?" I said in wonder. "You're saying that he had to fight four men first before he could even get to Obed?"

"Yes," Ania agreed. "One after the other with no rest in between. Clendon is the only man or woman to succeed in a Tribal Challenge in over three hundred years. His victory ended the blood-oath, since the five men who had sworn it were all dead, and as the new chieftain of the Hadrees, he began to bring peace to the Pith tribes, eventually uniting all of us."

Baine had called me then, and I had left on a patrol that would soon doom everyone in Gasterny to death. I had forgotten all about Clendon and the Tribal Challenge until now, and I stood in the darkness as the wind tugged at my beard playfully, staring out over the wall at the hundreds of cooking fires lighting up the Pith camp.

"Thank you, Einhard," I whispered. "I understand now, my old friend."

I turned away, heading for the keep and my bed. I would need my rest, for tomorrow, the fate of every man in Gasterny would hang on the strength of my sword arm.

15: Tribal Challenge

"Have you lost your damn mind!?" Jebido thundered at me the next morning.

It was still an hour before dawn, yet every man in the garrison was already awake. Many were filling their bellies for the needed strength food would give them or sharpening weapons that were already as keen as they would ever be as they prepared for the coming attack. Jebido, Baine, Fitz, and Lord Vestry sat with the king and me at a table near the dais. No one knew when we would get a chance to eat again, so there was no rationing of our food stocks this day. I had just informed everyone around the table of my plans, and each of their faces mirrored the incredulous look Jebido was giving me.

"Can you think of a better idea?" I asked my friend casually. I'd only had a few hours of sleep, yet that sleep had been especially restful and worry-free. I felt calm and wonderfully alive, even though I knew in another hour or two I might be lying dead in the fields to the east. I had a purpose now, one which did not include cowering behind walls waiting to be slaughtered. It was invigorating and I couldn't wait to set it into motion.

"Yes, you fool!" Jebido snapped, his eyes flashing. "I can think of a better idea. We kill every one of those bastards that comes over our walls until there's no more of them left to kill. That's my idea. What kind of lunatic rides alone against six thousand blood-thirsty Pith warriors?"

"A brave one," Tyden said with a sigh. He studied me with blood-shot eyes. I might have slept well, but clearly, the king had not.

"What makes you think Einhard will let us live, even if you somehow manage to win this challenge?" Tyden asked.

I shrugged. "I can't promise what he will do, Highness. I just know that was the message he was giving me. He wouldn't have offered it if there wasn't a way out of this for all of us."

"You seem to have overlooked something, Lord Hadrack," Lord Vestry said, surprising me. He rarely spoke at these gatherings, and it was easy to forget that he was even there.

"And what would that be?" I asked.

Lord Vestry shifted on the bench uncomfortably. "You said that any Pith might challenge for leadership of any of the tribes, yet I must point out that you are not a Pith."

I grinned and motioned to Jebido, who was staring at me with a dark expression. "Care to answer that for me?"

Jebido just snorted and looked away.

"When we swore an oath to Einhard," Baine explained to Lord Vestry. "He made us members of his tribe. So, what Hadrack is saying is correct. All three of us are considered Peshwin, which means he does have the right to call for a Tribal Challenge."

"As long as Einhard backs his claim, you mean," Jebido added with a growl. "If he chooses not to, then you'll be dead before you can even draw your sword."

"He will support me," I said confidently. "This was his idea in the first place."

"It could still be a ploy," Fitz suggested as he cut into an apple. Several moth larvae squirmed out from the severed fruit where his knife had passed. The young lord absently pulled them free and tossed them over his shoulder. "Maybe he knows you better than you think, Hadrack," Fitz said, pointing his knife at me. "Maybe he's just trying to draw you out there so that Lorgen can take his time to kill you."

"Not a chance," Baine said with a snort. "If Einhard suggested this, then that means he believes Hadrack can win."

"And if by some miracle you do manage to defeat five men, Lord Hadrack," Lord Vestry said, looking down at his hands. "What happens to us?"

"There's only one way to find out, lord," I said. I turned to Tyden. "Highness, this is the only chance we have. It might be slim, I'll grant you that, but any chance is better than none at all. Let me do this."

"Do you believe you can defeat them, Lord Hadrack?" Tyden asked. He leaned forward and put his hand over mine. "Because I have no wish to throw my best fighter to the dogs for no reason. I know you are brave, and I know you would gladly lay down your life for those in this garrison. But I also know you are an honest man. So tell me, Lord Hadrack, in all honesty, do you believe if you make this challenge that you can win?"

I smiled. "You have my word, Highness, that I don't just believe I can win—I know I can." I put my other hand over his. "You have my solemn vow that I will not fail you."

Tyden took a deep breath, withdrawing his hand as he sat back. "Then I accept your offer, Lord Hadrack. You have my permission to leave Gasterny and make this challenge. May The Mother watch over you and keep you safe."

"Thank you, Highness," I said. I glanced at Jebido, whose eyes were stained dark with bitterness, then I stood. "If you will all forgive me then, I'm going to go prepare. I want to be on my way before the sun rises."

Half an hour later, I stood with Angry near the gatehouse as I said my goodbyes. The king came to me first, and he drew me to him in a warm embrace. "Our prayers and hopes go with you this day, Lord Hadrack," Tyden said. He stood back, his hands on my shoulders as he studied me. "I was right to make you a lord. You have not disappointed me."

"Thank you, Highness," I said gratefully.

Next came Fitz and we locked arms as he wished me luck, advising me to take my own advice and keep my eyes off the Pith women while I fought. I laughed and assured him that wouldn't be a problem.

"Don't you go and get yourself killed," Baine said to me as Fitz stepped away. "There's still too much for you and me to do in this world. I'm not ready for us to move on to the next one just yet."

"We'll see each other soon," I promised him as we embraced. "Right here." I glanced at Jebido, who stood off to one side holding a shield and a lance. He scowled at me. "Any last advice before I go?" I asked my friend.

Jebido nodded moodily as he handed me the shield. "Remember what I taught you, and whatever you do, keep your temper in check. Use your brain and fight defensively. Smashing away at a man's guard might give you the win eventually, but you'll be winded when you have to fight the next man. That means he'll be as fresh as a morning flower and tickling your ribs with his sword while you're still trying to catch your breath, so stay calm and focused."

"Got it," I said as I swung up on Angry. "Anything else?"

"Yeah," Jebido grunted. "Don't lose." He handed me the lance, which had a well-used tunic hanging from the spearpoint. There wasn't a branch to be found inside Gasterny to use for parlay, so the tunic would have to suffice. "Remember," Jebido added. "Every man has a pattern. Study it and use it to your advantage."

I nodded to him, then gestured to the men at the gate that I was ready. The drawbridge began to lower as I guided Angry forward across the cobblestones. Men were lined up all along the ramparts watching me, though not one of them said anything. We all understood the only chance any of us had to live lay with me, but I'm sure most of those watching believed they were looking down at a dead man. I dearly hoped to prove them wrong.

I saw Tyris and Niko standing with Berwin above me, and I saluted them with the lance before I passed through the barbican. The skies to the east were glowing orange over the trees as the sun slowly rose, and I could see Piths moving about in their camp as they prepared themselves for the coming attack. I crossed the drawbridge and paused Angry on the other side as it slowly cranked back up behind me. A blanket of mist rose serenely from the moat and floated along the ground, and with that and the still faint light, I was certain that the Piths remained unaware that anyone had left the garrison. If they had posted a sentry to watch Gasterny, I didn't see him.

"We're on our own now, boy," I said to Angry as we started forward.

We quickly left the fortress behind, and I made it perhaps another hundred yards before the Piths finally noticed me. I could hear shouts of surprise echoing out in the still morning air, and then riders began galloping toward me.

"Easy now," I whispered to Angry as he snorted, shaking his head in warning at the approaching horses.

The Piths came on, perhaps as many as a hundred. They were screaming their war cries as they swept down on me, circling close on all sides and waving their hammers, axes, and swords. I continued at a steady pace right through them, looking straight ahead as I kept my features blank. A Pith warrior raced past me, cracking his war hammer against my shield as he went by. I didn't flinch or even acknowledge it. Another man rode past on the other side of me, this time using a sword. I felt the heat of his blade as it hissed past my ear. I stared straight ahead, fixing a cold smile on my lips as I guided Angry toward the camp.

The warriors surrounding me were playing a game, one which I knew well and understood. The Piths liked to see how close they could get to a man with their weapons before he balked. I had seen warriors standing tall, not moving a muscle as sword blades, axes, and war hammers grazed his skin while his brothers tried to unnerve him. I had also seen warriors inflicted with terrible wounds when a Pith misjudged his strike, so I prayed the warriors around me today all had sound eyes and steady hands. Another rider pulled up beside me. I could see out of the corner of my eye that it was a woman, and I did nothing as she took a knife and cut the tunic from the lance, then tore off, waving it over her head.

The Piths started to insult me as I rode, though their words were tempered by grudging respect for not showing any reaction or fear. Finally, we reached the outskirts of the Pith encampment, and the warriors started to fade back, giving me space as I dismounted. Many of the Piths had come out from the palisades, watching me in curious silence. I saw a youth no older than Peren had been the day that he had lost his head, and I crooked a finger at him. The Pith gawked at me, looking around self-consciously before he stepped forward.

I put Angry's reins into his hands. "This horse is the breath which gives me life," I said, using the Pith traditional words when handing over a horse. "Care for him well, brother, and the Master will reward you. Cause him any harm, and not even the Master can save you from my wrath."

The Pith blinked in surprise, looking down at the reins in his hands before he nodded. "It shall be done."

I smiled coldly. "Finish it properly, boy," I said with a snarl.

The youth colored. "It shall be done, brother."

"Good," I said in approval. "And fetch Einhard while you're at it. Tell him Hadrack of the Peshwin wishes to see him." The boy's mouth dropped open, and then he nodded uncertainly before leading Angry away. I stood, staring at the hundreds of unfriendly faces watching me as I waited. That wait didn't take long as Lorgen Three-Fingers strode through the palisade gates, staring at me in amazement.

"Well, if it isn't the wolf come crawling at long last," Lorgen said as he paused in front of me. The man was bigger than I had thought, almost able to look directly into my eyes. Lorgen's son, Nedo, followed his father through the gates with the four men of the chieftain's Blood Guard. I noticed the boy's feral eyes were aglow with excitement as he fingered his sword. Lorgen shook his head back and forth slowly as he studied me, then he chuckled. "You might have big weighty balls, Wolf, but that weight seems to have taken a great deal away from your brains. What do you expect to accomplish by coming here, except to find a quicker death?"

I saw Einhard pushing his way through the growing crowd of Piths. "Brothers and sisters, hear me!" I shouted, lifting my arms in the air. "I am Hadrack of the Peshwin, and as is my right, I evoke a Tribal Challenge!" I pointed at Lorgen as his eyes widened in surprise. "I challenge this man's right to lead the Amenti!"

"What!?" Lorgen snapped. "What game is this?" I could hear the confused murmur of hundreds of voices as the Piths reacted to my words. "You sniveling, filthy Ganderman!" Lorgen Three-Fingers growled as he drew his sword.

"Wait!" Einhard cried. "Stay your hand, Three-Fingers." Einhard strode toward us, his face angry as he glared at me. "How dare you!" he boomed as he halted in front of me. The Sword backhanded me across the face without warning, and I staggered in surprise beneath the powerful blow. "I saved your life, you ungrateful bastard, and the thanks I got for it was betrayal! And now you come here with your tail between your legs, trying to save your sorry ass with this Tribal Challenge nonsense!"

I felt blood on my lips, and I spat redness on the ground as I straightened to face Einhard, my hand on my sword hilt. I wasn't sure if this was all part of Einhard's plan or if he was genuinely angry, but either way, his striking me had the desired effect. Now I was angry too. "So, when it serves your purpose, you claim I'm not a Peshwin," I said with a laugh. "But that certainly wasn't the case when I fought by your side." I pointed at Einhard. "It was you who spoke the sacred words years ago that welcomed me into your tribe. Do you remember that, Einhard? Words that you assured me made me a brother to all Peshwins for life, no matter what." Einhard glowered at me, though I thought I could see doubt in his good eye now. "I may have returned to Ganderland, brother," I said. "But that was not my choice in the beginning. I have not forgotten what it means to be a Peshwin, even though it seems that you have."

"Enough of this talk," Lorgen Three-Fingers grunted. He put his sword to my neck. "Your death will not be quick, Wolf. No, it won't be quick at all."

"You cannot dismiss my claim, Einhard," I said, ignoring the cold blade at my throat. "Just because you don't like what I have to say does not make it untrue."

"You are a Ganderman," Einhard replied dismissively. "And we are at war with you. That nullifies your claim."

"I was born a Flin first," I retorted. "Now I am both Gander and Peshwin, and nothing you say can change that." I raised my voice so that I could be heard by as many of the Piths as possible. "I have spent time in the Rutting Rings, honoring the souls of my brothers and sisters as they found the path to the Master. I have fought beside warriors just like you and shed blood for them, and they for me. I have been an Other-Mate to a wonderful Peshwin woman whom I loved, and I have shared drink and laughter with many good friends who viewed me as one of them." I paused and winked at the listening Piths. "And I have lost more silver fingers in ill-conceived bets to those same friends than I care to admit." I heard laughter at that as I turned back to Einhard. "So make no mistake, Einhard the Unforgiving. I am a Peshwin as much as you are, and my right to call a Tribal Challenge cannot be denied by you or anyone else."

I could hear more than one Pith voice shouting out that I was right and that Einhard should allow the challenge to go ahead.

"Do you deny any of what I have said?" I asked Einhard when he remained silent.

The Sword glowered at me. "I do not," he replied reluctantly.

"And would any Pith alive allow anyone other than a brother or sister into the Rutting Rings?"

"They would not," Einhard conceded.

"Which can only mean one thing," I said smugly.

Einhard scowled as he thought about my words, his hands on his hips. Finally, he glanced at Lorgen Three-Fingers. "Lower your sword, Lorgen," he said. "As much as it pains me, Hadrack is correct. He has the right to call for a Tribal Challenge."

Lorgen's face turned red with anger, while behind him, Nedo was shouting something at his father that I couldn't make out with all the raised voices around us. Three-Fingers pressed his sword harder against my neck as he leaned closer to me, his breath smelling like rotting meat. "I should spill your blood right now, whelp," he hissed.

Einhard wrapped his strong hand around Lorgen's wrist. "Save it for the challenge, Three-Fingers. His death is assured, but it must be done in accordance with the law."

I smiled at the Amenti chieftain as he reluctantly sheathed his sword. "Don't worry, old man," I said as Lorgen turned on his heels. Three-Fingers paused at my insult, his shoulders stiff with anger.

"You'll get your chance to kill me. As soon as I've dealt with your Blood Guard, I'm coming for you."

Not long after that, I found myself standing alone with Einhard in his tent. The moment the tent flap closed, the blond man was on me, sweeping me up in one of those crushing embraces that I recalled so well. "You figured it out!" Einhard said. He lifted me off the ground, laughing as he shook me. "I wasn't sure if you would understand."

"Would you mind putting me down?" I managed to say. Einhard might be older, but it seemed to me, if anything, the Pith was even stronger than I remembered.

Einhard set me down, still chuckling. He stepped back as he studied my face. "You've gotten older," he said.

I grinned. "Which means so have you."

Einhard laughed as he looked me up and down. "Not just older, but bigger too. Much bigger." His face turned serious. "I never really believed you opened those gates, you know."

"Never?" I asked.

Einhard turned and poured some wine into several tins, handing me one. "Well, maybe a little at first. I was bitter after our defeat at the pass, so yes, I'm ashamed to admit that I did think bad things about you and Jebido and Baine." He paused then to drink. "By the way, how are they? Do they still live?"

I nodded and hooked a thumb over my shoulder. "Alive and well and waiting in Gasterny for me."

Einhard chuckled. "So, all three of you back where it all started." He shook his head. "How the Master toys with us mere mortals. You can only laugh at His sense of humor. Either that or spend your days weeping about it."

I shifted the tin in my hands uncomfortably, not in the least bit thirsty. "Einhard, as much as I have missed you and want to catch up with you, I do have five men outside that need killing first. Perhaps we could talk about that?"

"Yes, yes, of course," Einhard said with a wave of his hand. He set his tin down on a bench behind him. "How much do you know about the challenge?"

I shrugged. "Only that I must face the Blood Guards first and that there will be no rest for me in between each bout."

"That's right," Einhard agreed. "Three-Fingers can decide on the order of the combatants, but you, as the challenger, get your choice of weapons."

"For each battle?"

"Yes," Einhard said with a nod. He took a moment to open the tent flap and look outside before he let it fall back into place. "We still have time. I recommend you change weapons after every fight. It won't help much, but at least you'll get a chance to catch your breath. Delay things as long as you can."

"The men that I'm fighting," I said. "Can you—"

"I can and I will," Einhard said. "My guess is Lorgen will send his Sword against you first. He knows he won't get to torture you now, which I imagine must be eating away at his insides. So, since he won't get to see you suffer the way that he thought, I expect he'll send his best against you first in hopes the challenge ends quickly. The Sword's name is Umar the Bleak. He's as unlikeable a bastard as you're likely to meet, but a master with the sword. I'm sure you can beat him, but it would take a long time, and you would undoubtedly be dealing with a wound or two afterward. You can't afford that. Lorgen will expect you to use your sword, so I recommend you fight him hand to hand. He's big and strong, but so are you. Just don't let him get his hands on you."

I nodded, remembering my battle with Hervi Desh. He had been big and strong too, and most likely a more experienced fighter hand to hand than this Umar the Bleak, but I had beaten him anyway.

"Once you kill Umar," Einhard said. "Lorgen will probably send out the Eye. His name is Yaar the Windy." Einhard paused at the look on my face. "His farts are legendary," he explained. "It's said they are so loud it can even drown out thunder." I grinned as Einhard continued, "Yaar is a crafty little bastard, fast and deadly with either a war hammer or an axe. But the man is only passable with a longsword, so he should be easy pickings for you."

"All right," I said. "Who's next?"

"The Ear, Manek the Quiet," Einhard said. "He's the oldest man you'll face today, but don't let that fool you. He's still got plenty of strength left, and he's as deadly as they come. The good news for you is he's not as fast as he used to be, so he shouldn't give you any trouble." Einhard glanced at my father's axe strapped to my back. "I'm pleased to see you still have that. Use it against Manek."

I nodded. "And the last one?" I asked.

"The Shield," Einhard said with a sigh. "His name is Dace the Fearless." Einhard looked at me appraisingly. "Knowing Lorgen, he'll keep Dace for last, just in case you manage to get that far. Dace is big and stupid, but he's also mean and knows no fear. He will be a formidable opponent."

"What are his weaknesses?" I asked.

Einhard frowned, then he shrugged. "There aren't any."

"Wonderful," I muttered. "Any suggestions on how I fight him then?"

Einhard smiled. "I would recommend carefully."

"Thanks a lot," I muttered. "And what about Lorgen? How do I fight him?"

"Shield and sword, strength against strength," Einhard said immediately. "Lorgen was a mighty warrior once, but his time in the sun is coming to a close, and you are just the man to send him into the darkness." We both looked up as someone scratched on the canvas from outside. "It's time to go," Einhard grunted.

"One last thing," I said. "What happens after I win?"

Einhard paused. "What do you mean?"

"What happens to my men inside Gasterny after I win this thing?"

Einhard smiled, his green eye twinkling as he pulled aside the tent flap. "After you win this challenge, my dear friend, your king will surrender the garrison to me. If he does not, then I will kill everyone inside just like I promised I would."

16: The Blood Guard

We stepped outside into bright sunlight, with a persistent breeze whistling around us that swayed the tips of the trees back and forth in the forest behind Einhard's tent. Piths on foot and horseback were massed all along the riverbank and to the west, encircling the cleared area where the challenge was to take place. Colorful banners of mixed reds, yellows, blues, and greens flew from lances, announcing the various tribes that had come north with Einhard. I recognized the Hardees stag banner, as well as the soaring hawk of the Lemisk, the charging bull of the Cimbrati, and the serpent banner of the Ralisin. There were others amongst the massed army that I didn't know as well—a three-headed boar, a pouncing wolf, and a strange sea creature with a spiked tail. But for every one of those banners, hundreds more depicted the rearing bear of the Amenti or the fire-breathing dragon of the Peshwin.

Einhard and I walked to the center of the clearing where Lorgen Three-Fingers and his four Blood Guard awaited us. Lorgen looked furious, though his baleful glare was fixed on Einhard, not on me for a change. The burn scars from the Ascension Ceremony weeks ago could still be seen in the grasses, though rich green shoots were already working hard to eradicate them.

"You set this entire thing up!" Lorgen shouted, pointing at Einhard as we approached. "This was your idea all along, not the whelp's!"

Einhard and I paused in front of the Amenti chieftain and the Sword smiled that dangerous smile of his. "I can't imagine what you mean, Three-Fingers," he said innocently.

I ignored the two men as they cut back and forth at each other with words, focusing instead on the Blood Guard. I recognized Umar the Bleak immediately. He was the biggest of the four men, and he had been the one who had carried the parlay branch for Lorgen Three-Fingers. An older warrior with long grey hair and a grey beard twisted into three points would be Manek the Quiet, I guessed. Beside him stood a small man with fine scars crisscrossing his face. He had several war hammers and axes in his belt, and I assumed he was Yaar the Windy.

The last man would be Dace the Fearless. He was almost as big as Umar, with long brown hair pleated down his back like a twisted horsetail. Dace just stared back at me blankly when he saw my gaze on him. He wore a cloak of bear fur around his shoulders, making him look even bigger, and he was moving impatiently from foot to foot, as though eager to get on with killing something. The dark pits of his eyes studied me emotionlessly, showing not even the slightest hint of humanity in them. I knew instinctively that Einhard was right. Of the four, Dace would be by far the most dangerous. I turned my attention back to what Einhard and Lorgen Three-Fingers were saying.

"You spoke with the whelp in your tent!" Lorgen said hotly as spittle flew from his mouth. "I want to know why?"

"We were catching up on old times," Einhard said with a shrug. "I already told you that. Besides, what does it matter what we talked about in there?"

"It matters," Lorgen growled, "because I think you're lying to me. I think you told this bastard how to fight against my men."

"Now, why would I want to do that?" Einhard asked. "We are both on the same side, aren't we?" The Sword paused as he cocked his head to one side. "Or are we? I mean, you have openly defied our queen more than once in the last few months. I have even heard rumors that you covet the crown for yourself."

"That's a lie," Lorgen snarled in protest, though I could see the guilt clearly in his eyes.

"Is it?" Einhard asked. "Did she not specifically order you to raid only and not attack in force until the Pathfinders had read the captives' blood properly? Of course she did. Yet you went against her orders for your own selfish reasons, which could have put the rest of us in jeopardy. So, now that I think about it, maybe I am starting to wonder if we really are on the same side."

Lorgen pointed at me, his eyes filled with rage. "That bastard gelded my son! What was I supposed to do?" The Amenti chieftain held his clenched fist up. "I had their king in my hand, Einhard. My plan to draw him here was a good one, and you know it."

"Yes, you did have their king," Einhard said dryly. "And then you let a few hundred Ganders snatch him right out from under your nose and take control of the garrison." Einhard gestured to Gasterny. "A building we already controlled. Now we have to lose valuable warriors to get it back. Warriors we will need. If you hadn't been so negligent and had left men to guard that garrison, none of this would have happened in the first place. So I suggest you put the blame for this where it belongs, on your shoulders."

Lorgen Three-Fingers scowled darkly. "Then, if we must go ahead with this farce, I reserve the right to choose weapons."

"No," Einhard said without hesitating. "As the challenged, you set the order of your fighters, nothing more."

Lorgen cursed. "But you told him what—"

"That will be enough!" Einhard snapped. "My patience with you is running thin, Lorgen. All of this is your doing, not mine, so accept that fact and get on with it."

Lorgen Three-Fingers took a deep breath, glancing at me once before finally nodding. "Very well, Einhard," he said bitterly. He started to turn away, then came back to stand in front of me. "But my men will not be wearing any armor," he said with a sneer. "So, if your pet Gander here has any honor at all, he will do the same."

"That will be his choice," Einhard said, though I noticed he gave me a worried look.

Lorgen smirked at me, his eyes alight with challenge. "What's it going to be, whelp?"

"Will you also be without armor when I face you?" I asked, holding his eyes. "Or is that just for men who are your betters?"

Lorgen's face flushed, while beside me, I could sense Einhard grinning. "You'll never get close to me, whelp," Lorgen Three-Fingers snarled. "My men will take you apart one piece at a time, and when they're done, I'll feast on your brains and shit you out the next morning."

"You do have a way with words," I said with mock admiration. "But you didn't answer my question. Will you be wearing armor when I kill you?"

"It won't happen, whelp," Lorgen snapped, looking irritated now. "But if it makes your knees stop knocking, then yes, I agree I won't wear armor either." He grinned. "My son and I are looking forward to this. Nedo wants your balls. I think he plans on hanging them off his saddle."

Lorgen turned then and strode stiffly away while Einhard and I shared a look. "You know what they're going to try to do, don't you?" Einhard said.

I nodded. "Yes."

"Then make sure you stay away from the bastards," Einhard said under his breath. "Good luck," he added as he made his way toward the center of the clearing. He raised his arms, waiting until the massed Piths began to quiet down. "Today," Einhard shouted. "We recognize the right of Hadrack of the Peshwin to a Tribal Challenge. As is the custom, Lorgen Three-Fingers, chieftain of the Amenti, will now present his first Blood Guard." Einhard had said to expect Umar the Bleak, but instead, Yaar the Windy stepped forward. He was wearing only a simple tunic now, with his hands free of weapons. If Einhard was surprised, he gave no sign of it as he looked to me. "As the challenger, Hadrack of the Peshwin will now choose his weapon of choice."

"Swords only," I said as I unsheathed my axe, then began to strip off my armor and mail.

"I'll hold that for you," I heard someone say. I turned to see Saldor behind me, indicating my father's axe that I'd balanced against my leg. I paused, then nodded and handed him the weapon. "It's beautiful," he said, running his fingers along the carved figures with appreciation.

"I was hoping you had survived," I told him as I undressed. I looked at him sideways. "You're too good a man to be with the Amenti, Saldor. You should join with Einhard when this is all over."

Saldor grinned. "I might just do that," he said. He lifted the axe to me in salute. "Strength to you, Hadrack of the Peshwin, and may the Master look down on you with favor."

"The Tribal Challenge will begin now!" Einhard shouted, motioning Saldor away as he stepped backward, leaving only Yaar and me in the clearing. "It will not end until either the challenger or the challenged are dead."

Yaar the Windy came at me then, moving fast like a pouncing cat as he jabbed a short sword no longer than my forearm at my gut. His choice of weapon caught me completely by surprise, and I retreated under his furious onslaught as he continued to stab and slash, trying to get past my guard. I had said swords, but I hadn't specified anything beyond that, so Yaar was well within his rights to use the smaller weapon. I just didn't understand why.

The little man was blazing fast, dancing forward and back, and side to side as I worked feverishly to fend off his attacks. He always remained just out of my reach, and as my frustration grew with each miss of my sword, I began to grasp why he'd chosen the smaller weapon. I couldn't hope to match his speed with my bulkier, heavier blade, which Yaar had clearly known, and all I was doing was wearing myself down for nothing. I decided to wait the warrior out, planting myself in the center of the clearing while the smaller man circled me warily. Finally, when the Pith realized that I wasn't going to chase him any longer, he started a series of lightning-like feints, jumping toward me, then spinning away as I slashed at empty air. Yaar grinned his scarred face at me each time I missed, calling me slow and stupid like a blind, pregnant cow. I tried not to let his goading get to me, telling myself to fight this battle my way, but with every failure to make contact, I could feel Yaar's words of scorn gnawing away even more at my insides.

"Come on, you big stupid ox," Yaar said, coaxing me with his hand as I missed him by a wide margin once again. "Surely you can do better than this? I'm right here. All you have to do is catch me."

I roared, having had more than enough of the other man's taunting. I abandoned my earlier strategy and charged, swinging Wolf's Head left, then right as I descended on him, hoping to catch the little man as he dodged to either side. But Yaar anticipated me, and he dropped to the ground, rolling easily away. I tried to stomp in his grinning face with my boot as he twisted past me, but he was much too fast. Yaar nimbly rose to his feet and he chuckled, then motioned for me to try again. I knew the Pith could do this all day if he had to, which he seemed more than willing to do. With four more men waiting to fight me, I didn't have that luxury. I needed to put the smug little bastard down right now.

I returned to the center of the clearing, catching my breath as I studied my opponent. Piths were pressed in all around us, arguing and shouting as bets were being doubled and tripled by the minute. Find his pattern, I told myself, trying to drown out all the noise as I concentrated. The answer lies there, somewhere. I started to advance on the Pith slowly, forcing him to retreat and only reacting to his feints defensively. I watched the lithe movements of his feet through hooded eyes, not wanting to give away my intent. Yaar took a step back, then a second and a third before he skipped to his left three steps. Then two steps to the right, followed by a feint, fast and straight for my midsection before leaping away. I swung Wolf's Head clumsily, expecting to miss, but needing to keep up appearances. I even cursed in frustration, which drew a scornful laugh. Then the Pith moved in a similar pattern a second time, then a third before I was sure. I had him.

I began to stalk Yaar then, swinging and missing like a madman. I snarled in mock rage when the Pith danced away yet again and then did a contemptuous pirouette, playing to the crowd. The warriors watching hooted and howled with delight, enjoying the show, but I kept my attention solely on Yaar. I paused, waiting as my opponent took three quick steps backward before taking one to the left, then another, and then a third. I tensed. Now he moved to his right, one step, then the second. The moment he took his second step, I dove forward in a tight ball, coming up with Wolf's Head held outstretched roughly at waist height. The blade of my sword caught Yaar in the middle of his forward feint, cutting through the muscle and sinew of his belly before punching out his back. The little man whimpered, dropping his short sword as he looked down in shock at the cold steel that had gutted him.

"But, how did—" Yaar started to say.

I stood and put my boot on Yaar's chest and shoved back hard. The little man tried to say more just as blood erupted from his mouth, choking him. Wolf's Head popped free from Yaar's torn flesh with a wet sucking sound as steaming entrails fell from him and splattered at my feet. Then the Pith fell on his back and lay still.

I could hear groans and curses echoing across the field as silver changed hands, but I didn't have time to celebrate. Two warriors were dragging Yaar's corpse away while Umar the Bleak stepped forward, his eyes dark with purpose.

"Choice of weapons, Hadrack?" Einhard called out.

"No weapons," I responded, gratified to see Umar's features cloud with doubt for a moment. I tossed my sword to Saldor. "Just these," I said as I held up my hands.

"Then fight," Einhard commanded.

Umar advanced on me, his shoulders hunched, his balled fists held low by his hips. I grinned. This was more like it. I lowered my head and charged forward, catching the other man by surprise as I butted him in the stomach with the top of my head. I heard Umar gasp as air exploded from his lungs, and we fell awkwardly, with me lying on top of the warrior. I swung a fist for his head, my knuckles cracking against the other man's forehead. I felt pain shoot up my arm, afraid for a moment that I had broken my hand, but I didn't have time to worry about it as Umar flipped me off him with a grunt. He leaped to his feet, bellowing with rage, trying to cave in my skull with his boot. I twisted aside and rose, then ducked a wild swing. I dropped to one knee and punched as hard as I could with my aching hand, praying it wasn't broken as I caught Umar in the stomach. The Pith staggered backward, his eyes wide as he tried to draw in air. I didn't let him as I hit him again, this time using the edge of my other hand as I chopped savagely with it against Umar's vulnerable throat. The Pith's eyes fluttered, and he raised both his hands to his neck as I grabbed him by the hair, dragging his face down to meet my uplifting knee. Umar's nose shattered instantly, blood spraying over both me and the watching Piths as the big man collapsed, lying motionless on the ground. I stood over him, breathing heavily as the Piths started to cheer. I could hear some of them shouting for me to finish him. It seemed Umar was not a popular man. The big Pith's eyes were closed, but his chest was still moving, and I could hear a high-pitched wheezing coming from his mouth. I hesitated, flexing my injured hand as I stared at it. The little finger felt odd, pinching when I made a fist, but nothing seemed broken.

"You must finish him, Hadrack," Einhard said.

I nodded, not relishing this part, but it needed to be done. I sought out Lorgen Three-Fingers where he stood among his people, his face now the color of ash. I held the Amenti chieftain's eyes while I placed my boot on Umar's neck, then I stood, forcing all my weight down hard until I heard a satisfying crack. I stepped off the dead man and pointed at Three-Fingers. "How are your knees holding up, Lorgen?" I asked mockingly. I cupped a hand to my ear. "Because from where I stand, it sure sounds like they are knocking together to me!"

I made my way back to Saldor as Manek the Quiet entered the clearing. The grey-bearded warrior was perhaps Jebido's age, maybe slightly older. He'd taken off his tunic, revealing a sleek upper torso covered with battle scars and thick grey hair. The Pith's arms were heavily muscled, with his right forearm marred by a livid purple scar where something with teeth had latched on to him.

"Weapons?" Einhard asked, looking at me.

"Axes," I said as I held out my hand to Saldor for my father's axe.

"Better be clear about that this time," Saldor whispered as he handed me the weapon. "Manek is very good with one-handed axes."

I held up my father's axe to Einhard. "Two-handed axes," I added.

"Two-handed it is," Einhard acknowledged.

An Amenti held out an axe similar to mine to Manek. The older man took it, spinning it in his hands easily as he watched me with experienced and calm eyes. There would be no panic or mistakes coming from this one, I knew. I moved forward slowly, and so did he, until we met roughly ten feet apart in the middle of the clearing. Yaar had tried to use his speed on me, and it had failed, and now I would do the same thing to Manek, preferably with a different outcome.

I held the shoulder of the shaft just below the twin blades with my right hand, the pommel with my left. I lunged forward without warning with the butt-end of the shaft, hoping to catch Manek by surprise. The older man blocked me easily with the haft of his axe, then jammed his elbow hard into my face, staggering me. I felt my nose flatten as coppery-tasting blood filled my mouth. I shook my head to clear the sudden tears streaming from my eyes as I retreated, spitting blood. Manek came after me, sensing he had me as he swung his great axe in front of him like a scythe, trying to disembowel me. I snarled, dodging a slash that tore open my tunic yet somehow left the skin beneath it undamaged, then I hooked my blade on his and dragged the older man toward me. I had Manek suddenly off-balance, and I smashed my forehead into his nose, bloodying him now.

"Two can play that game," I grunted as we broke apart.

Manek grinned, showing surprisingly good teeth that were stained red with blood. "It does seem only fair."

I laughed despite the situation, finding myself liking the old bastard. "I killed your brothers without a second thought," I said as we circled each other. "But I'm actually going to feel bad about killing you. I think we could have been friends if not for this."

Manek chuckled. "That's funny, youngster. I was about to say the same thing about you."

He came at me then, roaring as he swung for my head. I was expecting it, and I ducked, then spun in a crouch, bringing my axe around fast and hard. The blade edge sliced open Manek's right boot at his calf, tearing a gaping wound in his flesh as it passed. I was off-balance from the swing, and the momentum of the axe pulled me to the ground as the old man screamed in pain above me. But even wounded, Manek saw me vulnerable, and he lifted his axe for the killing blow. I knew I couldn't bring my weapon up in time, and desperate, I dropped my axe and clutched the haft of his with both hands, stopping the descending blade inches away from my face. Manek cursed at me as he pushed down with all his weight, with warm saliva dripping from his open mouth splashing on my face. But, for all his experience as a warrior, I was younger and stronger than Manek. I twisted my body sharply as I held onto the haft, flipping him off his feet. Then I rolled on top of him as we fought for control of the axe. Slowly, ever so slowly, I gained that control until I had the wooden shaft pressed tightly against Manek's neck.

The older man was wheezing now, fighting to breathe as I leaned down and whispered in his ear, "I am sorry, brother," I said, meaning it. "I wish there was another way."

Manek's face was turning purple, his eyes bulging as he desperately tried to break my hold, but I had position on him, and I weighed more than he did, so there was nothing that he could do. Finally, once it was over, I stood above the old warrior's body as I slowly looked around at the now silent Piths.

"The Master will rejoice this day," I said to them, my chest heaving as I tossed Manek's axe aside. "For now, he will have a great warrior to sit by his side to drink beer and swap lies with until the end of time."

The Piths cheered then, and I could hear my name being chanted by many of the Peshwin as I stooped to pick up my axe before I walked slowly back to Saldor. I handed him the weapon, wiping the blood from my face as Dace the Fearless stepped into the clearing. "Any advice?" I asked the Cimbrati as I studied the Pith. The big warrior was dressed in a white tunic that hung down over his trousers. His face was blank, looking almost bored, but his eyes were molten pits of hatred.

"Don't die," Saldor said with a straight face.

I chuckled and nodded as I held my hand out for Wolf's Head. "That's sound advice, brother. Sound advice indeed." I turned to Einhard before he could ask. "Swords," I said. "The really long kind with the pointy end," I added, just to be clear.

Laughter arose at that, and I waited as Lorgen Three-Fingers pressed a broadsword into Dace's hand. The Amenti chieftain said something into the big Pith's ear, rubbing his back, and the warrior nodded, his face set in stone.

"Begin," Einhard called.

Dace the Fearless stalked toward me purposefully, his sword held low by his side. He struck without hesitating the moment he was in range, growling low in his chest as I blocked his blade. I felt the vibration of the collision all the way to my shoulder, and I realized the Pith was enormously strong. Dace swung a second time, his face showing no emotion, and again I blocked him, feeling that familiar shock to my arm. But this time, Dace lashed out with a boot at the same time, catching me in the chest. I stumbled backward into the mass of Piths watching and cheering behind me, and several of them shoved me forward, right back toward the oncoming warrior. I ducked as his blade brushed the top of my head, and I stabbed at the big man's leg, gratified to hear him grunt as the tip punctured his thigh. That was the only reaction I got from Dace though, and even as dark blood started to seep through his trousers, the warrior came after me with the same expression on his face.

I moved back, crouched and ready as Dace attacked with single-minded determination. The Pith warrior was hugely strong and unswervingly focused, but as the fight progressed, I realized that even though his swordcraft was very good, mine was better. I could beat this man. I just needed to be patient and careful until the right opening appeared. We fought back and forth across the clearing in silence, with the cheers of the Piths and the persistent clash of steel on steel the only sounds as we both searched for the momentary opening that would end a man's life.

Dace finally took an impatient backhanded swing at my face and missed, but that miss left him open and vulnerable for a heartbeat. That's all I needed. I swooped in, raking Wolf's Head down across his chest. The big man staggered from the blow, and he grunted as blood began to well up from the rent in his tunic. Dace paused to look down at the seeping wound, and then he cursed—the first words I had heard from him—before he attacked again. I parried an overhand strike, then a second as I gave ground, our blades ringing before I took the offensive, pressing the big Pith backward. Both of us were gasping for air now, and I could see blood dripping freely onto the grass from the Pith's wounds. I knew sooner or later the bastard would have to weaken.

Our blades met again, locking, and I twisted my wrists to get above his sword just as Jebido had taught me, using brute strength to force his weapon down and around, hoping to disarm him with a quick sideways motion. But Dace was a strong man, and he held on stubbornly as we struggled until finally he used his shoulder as a battering ram to knock me away. I stumbled back three paces, expecting him to keep coming, but the big Pith hesitated, and I saw the first sign of an actual expression cross his face. It looked like confusion. Dace blinked and wiped at his eyes, wobbling as his sword wavered. I grinned. The bastard had lost too much blood.

I waited just in case it was a ploy, but I guessed by the tense look on Lorgen Three-Fingers' face that it was not. His man was finished, and he knew it. Dace dropped to his knees, the sword in his hand falling limply to the ground, his eyes lowered. I cautiously approached and kicked his weapon away.

"You fought well," I said as I stood over the defeated Pith. "You have honored your tribe."

Dace looked up then and he smiled black teeth at me. "Honor has no place here," he spat. His eyes were full of hate and triumph as a knife suddenly appeared in his hand.

The wounded Pith lunged at me, heedless of my sword as his knife came for my face. I tried to twist away, but I wasn't fast enough, and I felt the sting of the blade as it raked along my skin, just missing my eye as it cut open my cheek. I cursed and fell backward as blood spurted while shouts of anger and protest arose from the watching Piths. Dace was on his feet, no sign of weakness now as he bellowed and barrelled toward me, his arms outstretched.

The bastard had deliberately aimed for my eye, I realized—not to win, but to cripple me enough that Lorgen could finish me off under the law. I felt an overwhelming rage take over me, and I brought Wolf's Head up and around as the big man ran at me, lopping off his right hand that held the knife. The warrior screamed in shock, gaping at me as dark blood began to gush from the stump. I didn't hesitate, and I rammed my sword's hilt into his blood-covered chest. The Pith fell to his knees as I quickly reversed Wolf's Head and struck again, taking the warrior's left hand this time.

Dace was sobbing now as I kicked him contemptuously onto his back. Then I started to work on him, cutting and slashing with fury as I took his feet one at a time, then his arms at the elbows, then at the shoulders. Dace had long since fallen silent as I worked, and he was probably dead by now, but I didn't care. I hacked and cut with a savage, single-minded rage as thousands of Piths watched in somber, awed silence. I kept slipping and falling in the bright red blood as I dismembered Dace limb by limb, but it didn't stop me. I don't think anything could have. Finally, there was nothing left to chop off the blood-drenched torso other than Dace's head. I stood, panting over what was left of the Pith warrior, my sword crimson and dripping. I spit in contempt on Dace's corpse, and then I took his head with one swing of my sword. I stooped and picked up the decapitated head by the hair and held it in the air.

"You see this, you bastard!?" I screamed at Lorgen as I shook the grisly remains at him. "This is the fate that awaits you, too!" I whirled the head by the hair, then threw it as Piths dodged aside. The gory missile landed three feet from Lorgen Three-Fingers, and I laughed at the look of dismay on the chieftain's face as he stared down at it. I stumbled back to Saldor, then turned and waited, my chest heaving.

"You truly are a Pith," Saldor whispered beside me in admiration.

"That's what I've been trying to say all along," I gasped. Several warriors started to drag Dace's torso and whatever else of him that they could find from the blood-soaked ground, giving me a much-needed moment to catch my breath. I glanced at my heavy rectangular shield where it lay in the grass. Einhard had said to fight Lorgen with sword and shield, but using the Gander one felt like a mistake to me. I had won over many of the Piths today, I knew, but fighting with something so obviously Gander might turn whatever good-will they now felt for me away. "I'll need a Pith shield," I said to Saldor. "I can't fight with mine."

Saldor nodded in understanding as he unstrapped his shield from his back and held it out to me. "I would be honored, brother, if you would accept this one."

"The honor is mine, brother," I replied, accepting the round shield with gratitude. Lorgen Three-Fingers reluctantly entered the clearing, already looking like a beaten man as he flexed his hands impotently by his sides while he awaited my choice of weapons. "Swords and shields," I called out to Einhard. "We end this like warriors with swords and shields."

Einhard nodded. "So be it," he said. "Swords and shields it is."

Nedo appeared with a yellow and red shield, as well as a sword. The youth said something briefly to his father as he handed him the weapons, then he gave me a baleful glare before stepping away from the clearing. The wound on my cheek was still bleeding, and I was having trouble breathing from my nose, but other than that, I felt in surprisingly good shape. I strode toward Lorgen Three-Fingers, brimming with confidence.

"Come, old man," I grunted. I smashed Wolf's Head on my shield. "Let's finish this."

The battle that followed did not last long. Lorgen Three-Fingers, for all his brave talk, proved to be a slow and unimaginative fighter. I could see before even the first blow was struck that the man had accepted his fate and his heart just wasn't in it. Lorgen had dishonored his people by putting that knife under Dace's tunic, and he knew that even if he managed to kill me, his tribe would no longer accept him as their chieftain. The Piths had a code of conduct when it came to man-to-man combat, and Lorgen had broken that code in a way that could never be forgiven. To this day, I can't understand why he did it, as he had to have known what the consequences would be, even if he had won.

When the deed was finally done, and Lorgen Three-Fingers lay dead, I dropped my sword and shield and fell to my knees in the center of the clearing. I closed my eyes as the Piths cheered me. I had won the Tribal Challenge, and with it, control of the Amenti tribe. But what was I going to do with that control? Would the savage warriors actually follow and obey me? I had no idea, and at the moment, I didn't even care. I just wanted to stay where I was and not move.

I heard a sudden commotion in front of me and I opened my eyes wearily. Nedo was running toward me with a sword clutched in his hand, his eyes mad with hatred. I reached for Wolf's Head desperately, already knowing that I was going to be too late. Then Nedo grunted as a thrown lance caught him in the belly. The youth staggered backward, letting go of his sword as he clutched at the haft of the lance with both hands before dropping to his knees.

"You bastard," Nedo managed to gasp out at me before he fell sideways and lay still.

A shadow fell over me and I looked up at Einhard's grinning face. "You owe me a life, puppy."

17: Calban

I rode Angry back toward Gasterny, the big black picking his way slowly through the fields as I tried to come up with a way around Einhard's demands. We were to surrender the garrison within the hour, and if we did that everyone inside it would be allowed to go home—everyone except King Tyden, that is. If we did not surrender, then the Piths would attack tomorrow morning with no quarter given. Einhard had promised me that he wouldn't kill the king and only keep him as a hostage, but I had little faith that he was being truthful about that. The Sword had not been able to protect Clendon the Peacemaker during the battle of Victory Pass, and I was certain that failure still weighed heavily on him. Killing Tyden in revenge for that failure would undoubtedly take away some of the sting of defeat, not to mention leaving our kingdom leaderless and ripe for the plucking.

I had briefly considered telling Einhard about Pernissy and First Son Oriell and what I believed would happen should Tyden die. But I knew if I did that, my words would fall on deaf ears, so I said nothing. I think my friend would have just found the predicament amusing anyway. The first thing that I did after being acclaimed chieftain of the Amenti was make Saldor my Sword—I could think of no man better suited for the job. He wasn't an Amenti, of course, but crossing over into other tribes because of marriage or opportunity was not that unusual for Piths, so he had readily accepted. I had hoped to use the Amenti to nullify Einhard's threat of sacking the garrison, but Saldor had quickly dashed that hope. He'd talked it over with some of the older warriors of the tribe, and though they had agreed my right to lead them could not be disputed, they had refused to side with Ganders over Piths in any way, even for me. However, the one concession Saldor did get from them was that if an attack on Gasterny became necessary, then out of respect for my position, the Amenti would not participate. It wasn't much of a victory, but it was better than nothing.

I could see the fortress's ramparts were lined with men as I drew closer, and could hear their faint cheers as they recognized me. They couldn't have possibly known what had occurred in the Pith camp from such a distance, so my appearance must have been a huge relief. Men began hugging each other and waving banners, some even dancing a jig as they lifted their weapons in salute to me. I couldn't help but smile wearily at the sight. Enjoy it while it lasts, I thought, the smile quickly fading.

The drawbridge slowly lowered to accept me back, creaking and clanking until it landed with a thump on the dirt ramp. I guided Angry across the bridge and through the barbican as men appeared on either side of me, tugging at my legs and boots as they sung my praises. Several of the braver men even attempted to pet Angry, which drew the predictable response. The stallion showed his displeasure by butting those men aside and narrowly missing another with his teeth before the joyful soldiers finally moved back to a safer distance.

I entered the outer bailey as Jebido rushed over to me and quite literally yanked me down from the big horse's back. Men began to press in close all around me, laughing and cheering as I felt rough hands slapping me in congratulations.

"See," Jebido shouted in my ear, grinning broadly as we embraced. "I told you if you listened to my advice, everything would be fine."

I laughed and kissed my friend on the head, then rifled his sweat-streaked hair as Baine, Fitz, and others came to embrace me. Some of the soldiers began to sing, standing arm in arm, while others threw their helmets in the air.

"Praise be to Lord Hadrack!" a man shouted from the watchtower.

"Praise to the Wolf!" another called, his fist raised. "Killer of Piths!"

Men on the ramparts began chanting my name then, which was soon taken up by almost everyone in the garrison. I found myself looking down at the ground in embarrassment, and finally, I pulled Baine closer to me so that he could hear. "Where is the king?" I asked.

"In the keep waiting for you with Lord Vestry," Baine responded. "He wanted the men to have the honor of welcoming you back first."

I nodded, then pushed my way through the crowd toward the keep.

"What's wrong?" Jebido asked, his features serious now as he fell in beside me. "I know that look on your face. Something is wrong."

I waited to answer him until we were all seated in our familiar places around the king's table, away from the noise and celebrations continuing outside. Then I told them in as few words as possible about the challenge, finishing with Einhard's demand that we surrender and hand over the king. Tyden sat at the head of the table listening as I talked, his hands clasped together in front of him on the worn wood.

"Well, that's that, then," Tyden finally said once I was finished. He looked tired, I thought, but even so, I could see a steely resolve burning in his eyes. His jaw was set in determination, something that I had become familiar with when his mind was made up. I knew Tyden planned on agreeing to Einhard's terms, but I had no intention of letting him, regardless of what he said.

"But I thought you told us this man was your friend?" Lord Vestry said to me, unable to keep the whine from his voice.

"He is my friend," I said. "But it's a complicated relationship."

Lord Vestry rolled his eyes. "Complicated? You lied to us, Lord Hadrack. You said the heathen would let us go if you won."

"He never said that!" Jebido snapped, rising to his feet in my defense. He pointed at me. "Look at him. He's covered in blood and half dead. This is a man who risked his life for us with no guarantees about what would happen afterward. It was a damn good try, and I know the bards will sing about it for generations, but in the end, it didn't change anything. So now all we can do is send those bastards out there a message with swords and shields that they will never forget before we die."

"We will not fight," Tyden said firmly. "I will turn myself over to Einhard as he has asked. That way, the rest of you can go free and organize a proper defense of the kingdom. I will not allow Ganderland to fall to these people. Not for any reason."

Everyone around the table instantly burst out protesting—all except Lord Vestry, that is, who had suddenly found something under a fingernail to take his attention away.

"That is not an option, Highness," I said just as firmly as the king had. "We all leave here together, or not at all."

"There is little choice, Lord Hadrack," Tyden said, sounding calm and relaxed. "Believe me when I tell you I have little desire to fall into the hands of those heathens a second time. But I will not sacrifice the lives of everyone else in this garrison, only to be captured in the end anyway." He looked at me and smiled. "Besides, they had me once before and you rescued me, so perhaps it can be done again."

"I have a better idea," Fitz said, looking around the table. "What if I go in the king's place?" Fitz held up his hands as both Tyden and I started to protest. "Listen to me, please." He waited until we had quieted down. "Think about it. Most of the Piths don't know what you look like, Highness. If you send me instead, you can get away before they realize we tricked them. If we stay and fight, then everyone sitting here knows what will happen. We will lose Gasterny one way or the other, but at least this way, you will be safe. It's the only option there is that has any chance of success."

"It won't work," I said with a shake of my head. I gestured toward Tyden. "Einhard saw him, and many of the Amenti know what he looks like as well."

Fitz snorted. "And what did Einhard see, Hadrack?" I opened my mouth to respond, but the lord didn't let me. "I'll tell you what he saw. He saw a young king leaning over the battlements with the sun above him dressed in armor and wearing a helmet." Fitz laughed. "As for the Amenti, they have a new chieftain now, I understand.

One who can tell them to keep their mouths shut. Besides, the last time most of those warriors saw his Highness, he was naked and riding a pony backwards." I saw Tyden flush at that as Fitz continued, "We are of the same build and close to the same age, so put me in the king's armor, and there is a good chance that no one will know the difference between us until it's too late." He winked and smiled. "Sometimes, people see exactly what they expect to see, Hadrack."

"It might work," Lord Vestry said thoughtfully. "But if I were you, Lord Fitzery, I would send one of your men in your place. No need to subject yourself to who knows what when a commoner will suffice to pull off this ruse."

Fitz stared at Lord Vestry with contempt. "Even if I chose to do that, lord, which I do not, I'd wager even a Pith heathen could quickly tell the difference between a nobleman and a common soldier."

Tyden sighed. "While I appreciate the offer, Lord Fitzery, I must, in all gratitude, refuse it."

"Nonsense," Fitz grunted. "It's the only way." The king's face turned dark as the young lord hurried to continue, "I mean no disrespect, Your Highness. But I have watched as Hadrack has willingly sacrificed himself more than once to save your life. Now the time has come for me to do the same. We need a man of nobility to play the part, and since Hadrack obviously cannot do it, and Lord Vestry is much too old, that leaves me as the only logical choice."

"They might kill you, Fitz," I said, torn between the need to keep Tyden safe and my concern for the young lord. "Even though Einhard is my friend, I can't guarantee your safety once he has you."

Fitz waved a hand dismissively. "If that is to be my fate, then so be it. I'm tired of letting you have all the glory. I have to say you're a little selfish in that respect, Hadrack. All I ask in return is the rest of you raise a mug to me before you send these heathens back to their lands with their tails between their legs."

It was an impassioned speech, spoken with eloquence and tempered by logic, and though we tried to poke holes in that logic, in the end, we all concluded that it really was our best and only chance. After that, there was little any of us could say except offer Fitz our thanks and admiration, then prepare for the handover of our imposter king and Gasterny. Would Einhard be fooled and believe Lord Fitzery was actually the king? I wasn't certain at first, but once the young lord was dressed in Tyden's freshly polished armor with a red cape embroidered with gold, my confidence was bolstered somewhat. We even hammered out a crude crown from a shattered breastplate for Fitz to wear since the king's had been lost in the battle at the bridge.

We met Einhard, Saldor, and two other Piths that I didn't know outside the walls of Gasterny less than half an hour later. The four warriors waited in a line, sitting silently on their horses as they watched us approaching. Einhard's expression was devoid of emotion, showing neither suspicion nor satisfaction at our surrender. I wondered what was going through his mind. Had he already seen through our ploy and was just waiting to vent his anger once we were close enough? Or did he just see a king riding toward him the way that we wanted? I tried to keep my expression as neutral as Einhard's, though inside, my stomach was churning.

Baine and Jebido rode to either side of me, their faces dark and serious. I had brought them along in hopes of distracting Einhard so that he wouldn't focus too much on Fitz, who was riding Tyden's white mare to Jebido's right. The young lord sat his horse as straight as an arrow, with his nose in the air and his cape wrapped tightly about him. His battered and tarnished crown barely reflected the sunlight, but even so, I thought he looked every bit the part of a king. Someone had found one of Tyden's torn and frayed eagle banners and had draped it under the mare's saddle, where it hung down to either side, flapping in the wind.

"So," Einhard said as we stopped in front of him. He smiled. "I'm glad to see that common sense has not been completely bred out of the king's of Ganderland just yet."

"You have won for the moment, heathen," Fitz said with scathing contempt. I had to suppress a smile of my own. He even sounded like Tyden. "But don't get too comfortable in your victory, dog.

There will be dark days ahead for you and your rabble soon enough, mark my words."

Einhard grinned. "I'll try to remember that, Your Highness," he said before focusing on Jebido. "It's good to see you after so long, old friend."

"I wish I could say the same thing," Jebido grunted back.

"Still the same old Jebido, I see," Einhard said with a laugh. He shifted his gaze to Baine. "But this one is different now." Einhard stroked his beard thoughtfully as he studied my friend. "I recall a boy full of laughter and mischief. But that boy is gone, it seems, and a man has taken his place." Einhard inclined his head slightly toward Baine. "A man who has seen both pain and death, I would guess, and has clearly beaten both."

"Pain can always be beaten," Baine said, his eyes dark and threatening. "But death comes for us all." Baine smiled, but there was no humor in it. "Even for you, Einhard the Unforgiving." The last time I had seen Baine's eyes look that way, he'd been describing how he had found the informant who'd told the imposter Outlaw of Corwick about our gold stash under the floorboards at Witbridge Manor. I had been saddened to learn that Ira, the eldest son of Ermos, the village blacksmith, had betrayed that information. I had liked the youth and had been grooming him to join our band.

Einhard and Baine stared at one another for a moment longer, and then the Pith leader broke the spell as he switched his gaze back to Fitz again. "Your Highness," he said, gesturing to the east. "If you would be so good as to accompany my men to my camp, then we can get on with the important business of sending your soldiers back to their homes and wives."

"Very well," Fitz said with a sniff. He edged his horse forward as the two Pith warriors moved to either side of him, one of them grabbing hold of the mare's reins.

"Remember, Lord Hadrack," Fitz called out as the three men rode off. "Don't forget to raise that mug to me." Then he turned away, staring forward at the Pith camp as they cantered across the field.

"What was that about?" Einhard asked.

I guided Angry as close to Einhard's horse as I dared, afraid the big black would lash out at the other animal. "The king is convinced you are going to kill him," I said. "I told him you promised me his life would be safe, but he doesn't believe it." I paused, letting Einhard see the threat in my eyes. "I gave the king my word that if you lied to me, then nothing will stop me from avenging his death, not even our friendship."

"Well," Einhard said with a chuckle. "I guess I'd better not let anything happen to him, then." We sat there for a moment longer, and then the Sword sighed as he turned his horse. "You have two hours to clear your men from the garrison, Hadrack. If anyone is still inside after that, they will die." He hesitated as sudden sadness crossed his features. "I hope we never meet on the battlefield, my friend. I truly do. You are like a blood brother to me."

"I feel the same way," I said, fighting to control my emotions. "But if we do meet, I won't let that stop me from killing you."

Einhard grinned, the sadness gone now as the confident warrior returned. "I didn't think it would. Neither will I." Then he kicked his horse into motion, galloping away.

Baine, Jebido, and I watched him go, and it took me a moment to realize that Saldor was still with us. "Aren't you going with him?" I asked the Cimbrati.

"I am," Saldor said. He turned to watch Einhard's retreating form. "He will be furious with you once he realizes."

"Realizes what?" I asked innocently.

Saldor grinned and shrugged as he turned his horse to follow after Einhard. "Nothing, Hadrack the Wolf. Nothing at all."

Three days later, Baine, Jebido, and me, accompanied by the king dressed as a common archer, crossed over the bridge leading to Camwick. We had left Lord Vestry in charge of the rest of the men and had pressed on ahead just the four of us, intent on putting as much distance between King Tyden and the Piths as possible. The fear of Einhard coming after us had receded after the first day, but I knew I wouldn't be able to relax until Tyden was safely behind the walls of Corwick Castle.

The town of Camwick seemed quiet, almost somber as we entered, with the normally busy streets practically deserted. Only a few shopkeepers and merchants were out hawking their wares, all of them women, I noted. Even they seemed to be just going through the motions, as there were few if any customers. In fact, as I looked around, I saw nothing but females except for an old man with one leg hobbling with a crooked staff down a side street.

"What's this all about?" Jebido muttered uneasily.

I paused Angry when I saw a familiar face. "Trula," I called out. The girl turned, a basket in her hands. Trula was a weaver specializing in caps, laces, and tassels. Shana had used her services on more than one occasion. "Where is everyone?"

"Why, gone to join the call to arms, my lord," she said as though it were obvious.

I blinked at her in bafflement. Tyden had taken some of the young men of the town with him when we marched on the Piths, but the survivors I had sent back weeks ago should have returned by now. I didn't see them or any of the older men either.

"Who issued the call to arms?" I demanded.

"Why, Lady Shana did, my lord."

I could feel my mouth opening in astonishment and I had to force it closed. "Where is she, Trula?" I asked, feeling anxious now.

The girl pointed to the castle in the distance. "Up there, I expect, my lord."

I cursed under my breath, then urged Angry through the empty streets at a gallop as the others followed closely behind me. We left the town behind and climbed the road to the castle, where Ubeth awaited us in the outer bailey.

"My Lord!" the bald gatekeeper said, looking relieved when he saw me. "I'm glad you're back."

I quickly dismounted, and Ubeth's breath caught in his throat when he saw Tyden as he jumped to the ground. The gatekeeper dropped to one knee. "Your Highness," he said in awe.

Tyden clapped him on the shoulder. "On your feet, there's a good lad."

"It's an honor, Your Highness," Ubeth said as he stood. "I saw you and your brother once years ago when your father came to visit Lord Corwick."

"Ah," Tyden said. "I remember that visit. I almost went mad with boredom."

"My Lord!"

I turned to see Putt hurrying toward me, his face twisted with anxiety. Something was very wrong.

"What's happened, Putt?" I demanded. "Is Shana all right?"

Putt's eyes dropped. "My Lord, I think it best that you hear it from the lady herself."

I put my hand on Putt's shoulder and squeezed, ignoring the look of pain on the red-haired man's face. "You'll tell me now, Putt, or you can find other employment."

Putt nodded, not able to meet my eyes. "I am truly sorry, my lord, but the baby didn't make..." He trailed off weakly as I groaned, feeling as if I had just been kicked in the stomach. "She's all right, though, my lord," Putt hastened to add. "Perfectly fine, but—"

"But what?" I growled.

Putt took a deep breath. "But that's not all, my lord. Calban has fallen." I just gaped at him, not certain that I'd heard correctly.

"How?" I heard Jebido whisper in disbelief behind me. "How could the Piths have gotten that far north?"

Putt glanced at him reluctantly. "It wasn't the Piths, Jebido," he said.

"Tell me," I grunted low and harsh. I felt unsteady on my feet, overwhelmed by all the bad news, but I could tell by Putt's expression that there was still more to come.

Putt took a deep breath. "Cardians came by sea, my lord," he explained. "They were masquerading as Afrenian silk traders. By the time anyone suspected anything was amiss, it was too late."

I closed my eyes in dismay, knowing that if I hadn't drawn men away from the castle, Calban would not have fallen. "Who led them," I demanded, certain even as I said the words what the answer would be.

"Lord Boudin," Putt responded. He hesitated. "And that bastard Pernissy was with him as well, my lord."

18: Daughter Gernet and the Truth

I was told that Lady Shana was meeting with Wiflem, Finol, and several other of my senior men in Corwick Hall. She clearly hadn't been made aware of my arrival yet, and her face was set with intensity and determination as she leaned over a table, studying several maps while Wiflem talked. Shana looked up at the sound of our boots as we strode into the hall, and I saw her body sag with relief when she saw me.

"Hadrack!" Shana cried out. She was dressed in a man's light mail tunic, thick woolen trousers, and heavy leather boots. I was surprised to see a short sword belted around her waist as well. Shana ran to me, unashamed as she flung herself into my arms. I held her, pressing my lips to hers, while around us, men smiled or looked politely away. Shana finally broke the embrace, her hands clasped around mine as she looked up at me.

"You lost the baby," I blurted out before she could say anything. No one has ever accused me of being discreet, and I instantly regretted my words, cursing myself for being a complete fool. Shana blinked in surprise, her face falling. I could see she was fighting back sudden tears and I cursed myself yet again. "Putt told me," I hurried to explain as I gently rubbed the smooth, lily-white skin that covered the back of her hands. "I am so sorry, my love."

Shana fought to control her emotions, and finally, she nodded, her features etched in sadness and regret. "So am I, Hadrack. But now is not the time to talk of it. There will be time for that later when we are alone and can grieve properly." She withdrew her hands from mine and turned, gesturing to the men standing around the table. "I was in the process of preparing an army to go to your aid."

I couldn't help but smile despite the somber moment. I shook my head in admiration, understanding the armor and sword she wore now. "You were going to lead men into battle to rescue us from the Piths?" I asked.

"And why not?" Shana demanded, her blue eyes flashing. Nothing got Shana's fire burning more than being dismissed simply because she was a woman. I hadn't meant it that way, of course, but if her sudden anger at my words helped deflect her sadness away from our dead child for a time, then I would gladly accept it. "You would do the same for me," Shana added, her chin lifted in challenge.

"Well, that's true," I agreed. "It's lucky for the Piths that they decided to let us go. I wouldn't have envied them having to face you on the field of battle." I gestured to Tyden, who stood behind me, still dressed in a worn, stuffed doublet, filth-stained trousers, and grey stockings. "We had to surrender Gasterny to Einhard of all people, but the king is alive and well."

Shana gasped in surprise as she dropped to one knee while the men around the table did likewise. "Your Highness," she said. "My apologies, I did not see you standing there."

"Hello, cousin," Tyden said with a wry grin. He stepped forward and lifted Shana to her feet before embracing her warmly. "I had thought I would never get to see your beautiful face again, Lady Shana. But The Mother has other plans, it seems." The king glanced at me. "As does my protector, Lord Hadrack." Then his face turned serious. "Tell me what has happened at Calban, cousin."

"We had only just arrived at the castle, Highness," Shana said, her face clouding. "It was less than a week after we left Corwick, I think." She glanced at Putt, who nodded. "A trading ship arrived from the north, claiming to be from Afrenia. We had little reason to doubt their story, since the ship was laden with silk, so we allowed them to dock to replenish their supplies. The traders came late in the day and as is the norm, asked to stay the night."

"And they opened the gates for the others," I said as I stood with my arms crossed over my chest, listening. The quickest way to get inside a formidable castle like Calban was not with ladders, swords, and siege engines, but with trickery, as the men stationed at Gasterny had also learned to their dismay.

"Yes," Shana agreed. "There was no moon that night and the skies were rain-filled. The sentries clearly saw nothing, though I imagine they were spending more time trying to stay warm and dry than looking out to sea. Had they looked closer, they might have seen the Cardian ships riding in on the tide."

"Those sentries were probably long dead by then, lady," Jebido said bluntly. "Letting them live to sound the alarm would have been too risky."

"Oh," Shana said, looking crestfallen.

"Did you see how many ships the Cardians had?" Tyden asked, his cheeks flushed with anger.

Shana sighed. "Not really, Highness. It was very dark and I was confused." Shana gestured to Putt. "Perhaps Putt can help with that answer, Highness, as I owe my life and freedom to this man's quick thinking. It was he who had us escape through the tunnel beneath the keep, and, along with his men, they ferried my court ladies and me to *Sea Dragon*, where we hid in the hold until morning."

"You have my gratitude for my cousin's safety," Tyden said, turning to Putt and taking his hand.

"And mine, my friend," I said, feeling badly now about how I had spoken to him earlier.

Putt grinned sheepishly and he shrugged. "I would rather have faced a thousand Cardians, my lord, than let anything happen to Lady Shana." He turned back to Tyden. "As to your question, Highness, I saw at least ten longships moored at the wharf and beached on the sands the next morning when we sailed away."

"The Cardians let you go?" I said in surprise.

Putt grinned. "Of course not, my lord. But what ship can catch *Sea Dragon* once she has a good wind behind her? Besides, I think most of them were drunk by then."

"Did you say ten ships?" Tyden asked. He raised an eyebrow, looking around. "How many men is that?"

"At least five hundred, Highness," Putt answered grimly. "Assuming fifty men per ship, which is likely."

Tyden sat down at the table, his elbows propped up on the hard oak planks as he rubbed wearily at his face. "So, not only have we lost Gasterny to an army of Piths in the south, now we have a second army in the north who have taken Calban." He looked up, his eyes red-rimmed and puffy. "What is happening here? Can someone please tell me that? Are the Piths and Cardians working together now?"

"I doubt it," I said. "We already knew Pernissy and this Lord Boudin were up to something, and I think the Piths attacking us was just the excuse they needed."

"I hope you are right, Lord Hadrack," Tyden said as he glanced down at the maps before him. "But even if you are, it does little to settle the ache of dread in my gut." He turned one of the maps around and studied it, frowning as he ran his hand across the surface absently. "The question before us now is, what do we do?" He fixed his gaze on Shana. "This army you are forming, cousin, how many men do you have?"

"Three thousand currently, Highness," Shana said. "I was hoping for more, but many of the lords I contacted refused to send men. They said they needed those men to defend their own lands when the Piths came."

"Two-faced bastards," Tyden grunted. He drummed his fingers on the table moodily, then glanced at me. "Any suggestions, Lord Hadrack?"

"Yes," I said. "You need to return to Gandertown right away, Highness. The fact that the Cardians came with that many men means that they are serious, and I fear Calban might have just been a target of convenience, not the primary one."

Tyden frowned in confusion. "Please explain," he said.

I started to pace, my hands behind my back as I thought. "We all know Pernissy covets the crown, Highness," I said. "He always has, and he would gladly take it by force if he could. I think he has made a deal with the Cardians to do just that. Pernissy knew you would be traveling south for my trial, since he's the one who arranged the entire thing in the first place. I think he planned on making a play for the throne during your absence. But then the Piths attacked, and like a fool, I drew men away from Calban. That changed the bastard's plans. Calban is on the west coast, close to Cardia, and if Pernissy and Lord Boudin could take it, they could use the surrounding beach to land more men, supplies, and horses there with impunity."

"So, you're suggesting that we are dealing with two separate invasions at the same time," Tyden said, looking overwhelmed. "Either one of which might be more than sufficient to destroy Ganderland."

"Yes, Highness," I said. "That is what I think. That's why you must return north as soon as possible. Now that the Cardians have a foothold, I'm sure those five hundred men will grow. Pernissy knows how well defended Gandertown is and that he'll need at least twenty times that number if he wants to take it." I moved to the maps, studying them before selecting the one I wanted. "This is Calban, here," I said as men crowded around the table. "Taking the castle gives Pernissy a strong western base to work from now, but it also offers him an uncomfortable problem. He's secure in his position but far away from what he's really after—Gandertown. The only way he can take the city and throne is to move his army halfway across the kingdom."

"Why didn't he just sail his ships around the northern tip and land men there, my lord?" Finol asked, his white eyebrows furrowed as he studied the map. "Gandertown is only two or three hundred miles away to the south from there that way. Wouldn't that have been easier?"

"That might have been his original plan," I conceded. "But I doubt it would have been easier. Far from it, in fact. At this time of year, the storms on the Northern Sea would probably have taken half his ships, even if he hugged the coastline."

"And those coastlines are unforgiving up there, my lord," Wiflem added. He grimaced. "I spent two miserable years in the north, so I know. There are only a few suitable landing sites he could use, and each one of them is guarded by garrisons."

"He could have sailed down the White Rock," Baine ventured forth, following the river with his finger.

Wiflem shook his head. "The Screech Falls lie half a mile from the river mouth. He would never have made it."

"All of which explains why Pernissy latched onto Calban the moment he saw the opportunity," I said, tasting the bitterness in my mouth. "Which brings us back to the bastard's dilemma. Pernissy can either have his men pick their way through rough mountainous terrain until they get to the Silver Valley, right here," I said, pointing to a gap in the route through the Father's Spine mountains that I knew intimately. I had taken that same route with Sabina during the Walk last year. I swept my hand to the south. "Or he can travel southeast around the mountains and cross the White Rock at this bridge." I looked up. "But I don't think he is going to do that. Going around would add several weeks to the march at the very least." I tapped the map confidently. "No, Pernissy will go northeast," I said, knowing that I was right. "It's riskier for him, but he'll be impatient and want to get to Gandertown as soon as possible."

"So, you're suggesting trapping his army in that valley," Jebido said, looking thoughtful.

"Yes," I nodded. I turned to the king. "But to do that, Highness, you have to move fast and organize against him. If Pernissy gets to Silver Valley first, then he'll be hard to contain once he's free of the mountains."

"But what about the Piths?" Tyden asked. "What is to stop them from taking the entire southland while we fight the Cardians?"

"Me," I growled.

King Tyden left the next day, accompanied by Putt and twenty of my men-at-arms. The king was to stop at Halhaven first and inform Daughter Gernet of what was occurring, then travel to Gandertown to begin the defense of the north. Lord Vestry and the rest of the survivors from Gasterny arrived three days after the king's departure. Lord Vestry claimed that he was unwell and could not take part in a second expedition against the Piths and would be going home instead. I can't say I was saddened to see him go, but he did leave what men he still had left under his command with us, so I sent them and the others to the western fields where the rapidly growing new levy was encamped. The king promised me the lords who had refused to send men to Shana would be reminded of their duty, forcefully if necessary, and that they would come this time. He'd also made it clear that I would be in charge of those lords, which I had immediately protested.

My many failures the past few weeks had been weighing on me, culminating with my foolish decision to draw men away from Calban. A decision that had ultimately cost me a child. Shana was adamant that it wasn't my fault, but I knew better, and the deep bitterness I felt was eating away at my confidence minute by minute. Shana and I had spent our first night together huddled in her rooms, mourning the loss of what I now knew would have been my son. The pain from that loss still hurts me to this day, more so than any physical wound I have taken over my long life. I have always wondered what might have happened had I not called for those men and given Pernissy the opportunity that he so desperately needed.

I had tried to explain my feelings to the king—about how I felt that I'd let everyone down and had no right even to be a lord, let alone be left in charge of them. But my words had been clumsy and wandering, filled with self-doubt and recrimination, and the king would hear none of it. He had told me rather harshly that I was a leader of men whether I liked it or not and that my job was to lead, not to whine. Sometimes men who lead will make errors that cost lives, he'd said, and when that happened, you needed to learn to live with it and move on. I knew Tyden was right to be so blunt with me, just as I had been right to be equally direct with him back in Gasterny. But as I had watched the king ride away, all I could think about was that my son would never get to smile or feel the wind on his face or any of the other things that we, the living, take so easily for granted.

Tyden was as good as his word, and as the days went by, more and more of the southern lords appeared. Though I noted there were few actual experienced fighters among the men they brought with them. I rode out each morning to take stock of the expanding army, always returning to the castle in disappointment. How could forty and fifty-year-old men dressed in padded jackets or simple leather armor hope to stand up to Piths? Our scouts keeping an eye on Einhard's forces had reported little change at Gasterny, though their numbers did seem to have swelled somewhat. That part worried me greatly. How many more Piths could Einhard call upon? Was the already substantial army at the garrison all there was, or were there still more on the way? It was a particularly unnerving question, considering the relative inexperience of most of the men I knew I would soon have to send against them.

I had managed to come to terms with my self-doubts as the days passed, thanks in great part to Shana's unflinching support and faith in me. Her unwavering strength, determination, and clear-headed thinking were just what I needed to help me start to regain my confidence. I don't know what I would have done without her by my side.

Four days after King Tyden left, Daughter Gernet arrived in Corwick. She was accompanied by ten House Agents led by Malo and several Daughters with a small flock of Daughters-In-Waiting attending them. I was surprised to see that Jin wasn't among the apprentices.

"What are you doing here?" I demanded as Malo helped Daughter Gernet down from the small wagon that led the procession.

"It's good to see you as well, Lord Hadrack," Daughter Gernet said with a sniff.

I ignored her, turning my angry gaze on Malo. "The Piths could be here any day," I said to the House Agent. "You should have known better than to bring them here."

"And you should know when to keep your opinions to yourself," Malo grunted.

I hadn't seen the House Agent since the king's coronation, and it was clear to me that the bastard hadn't changed much. I turned away from him in disgust. "Daughter, it's dangerous to be riding about these days. You must return to Halhaven."

"Must I?" Daughter Gernet said, the ghost of a smile upon her lips. "The last I knew, Lord Hadrack, your nobility does not give you precedence over matters of the House."

"And how is putting yourself and everyone accompanying you in danger a House matter, Daughter?" I asked.

Daughter Gernet turned away then, not answering. "Hando," she said to a thickly built House Agent. "You and Therin will see to the horses and wagons."

"Yes, Daughter," the House Agent said with a bow.

"Now then," Daughter Gernet said to me, taking my arm. "You must take me to that charming wife of yours, Hadrack. We had such delightful conversations when we were in Gandertown together." I sighed, knowing whatever the Daughter's reasoning for being here was, she had no plans on revealing it to me just yet.

A great feast was prepared for our visitors, and we dined in Corwick Hall, inviting many of the lords camped to the west to join in the festivities. The elaborate feast might be the last one for many of us, I reflected sourly as I watched two of those lords dancing with Hesther and Hamber. The girls were unquestionably ugly, but I noted their dancing had improved considerably under Shana's tutelage. Daughter Gernet was placed in the position of honor in the center of the long table on the dais, with her fellow Daughters sitting on the ends. I sat to one side of Daughter Gernet and Shana the other. Malo sat beside me, saying little as he tore into his food like a man who hadn't eaten in a week. I would have found it remarkable had I not known the House Agent as well as I did. Malo's appetite was legendary, and he could eat twice as much as the average man. My wife and Daughter Gernet ate little, hunched together like thieves in the night as they talked endlessly. I found their laughter and carefree attitude hugely annoying.

"You don't seem to be enjoying yourself much," Malo said around a leg of lamb. He pulled the last of the meat from the thin bone with his teeth and threw the leg aside, wiping his hands on his trousers as he studied me.

"Why did you come here, Malo?" I asked, unable to keep the distrust I felt for him from my voice. "Whenever you show up, trouble soon follows."

Malo laughed as he speared a bloody slice of roast beef with his knife. "You are a suspicious fellow, my old friend."

"For good reason," I growled.

Malo paused with dripping meat halfway to his lips. "What if I told you we came here to support you?"

"Then I would say that you were lying," I responded as I toyed with my wine goblet.

"Well," Malo said around a mouthful of meat, "then you would be wrong." He pointed his knife at Daughter Gernet. "She brought you three hundred House Agents to help fight the Piths, you stubborn ass."

I stared at Malo in astonishment. "You're joking?"

Malo shook his head. "No, I'm not. They have already joined your camp. Daughter Gernet spoke with the king before he went north and promised him she would help in any way that she could. This is her way of helping, so you might consider yanking your foot out of your mouth long enough to thank her, Hadrack."

I sat back in surprise. Three hundred House Agents was no small thing, and they would be invaluable to me when we faced Einhard. I felt my animosity toward Malo starting to cool. "So, that's the only reason?" I asked, more out of habit than suspicion now.

"The only one that I'm at liberty to tell you," Malo said with a wry smile.

I cursed under my breath as the House Agent began forcing more food into his mouth, our conversation apparently over. Musicians played lutes, violins, and flutes on the landing above me that led to the spare rooms, while a servant girl stood at the bottom of the stairs and sang a haunting song about the fall of the Flin dynasty. I glanced at my wife, who remained deep in conversation with

Daughter Gernet. I decided I needed to be alone for a while, so I stood unnoticed and quietly made my way from the hall and stepped outside.

I stood in the inner bailey as music and merriment filtered out from the keep, staring up at the White Tower that rose above me like a boney finger in the moonlight. I had kept Grindin in that tower, expecting at some point to kill the little bastard, but circumstances had let him escape my justice, at least for now.

"It's usually considered rude for the host to leave the party first, Lord Hadrack."

I turned as Daughter Gernet walked slowly down the ramp toward me. "I have to piss," I grunted, hoping she would take that as a hint and go back inside.

"Do you now," Daughter Gernet said in amusement as she paused beside me. "Then, by all means, please go ahead. Don't let my presence stop you. It's nothing I haven't seen many times before, after all."

"It can wait," I muttered, unable to keep the irritation from my voice.

Daughter Gernet chuckled softly to herself as we stood together, saying nothing. Finally, I turned to her in exasperation. "What is it you want from me, Daughter?"

"What makes you believe I want something from you?"

"Because everything you do has a purpose to it," I replied. "Malo already told me about the House Agents, in case that's why you came out here to talk to me."

"Ah," Daughter Gernet nodded. "I thought he might have. And are you not pleased?"

"Of course I am," I said. "We're going to need all the help we can get."

"So, if you are aware of the reason I came to Corwick, then why accuse me of having an ulterior motive?"

"Because, Daughter," I said. "Malo is more than capable of bringing those men to me on his own. You didn't need to make the journey, yet here you are anyway. Which can only mean there is another reason for your presence here."

Daughter Gernet sighed, surprising me by running her hand gently through my hair. "You are so much like your father, Hadrack. Strong-willed, honest, and honorable almost to a fault." She let her hand fall away. "I miss him terribly, you know."

"Yet, in all the years we have known each other," I said bitterly. "You still refuse to tell me how you knew my father."

Daughter Gernet hesitated as she clutched at the Blazing Sun pendant hanging around her neck. "It was necessary, Hadrack. I have not kept this information from you out of spite. Please believe me."

"If that's true," I said. "Then tell me right now. Why continue to keep it a secret?"

The priestess sighed again, wrapping her arms around herself. "It's getting colder at night now, don't you think?" she said. I snorted in frustration and looked away, determined not to respond. "Do you know the history of the White Tower, Hadrack?" Daughter Gernet finally asked to break the silence.

I shrugged, angry now. "Why would I care to?"

Daughter Gernet seemed not to have heard me. "Brimal Corwick built it originally," she explained as she looked up at the tower. "No one seems to know why, exactly. He was said to be a contemplative man, obsessed with book-learning and reflection, so perhaps he built it as a type of sanctuary. We probably will never know for certain."

"That's fascinating," I said sarcastically.

"After Brimal Corwick's death," Daughter Gernet continued, unfazed by my sarcasm. "The White Tower sat empty for years, though I had heard that his son used it from time to time as a sort of brothel." She glanced at me. "He was a wicked man, that one," she said primly. "Some even claimed that he had a little Pith blood in him, which would explain a lot, I suppose. The White Tower was used for many things over the generations that followed. Once even as a Holy House, until the reign of Kerlt Corwick, who stored imported oats from Parnuthia in it for his prized horses." She leaned forward conspiratorially. "Kerlt was quite the whore-jumper himself as well, you know, though at least he had the decency to take his pleasures outside of the castle most nights."

I sighed and stared up at the star-filled sky, barely listening. Just what I needed, a lesson in history on the Corwick family.

"But Kerlt's humping days came to an abrupt close one night when he got caught with his pants down," Daughter Gernet continued. She winked at me. "Quite literally, as the husband of the fishwife he was rutting with caught them in his bed. Kerlt tried to talk his way out of it, of course, since he was unarmed and rather indisposed at the time. But sleeping with another man's wife can have consequences, even for a lord, and for Kerlt, that consequence turned out to be a sharp blade between the ribs. Kerlt's son, Coltin, became the Lord of Corwick after that." The light wind around us suddenly gusted, lifting the hem of the priestess's robes playfully as she steadied herself against me with her hand. "You remember Coltin Corwick, I imagine, don't you Hadrack?"

I nodded. Coltin had been the first Lord Corwick that I had known as a child, before the Border War and Pernissy.

"I imagine he must have been an old man when you knew him," Daughter Gernet said wistfully. She chuckled, remembering. "But he wasn't always old. In his youth, he was a dashing, handsome man who could make any girl swoon just by looking at her." The priestess shook her head fondly. "Myself included, I must confess, though he was approaching middle-age by the time I was old enough to appreciate his charms."

"I wonder if there might be a point to all of this soon?" I said. My story about a full bladder earlier had been designed to rid myself of the priestess, but it was now becoming uncomfortably true.

"My point, dear boy," Daughter Gernet said. "Is that it was here, in this very castle ruled by Coltin Corwick, that I first laid eyes on your father."

I could feel my eyebrows rising in surprise. "My father lived here?"

"He did," Daughter Gernet confirmed. "For a time, anyway." Her lips twitched in amusement. "Should I continue, or have you had enough lessons for one night?"

"No," I said eagerly, my pulse racing. "Please, go on."

"Coltin, like many of the Corwick men before him, had an eye for the ladies," Daughter Gernet said. She sniffed. "It's not all that surprising, I suppose. Most men do." She eyed me up and down with sudden disapproval. "If your sex is not busily hacking the limbs from one another, or passed out drunk, then you are off humping the leg of the first pretty girl you see like a mindless dog."

I grinned despite myself at the look on the priestess's face. "That's a little harsh, don't you think?" I said.

Daughter Gernet's features softened somewhat. "Perhaps it is, my dear. Not all men are like that, I suppose. Take you, for instance. Sometimes, with the guidance of a good woman like your Lady Shana, even wild beasts can be tamed to a degree."

"You were speaking about Lord Corwick and my father," I said, refusing to get drawn into a debate about the virtues of men and women.

"Yes, I was," Daughter Gernet said, focusing back on the White Tower. "As I said, Coltin liked his women, though he seemed to be mainly interested in peasant girls. He took great delight in wooing them into his bed. I can't imagine why. Anyway, Coltin was eventually married to a witch of a woman named Esmira. She gave Coltin a son, Jesip, but she was so torn up inside after the birth that she couldn't have any more children." I nodded. I remembered Jesip vaguely. He had died with his father in the Border War. "Then, one day, Coltin met Luna and everything changed for him. His wandering eye became fixated, as was his heart, on one woman, and one woman alone."

"Who was she?" I asked, although I already suspected what the answer would be.

"Luna was your father's mother," Daughter Gernet said as she watched me closely.

"Did she and Lord Corwick marry?" I asked, my voice strained and shaking as I realized the implications of what I was hearing.

"They did not," the priestess said soberly. "Esmira came from an influential and well-connected family to the north, and with her union to Coltin Corwick, it gave the Flin king control over territories that he had long coveted. When Coltin went to the king for an annulment of his marriage so he could marry Luna legally, he was refused. The king advised Coltin to keep Luna as a mistress until he tired of her, and then find himself another girl with which he could amuse himself."

"But he never did get tired of Luna," I said softly.

"No," Daughter Gernet replied with a regretful shake of her head. She glanced upward. "Coltin brought Luna to the castle to live in the White Tower. I can only imagine what it must have been like for Esmira to see it every day, knowing who dwelled inside and why. After a time, a son was born to Luna, who Coltin adored even more than his firstborn son, Jesip."

"My father," I whispered.

"Yes," Daughter Gernet agreed. She put her hand on my arm. "You were right, Hadrack. I did have another reason for coming here. King Tyden told me of your doubts and that you feel you do not belong in the company of lords. But I am here to tell you that you do. You are the last of the Corwicks, Hadrack. And you are as much a lord, if not more, than any of those fools dancing inside."

"But why didn't you just tell me all this before?" I demanded, still reeling from the knowledge that I was a descendant of Castis Corwick. "What harm would it have done?"

"Because I made a vow once too, Hadrack, much as you did. I swore the truth of who Alwin was would never pass my lips."

"But why?" I asked in confusion. "I don't understand."

"Because Esmira was a mean, vindictive woman, Hadrack. Just think what it must have been like as her husband displayed his unfaithfulness and disdain for her every day. Coltin rarely gave Jesip attention, either, favoring young Alwin in all things over his firstborn son. That was a mistake that Lord Corwick should not have made, and eventually, Esmira's hatred and jealousy got the best of her."

"What did she do?"

Daughter Gernet grimaced. "While Coltin was off hunting one day, Esmira had men she'd hired seize Luna and take her into the woods to the east. There they raped the poor girl in every vile way possible, then dismembered her body, each man riding twenty miles on the points of the compass before dumping her remains on the ground."

"Mother Above," I whispered in horror. "What of my father? How did he survive?"

Daughter Gernet smiled sadly. "That is where I come in, Hadrack. My father was the lord's bailiff, and when he came to the castle on business, my family would sometimes accompany him. Alwin and I were young children when we first met, and we quickly became friends since we were both of the same age. We were playing together along with my two sisters the day Luna was dragged from the White Tower. Alwin tried to go to her aid, but somehow I knew those men would kill him, so together with my sisters, we managed to hold Alwin down until they had ridden off with Luna."

"And then what did you do?" I asked.

"Then we ran," Daughter Gernet said. "We ran to our village in the hills and waited for Father to come home." Daughter Gernet swallowed, her eyes fixated on the ground now, though I could tell she saw nothing but the past. "The men who had taken Luna returned to Corwick Castle later that day," the priestess said. "They couldn't find Alwin, so instead, they grabbed the first boy of a similar age and build that they saw and killed him, cutting him up so badly that it was impossible to tell who he was. Esmira didn't suspect a thing, and though Coltin grieved the loss of the woman and son he loved when he returned, he could not change what had happened."

"You mean he did nothing?" I snorted, amazed.

"Not to Esmira," the priestess said. "The power her family wielded was enormous, and he could not risk their wrath or the king's. But the men who had taken Luna all died hideous deaths, as did anyone else who Coltin suspected was involved. My father brought Lord Corwick to our village sometime later, and the look of joy on his face when he saw Alwin is something that I will treasure all of my life."

"So, he took Alwin home, then?"

"No," Daughter Gernet said. "He feared for the boy's life, so though I could tell it pained him greatly, he left Alwin with us. He made my entire family swear on The Mother Herself that we would never tell anyone who Alwin really was in case Esmira or her family found out."

"But that happened ages ago," I protested. "Why couldn't you have just told me all this now that everyone involved is dead?"

Daughter Gernet held up her pendant. "Because I am a priestess," she said. "Soon to be the First Daughter, and a vow to The Mother cannot be taken lightly, nor easily broken."

"But you were just a child," I said. "You can't be held to that vow after so long."

"As were you when you made your own vow," Daughter Gernet said, one eyebrow raised. "Does that mean it is any less relevant now, simply because you are older?"

"No," I grumbled, knowing it was a fair point.

"Besides," Daughter Gernet said. "Everything worked out in the end without my having to speak of it. I only do so now because of the dire circumstances Ganderland finds itself in at the moment. The kingdom needs you at your best, Lord Hadrack, and having you doubt yourself in any way cannot be tolerated. Even if it means breaking a solemn vow to The Mother that I have carried for most of my life."

I had heard something in her words and I looked at her suspiciously. "It was you who suggested King Tyden make me the Lord of Corwick, wasn't it?"

"It was," Daughter Gernet confirmed. "You are the rightful lord of this place, Hadrack, so after what you had done for the king, it seemed fitting. It also allowed me to set things right for Alwin while keeping my vow of silence intact."

"Does he know?" I asked.

"Does who know what?"

"Tyden," I replied. "Does he know who I really am?"

The priestess shook her head. "He does not, and my advice is that you never tell him."

"Why not?"

Daughter Gernet sighed. "Because he is a good man, Hadrack, but he is also a Raybold, which means you need to be cautious." I just stared at her blankly until she continued, "The Raybolds were the powerful family I spoke of who arranged Esmira's marriage to Coltin Corwick."

I blinked in surprise. "Are you saying that Esmira and Tyden were related? That she was a royal?"

Daughter Gernet shook her head. "The Raybolds weren't royalty back then, just a very powerful family with vast lands situated between Ganderland and the Flins. Neither king wanted to anger the Raybolds, which gave them unprecedented power to do whatever they wanted."

"But you said the Raybolds allied themselves with the Flins, not Ganderland."

"At first," Daughter Gernet agreed. "But things changed when Jorquin Raybold became head of the family. Jorquin was a greedy, self-centered man who was never satisfied with whatever power and riches he already had. He always wanted more. Jorquin staged a coup in Ganderland and seized the throne, then turned his eyes toward the Kingdom of the Flins. But though he coveted the southern lands, the man still had a modicum of honor left in him, I guess, and it was that honor that kept him from attacking the Flins in force."

"Because of Esmira and Coltin Corwick's union," I said, understanding now.

"Yes," Daughter Gernet said. "Many years went by, and though the odd disagreement arose between the two kingdoms, they rarely amounted to much. For always, there was Esmira and Coltin to point to as a reason for peace." Daughter Gernet shook her head sadly. "Their lives were miserable, Hadrack. Those two people hated each other, but they both knew they were all that was standing between an all-out war, and, for that reason, they somehow managed to tolerate each other."

"But war came eventually," I pointed out.

"Indeed it did," Daughter Gernet agreed. "Esmira fell ill, and though her condition was said to have been treatable, Coltin had

had enough. He decided to leave her fate and that of the kingdoms in the hands of the First Pair."

"She died," I said, knowing it could have gone no other way.

"She did," the priestess confirmed. "Jorquin learned of her death, and they say the news struck him hard, though I have my doubts about that. He hadn't seen his half-sister in many years, so I can't imagine he was that heartbroken over it."

"But grief can be a convenient tool if you are conniving enough to use it," I said.

Daughter Gernet smiled. "You are a smart one, aren't you, Hadrack. Jorquin learned that Coltin did nothing to help his sister, and he proclaimed the alliance between the kingdoms void because of that failure to act. Jorquin vowed revenge for his sister's death and that he would do everything within his power to rid the world of every last Corwick. Including his own nephew, who he said had conspired with his father to murder Esmira."

"Was that part true?" I asked.

Daughter Gernet shrugged. "Does it matter? King Jorquin used the entire affair as an excuse to invade the Flin kingdom, and he was as good as his word. He hunted down every living Corwick and had them executed."

"All except my father," I whispered.

"All except your father," Daughter Gernet agreed, looking tired and drawn now. She put her hand on my arm. "And now you know everything, child."

19: Friendship or War?

I was a Corwick, just like my father had been before me. Nothing had prepared me for such an unexpected revelation. The knowledge that my father had been so much more than he seemed was both deeply gratifying and deeply saddening at the same time. I understood the reason now why he never told anyone of his heritage, afraid for the lives of his family should the Raybolds learn he lived. But even so, I wish that he had shared that part of his life with me. How difficult it must have been for him, carrying the burden of being a bastard child to a mighty lord on his shoulders for all those years. I can't imagine what must have been going through his head each time he was summoned to Corwick Castle with the other village elders, knowing that if not for a cruel and unforgiving woman, he would have had a much better life.

Daughter Gernet left for Halhaven the morning after the feast, but I managed to pull her aside before she departed. I still had one last question that needed answering.

"How did my father hurt his leg?" I wanted to know.

Daughter Gernet seemed more restrained in the light of day, but with a little prodding from me, the answer came. "Alwin was sixteen and already big and strong, so he was recruited to be a soldier."

"Inside the castle?" I asked, surprised that Lord Corwick would take that chance.

Daughter Gernet snorted. "Of course not. Coltin was no fool. He stationed Alwin at Knoxly Manor, where the boy could be properly trained away from prying eyes."

"Oh, I see," I said, nodding. That made sense. "And his leg?"

"Coltin was feuding with the Lord of Welis over some land or some such silly thing. I can't remember what it was exactly."

"Lord of Welis?" I grunted, realizing that would probably have been Fitz's grandfather.

"Indeed," the priestess said. "The two hated each other. Alwin was around nineteen or twenty years old, I think, when that hatred finally boiled over into armed conflict. During the skirmish, Coltin became entangled in his horse's stirrups, and if not for Alwin, he would probably have died."

"My father saved him," I said, knowing that I was right as I pictured the desperate scene.

"He did," Daughter Gernet confirmed. "Your father leaped from his own horse onto Coltin's and cut away the strap, freeing him, but the horse panicked and reared backward and fell, crushing your father's leg beneath it."

I bowed my head, remembering the constant look of pain on my father's face as he dragged his useless leg along. I had always wondered how it had happened, and now I knew.

"Your father could only show so much gratitude to Alwin because of the threat of the Raybolds," Daughter Gernet said. "He did what he could for the ruined leg, but the boy's exploits hadn't gone unnoticed. Coltin had no choice but to make some form of public gesture of thanks for what Alwin had done for him."

"The axe," I whispered.

"Yes," the priestess agreed. "After Alwin had recovered as much as he ever would, Coltin chose a day when Esmira was under the weather to present a special axe to him. The woman didn't spend much time involving herself with castle business, anyway, but it was still better to be cautious. Coltin didn't know what to do with the boy after that. But he couldn't stand the thought of sending him away, so he built him a house and gave him land to work in the village of Corwick. He knew Alwin could live there the rest of his life and never be noticed by Esmira."

"And that's where he met my mother."

"Yes, that is where he met the love of his life." I could see something in the priestess's eyes when she said that, a quick flicker before it was gone. Daughter Gernet put her hand on my shoulder. "Do not feel sorry for your father, Hadrack. He loved your mother deeply and told me more than once that he would gladly do it all again, including losing the use of his leg if it meant he could be with her." I felt tears forming in my eyes when she said that, and I nodded, unable to speak as Daughter Gernet climbed into the wagon. "Do not grieve for them, child," the priestess said to me kindly. "They are together now with The Mother, and that knowledge should be a source of joy for you, not sadness."

Daughter Gernet had left then, along with her priestesses, apprentices, and the House Agents guarding them, though Malo decided to stay and help with the offensive against the Piths. I wasn't keen on having the House Agent's dour personality around, but could not say no to a man as skilled as he was with a sword.

That had been over three weeks ago, and now, as I sat Angry in the western fields and surveyed my army of close to twelve thousand men on the march, the time for war had come. The Piths had broken camp over a week ago, heading northwest, with an army that had grown to over ten thousand warriors. Strange men in armor had been sighted within the Pith encampment two weeks before the departure. The arrival of those soldiers had coincided with furious activity beginning within the trees near Gasterny. Those men, it turned out, were Afrenian mercenaries. The Afrenians did two things very well, I was told—weave silk, and build siege engines.

The Piths building siege engines had caught me off-guard, I have to admit, but in retrospect, I probably should have seen it coming. Many of the towns Einhard would need to conquer were protected by thick walls and well defended. He couldn't afford to leave those towns undefeated as he forged further into Ganderland, as it would leave his rear vulnerable to attack. So, his only recourse was to build the engines and take each of the towns one by one. Capturing those towns would not only eliminate any potential threats to his rear, but also work as a network of supply lines, helping to keep his army well-stocked with grain, weapons, and food. Most armies on the march depended on foraging to fill their bellies, but a savvy enemy could just burn everything in their path, leaving nothing for the invaders to scavenge. Men don't fight well on empty stomachs.

Starving Einhard once he got deeper into Ganderland had been my initial plan, but now I knew it wouldn't work. I didn't have the time or the men to retake those towns or try to break his supply chain.

The Piths under Einhard were evolving, I realized bitterly, knowing that I'd probably had a hand in that to some degree. Einhard and I had talked of war and strategies many times while in Gasterny together, and it had been me who had repeated to him what Jebido had told me about siege engines and the destructive force that they could wield against a fortified town. Einhard had scoffed at the idea back then, but he was older and wiser now and was determined to win this war no matter what. If siege engines built by unscrupulous men from another land could hand him that win, then I knew he would gladly shunt aside the old ways of his people to do it.

My scouts reported that the Piths reached the small town of Kamlee first, where Einhard's demands for immediate surrender were rejected. Kamlee fell quickly, with everyone inside its walls being slaughtered as an example to any others who might choose to resist the Piths. I grieved for the dead of Kamlee, but as Tyden had told me, men who lead need to make choices—tough choices. I could not afford to chase after a highly mobile force like Einhard commanded with my slower army. The men we had gathered were all that stood between the Piths and the north, so I needed to be smart and not let emotion cloud my judgment. I would meet Einhard in a place of my choosing, not his. One that I hoped would give us an advantage over his more experienced warriors.

After Kamlee fell in such horrific fashion, towns and castles began to submit one by one as Einhard kept his force heading steadily northwest. It quickly became apparent that my old friend was aiming straight for Halhaven, the seat of power in Southern Ganderland. It was there, on the grassy plains called Land's Edge ten miles west of Halhaven, that I planned on destroying him.

Einhard's current route would lead him to the mining town of Lorimire next, then after that through the lands of Lord Vestry before he reached Halhaven. I grimaced when I thought of the timid lord, knowing he would soon live to regret deciding to return home.

Hopefully, the Piths would be delayed long enough as they dealt with him for me to get my troops into position.

"So, what do you think?" I asked Jebido as our army slowly trudged past us. "You didn't say much earlier."

"It's as good a place as you are likely to find," Jebido said noncommittedly.

I pictured the plains surrounded by foothills where I planned to meet Einhard. The White Rock dissected Land's Edge as though someone had taken a finger and dragged it through the soil in an almost perfect line, with only two fords of solid rock within half a mile of each other for many miles in either direction. I knew if the Piths were allowed to cross that river with their siege engines, then it would be a short march for them to the gates of the city. Einhard would have a choice when his scouts saw us waiting for him on the opposite bank. He could change directions and follow the river until he found another suitable place to cross, or he could march straight ahead and try to wipe my forces out.

Einhard was an intelligent man and a charismatic leader, but he was also a Pith, with a Piths' natural arrogance, and I knew he wouldn't want to wait. Going north or south along the river looking for another ford or bridge would take him many days out of his way, with no guarantees that we wouldn't shift our forces to meet him, putting him in the same situation. I was the only real threat left to his total victory in the south, and if he could defeat me quickly, then Southern Ganderland would be his for the taking. No, my old friend would not turn, even if it was the sounder strategy. Einhard's natural competitiveness and disdain for most Ganders meant he would forge ahead, eager to match shield against shield and sword against sword with us. I planned on having a few surprises in store for him when he did.

I had told no one about my conversation with Daughter Gernet, not even Baine and Jebido, my two closest friends. I wasn't sure why I hadn't said anything, but the priestess's revelation about my father had profoundly affected me. Gone now was the self-doubt and insecurity that had been plaguing me these past months. Those feelings had been replaced by a quiet confidence and a better understanding of my place in the world. It wasn't bravado or arrogance that I was feeling, but rather a deep-seated sense of belonging. I knew the discovery that I was a Corwick hadn't changed who I was as a person, but it had finally put to rest my need to question every one of my decisions, wondering what an actual lord would have done.

The days of insecurity were gone for me and, from that moment forward, I have never doubted myself ever again. Though, I am saddened to say I would still make mistakes in the future that would end up costing many good people their lives.

"You think my choice of battleground is a bad one?" I asked Jebido.

"It's a fine spot," Jebido said. "As long as Einhard does what you want."

I frowned. "You think he'll try to go around us?"

Jebido shrugged as he kicked his horse forward. "I know I would. But I'm not really a Pith, now am I?"

We arrived at our destination six days later, well ahead of Einhard's forces, whose siege and baggage trains had become bogged down in muddy roads after three solid days of rain. It was a blessing from The Mother, we all agreed, as the weather had given us even more time to prepare than I had expected. Conscripts bolstered my army from Halhaven and the surrounding countryside, and we now numbered sixteen thousand men. I had seven thousand infantry, four thousand men-at-arms on horseback, and five thousand archers. It was a formidable force, one that even Piths might raise an eyebrow at, which troubled me. I wanted the Piths overconfident, believing us to be weak.

I decided to post a thousand men-at-arms several miles to the north along the river, and a further thousand to the south, splitting the remaining two thousand and sending half of them to wait out of sight to my rear as a reserve force. As confident as I was that Einhard wouldn't try to find another route, I respected Jebido's experience and instincts on the matter. Sending those men away would not only protect my flanks and rear, but hopefully fool Einhard into thinking that I had a much weaker force than I did.

I had sought out Gerdy soon after returning to Corwick and had plucked him from the ranks of the levy, tasking him and those having a similar talent as he with making as many longbows as possible. I knew a man with Gerdy's skills would just be wasted if we threw him into a shield wall to die. There were a wealth of strong, eager young men in my army to choose from now, and my force of Wolf's Teeth boys quickly swelled to well over five hundred.

Almost a quarter of the bowstaves Gerdy and his fellow bowyers made were of undried wood out of necessity, however. The little man had explained to me about wood memory, which he warned would only allow me limited usage from the green bows. With each shot, the bowstave would lose its ability to fully flex back to its original position, with many of them forming an elbow, where eventually a breakage would occur. At best, he'd said, I could expect four to five volleys with the green bows before they became unusable. Of course, I would have preferred more, but hopefully, those volleys would suffice and have the effect I needed when the moment came.

That moment arrived three days later, when our scouts reported seeing the vanguard of the Pith army approaching in the early dawn. The day had begun cloudy and cool, with a light breeze blowing from the southwest.

"Good weather for it," Jebido grunted as we stepped out from my command tent together. "Nothing drains a man more than fighting in armor under a hot sun."

I nodded my agreement as horns sounded, signaling the men to take up their positions. The forces directly under my command were assembling in front of the larger ford, consisting of three thousand infantry armed with pikes and shields, five hundred mounted men-at-arms with lances, and twenty-five hundred archers. The infantry were broken up into units of roughly two hundred men, each one led by a lord or experienced soldier who understood my battle plans intimately. One of the biggest failures we'd had at Gasterny was the lack of training and communication between our forces. That lack had ultimately led to our rout, which might have been avoided if we'd had a better-defined chain of leadership for the common soldier to follow. I was determined that this time there would be no confusion. Now that capable men commanded those smaller units, I could move them quickly and efficiently wherever I needed as the battle wore on.

I had stationed an equal force of men at the smaller, northern ford under the command of Wiflem, with one thousand more infantry waiting in between the two fords as additional reserves. Two thousand archers were spaced out along the riverbank in front of the reserve infantry, including my Wolf's Teeth. Baine and Tyris were each in command of a thousand of those archers, who would have an unimpeded view of the fords to the north and the south. The Piths would be well within the range of the longbows before they even reached the water, with the smaller bows coming into play afterward once the mounted warriors entered the river.

That river was swollen greatly from the rains, and the first line of wooden palisades made from sharpened stakes that I'd built on the banks encircling the fords were now a foot deep in the water. Normally, the rocky ford was covered by only a few inches of water, which probably explained why no one had ever bothered to build a bridge here. I nodded in approval. The deeper water level and muddy riverbanks would make it even more difficult for Einhard to cross. A second line of palisades encircled the first one fifty feet back, built on solid earthworks with a deep trench in front that bristled with additional stakes pointing upward at an angle. A berm of dirt and sod blocked the view of the trench from the enemy.

The Piths could try to go around my defenses, of course, but they would have to stay close to the ford on either side to have any chance at success. The water deepened remarkably fast after that, with treacherous currents just waiting for the unwary. We had sounded the river extensively when we arrived, and I knew if the Piths tried to go around, their horses would immediately be up to their bellies in water and moving slowly. Ten feet further out and they would be swimming and hopefully floundering as they fought the strong-flowing river. I doubted the Piths would choose to attack that way, though, as it would leave them vulnerable and easy targets for my archers. Sometimes, the best fortification you can have is the one that nature already provides for you.

The hardest part for me about this day was going to be sitting and watching from afar as I sent men to their deaths. I needed to see what was happening throughout the battle to make adjustments when needed. I couldn't do that in the thick of the conflict, as Jebido had adamantly explained to me more than once.

"Have I forgotten anything?" I asked my friend as he and I mounted our horses and rode to a small knoll a hundred and fifty yards back from the river. The knoll gave us an unobstructed view of the battlefield and the far riverbank, and it was here that I would stay for the duration of the fighting to watch my plans unfold. Ten youths on foot wearing boiled leather armor stood along the knoll's crest, all of them looking excited and nervous at the same time. Several more youths waited on horseback at the base. It would be their task to relay my commands to the lords along the frontlines and my reserves, as I did not trust the horns to be heard once the battle began.

My friend shook his head. "You've thought of everything, Hadrack. Einhard would be a fool to attack us now."

"Well, we both know he isn't a fool," I grunted as I stared moodily down at the river and my bristling army. "But he is a proud and stubborn man, which is what I am counting on."

It took several hours for the Pith army to make its way along the road that wound through the western foothills. The sun had burnt away the clouds long ago, and I could feel the sweat from the leather lining inside my helmet dripping down my neck as we waited and watched the endless line of warriors approaching. I was trying not to let the surprise and dismay I felt at the vastness of the Pith army show on my face, though I could hear men muttering down by the palisades as more and more of the warriors appeared from the west.

"Well, you were right," Jebido finally said sarcastically. "Einhard won't be going around us today. But somebody sure needs to have a talk with your scouts." Jebido nodded his head toward the river. "Because that, my boy, is a lot more than ten thousand men."

I grunted in agreement, not trusting my voice to speak. Inside, I was reeling at the size of the force opposing us, with the first tingles of uncertainty starting to flutter in my gut. There had to be double the amount of Piths from what I had been expecting.

"We stick with the plan," I said. "Whatever happens, we hold our bank of the river, no matter what."

"Do you want to send for the reserves?" Jebido asked, his face looking strained and serious now.

I paused, thinking, then I shook my head. "Not yet. I don't want Einhard to know about them until it's necessary."

"Speaking of the bastard," Jebido said as he pointed.

I watched as Einhard slowly made his way on horseback toward his side of the riverbank. He was carrying a parlay branch, which didn't surprise me in the least. I started to urge Angry down the embankment.

"Want me to go with you?" Jebido shouted from behind me.

I just shook my head and kept riding. Einhard was alone, so I would meet him alone. I could feel thousands of pairs of eyes on me as the big black made his way through my massed forces. Most of those eyes appeared anxious, I thought, which seemed justified given the unexpected size of the army opposing us. A soldier offered me his spear that bore a pennant with my wolf emblem on it, and I accepted it, thanking the man as I kept going. I reached the palisades and skirted them as Einhard paused his horse in the ford halfway between his side and mine. Angry snorted with displeasure at the coldness of the river, but he forged ahead just the same until the water was well past my knees. I guided the big black north toward the ford, then finally stopped five feet from Einhard. We both sat in silence as we assessed one another.

Einhard was dressed in splendid plated armor and mail, with a golden helm topped by a red and black plume. He wore a black cloak lined with wolf fur. He grinned at me. "I imagine you're surprised to see so many men along with me, my old friend."

I nodded. "Yes, I was expecting there would be a lot more of you to kill than just these few."

Einhard burst out laughing. "You truly are an inspiration, Hadrack. I do not believe there has ever been a time when you haven't delighted and amazed me in some way."

I shrugged. "It's a talent, I guess."

"Indeed," Einhard said. He let his gaze roam over the fortifications behind me. "Is all of this just for me?" he asked.

I smiled. "Send your men across the river, and you'll soon find out."

"All in good time, Hadrack," Einhard said. "All in good time." I saw him focus on the knoll. "Is that old Jebido way up there?"

"It is," I said. "He says to say hello and that you're a turd-eating bastard."

Einhard chuckled. "I hope he plans on staying up there, as that might be the safest place for anyone today."

We both fell silent after that, with Einhard's shimmering black stallion eyeing Angry with just as much disdain as I knew my horse felt for him. "It doesn't have to end like this," I finally said. "You can still turn back and return to Alesia and your son. The Ganderland that slaughtered your family is long gone, Einhard, and we are all better off for it. King Tyden is not the man his father was. He is good and just, and all he wants is peace between our two nations."

"Ah yes," Einhard said with a sigh. "King Tyden." He waggled a finger at me. "You tricked me, Hadrack."

"It was necessary," I said. I paused, feeling a sharp jolt of apprehension in my chest. "Did you kill Fitz when you found out who he really was?"

Einhard looked at me in mock surprise. "Now, why would I go and do that? Even though you lied to me, Hadrack, I promised you the man's life was safe." Einhard smiled. "Besides, I rather like the little fellow, all things being equal."

I couldn't stop myself from grinning with relief. "Fitz is an interesting character," I agreed. I looked behind Einhard at the massed Piths. "Is he with you?"

Einhard nodded, his face hardening. "I'll set him free once you surrender to me."

I took a deep breath and let it out slowly. "So, no peace, then?"

"Of course not," Einhard said. "The Pathfinders have been clear, Hadrack. Ganderland must fall. You and I are simply pawns in all this, just like in that game you taught me years ago."

"But we don't have to be mindless pieces like those on that board," I said. "We can choose another path, one which the Pathfinders were too blind to see." I sighed in frustration at the unimpressed look on my friend's face, then swept my hand around us. "Look at what is about to happen here, Einhard. All because of some fickle gods who rarely pay any attention to what we do anyway. Is all the death, misery, and bloodshed we are about to set into motion today worth it just to appease those aloof gods?"

Einhard shrugged as he smiled his dangerous smile. "I am just a man, Hadrack of Ganderland. A simple man with so many faults and failings that they are too numerous to mention. But, one thing I know for certain is that my god is not fickle, nor is He aloof." Einhard sniffed then with disdain. "Perhaps the reason yours are, my friend, is because they do not exist."

I bowed my head, knowing there was nothing left for me to say. "So, that's it, then?"

"It is," Einhard growled. "Surrender to me now, and I promise to be merciful with your men. Do not, and there will be no quarter given to any of you."

I returned his hard stare with one of my own. "So be it," I said, feeling a deep sadness inside.

"So be it," Einhard repeated. I thought I saw regret cross his features for just a moment, then that moment passed and he turned his horse away. Einhard paused abruptly, and I heard him curse as he saw the faint black smoke that was beginning to drift over the foothills from the west. He turned to glare back at me. "What have you done, puppy?"

"You didn't think that I would let you bring your siege engines here just so they could destroy my defenses, now did you, old friend?" I asked mockingly.

I turned Angry away before he could answer, heading for my side of the river with Einhard's molten gaze burning into my back the entire way. I paused at the riverbank and jammed the butt end of the spear I held into the soggy soil as my men finally broke their silence and began to cheer. The iron point twinkled in the sunlight as the wolf pennant below it snapped and crackled in the wind. I glanced one last time at Einhard, who still sat his horse watching me as he smoldered in helpless fury.

I knew by the look on his face that only one of us was going to survive this day.

20: The Battle of Land's Edge

"I guess Einhard didn't see that coming," Jebido chuckled when I returned to the knoll. "Maybe he would have if he had two eyes instead of one."

I didn't say anything as I studied the thick smoke rising to the west. I had sent Malo and his three hundred House Agents deep within the foothills many days ago, with instructions to stay out of sight until the enemy army had passed. I had bet that the Piths would leave the baggage and siege trains behind in their eagerness to reach my forces, especially with the soggy roads, and I had been right. Einhard, being a cautious man, had undoubtedly left a rearguard to watch over the Afrenian mercenaries and their toys. But I knew he was not expecting any kind of serious attack, since as far as he was aware, my entire army lay entrenched on the far side of the river. Nor would that rearguard who were most likely drawn from Pith youths have been prepared to deal with men like the House Agents, who were even more ferocious warriors than the Piths themselves. Now, all I could hope was that Malo had succeeded completely in his task. If even one of those siege engines had survived his attack, then it would make short work of my fortifications, and we would all die.

"Fitz is alive," I grunted. I glanced at my friend. "Einhard kept his word."

Jebido nodded. "Well, that's some good news, at least. Where did all those Piths come from?"

"Einhard didn't say," I responded. "And I didn't ask him." Angry snapped at a horsefly in irritation and it took me a moment to regain control of him. "He promised no quarter for any of us," I added in a flat voice.

"Ah," Jebido said with a grimace. "That's hardly surprising."

"No," I agreed.

The Piths were massing in the fields in a long line well out of range of my Wolf's Teeth. I could tell they weren't preparing to attack yet, but it was clear Einhard had been warned about what the longbows could do. I wondered if the Piths were waiting for a siege engine to appear, lumbering down the road like some great, fearsome beast. Had Malo failed me in the end? It was agonizing to be sitting helpless on that knoll, not knowing the answer to those questions. Purple-robed Pathfinders paced on foot all along the riders' front ranks, chanting loudly and waving small round pots hung from silver chains that billowed clouds of white smoke. I knew incense burned inside those pots, which was meant to represent the breath of the Master and give strength to the warriors. I dearly hoped that this day it proved to be ineffective.

My army stood fingering their weapons and watching the Piths, their cheers from earlier now extinguished as sober reality began to set in. I could hear indifferent birds chirping as they flew overhead and the creak of armor and weapons shifting in sweating hands, along with the occasional tortured rattle of men retching. Nothing plays more with the mind of a soldier about to go into battle than waiting for it to start. Once the action begins, you no longer have time to dwell on all the terrible things that can happen during the fighting. But before that, during the waiting time, that is when a man's imagination can become worse even than the enemy itself. The key is to get to the fighting before the fear of the unknown turns bowels into steaming brown liquid that rolls down legs or starts hands shaking so much that men can't even grasp a weapon anymore. My strategy depended on the Piths bringing the fight to us, however, and not the other way around, so all we could do was wait and let the cunning phantoms within our own minds play havoc until the bloodshed finally began.

The army we'd gathered had undergone a fair amount of training during the wait in Corwick, but that training had essentially ended the moment we set out for Halhaven. It's impractical to ask exhausted men who have marched all day long to practice battle formations at night, and I prayed that the training they'd had would be enough. Hopefully, the men I'd chosen to lead my various troops would be able to steady them when the Pith advance finally came.

My biggest concern now—and perhaps the biggest flaw in my overall strategy—was that Einhard would try to overwhelm one of the fords while ignoring the other one. It hadn't been as big a worry when I thought he had a much smaller force, believing with my fortifications that we could hold them off. I had even placed reserves in the center to bolster either ford just in case he tried that. But now that Einhard had twice the number of warriors than I had been expecting, I knew even those reserves might not be enough to hold back the Piths.

"He's going to go for one of the fords," Jebido said, clearly having the same thoughts as me.

"Probably," I grunted. I looked at him. "But which one?"

"Ours," Jebido said confidently, gesturing to the defenses below. "The passage is wider and the current isn't as strong as it is at the northern one. He'll be able to get more men across faster here."

And that's exactly what he did.

The Pathfinders finally finished their chanting, and the Piths began to cheer as the purple-robed priests left the field. I signaled for the men below to take their final positions just as the Piths started to draw their weapons. Fifteen hundred pikemen marched forward to the second palisade, encircling it seven ranks deep, with the first few ranks leveling their spears across the wooden barrier. Bundles of additional spears were interspersed along the back line to be used by the last two ranks as throwing weapons. Two units of two hundred men each set up a shield wall at an angle on either side of the palisade, protecting the main body's flanks in case the Piths tried to get across the river through the deeper water. The rest of the pikemen formed a wall fifty feet back from the main force, protecting my archers from the Pith arrows that I knew would soon start to fly. Behind them, the mounted men-at-arms waited patiently with their great lances ready in case any Piths managed to breach our lines.

"You," I shouted at one of the young riders. "Go tell Baine to join his archers with Tyris'. The Piths won't be attacking the northern ford. They're sending everything at the southern one."

"Yes, my lord," the youth said, his eyes wide with excitement as he pounded away. I glanced behind me to our supply wagons, where hundreds of boys waited with armloads of arrows. I expected it to be a long day, and those boys would likely get little rest as they ran back and forth, restocking the arrow bags of the archers on the front lines with more shafts.

Jebido nudged my arm. "Baine is moving, Hadrack," he said.

I could see my friend in his familiar black leather armor leading his men along the shore from the north, where they quickly meshed with Tyris' men. The Wolf's Teeth were in the forefront, far enough back that the lighter Pith bows couldn't reach them, but well within striking distance of the ford with their longbows.

Drums began to pound across the river, and I glanced at Jebido. "Here we go," I grunted.

I do not believe I have ever felt such nervousness heading into a battle. My hand itched to draw Wolf's Head and rush to the front of the line, and it took all of my willpower not to as the Piths finally charged with a roar that rose from twenty thousand eager throats. The ground began to shake even though we were almost a mile away across the river. I could only stare, mesmerized by the sight of so many warriors and horses bearing down on us all at once. I had briefly considered drawing more men from the northern ford or my reserves in the middle when it became clear where Einhard would attack, but I decided not to in the end. Einhard was undoubtedly expecting me to do just that, and I wanted to send him a clear message that I believed my defenses were sound and that I wouldn't need them. Besides, I was certain the moment I drew those troops away that the mobile Pith warriors would shift toward the weakened northern ford and attack it instead.

"Mother protect us," I heard Jebido whisper in awe beside me.

The lead Pith riders were fifty yards from the shoreline when the first of the arrows from the longbows started to fall amongst them. Warriors were snatched from their saddles all along the line, but they came on regardless, pressed in so densely that I could see nothing but flying clods of grass and dirt, sweat-streaked horseflesh, and whooping men. The lords in the front ranks began shouting at their men to raise shields as Pith archers on the flanks sent a withering barrage of arrows toward my defenses at the palisades. But the soldiers positioned there followed their training better than I could have hoped for, and the heavy shields of the pikemen just shrugged off the Pith shafts. Not one of our men fell under that first hailstorm of arrows. I could hear them cheering and mocking the Piths now as the lead riders surged into the shallow water covering the ford as it sprayed upward in sheets around their horses' hooves.

Twenty-five hundred archers were spread out behind the second line of pikemen further up the riverbank, and those archers began to shoot at an angle into the air, aiming over the barricade of stacked shields in front of them. The archers' position on the field was not a coincidence, as we had tested their maximum range until we knew where they needed to stand to have their arrows land in the middle of the ford. The Pith archers wouldn't be able to protect the flanks of the warriors coming across that ford effectively because of the deep water, which meant they would probably follow along behind in their traditional place instead. That would put them at the back of the ford, far enough that they wouldn't be able to target my Gander archers. The lead Piths would then be trapped in a tightly confined space in what I expected would soon be a sea of slaughter, while my archers shot from behind the safety of a shield wall into the massed warriors with impunity.

I watched as hundreds of iron-tipped shafts filled the sky, turning it dark before they began to arc downward like deadly rain on the heads of the onrushing Piths. Warriors and horses fell in droves, thrashing and screaming as the White Rock began to turn red with blood. Impatient Piths waiting on the far bank to cross the crowded ford leaped their horses into the river to either side instead, waving swords, war hammers, and axes as they tried to flank us. But the incredible horsemanship the Piths displayed on land was neutralized by the pressure of the water, and few managed to make it to our side before they were cut down. Those that did were greeted by a solid wall of shields and spears, and not one warrior gained a foothold on the bank.

The lead Piths reached the first palisade, trying to leap over it, but most horses—even those as well-trained as the Piths' warhorses—will almost always balk at an obstruction of that size. Men were flung from their saddles onto the waiting sharpened points of the barricade, with their riderless horses milling about, adding to the confusion. Waves of arrows and thrown spears continued to pour into the Piths as they cursed at us in defiance, hacking at the wooden palisade with both axes and swords. I shook my head in admiration as a giant, bare-chested warrior with a bald head balanced himself on his saddle, then leaped agilely to the top of the barricade. He roared, shaking his war hammer at the skies before an arrow transfixed his throat and he fell back into the carnage behind him.

"That was foolish," Jebido muttered beside me.

I nodded but kept silent. The Piths had already suffered huge losses and the battle had only just begun, yet I took no pleasure from it. It's one thing to be in the heat and thick of a fight like this, relishing every breath you take as you match yourself strength for strength and skill against skill with other men. But it's an entirely different thing to watch everything from afar, safe and secure, while men you would gladly call friends in a different situation do everything they can to kill and maim one another.

Finally, after many long minutes of nothing but slaughter and mayhem, drums started to sound from the opposite shoreline before the Piths began a confused and disorientated withdrawal. Our cheering archers and spearmen made them pay for every foot they took backward. Hundreds of Piths lay dead and dying all across the ford and in the river. Some of the corpses were being swept along by the current to the south, but most remained where they were, weighed down by armor. A hush began to fall over the battlefield, the cheers lessening one by one as the full extent of what had happened to our adversaries became all-too clear.

"Damn," Jebido muttered. He spat on the ground and wiped his mouth. "What a waste."

The Piths had drawn back to the base of the closest foothill, though some of the more daring had already returned, riding back and forth along the far bank in rage as they sent the odd arrow our way. I saw one woman halt along the shoreline and bare her large breasts, which brought forth the expected whistles of appreciation. Men in the front rank lowered their shields to get a better look, but before either Jebido or I could shout a warning to them, the Pith loosed three arrows in rapid succession. Two pikemen in the front rank immediately fell as the rest ducked back beneath their shields in sudden fear. Our archers tried to bring the bare-breasted Pith down, but she just twisted her horse nimbly to the side and then galloped away unscathed, leaving only her mocking laughter behind.

The boy who I'd sent to Baine earlier had returned, and I turned to him. "What's your name?"

"Culbert, my lord."

"Whose son are you again?" All the runners today were offspring of the lord's down in the field.

"Lord Rupert, my lord," Culbert answered. His face turned angry. "Father said that I was still too young to fight, but I want to help."

"I'm glad to hear it, Culbert," I said. "And help you shall. I want you to ride south and tell Lord Stegar to expect Piths." Lord Stegar was a small, intelligent man with three sons and a vast holding southeast of Corwick. All of his sons were equally as capable as their father, and I had placed all four men in positions of importance.

Jebido frowned at me." I thought you said Einhard wouldn't go around?"

"I said he wouldn't go around at first," I replied. I gestured to the ford. "Now that he has lost his siege engines and this has happened, he's going to be looking at alternatives." I knew the next likely place a force could cross the White Rock was a bridge three hours hard ride to the south from here. That bridge was too small to get siege engines and larger wagons across; that's why I had discounted it as an avenue for Einhard earlier. But it was more than big enough for horsemen to ride single file. I examined Culbert's young mare. She had fine lines and looked fast enough to get the job done. "After you speak with Lord Stegar, follow the river south until you come to a narrow stone bridge. If the Piths haven't already crossed, then wait until you see how many there are before riding back to inform Lord Stegar."

"Yes, my lord," Culbert said.

I glared at the boy. "Don't do anything stupid. Dead heroes won't help me win this battle. Just find the Piths, assess their strength, then return to Lord Stegar. Tell him I said to fall back here if there are too many of them for him to handle on his own."

"I understand, my lord," Culbert said, his face etched with determination. "I won't fail you."

I nodded and motioned the boy off as a rider appeared across the river, heading for the ford.

"Is it Einhard?" Jebido asked, squinting.

I shook my head as I urged Angry forward. "No, I think it's Saldor."

I rode Angry to the water's edge to the left of the fortifications as the Cimbrati paused his horse well out of bowshot range. The higher ford was shedding water all along its length like a miniature waterfall as it fell into the lower part of the river, where it swirled and gurgled in tiny whirlpools. Saldor was holding a spear with an Amenti banner attached to it in his right hand. He lifted his free hand to me in greeting.

I lifted mine back. "What can I do for you, brother?" I shouted across the distance.

I saw the warrior shrug. "I come with a request, great Chieftain." His words seemed to float over the water as my army waited, listening in breathless silence, while in between us, wounded men and horses moaned and whimpered all across the ford.

"I thought you told me that the Amenti would never lift arms against me," I called back.

"And we have not," Saldor replied. "Nor will we while the Wolf lives."

I grunted in acknowledgment. "Then, what is it that you want?"

Saldor shook his head. "It is not I who asks, Chieftain," he said. He gestured behind him. "The Sword of the Queen requests that you allow us time to clear our dead and wounded from the battlefield."

I hesitated for a moment, and then I shook my head. "Denied," I said in a gruff voice. Even from where I sat Angry, I could see Saldor's face harden with disapproval. "But," I added in a more conciliatory tone. "I consent to ten Amenti recovering the wounded and dealing with any horses that remain alive. You have one hour. The bodies of the dead will stay to remind the Sword of the mistake he made in fighting us."

"It is a fair bargain," Saldor said after a moment of thought. "I believe he will accept your terms."

I thought I could see the Cimbrati smiling with admiration as he swung his horse around. I cupped my hands around my mouth. "One last thing," I shouted. Saldor paused his mount as he looked back at me. "The next time Einhard wants to beg me for a concession, you tell him to come see me himself, preferably on his knees."

Saldor hesitated, then he nodded. "I will tell him, Chieftain."

I returned to the knoll then as my forces began chanting, "Wolf! Wolf! Wolf!" They were loud and raucous as they cheered me, for many of them had heard what I'd said to Saldor and had passed it on. An army is only as strong as the commander that leads them, and I had wanted my men to know that I was not afraid of the Pith warriors and their superior numbers. Einhard would be smarting from his recent failure just now, and hearing those chants would only add to his anger—that and my taunt once Saldor relayed it to him. I had said those words deliberately, knowing what effect they would have on the Sword. I wanted Einhard to react with emotion and anger right now, and, because of that, hopefully make poor decisions in the hours to come.

I smiled grimly as I watched Saldor disappear within the mass of teeming warriors. I had never wanted Einhard or the Piths as an enemy. But sometimes choices are taken from a man, and all he can do is deal with what lies in front of him, regardless of how unsavory it might be.

"What did Saldor want?" Jebido asked me when I returned to him.

"To clear the injured and dead from the ford," I responded. Jebido looked at me sharply and I raised a hand. "Don't worry. I told him he could only remove the wounded and put any horses still alive out of their misery." Jebido looked relieved, though I thought he should have known me better than that. Removing the corpses would have done nothing for me, but it would have been a great benefit to Einhard's side. The bodies lying twisted and broken in the water would only help slow the Piths down on their next attack, so why would I possibly consent to allow them to be moved?

"He's trying to buy time," Jebido muttered.

"Maybe," I said. I looked south, wondering what was happening in that direction. Had Einhard actually sent men that way to get around us? And if he had, how many would be coming, and when? It was a three-hour ride at a gallop to the bridge from here and three hours back—a long time. If Einhard had sent those men only recently, then it would be close to dusk before they would arrive. If he had sent them earlier than that, then Lord Stegar might even now be engaging them. There was no way for me to be certain, and I didn't want to waste my remaining mounted messenger to find out. I would just have to depend on Lord Stegar to handle whatever situation arose on our flank.

I had told Culbert's father, Lord Rupert, who was in overall command of my front rank, to expect Piths coming to retrieve their wounded. My orders were to let them be, so when the ten Amenti led by Saldor began helping wounded men from the ford and plains, not a single Gander raised a hand against them. It took a little less than the allotted hour for the Amenti to move all the wounded away and deal with the injured horses, and the moment they were done, the drums began to roll again. This time, Einhard had broken his forces into two groups, one of which started toward the north, where Wiflem's still untested men and the smaller ford they protected awaited. The second group remained in place, facing us as their eager warhorses pawed at the ground.

I glanced at my messenger, who sat his mount chewing on his filth-encrusted nails. "Go tell Baine that I want him to shift his archers back to their original position."

"Yes, my lord," the boy said, looking startled that I'd spoken to him before galloping away toward the river.

"I guess Einhard's thinking he has twice the chance to break through this time," Jebido said.

"Probably," I grunted, feeling uneasy. I couldn't see Einhard anywhere within the throng of warriors, but I knew I was visible to him where I watched from the knoll. I was certain that I could feel his cold gaze upon me. I wondered what he was planning.

Baine's men were still moving into position when the Piths began their charge toward the southern ford. The northern horde began their attack moments later, and both forces reached the riverbank at the same time with a volley of our hungry arrows waiting there to greet them. And just like before, Piths began to fall, though this time, something appeared to be different. I realized that all the warriors on the forefront of the attack were heavily armored, and as they forged into the water, they made no effort to assault the palisade, but instead leaped from their saddles to form a shield wall across the ford. The suddenly riderless mounts swarmed in front of that wall of men, panicking as they were now trapped between our barrier and their own riders while arrows hissed and whipped around them. Some of the terrified horses crashed through the rapidly-forming shield wall anyway, ripping gaps in the line, but most spilled out to either side of it into the deeper water beyond the ford.

More Piths were arriving along the shoreline on foot to either side of the ford, and they splashed into the water, shouting and waving their weapons at the terrified horses as they tried to fight their way back toward the western side of the river. That left the animals only one remaining option for flight, and they turned and headed our way.

"Pull back!" I called out to my men, knowing what was about to happen. But my words were lost to the noise of battle and the screams of the horses. "Stay here!" I grunted at Jebido as I propelled Angry down the embankment, shouting at my flanks to give ground and let the horses pass. But no one heard me. I hadn't even reached halfway to the river before the first of those horses came barrelling out of the water and up the bank, causing instant pandemonium as the wall of pikemen to either side of the ford buckled beneath them.

I was cursing as I rode, knowing Einhard was using my strategy at Gasterny against me as I tried to get Angry through the lines of panicking men. I could see hundreds of Piths in the river now, many of them holding their bows over their heads as they waded through the almost chest-high water near the ford. Others stripped of armor were diving into the river further down, fighting the pull of the current as they tried to swim across with axes and swords strapped to their backs. If they got behind us, I knew we were finished.

"Form up!" I screamed, launching myself off Angry and grabbing the first man I saw who had turned to run. I shoved him forward. "Make a line, damn you! Hold this shore or we all die!"

The lead Piths had almost reached our side of the river, while more continued to pour into the water from the opposite bank. Many of the Piths' terrified horses had punched through my front lines into the rear ranks, creating mayhem everywhere. I glanced behind me to my secondary line, where Lord Stegar's youngest son, Brock, stood watching in wide-eyed indecision as panic-stricken horses swept through and around his men.

"Brock!" I shouted, waving Wolf's Head to get his attention. "Send the archers back fifty yards." I pointed south with my sword. "Move half your men there and form a wall. Keep those bastards from getting around us! Then shore up my lines with the rest."

I wasn't sure by the look on the young man's face if he had fully understood what I wanted, but I had no time left to worry about it. The Piths had reached the riverbank, and they came out of the water on either side of the ford, dripping and furious as they threw themselves at our disorganized walls. Many of the warriors were falling to our arrows, but even more continued to wade and swim across the river. I glanced to my right as the enemy shield wall at the ford slowly advanced toward the palisade, knowing we were in trouble.

I could hear myself cursing as I ducked beneath a Pith's wild swing, then gutted him and kicked him back into the water. A female archer descended on me, screaming as she struck her bow across my face. I barely noticed as I grabbed her by her leather breastplate and swung her around, flinging her back into several more warriors struggling to navigate the muddy shore. All three of them fell as I continued to shout at my men to hold the line. A wild melee began then as more and more Piths swarmed out of the river, hacking and slashing at Gander shields as they tried to gain a foothold.

Pikemen were falling on both sides of the palisades as the lead Pith archers finally reached shallower water and began shooting up at us. Above the riverbank, the already soggy ground had turned from slick grass into clinging muck beneath the churning boots of the combatants. I glanced to the ford, where the Pith shield wall had halted only feet from the first barricade. The Piths were trying to set the wood on fire as archers behind them raked our lines with deadly shafts. But we'd smeared river mud all over the poles and beams that morning, and they quickly gave up when the wood wouldn't take the flame. Warriors started hoisting men into the air then, flipping them over the shield wall and onto the barrier. Many were cut down, but some managed to leap into the gap between the two fortifications. Once there, they were forced to climb the berm only to face the trench's bristling stakes below and then Lord Rupert waiting behind the barrier with his pikemen.

Brock had understood what I'd wanted after all, and hundreds of additional spear-wielding men suddenly bolstered our faltering shield wall. While behind them, my lancers spun and whirled, skewering any of the enemy who had managed to get past our lines. More pikemen had shifted to the south as I had instructed, engaging with the nearly naked Pith warriors who'd managed to swim the White Rock. The archers further up the slope were shooting over our heads with devastating effect, their barbed shafts sending Piths reeling backward into the water all along the embankment.

A warrior brandishing a double-bladed axe came roaring up the bank in front of me, the axe held over his head. My right boot was almost ankle-deep in the muck, and I kicked forward without thinking, sending a great gob of ooze into his face. The man sputtered, pawing at his eyes with one hand as I slashed through his leather breastplate with Wolf's Head. The Pith screamed and fell, dropping his axe and rolling back down the embankment, while the man coming up behind him was forced to leap over the wildly tumbling body. I impaled the off-balance warrior with my sword, sending his corpse after the previous one as two more Piths rushed at me. I kicked one in the face, and he fell while I used the edge of my shield on the other one, slicing open his cheek with the metal-rim before I cut him down.

The battle raged back and forth all across the riverbank at a furious pace as the Piths desperately fought to drive our line from the crest. My men faltered at times, our wall of shields and spears sagging under the pressure, but other than the odd man who got through and was quickly dispatched by the lancers, the screaming warriors could not break us. I stood closest to the ford where the bulk of the Piths were crossing, shouting encouragement to my men as I fought. I took on all-comers one by one as they surged out of the water, bellowing with the pure joy of battle, while the pikemen to my left and behind chanted my name. Bodies were piling up quickly all along the shoreline and the crest of the bank, with many dead Piths floating along the red-stained river as the current tugged at them. Finally, the endless waves of Pith warriors coming up the incline began to slacken, and those still forging their way toward us through the river hesitated, then began to head back to the western bank.

"Kill the bastards!" I heard Brock shout from beside me, his eyes alight with battle fury as he hefted his spear over his shoulder, then threw. The missile caught a female Pith in the back, and she fell, flinging her hands in the air as more spears sought out the retreating Piths.

I took a moment to catch my breath, patting Brock's shoulder in gratitude. Our pikemen and lancers to the south had made short work of the unarmored swimmers, I saw with relief, but the Pith shield wall at the ford remained intact. I could see warriors there hacking awkwardly with axes at the wood, but they had to lower their shields to do it, and most of them only got in a blow or two before an arrow or spear took their life. I glanced to the north, where a similar shield wall bristled in front of the smaller ford's barrier. Black smoke and weak flames were welling up from the fortification, as somehow the Piths had managed to set it alight despite the caked mud. The Piths had also gained a foothold on the shore north of the ford, forming a shield wall as more warriors waded out of the water to join its ranks. The entire river from ford to ford was filled with Piths making their way forward through the chest-deep water. Baine and Tyris had wisely drawn their archers back, raking the slow-moving enemy with waves of arrows while my infantry reserves knelt in a shield wall bristling with spears along the shoreline in front of them.

"Stay here in case they try again!" I shouted at Brock. "And keep your eyes to the south."

I located Angry and leaped on his back, heading north. I saw the Piths at the southern ford wrapping ropes around the wooden barrier as I galloped past. I smiled, knowing that they were going to attempt to yank it out of the way with brute strength, though I had expected them to use horses for the task. But I was ready for that. We'd lashed horizontal poles to the base of the palisade when we built it, then tied them to more poles buried in the ground. After that, we attached thick cables to those poles and ran them along trenches that angled up the slope to where the berm would eventually be situated. Then we'd sunk additional poles deep into the ground there, attaching the cables from the first palisade to those sunken poles before filling in the trenches and building the berm overtop. The Piths could pull on that barricade all day long if they wanted, but, unless they could move the tons of dirt pinning those poles down, the barrier wasn't going anywhere.

I reached the line of archers, sweeping past Baine and Tyris without stopping. I knew the pikemen protecting those archers could handle the Piths trying to cross the river and that they had things under control here. The smaller ford was another matter, though, and as I drew closer, I could see that the Gander line along the northern bank was in disarray. The Pith shield wall had grown considerably larger, and they had managed to push our flanking force backward at an angle, where they were now becoming tangled up with the last few ranks protecting the fortifications. The Piths had just breached the first barrier at the ford as well, pouring over the smoking ruins of the palisade toward the berm.

My lancers were waiting in frustration to the rear of the milling pikemen, unable to get through all the confusion to charge the Pith shield wall. I saw Niko in amongst them and I galloped toward the youth.

"Where is Renald?" I demanded. Renald was another of Lord Stegar's sons. I had left him in charge of the lancers here.

"Dead, my lord," Niko said.

I nodded. "And Wiflem?"

Niko pointed ahead into the mass of sweating, fighting men. "In there somewhere, I think, my lord."

"All right," I said with a grunt. "You and your lancers, follow me."

I whipped Angry about, heading back to the east around a small stand of trees as Niko and almost five-hundred lancers and men-at-arms followed. Finally, I cut to the north again and rode until I was far enough, then I swerved back toward the river. The Piths were standing a hundred feet to the south of us now, a dark mass of determined men that were fighting like demons as they slowly gained ground on my forces.

I lifted Wolf's Head and pointed at the rear of the enemy shield wall. "Kill the bastards!" I screamed. "Kill them!"

I could hear the warriors crossing the river shouting at their brothers on the shore in warning, but we were on those Piths too fast for them to be able to react in time. A shield wall can be a formable thing when faced head-on, but it is only as strong as its individual parts. Get behind or flank such a formation and, if even one man falters, it will quickly disintegrate like a straw house in a tornado. We crashed into the back of that Pith shield wall at full speed, with sharpened lances slicing through armor, bones, and shields as easily as if they were made of parchment. I was in the forefront, hacking down at the Piths to either side of me with Wolf's Head as Angry kicked and butted anyone foolish enough to remain in his path.

Our initial charge had shattered any semblance of the enemy shield wall, and lancers were now whirling within the midst of the shocked and confused remnants of that wall, slaughtering men at will. It had quickly turned into a complete rout, with no quarter given or asked for as we butchered men trapped between our two forces without remorse. Finally, only a few Piths were left alive on our side of the shore, and I guided Angry away, letting the lancers and pikemen deal with them. The Piths who had been crossing the river had turned long ago, cursing us as they headed back to their side, while at the ford our defenses had contained the attack there, though the surviving Piths still fought in vain to breach the second palisade. Finally, the drums began to sound from the west and the Piths started to withdraw, climbing back through the smoldering remains of the first palisade before crossing the ford as Gander arrows, spears, and cheers sent them on their way.

"My Lord," Niko said to me in warning. He gestured to the east, where three lancers had cornered a snarling Pith beneath an oak tree. The Pith was slashing at the lancers' iron-tipped spears with his sword, while the Ganders laughed, clearly toying with him.

It was Einhard.

"Hold!" I shouted, urging Angry forward. "Lower your weapons," I commanded. The lancers did so reluctantly. I motioned them back as I dismounted and walked toward Einhard. My friend was taking in great gulps of air as he watched me warily. His fine helmet was gone, and his cloak was torn and bloody. I noticed he was putting little weight on his left leg as he shifted toward me, his sword ready. I sheathed Wolf's Head. "Put that away," I said in irritation.

Einhard hesitated, then he lowered the weapon to his side. He smiled bitterly. "I thought we had you for a moment there, puppy."

"You almost did," I agreed. I glanced to the smoking ruins of the palisade and the bodies littering the shore and ford there, feeling suddenly weary and sick of it all. I shook my head as I turned back to Einhard. "I told you before we don't need to do this." I stepped forward and put my hand on his shoulder while Niko called out in protest behind me. Einhard's sword remained by his side, but it would take him only a moment to lift the weapon and impale me. I focused on my friend's face. "No more fighting, Einhard. Take your men and go home to Alesia and your son. You've lost. Now it's time for Ganders and Piths to live in peace."

"Lost?" Einhard said with a snort. "You think you've won because you have me?" He shook his head. "This is only the beginning, puppy." He pointed west. "The tribes won't stop just because I'm dead, Hadrack. They will keep coming until every one of you has been slaughtered and your kingdom falls to dust. The Pathfinders have seen the truth written in blood. That truth does not include peace with Gandermen, ever."

"You are a fool," I said, bitter and angry now. "You could end this war right now, but you're too blinded by hatred and the need for revenge to see clearly."

"And you have become soft," Einhard retorted. He put his hand on my chest and pushed me backward as he raised his sword. "I've had enough of your talk. We end this like men."

I just shook my head, knowing nothing I said would ever get through to him. "I will not fight you, Einhard."

"No?" Einhard said, mockery in his voice now. "And why not? Are you afraid?"

I sighed in resignation and shook my head. "No, my old friend, I am not afraid of you." I stepped out of his way and gestured toward the river. "But I owe you a life, as you pointed out to me not that long ago. Consider that debt paid in full now. All I ask in return is that you don't send any more attacks today. There are wounded men on both sides of this stupidity who need our help right now more than we need to kill each other."

"And tomorrow?" Einhard asked, looking thoughtful. "What happens then?"

"Then you get your wish," I said in a tired voice. "And we end this like men."

Einhard hesitated, studying me. Then he nodded. "Very well, Hadrack," he said. "We have an agreement. No more attacks until the morning."

I watched the Sword limp away into the river then, feeling an overwhelming sense of sadness taking over me. Whatever friendship he and I had shared once was gone now, I knew, and there was nothing left between us except the promise of more violence and death. It was a depressing thought. I gathered Wiflem and the other leaders together, informing them that the Piths would not be attacking again today. My men were skeptical at first, but while Einhard was many things, I knew he was not a man who would go back on his word once it was given. There would be peace between us, at least for the remainder of this day, anyway.

The Piths had sent a flanking force south to the bridge this morning just as I'd guessed, but Einhard had erred by only dispatching four hundred warriors. I assumed he had only wanted them to be a distraction, hoping to take our attention away from the river. Culbert had managed to reach the southern bridge first, and he'd hidden himself in the trees, only riding back to warn Lord Stegar once he was certain of the Piths' numbers. The lord immediately moved to meet the advancing Piths, ambushing them in a dense woodland six miles from the bridge. The surprised warriors had fought ferociously, Lord Stegar told me later, and his men-at-arms had suffered many losses. But in the end, the Gander numbers had been too great and the Piths were destroyed.

The attack at the southern ford had failed to remove the barrier, just as I had known it would, and bodies lay stacked all around it as a reminder of that failure. We had managed to repulse the Pith attack at all points along the river twice today, but had lost hundreds of men in the effort. The Piths had lost many more, of course, but their numbers still seemed endless. Despite my words of confidence to Einhard, I knew there were no guarantees that we would be able to do it again when the fighting resumed in the morning.

Saldor and his Amenti returned for the wounded a second time while the Piths retreated to the base of the western foothills to set up camp. This time I chose not to talk to the Cimbrati, sending Jebido in my stead. We had gained valuable time from Einhard, and that time would be spent repairing and shoring up our defenses, as well as caring for our own wounded and dealing with the dead.

I had become increasingly morose and moody ever since letting Einhard go, and as the sun slowly began to sink behind the foothills, I finally retreated to my tent to be alone for a time. Jebido brought me clean water and bandages, although he was astute enough to sense my mood and leave quickly afterward. I had taken more than one wound during the fighting, though none were serious, and I cleaned and dressed them with methodical movements, not really paying attention. Ganders had defeated Piths twice in open battle today, and I knew I should feel a deep sense of satisfaction and pride in what we had accomplished. But all I could think about was the look on Einhard's face and the inevitableness of what was going to happen in the morning.

I stood, shirtless now and filled with a sudden, restless energy. I started to pace, trying to put myself in Einhard's boots and predict what he would do next. That's when a man with three white scars on his face stepped into my tent, and the world that I knew changed forever.

It was Rorian.

21: Rorian

The last time I saw Rorian, I was leaving Sea Dragon to enter Calban and join the Walk with Sabina. The bargain Malo had struck with the scholar to learn the codex's location had been honored, and he had been allowed to return to his own lands with his wife and gold. I hadn't seen him since and hadn't once thought about him—until now. I had only known Rorian for a few days, but that had been more than enough for me to develop a healthy dislike for him, though admittedly, it had been tempered by a grudging respect.

The Rorian that I had known then was big and strong, with a cocky self-assuredness that had annoyed me constantly. But this Rorian was very different. He was thin, almost emaciated now, with long hair and a scraggly beard, both of which were caked with dirt and blood. I might not have recognized him at all if not for the distinctive scars. Rorian was dressed in a tattered, filth-encrusted robe and was unarmed, holding only a crudely carved staff that he used to support himself.

We stared at each other for a moment—me in surprise, him with what looked like relief.

"Thank The Mother!" Rorian gasped. "I found you." He wobbled then and fell to his knees, one hand held out to me.

I moved to him automatically, grasping his outstretched hand, which felt hot and dry. "What are you doing here?" I demanded, wondering how the man had made it through my camp without being challenged.

"Water?" he whispered as I helped him to his feet.

I guided him to a stool and poured some wine instead, since I had used all the clean water on my wounds. "What is this about, Rorian?" I asked.

Rorian downed the wine first, gasping as he drained the last of it. Bright red liquid dribbled off his beard, but he seemed unaware. He grabbed my wrist and drew me closer. Rorian might be thinner now, but his great strength remained. "I have been trying to find you for a month now, Hadrack."

I frowned, pulling my hand away. "Why?" I asked, not hiding my suspicion from him.

"Because of that bastard," Rorian grunted. He glanced around before sighting another wine bottle on a table nearby and poured himself a second mugful. He drank it all in one gulp, then sighed. "There, that's better."

"Rorian," I growled, getting annoyed now. "You had better start talking before I have my guards drag you out of here."

Rorian held up a hand. "Trust me, Hadrack. You are going to want to hear what I have to say." He got up, limping to the entrance to peer outside, then shuffled back to the stool. He fished around inside his robe, then withdrew a cloth bundle and set it on the ground. Then he just stared at it, biting his lips and shaking his head.

"Well?" I finally grunted in exasperation. "Are you going to tell me what that is, or do I have to guess?"

"Can't you feel it, Hadrack?" Rorian said, not looking up at me as he stared at the bundle. "Can't you just feel the heat of the lie burning through the cloth?"

I snorted. Rorian had clearly lost his mind. "You have one minute, Rorian," I said. "After that, I'm throwing you out of here on your flea-bitten ass."

Rorian looked up at me then. "I think you were always meant to have this, Hadrack. I think it was planned all along. I don't know which of the gods conspired for you to have it, ours or theirs. But now my part in this is done." Rorian looked away from me, brushing long hair from his eyes. "Either way, it's your problem now, and maybe I can get some sleep."

"What exactly are you talking about?" I demanded. Whatever Rorian's problem was, I had a battle to prepare for and had no more time to waste on riddles.

I grabbed Rorian by his stinking robes, about to throw him out of my tent, when he whispered up at me, "Remember Waldin?"

I hesitated, stepping back as I looked down at the cloth bundle. "No," I said in surprise as I realized what Rorian was implying. I looked at him. "It isn't?"

"It is," Rorian replied. His feet were encased in worn leather sandals and he pushed the bundle toward me with a filthy toe. "It's yours now, Hadrack." He shuddered. "Good riddance."

I knelt, curious as I carefully unwrapped the cloth. Inside was a thick, leather-bound book the size of my hand. I closed my eyes. It was Waldin's copy of the codex, just as I had feared that it would be. After so many bad things had happened trying to find the damn thing, now here it was in my possession when it no longer mattered. I stood, glaring down at Rorian as I held up the book. "Where did you get this?"

"You know where."

I nodded, having a pretty good idea. "You went to the Ascension Grounds?" I asked, impressed despite my dislike for the man. It would have taken a brave man with nerves of steel to go searching for the codex with all those purple-robed priests and Piths around.

"Yes," Rorian simply said.

I fingered the codex as I thought. "How did you know where to find it?"

"Waldin's journal," Rorian answered. "The Sons kept it, though I don't think any of them bothered to read it. I saw Verica's drawing and figured that since she wrote she was going south, it might have something to do with the Piths. I eventually found a Pith village and the people there told me where the place on the drawing was, though I had to go about getting that information carefully." He smiled, a hint of the arrogant man I remembered in his voice now. "I was pretending to be one of them, after all, and it was something that I should have known already. It took a while once I found the Ascension Grounds, but I finally located the codex underneath a carved stone marked with a large W. I assumed that was for Waldin. The codex lay beneath the stone in a hollow. It looked as though no one had touched it in generations."

"You actually got Piths to talk to you?" I said, surprised that they hadn't just killed him outright. Piths were naturally suspicious of strangers. Especially ones who didn't look like a traditional Pith.

Rorian gestured to his dirty robe. "No Pith would refuse speaking with a Pathfinder, Hadrack." He smiled at the look on my face. There were streaks of faded purple in his robe that I hadn't noticed before. "I told you once that I have special talents," Rorian added. "I wasn't joking when I said that."

"But why go all that way and risk your life?" I asked. "You were paid handsomely for your help the first time."

Rorian sighed. "There is never enough money in the world, Hadrack. An opportunity was offered to me, and I took it."

"By the same bastards who hired you before?" I growled in disgust.

Rorian shook his head. "No, not them. This was a contract from a rival client."

"Who?"

"His name is Lord Boudin," Rorian said.

"Him again," I grunted, feeling a deep-seated hatred for a man that I had never even met. "Isn't he a Cardian as well?"

"He is," Rorian said. "He and my prior employer have been competing to find the codex for some time." He glanced up at me. "I believe you met several of Lord Boudin's operatives during the Walk, if I'm not mistaken?"

"Emand and his bitch of a wife," I replied, understanding now.

"Yes," Rorian agreed. "Lord Boudin's spies learned my wife and I were taking the Walk. He correctly guessed that I might have an idea where the codex was, but he couldn't locate me to, um, ask politely to tell him what I knew."

"So he sent Emand and Laurea to befriend you and try to find out that way."

"In a round-about way," Rorian said. "They were instructed to kill me once I found it, but you got in their way. Lord Boudin only learned you had taken my place after the Walk began. He managed to get word to Emand, who clearly was not as competent as his reputation had led people to believe."

"Yet, after all that, you still agreed to work for Lord Boudin?"

Rorian shrugged. "Business is business, Hadrack."

I nodded, not the least bit surprised by his answer. I had given little thought in the past few months about what Emand and his wife were doing on that mountain. Now I knew why they had been there, though I still had more questions for Rorian.

"What does Lord Boudin want with the codex?" I asked. "He captured Calban weeks ago and plans to seize the throne with that bastard Pernissy's help, so I don't see what good it will do him now."

Rorian's eyebrows rose in surprise. "Really? I hadn't heard anything about that."

"They might have already marched on Gandertown by now for all I know," I said.

Rorian stroked his beard as he thought, absently pulling something dark and clingy from the tangled hairs before flicking it away. "So, Lord Corwick is working with Lord Boudin now. That's interesting." I bristled at the name and Rorian added, "I mean Pernissy Raybold, of course."

I grimaced. It had slipped my mind that Pernissy was a Raybold, which just added another layer to the hatred that I already felt for him. "That sniveling worm, Son Oriell, is helping the bastards," I said as an afterthought.

"That's right," Rorian said, his eyes lighting up with sudden understanding. "I had forgotten that the First Son and Pernissy were allies. That would explain why they still want the codex. Even if Pernissy were to take the crown, he would still have to deal with a hostile House led by the Daughters. He and Lord Boudin must be hoping the codex can change that by naming The Father." Rorian grimaced. "They are going to be very disappointed."

"Good," I grunted, pleased Son Oriell would never gain the kind of power that he so obviously craved. I lifted the codex. "But why bring this to me if it names The Mother? Why not just take the codex back to Lord Boudin and collect your payment? It's meaningless now."

Rorian sighed as he stood. "Because I can't allow a man like that to get his hands on it now that I know what is inside. I can be an unscrupulous bastard sometimes, but even a man like me has a line that he will not cross." He closed his eyes for a moment, wobbling with fatigue before he looked at me again. "I almost destroyed the codex so many times on my journey back to Ganderland. But in the end, I couldn't bring myself to do it. It was as if the gods were watching and judging me, Hadrack. I couldn't shake the feeling that terrible things were going to happen if I rid myself of it." Rorian shook his head, suddenly looking miserable. "I wish that I had never laid eyes on the damn thing. But you can't unsee something once you have seen it, much as I dearly wish otherwise. After I read the codex, I wandered for a time in the land of the Piths, not knowing what I should do. But then I reached a village, half-starved and out of my head where I heard tales of a great Pith victory at Gasterny and that a Peshwin named Hadrack, who was also a Ganderman, had won a Tribal Challenge. That is when I knew you were the man I could entrust the codex to."

"Why me?" I asked with a frown. Nothing but misery had followed the codex since I'd first learned of its existence, and I wanted nothing more to do with it. "Why not give it to Daughter Gernet or the king and let them deal with it if the words inside are so troublesome?"

"Because you are both a Pith and a Gander, Hadrack," Rorian said. "Which gives you a unique perspective on this that no one else has. You are also a man who cares nothing for power or wealth, which will allow you to view this objectively. I saw something different in you when we first met, and even that bastard House Agent told me that there was something special about you." He tapped the codex with a finger. "Whoever possesses this book will hold the power in their hands to change everything we believe in, if they dare to reveal it. I know my weaknesses, and it's a responsibility that can't be left up to me. That is why I had to find you and give this to you and no one else." Rorian put his hand on my shoulder. "You are as honest and as morally incorruptible as any man that I have ever met, Hadrack of Corwick. Read the codex, and then you will understand everything." He sighed and dropped his hand. "I am sorry to do this to you, but you are the only one I trust to decide what is the right thing to do. I wish you luck."

Rorian left then, and I stared after him in bemusement for a while, then I sat and started to read by the light of a single candle. The words inside the codex were small and precise, written efficiently. There was little that I found interesting in the beginning. Merely daily musings from the First Son and Daughter about what life had been like at the Complex on Mount Halas many centuries ago. Then I came to the section that had ignited a war between the two sides of the Holy House, and my mouth dropped open, not certain that I had read the words correctly. I started over from the beginning again, hoping that I had misunderstood somehow as growing horror gripped me. But the words were just as clear the second time around as the first, and as much as I wished it, there could be no misunderstanding what they meant. I sat back on the stool and stared at the codex in my lap in dismay, my heart thudding in my chest. Now I understood why Rorian had looked so haunted and why he had been so eager to rid himself of the codex.

The Father was not named the supreme god, just as I had expected, but neither was The Mother. There was a third, even mightier god than either one of the First Pair. This god formed our world out of eternal darkness, creating a blazing sun to add warmth and light to the sky and a foundation of rock to bear the weight of all life that would soon rise from the lands and seas. He then created The Mother and The Father from the soils of this new world, charging them and their descendants to be the stewards of all that He had made. This greater god had forged many worlds in this manner across something called the cosmos, and He was known by many different names.

But I only recognized one of those names.

The Master.

Everything Rorian had warned me about the codex was true, and I spent hours pouring over the revelations within its pages. Why had the truth been kept from us? When had any mention of the Master been cleansed from the House's writings and teachings? And on whose orders? It was a mystery that I didn't expect would ever be solved. If not for Waldin discovering the codex where it had lain hidden for centuries, no one would have ever known. I fully understood the dilemma Rorian had found himself in now, and I cursed the bastard as I stared down at the only evidence there was that the Master had been the beginning of us all. The Piths had been right all along, I realized. I felt a thud in my gut. Which meant Einhard had been right all along, too.

I glanced at the candle that flickered and twisted beside me, knowing that it would take only moments to set the ancient pages alight and the problem would be gone forever. But did I have the right to do it? Who was I to decide such a thing as big as this? I stood and carefully placed the book on the table beside me, then turned my back. I closed my eyes and rubbed them with the palms of my hands as I tried not to think about what I had read. Rorian was right, though. Once you have seen something, you can never unsee it again.

Waldin had left cryptic messages in his journal, talking about the great lie, but I had given his words little attention at the time. I had been focused on finding out what he had done with the codex and nothing else. But Waldin and Verica were the only ones who had known the truth about the Master—them, and I suppose those few who had escaped Oasis with the Daughter-In-Waiting. Had Waldin finally returned to Mount Halas only to find Verica gone and her message in his journal waiting for him? It seemed unlikely since, in my opinion, he would have taken it with him when he left. But what if Waldin had learned where Verica went another way? What if she had gotten word to him and he had never gone back to Oasis and instead had traveled south to join her?

My eyes snapped open as a sudden realization hit me. Verica had fled with the codex to where the Piths' lands now lay. If Waldin had gone to her there, it was altogether possible that many of the Piths could be his and Verica's descendants, which, after what I'd read about those two, would explain a lot about Piths. It was a sobering thought to realize that Waldin was probably responsible for how the tribes viewed the rest of the people in this world now. Why Waldin and Verica had decided not to include The Mother and The Father in their teachings was something that I knew I would probably never learn.

I turned, pausing to pull on a tunic before I grabbed the codex and headed outside. I didn't know where I was going—I just knew I needed to be out in the open where I could think clearer. Morning was still hours away and the night air was crisp. I could see my breath as I walked through the camp as a half-moon lit my way, with twinkling stars filling the sky. The Piths believed that an Ascension Ceremony was necessary to lead a soul to the Master, but I now knew they were mistaken in this. Like ours, Pith souls went either to The Father to burn and be reborn or to The Mother once it was pure enough, where She would then send the cleansed soul on its way along the final path to the Master.

Not Ascending a soul did not mean it would be lost to wander the paths forever as the Piths believed. In fact, there seemed no real purpose for the Ascension at all that I could tell from what I had read. Perhaps the ceremony's roots lay at the feet of Waldin and his perversions. I wasn't sure. I felt a momentary glow of happiness as I thought of Ania, Eriz, and all the others who had fallen at Gasterny and had never been Ascended. Ania had been so terrified of just such a death, and I could rest easy now, knowing that she was not lost along the dark paths like she had feared.

That glow quickly faded, however, as I realized the enormity of the burden that I carried. What was I going to do? I felt suddenly very small and insignificant beneath the expanse of the sky as I clutched the codex to my chest while I moved through the camp. Soldiers slept everywhere on the ground and around the dying embers of campfires, with only the shadowy forms of the sentries in the distance moving to break the stillness of the night. Einhard had promised no attack would come until the morning, but he hadn't said that the sun had to be up when it did, so we were taking no chances.

I headed down to the river, picking my way through hundreds of snoring soldiers that slept on the flattened and churned-up grasses near the palisades, where only hours before they had stood battling for their lives. A few of the men were awake, talking quietly to one another, but they barely glanced at me. No one was expecting a lord dressed in a simple tunic to be wandering among them at this time of night. The fortifications around both fords had been repaired and strengthened considerably. We'd also placed sharpened stakes in the mud along the embankments to either side of them as an added defense in case the Piths tried a similar tactic as before. It had been Baine's idea, and I dearly wished we had thought of it sooner, as it might have saved a great many lives.

"Out for a stroll, are you, my lord?"

I turned to see Wiflem approaching. "Just checking over the repairs," I said. I shrugged. "I couldn't sleep."

"Me neither," Wiflem said. "Care for some company, my lord?"

I hesitated, about to refuse, but then something changed my mind and I nodded. Wiflem followed me as I made my way down to the riverbank to stand on the muddy crest. Bodies of Piths lay everywhere along the shore, with more corpses of men and horses lying in the water all along the raised bed of the ford. The current had managed to push some of those bodies over the edge into deeper water, though most remained, held in place by their armor, which glinted and flickered in the moonlight as the water lapped gently against mail, helms, and metal plating. The odd leg or arm on the corpses swayed along with the current, which was the only sign of movement on the water in an otherwise silent night. I knew in a few hours, once the sun rose, those corpses would start to swell and stink in the heat that was sure to come.

"You look perturbed, my lord," Wiflem said, eyeing me with concern.

I gestured to the many fires lighting the Pith camp across the river. "Should I not be?"

Wiflem shrugged. "Perhaps. But we have the upper hand now, my lord. Men believe in you and that we can win this fight. The Piths, on the other hand, have learned we are warriors to be feared. That will make them doubt when they try again in the morning. A confident soldier who believes in their leader will always triumph over one with doubts."

"Have you been taking lessons from Jebido?" I asked, unable to keep a smile from creasing my face.

"I have not, my lord," Wiflem said seriously, not realizing that I was teasing him. "Though Jebido's experience and knowledge is certainly worthy of listening to at any time."

"That it is," I agreed as I fingered the codex.

"Is that a prayer book, my lord?" Wiflem asked, glancing at the leather-bound tome.

"Something like that," I mumbled. I studied him as a thought struck me. "How old are you, Wiflem?"

Wiflem blinked in surprise. "I am thirty-three, my lord."

I nodded. "And in all those thirty-three years, have you ever doubted what you were taught about the gods who watch over us?"

Wiflem's eyebrows furrowed. "Doubted, my lord? Why would I have reason to?"

"You have seen much in your life as a soldier, I imagine," I continued. "Great pain, hardship, cruelty, and suffering, along with all manner of other vile things that one person can do to another. Yet you claim your faith in those gods has never faltered even once, despite all of that?"

"No, my lord," Wiflem said firmly. "Not once."

I took a deep breath. "But what if I told you your beliefs were all wrong. That I could prove what you have been told your entire life was nothing but a lie? Would you still look upon those beliefs the same way after that?"

Wiflem scratched at his beard as he thought. "It is an interesting concept, my lord. Yet I fail to see why such an exercise in critical thinking is needed at a time like this."

"You might soon enough," I muttered. I stared across at the Pith camp, wondering if Einhard was awake in his tent, tossing and turning as he worried about what the coming dawn would bring. Then I snorted, knowing Einhard would be worrying about nothing at all. The Master and the Pathfinders had guaranteed him total victory over Ganderland, and he would believe his triumph over me in the upcoming battle was already assured. I paused, clutching the codex tighter to my chest. The Pathfinders had shown the Piths the way through the blood of Gander priests and priestesses, Einhard had said. But that way was wrong, I knew now, and the proof of that wrongness lay in my hands. I closed my eyes for a moment, aware now of what I had to do. Finally, I focused on the silent soldier beside me. "Go saddle Angry and bring him to me, Wiflem."

Wiflem gawked at me. "Your horse, my lord? At this time of night?"

"Yes," I said, my eyes fixed on the Pith camp.

"But, where will you be riding, my lord?"

I remained focused to the west. "There," I grunted.

Wiflem followed my gaze and he shifted uncomfortably. "Do you mean to try a night sortie, my lord? Because if so, I would not recommend—"

"No sortie," I snapped, cutting the older man off. "Now get me my damn horse."

"Yes, my lord," Wiflem said with a slight bow before turning and striding away.

It took Wiflem less than ten minutes to saddle Angry and bring him to me, but long before he arrived, I heard footsteps behind me. I sighed. "Don't start, Jebido," I said, not bothering to turn as he stopped beside me.

"What's this nonsense Wiflem tells me?" Jebido demanded. "You're actually going to ride over to the Piths?"

"That's just stupid, Hadrack," Baine said from my other side. I hadn't seen him moving in the darkness, dressed as he was in black leather.

"I'm starting to think you have a damn death wish," Jebido growled. "What possible good can it do to sacrifice yourself like this?"

I turned to face him. "I can end this war, Jebido. Right here and now, forever. I just need to talk with Einhard to do it."

"Then wait until the morning," Baine said. "Talk to him from the safety of the ford like before."

I shook my head as Wiflem appeared, leading Angry. "This can't wait until the morning."

Jebido grabbed me by the wrist of my hand that held the codex. "I'm not letting you go, Hadrack."

I took my free hand and pried his away, not letting up on the pressure when I saw my friend wince in pain as I squeezed. "You don't have a choice," I said.

"You stubborn bastard!" Jebido hissed. I let him go as he rubbed his wrist, staring at me with fury in his eyes. "Then if you are so bent on dying tonight, you'll have to deal with Baine and me dying as well. Because we are going with you."

"No, you're not," I growled. "I have to do this alone." I moved to Angry and swung myself into the saddle as Wiflem held the horse's bridle, his face set with disapproval.

Jebido kicked at the ground in frustration, then spread his arms as he blocked my path. "What has gotten into you, Hadrack? Why are you so determined to get yourself killed?"

I ignored him. "Wiflem," I said in an even voice.

"My Lord?"

"Have your men detain Jebido and Baine until I get back. If I see them or anyone else following me, I will take your head."

Wiflem lowered his eyes. "Yes, my lord."

"Good," I grunted as I urged Angry around Jebido toward the riverbank.

"You fool!" Jebido shouted at my back as I rode away. "You damn stupid fool! You're not even armed!"

I kept riding, focusing on the far bank where Einhard, thousands of Piths, and hopefully, the end to a war all awaited me.

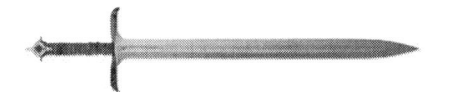

22: The Codex and the Piths

It didn't take very long for the Pith sentries to notice me. Cries of alarm sounded, followed by warriors on horseback galloping toward me. The last time that I had ridden alone toward a Pith camp, they had only tried to intimidate, not hurt me. But this time, the first man to reach me didn't even pretend that his intent was anything but my death. I shouted at him to stop and that I only wanted to talk with Einhard, but he just spat a curse and swung a war hammer directly for my head. I managed to twist to one side in the saddle, avoiding the worst of the blow. The edge of the iron face of the hammer still grazed my temple, though, with the metal shaft cracking painfully against the meat of my shoulder before deflecting away. I fell from Angry's back, landing heavily in the dew-covered grass as the Pith leaped nimbly from his horse. He came for me then, growling as he pounced on top of me, the sharpened beak of the hammer now pointing down as he lifted his weapon for the killing blow. Then a second warrior appeared, and he clasped his hand around the first man's wrist and twisted, eliciting a grunt of pain before the hammer dropped from numb fingers. It was Saldor.

"Chieftain," Saldor said to me as he pushed the injured Pith away with a contemptuous shove. "Are you lost, or have you become deranged?"

"Neither," I assured Saldor as he helped me to my feet. I felt around, relieved to find the codex still tucked safely away in my trousers, knowing that the words inside were all that stood between me and a quick death. Would Einhard listen to what I had to say, or even care for that matter? I was betting my life that he would, though I doubt even Saldor would be willing to take that wager right about now.

Warriors on foot and horseback poured out from the camp and began to swarm all around the two of us in a sea of outrage, their faces half-seen in the light of torches as they shouted angry words at me. But suddenly, there were Amenti among them, pushing back against the surging crowd as they began to form a protective cordon around where we stood.

"Why have you come here, Chieftain?" Saldor asked. "What you are doing is very dangerous and foolish. You must turn back. I can't guarantee your safety for much longer."

"I have to speak with Einhard tonight," I told him. "It can't wait."

Saldor hesitated, then he shook his head. "He won't speak with you. Go back to the river while you still can."

"Yes, he will talk to me," I said, trying to sound confident. "And as my Sword, I am depending on you to get me to him."

Saldor took a deep breath, then he nodded. "Very well, if that is what you really want. Mount your horse, my chief, and do nothing that might anger our brothers further. I will try to get you through to Einhard." He grimaced. "But don't blame me if his reaction is not what you expect."

Saldor and I rode deeper into the Pith camp together, with the Amenti warriors pressing in tightly around us on all sides, shielding me from the members of the other tribes who cursed the Amenti and called them traitors. Someone threw an axe from the crowd, which clanged loudly off the boss of Saldor's shield. I hunched low in my saddle, afraid that soon arrows would start to fly as well. Riders and men on foot from both sides pushed and shoved against one another in a teeming mass of confusion, with the Amenti working furiously to clear a path for us using the flats of their swords. But a solid wall of Piths had now moved to block our progress, refusing to step out of the way as they struck back with their own weapons. Both sides were being careful not to kill or injure one another, but I knew if we didn't break free of the mob soon, that would change and blood would start to run.

"Enough of this!" a voice rang out over the uproar. "Make way! Make way, I said!"

The Piths began to step aside, revealing Einhard limping toward us. He was dressed in light mail and a naked sword was clutched in his hand. He paused to stare up at me incredulously as he took in my lack of armor and weapons. "Have you lost your mind, Hadrack?" he finally said.

"That is what I asked him," Saldor muttered.

I jumped down from Angry and made my way toward Einhard. "I need to speak with you," I said. "It's urgent."

Einhard just glared at me in disbelief. "Your arrogance astounds me, Hadrack. Our debt of life to each other is paid. Do you really think that just because we were once friends and I made you a Peshwin that you are safe here?"

"No," I said. "I think nothing of the kind."

"Then why would you come here, alone and dressed like this if you didn't think that I would show you leniency?"

"Because I know the truth now, Einhard," I said. I pulled out the codex and held it up. "You were right all along, my friend. The Master created the world just as you told me."

Einhard blinked in surprise, then his eyes narrowed. "What are you up to, Hadrack? What trickery are you planning now?"

"Look at me, brother," I said forcefully. "Look into my eyes and you will know that this is no trick. The Pathfinders were wrong. They misinterpreted the blood, and we are fighting each other for no reason. Gandermen and Piths were never meant to be enemies. We are all brothers, born of the same gods. I can prove it if you will just listen to me." Einhard's face was set in stone, impossible to read. I moved closer to him. "We have all been misled, Ganders and Piths alike, and the time has come to set things straight." I spread my arms. "That is why I'm here, alone like this, asking for nothing except that you listen to me. Do that, and I promise you won't regret it."

"And if I don't believe what you have to say?" Einhard growled.

I let my hands drop to my sides. "Then you can do with me what you want." Einhard studied me, his one eye hard and cold. "Please, for all that we have meant to each other," I said. "Just listen. That's all I ask."

Einhard shifted his gaze to Saldor behind me. "Bring Hadrack to my tent in twenty minutes. See that he behaves. If there are any problems, I will hold you responsible."

"Yes, brother," Saldor said.

The warriors from both sides slowly began to disperse at Einhard's sharp command. I could see many of them looking at me with resentful eyes, even some of the Amenti. I tried not to focus on their hateful glares, and instead, I worked on what I wanted to say to Einhard while we waited. I figured I only had a few minutes to convince him, or, if not that, at least pique his interest. Beyond that, there was no telling what the volatile Sword might do. I wasn't all that keen to find out.

Finally, we were summoned by a monstrous Pith who reminded me vaguely of Eriz, and Saldor and I paused outside the entrance to Einhard's tent.

"I will wait here," Saldor said. "Call if you have need of me."

I put my hand on his arm. "Thank you, Saldor. You have been everything I could have asked for in a Sword and much more." I turned to go inside, then thought of something and paused to look back. "Is there a senior Pathfinder here, Saldor? One who the others listen to and respect?"

Saldor pursed his lips as he thought. "None are above the other, Chieftain. But if I had to choose, I would say Malakar would best fit the description that you give."

"Can you see if he can join us?"

Saldor inclined his head. "I will ask, Chieftain."

I stepped inside to see Fitz pacing back and forth in the light of several fat candles. "Hadrack!" he called out as he rushed forward to embrace me. "Einhard told me you were coming, but in all honesty, I thought he was just playing one of his cruel little jokes on me. I didn't think even you would be so foolish as to come here alone." He laughed. "I should have known better."

I glanced at Einhard, where he stood at the back of the tent with his arms behind his back as he glowered at me. I nodded to him, then turned back to Fitz. "I'm surprised to see you looking so healthy and fit, my friend. I guess captivity suits you."

Fitz shrugged. "I gave Einhard my word I wouldn't try to escape. I have the run of the camp, so to speak." He leaned forward, a hand cupped to his mouth, though he didn't bother to lower his voice. "Don't let that cranky face fool you, Hadrack. He's delighted to see you."

"Looks to me like he's hiding it well, then," I said sarcastically.

Fitz laughed and drew me further into the tent. "Care for some wine, Hadrack?"

I nodded and Fitz busied himself pouring us wine. I noticed a chatrang board with crudely formed figures of stone and wood sitting on a stool. "You're still playing?" I said to Einhard, surprised. I had actually thought he'd just been humoring me in Gasterny when we played together.

"It passes the time at night," Einhard muttered. He gestured to Fitz. "My slave here reintroduced it to me."

"Tut, tut," Fitz said with a chuckle. "Slave is such an ominous word." He handed Einhard a mug of wine, then me. "I prefer something closer to reluctant servant, if you don't mind? It just has a better ring to it, I think, all things considered."

"Shit still smells bad no matter what you call it," Einhard grunted.

"True," Fitz agreed with a grimace. "You certainly do have a way of cutting directly to the heart of an issue sometimes." His face brightened as he raised his mug. "Here's to friendship, then." Neither Einhard nor I moved as Fitz snorted impatiently. "Enough of this silliness, you two. You're both stubborn idiots, and you aren't fooling anyone. Now drink your damn wine and stop acting like spoiled children." I drank reluctantly, then Einhard slowly brought his mug to his lips. "Good," Fitz said, looking pleased. "Now that we have that settled, why did you risk your life to come here, Hadrack?"

"He suddenly believes in the Master now," Einhard said, his voice deep and suspicious. He swirled the wine around in his mug, then downed it in one gulp. "It's awfully convenient timing, don't you think? Hadrack knows we are going to smash him tomorrow, and he's looking for a way out."

I bristled at that. "We already sent your men running with their tails between their legs twice," I snapped. "And we can easily do it again."

"You think so, do you?" Einhard growled as he slammed his mug down on a table.

"I know it," I said, glaring back at him.

"Why do I even bother?" Fitz muttered with a sigh. He turned to Einhard. "You said you would be nice."

"This is me being nice," Einhard grunted.

"And you," Fitz scolded, turning to me. "How can anybody have a serious conversation with you when you look at them like that? Frankly, those grey eyes of yours are unnerving."

"I'm not doing anything," I protested. "It's him. He's the one not willing to listen."

"You're here, aren't you?" Einhard rumbled. "I could have just had your throat slit and left you where you fell."

I was about to respond angrily when both Einhard and Fitz looked past me in surprise. I turned. A tall, thin man with a bald head and looped rings in his ears stood just inside the entrance. He wore a bright purple robe and had an oval, intelligent-looking face. This, I guessed, would be Malakar.

"You wished to see me, Sword?" Malakar said.

Einhard turned his sarcastic gaze on me. "No, I did not. I believe we have the puppy, here, to thank for your presence."

Malakar blinked, looking back and forth between us. He gestured the way that he had come. "Shall I leave, then?"

Einhard took a deep breath, then let it out noisily as he waved a hand. "No, Wise One, you are here now. You might as well stay and hear what he has to say." Einhard folded his arms over his chest, staring at me in challenge. "I doubt this will take long."

"Very well," Malakar said. He swept past me, lifting the hem of his robes to sit cross-legged on the furs lining the floor of the tent. He glanced at Fitz with little warmth in his eyes. "Can you not see my throat is parched, slave? How long must a man wait to quench his thirst?" Pathfinders might be the equivalent of Gander priests, but they were still Piths and liked their drink as much as any other of their brethren.

Fitz hurried to get the Pathfinder some wine, and I waited until he had drunk his fill before I began. "As I explained to Einhard earlier," I said. "I know now that the Piths have been right all along. The Master is the Lord of us all. He made our world from nothing and gave life to everything that inhabits the lands and the seas."

Neither Einhard nor Malakar showed much reaction to my words, though Fitz looked shocked. "Hadrack," he said, blinking in confusion. "What are you doing? You risked your life to come here just to say that?"

"You are pandering to us," Malakar said bluntly, studying me with unamused eyes. "You speak the obvious in some misguided hope that it will distract us from the coming battle." He shook his head. "Piths are not so easily fooled, Ganderman."

I shook my head. "No, Wise One, that is not my intent. If someone had asked me only a few hours ago if I believed in the Master, then I would have laughed at them and told them no."

"Have you had a vision, then?" Malakar asked, looking suddenly interested now. "Has the Master visited you and told you to lay down your arms and accept Pith superiority?"

"No," I said. I withdrew the codex. "Inside this holy book written by Ganders is the proof that the Master created our world."

I heard Fitz gasp. "Is that the codex?"

"It is," I said. "But before I explain what it says, I need to tell a story about a man and a woman who lived long ago and a quest I participated in to find this book and end a war." I glanced at Einhard. "It's a long story, my friend, but one that I think you will appreciate. Though I'll need you to let me live long enough so that I can tell it."

Einhard merely nodded, his features unreadable as I began to talk. I told them about a Son-In-Waiting finding the original codex and concealing it hundreds of years ago inside another book. Then of how the pages were mostly unreadable when it was finally found, all except one page that had helped to start a civil war. Next, I told them of the copy the Son-In-Waiting had made of the codex and how the scholar, Rorian, who was working for the Cardians, had eventually concluded that it was hidden somewhere on Mount Halas. Then I described the harried pursuit we had undertaken over land and sea to catch Rorian. I could see Einhard's cold features starting to thaw as I talked, the warrior in him appreciating the many trials we had faced along the way. I told them then of the Walk and what Sabina and I had gone through on that heartless mountain, only to find the cave empty in the end except for a single journal.

"This man that you spoke of," Malakar said when I finally paused. "This Son-In-Waiting. What was his name?"

"Waldin," I replied.

Malakar and Einhard exchanged a look, and I thought I could detect a change in both their demeanors. "And the woman that he wrote about in this journal?" Malakar asked in a soft voice. "What was her name?"

"Verica," I answered.

Silence hung over the tent for a moment, then Einhard snorted. "It's a trick, Wise One. Hadrack has spent many months among Piths. He must have heard the story of Waldin and Verica from one of them."

"Perhaps," Malakar said as I stared at him in confusion. I noticed the bald man was sweating now, beads of moisture pooling across the dark skin of his head. The Pathfinder slicked some of the sweat away with his hand and wiped it on his robe. "Did you hear those names from Piths as the Sword suggests, Ganderman?" he asked.

I shook my head emphatically. "No, Wise One. I swear that I did not."

"Waldin and Verica are the names given to the first Piths," Malakar explained. "Their time goes back to the beginning of us all, and it is said that the Master created them in His likeness." He sniffed. "And now you come here expecting us to believe that they were Gandermen all along?"

I rolled my eyes, realizing that Waldin and Verica had instilled themselves as the Piths' First Pair. "I swear to you on The Mother and The Father that it is the truth," I said.

Malakar frowned with displeasure. "What do those meaningless gods matter now if, as you say, you believe they no longer exist?"

"Because they do exist, Wise One," I said. "And so does the Master." I flipped open the codex and read the passages that explained it all, not stopping as Fitz dropped to his knees, moaning softly with his hands over his mouth as he listened in disbelief. Finally, when I was done, I gently closed the book and held it up. "Just hours ago, the scholar I mentioned earlier, Rorian, appeared in my tent and gave me this. He found it under a stone with a special mark on it in the Ascension Grounds." I fixed my gaze on Malakar, whose face had drained of all color. "I imagine you know which stone I mean, Wise One?" Malakar simply nodded, his eyes on the codex. "I didn't want to believe any of this at first, either," I said. "In fact, I strongly considered destroying the codex and forgetting all about it."

"You should have, Hadrack," Fitz whispered. I could see tears in his eyes. "You have ruined us all."

I shook my head. "No, this will not destroy us, my friend." I lifted the book. "This is our salvation. This codex proves that we are all brothers under one god and that there is no longer a reason for us to fight anymore."

"You are naïve, Hadrack," Einhard growled. He strode toward me aggressively. I clutched the codex to my chest, afraid that he might try to take it. "Do you really think that this proves anything?" He stopped in front of me and gestured to the codex with contempt. "That somehow a few Gander scratches on some parchment mean anything to Piths?"

"Doesn't it?" I asked, ignoring Einhard as I focused on Malakar. "What does the Pathfinder have to say about it?"

Malakar stood stiffly, his face showing the anguish that he felt inside at what he had just heard. "My brothers and I must speak with the Master immediately to make sense of all this," he said. "Sword, I require you to assemble the chieftains to join us as well."

Einhard frowned. "Wise One, I do not believe that the situation warrants—"

Malakar's eyes flared. "In this, you have no say, Sword. No one disputes that your voice is heard above all others except for the Queen in matters of war. But when it comes to the spiritual, your voice is silenced, and the word of the Pathfinders takes precedence."

Einhard flushed, his face turning angry, then he swallowed that anger and inclined his head. "You are, of course, correct, Wise One."

"What about me?" I asked. "I'm a chieftain, too."

Malakar hesitated as he headed for the entrance. He studied me for a moment, then shook his head. "Your presence will be too distracting. You will stay here with the Gander slave until we return."

"And when will that be?" I demanded.

"That is up to the Master to decide," Malakar said. "He will speak to us when He is ready."

"And then what?"

Malakar shrugged. "And then, Ganderman, you find out if you live or die."

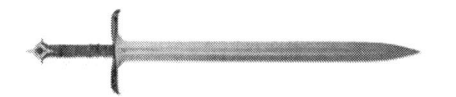

23: To Brothers, Friends, and Peace!

Hours went by as the skies lightened and the sun slowly rose, but still, there was no sign of either Malakar or Einhard. Two armed Piths stood outside the tent, preventing Fitz and me from leaving, though I wouldn't have tried to escape anyway, even if they hadn't been there. I was the one who had set all of this into motion, after all. To run now would only undermine the reason why I had come here in the first place. Would the Pathfinders see the truth and take the path to reconciliation and peace, or would they choose to turn a blind eye to it all in favor of destruction and war? I could only wait and wonder as I paced back and forth.

"You are going to wear a hole in Einhard's furs if you keep that up," Fitz said. He was sitting on a bench, the codex lying open on his lap. The pages inside were hundreds of years old, brittle and easily torn. Fitz had pleaded with me to let him read it, and I'd finally relented after he had repeatedly promised that he would be careful.

"I'm sure Einhard can find more furs," I grunted.

Fitz had quickly gotten over his shock about the Master and the First Pair. If anything, he seemed almost buoyant about the entire thing now. I found his enthusiasm quite annoying as he continuously read passages to me that I already knew off by heart.

"This part is truly fascinating, Hadrack," Fitz said, his eyes aglow with excitement. "To think that there are other worlds just like ours in this…" He paused to glance down. "In this place called the cosmos. It's staggering to imagine all the possibilities that entails."

"What possibilities would those be?" I asked, not really caring as I stopped pacing to look at him.

Fitz blinked at me in surprise. "What possibilities, my friend? Don't you understand what this means? If there are other worlds like ours, then maybe there is a way to go there and see them for ourselves."

"Why would anyone want to do that?" I asked.

"Why?" Fitz repeated with a snort. "Do you really have to ask that question? For the adventure of it all, of course." He looked up at the ceiling dreamily. "I wonder what those other worlds are like? Maybe they're cold and wet like Cardia is said to be, or hot and covered in white sand like the Afrenian desert." He grinned. "Or maybe it's just sunny and warm there all the time, with plenty to eat and buxom young women bounding naked through the meadows everywhere you look."

"I think you've had too much wine," I muttered sarcastically as I returned to my pacing.

"Your problem is that you have no imagination, Hadrack," Fitz replied with a sniff.

"No," I said as I stabbed a finger toward the entrance. "My problem is that I have no idea what is going on out there." I couldn't stop picturing what might be happening at the Pith meeting and what my forces might be doing. What were Jebido and the others thinking, staring across the river hour after hour with no attack coming and no sign of me anywhere? Did they believe I was long dead? I knew there would be a great amount of unease on the Gander side right about now, with nothing for them to do but wait and hope.

"The Pathfinders will make the right choice in the end, Hadrack," Fitz said as he carefully turned a page. "You will see." He grunted in surprise. "Listen to this. It says here that the Master lives in a place known as Beyond in the Third Realm."

I nodded, having read that also. We already knew that The Father dwelled in the realm Below, and The Mother in the realm Above. But now, there was a third, much bigger realm than the other two called Beyond.

"Why do you suppose they did it?" Fitz asked, looking pensive now.

"Why did who do what?"

Fitz motioned to the codex. "Whoever it was that decided to hide the truth from us. Why would they do that?"

I shrugged. I had wondered the same thing myself many times, of course, but hadn't been able to come up with an answer that made any sense. "I don't know," I said. "That will be up to the Daughters and Sons to figure out if they can, I guess."

"You know they're not going to be very happy about all of this," Fitz warned.

"That's not my problem," I replied. "They will just have to learn to live with the truth like everyone else."

Einhard stepped into the tent then, ending our conversation abruptly. Fitz stood in surprise at the Sword's sudden appearance, the book falling from his lap. My friend cursed and dropped to his knees as he gently scooped it back up from the soft furs.

"It's all right, Hadrack," Fitz said, looking relieved as he stood. "No harm done."

"Give me that," I growled as I grabbed the codex from him. I turned to Einhard. "So? What did they say?"

Einhard wrapped his arms around me without warning, giving me one of his breathtaking embraces. "It would seem that the Master Himself is watching over you, puppy."

I closed my eyes in relief, feeling all the tension leaving my body. The Piths had taken the correct path toward peace. I returned Einhard's embrace, matching him squeeze for squeeze before finally I stepped back. "The Master spoke to the Pathfinders?" I said.

"Yes," Einhard nodded. "In His usual vague way, of course. But it was enough to confirm that some of what you claim might be true."

"Some?" I said with a frown, feeling a sudden lurch in my chest. "Might be? What does that mean?"

"It means that not all the Pathfinders agree as to what He meant," Einhard said.

I took a deep breath, afraid by Einhard's expression that despite everything, I had failed in the end. "Which means what, exactly?" I asked.

Einhard moved to the table and poured himself some wine. "It means the Pathfinders will return to the Ascension Grounds, where they hope to get a clearer answer from the Master about all of this."

I nodded, trying not to show my anxiety. "And what about you and your army? What will you be doing?"

"We will be returning with them, Hadrack," Einhard said. "Our war with Ganderland is over, at least for the time being." I started to break out in a grin just as Einhard frowned. "But should the word of the Master be interpreted differently, then we will return. Nothing will stop us from destroying Ganderland if we do come back a second time." He tapped the codex. "Not even you and your little book of scratches."

"I never wanted any of this, you know," I said.

"I know that," Einhard replied. He looked down at his mug. "I have always believed the Master meant for us to wage this war on your people, Hadrack. It has not been easy for me to hear that those beliefs might have been wrong all this time. But despite what we have learned, I am still not convinced we won't be back, though I am glad that you and I don't have to cross swords today. I had no wish to kill you."

I chuckled. "I'm not so easily killed, old friend."

Einhard nodded, the hint of a smile on his lips. "I know. Neither am I."

We stood staring at each other then, both grinning like fools, until finally I asked, "So, what happens if you do come back? Do we start this all over again?"

Einhard raised his mug. "That, my friend, is something we can worry about another day."

"Well, there you have it," Fitz said, beaming as he approached us with two mugs of wine in his hands. He handed one to me. "Now, let's do this properly." He lifted his mug. "To brothers, friends, and peace!"

"To brothers, friends, and peace!" Einhard and I echoed as we banged our mugs together.

It was already well past midday, and Fitz and I had almost made it to the western side of the ford, when suddenly I paused Angry as a thought struck me. Fitz and his borrowed horse continued onward, the young lord oblivious of me as he continued with his mostly one-sided conversation. Thousands of Ganders were lined up at our defenses, cheering as we approached, and it took a moment for Fitz to realize that I wasn't beside him. He rode back to me with a puzzled look on his face.

"What's the matter?"

"Son Oriell," I grunted.

"Where?" Fitz asked, looking around.

"Not here," I said. I felt for the codex where it lay nestled in the band of my trousers, assuring myself that it was still safe. "Son Oriell is the problem. The bastard is probably in Gandertown right now, working to undermine things on behalf of Pernissy like the little weasel that he is."

"Most likely," Fitz agreed. He glanced across the river, where our men continued to cheer and wave, urging us to keep riding. "I'm not sure this is the time to bring that obvious point up, though, Hadrack. Perhaps we can address it once we're safely out of the reach of those heathens. What do you say?" He looked over his shoulder at the sprawling Pith encampment. "Just because Einhard has promised peace doesn't mean some angry warrior with a grudge to bear won't come riding our way soon."

"What happens when the House learns what's in the codex?" I asked, ignoring his concerns.

Fitz shrugged. "Well, I would guess it's going to be a pretty traumatic time for everyone. But people will get used to the idea of a third god, eventually. Just like I did."

"Not everyone can just shrug things off as easily as you do, Fitz." I fixed my gaze on him. "What about all those Sons and Daughters, and all those eager apprentices and their endless lessons? What happens to them when they realize everything that they have been taught their entire lives was a lie?" I sighed, thinking of Jin and how devastated I knew she would be. "And now that we know the Master created the First Pair, does that mean the Pathfinders should by rights gain control over the House? And if not them, then does it go back to how it was with the Sons and Daughters being equals and resentful of one another? We could have three factions vying for control of the House instead of just the two once this comes out."

Fitz scratched at his scalp. "I hadn't really thought about that," he admitted. I could see worry rising in his eyes now. He groaned. "What a mess. No Son or Daughter is going to accept bowing to Pathfinders, Hadrack. This thing could still end up in a war."

"I know," I said with a frown. "But whatever happens, you can bet Pernissy and Son Oriell will still try to use the information in the codex to their advantage somehow."

"Then we don't tell anyone," Fitz said firmly.

I glanced at him, assessing how serious he was. I had already come to that conclusion a few minutes ago, but I'd wanted Fitz to reach it on his own without any obvious prodding from me. "So, you're saying we keep our mouths shut about this," I said, looking as though the thought had never occurred to me.

"Only for now," Fitz hurried to say, mistaking my look for one of disagreement. "It's going to take the Piths weeks to return to their own lands. Then maybe months before they know for sure what the Master wants. Why turn the House and kingdom upside down with turmoil now when it will do nothing but help to weaken us against our enemies?"

I nodded to him in admiration. "I hadn't thought about it like that, my friend, but you're right. Telling anyone about all of this now does nothing for us." I tapped the leather-bound tome through my clothing. "I'll keep it with me for now. Once we've dealt with

Pernissy and know what the Piths plans are, then I will give it to Daughter Gernet."

"A splendid plan," Fitz said, grinning. "I'm glad I thought of it."

I smiled as I motioned Angry toward the river again. "So am I, Fitz. So am I."

Fitz and I were treated like conquering heroes when we got back to the camp, though I was surprised to see Malo amongst the cheering men as I wearily dismounted. After destroying the siege engines, I had instructed Malo to take his men north and find a crossing over the White Rock before joining my rear reserves until he heard from me. The House Agent shouldn't be here, I knew, and he was the only one not cheering as he stood regarding me with his arms crossed over his chest and a dour expression on his face. Nothing ever seemed to please that man.

Jebido was the first to greet me, and I forgot all about Malo as my friend put his hands on my shoulders and shook me. "I swear, boy," he said. "You have more lives than a barnyard cat."

I grinned, then waved for silence until a hush fell over the assembled soldiers. "Men of Ganderland!" I shouted. "I have negotiated a peace with the Piths! The war is over! They are returning to their homeland with their dead tomorrow!" A roar rang out at that news, and I raised a hand to the men as they hailed me before finally I turned away.

"How in the name of The Mother did you manage that?" Jebido asked in wonder as Baine pushed his way through the jubilant soldiers to embrace me.

"It's a long story," I said, watching as Fitz stood on his horse's saddle, balancing precariously. I guessed it was something the Piths had taught him during his captivity. He waved his arms at the assembled army, urging them to even louder and more boisterous cheers. I put a hand on Jebido's and Baine's shoulders. "One I might even tell you two about someday."

"What is that supposed to mean?' Jebido grunted, his smile dissolving.

"It means that I am tired," I said. "I've been up all night, and I need some sleep."

I made my way through the cheering soldiers toward my tent, with Jebido and Baine following and Fitz hurrying to catch up. Then I groaned when I saw Malo waiting outside the entrance.

"We need to talk," Malo said.

"Another time," I replied, in no mood for the House Agent as I pushed my way past him and into the interior.

"It needs to be now," Malo insisted as he followed me inside.

I sighed, turning to face Malo as Baine, Jebido, and Fitz entered behind him. "What do you want?" I asked in a tired voice.

"Why did Rorian come to see you?"

Both Jebido's and Baine's faces registered their surprise, though luckily, no one was looking at Fitz. He already knew about Rorian, and that fact showed plainly on his features.

"What makes you think he was here?" I asked, hiding my own surprise.

"Because I saw him in Halhaven," Malo said. "The bastard wouldn't answer any of my questions."

"So, naturally, you assumed his being there had something to do with me," I grunted. "What kind of sense does that make?"

"The kind where after some prodding with my sword," Malo said, his eyes hard and cold, "Rorian eventually told me to ask you. That's all he would say." The House Agent glared at me. "So, here I am asking."

I glanced at Fitz, who just shrugged and looked away. Did I dare tell Malo? The House Agent was unpredictable, and I wasn't sure how he would react if I told him why Rorian had come here. But he was also like a dog on a bone when he sensed something was afoot. Other than the truth, I didn't have an answer for him that made any sense, and I could tell by the set look on Malo's face that he had no intention of leaving until he was satisfied by my explanation.

"What do you think?" I asked Fitz.

The young lord shrugged. "You know him better than I do, Hadrack. Will he see things our way?"

"What are you two talking about?" Malo demanded, his face angry now. "See what your way? Does this have something to do with the codex?"

"That's quite a leap," I said, stalling for time as I thought furiously. Malo was no fool, and he had quickly deduced that the only thing I had in common with Rorian was the codex. I knew he was just guessing, of course, but now that the bone was out there, Malo was going to keep sniffing at it until he found some meat.

"Is it?" Malo challenged. He looked at Baine and Jebido. "Does anybody else find it strange that the Piths have decided to return home just hours after that bastard Rorian shows up?" The House Agent folded his arms, glowering at me. "I'm not leaving here until you tell me what's going on, Hadrack."

"What if you can't handle it?" I asked. "What if what I know could bring down the entire House and kingdom around our heads if I tell you? Would you still want to know about it then?"

Malo suddenly looked uncertain. "What nonsense are you talking about?"

I slowly withdrew the leather-bound tome from my trousers and held it up. "You were right, Malo. Rorian came here to give me Waldin's copy of the codex. Lord Boudin hired him to find it."

"That bastard again," Jebido grunted. He scratched at his beard. "But if Lord Boudin is paying him for it, why did he give the codex to you, Hadrack?"

I glanced at Malo. "Because of what it says inside. It seems even Rorian has a conscience, and he couldn't bring himself to hand it over to Lord Boudin. He decided that I was the best person to decide what to do with it."

"Because it names The Father," Malo whispered in dismay, his face paler now.

I shook my head. "No, it does not."

Malo blinked in confusion. "Then, I don't understand. What could be so damning in there to cause a man like Rorian to pass up gold?"

"Let me ask you something, Malo," I said instead. I lifted the codex. "If I tell you what is inside, what are your obligations to the House?"

"I'm not sure I understand the question," Malo said.

"What I mean is, as an agent of the House, would you feel you must report whatever you learn to Daughter Gernet, regardless of the potential damage it will bring to everyone involved?"

Malo took a deep breath. "Hadrack, if the codex does not name The Father, then whatever information it does contain can eventually be dealt with by the House. As long as the Daughters retain control, then I don't see the problem."

"That's because you're looking in the wrong direction," Fitz muttered under his breath.

"Answer my question, Malo," I said. "You took an oath when you became a House Agent. Will that oath require you to report on the contents of the codex, regardless of the consequences?"

Malo removed his helmet and rubbed his scalp vigorously as he thought. Finally, he grunted assent. "It would require that, yes."

I sighed. "Then believe me when I tell you nothing good can come of you knowing. For the sake of the House and the kingdom, go back to your men and forget all about this."

Malo shook his head. "You know I can't do that, Hadrack."

"What I know is you are a stubborn fool!" I shouted in frustration. I glared at the House Agent. "What will it finally take for you to trust in me? Have I not done enough these past few years to warrant it? Time and time again, I have proven my loyalty to the king and the House, yet always you doubt me."

"I trusted in you after Halhaven," Malo pointed out.

He was talking about after I had pretended to murder King Tyden, of course, and how he had caught me in the street outside the Grand Holy House. Malo had almost killed me then, but I had convinced him to let me go. I needed to convince him again. "And look how well that worked out for everyone," I said. "This is the same thing. All I am asking is that you walk away right now. I won't keep the information in the codex secret forever. Sooner or later, it has to come out. But if you reveal it now, I promise you it can and will destroy everything you stand for. Do you want that on your conscience just because you're a stubborn bastard?"

Malo hesitated, looking from one tense face to another. "Do you swear that you will hand over the codex to the House when you feel that the time is right?"

I put my hand on his shoulder and looked him in the eye. "I promise the moment there are no longer any threats to Ganderland that I will give it to you personally, Malo. After that, it will be your burden, not mine. You have my word."

"Very well," Malo said. "But if you are lying to me in any way, Hadrack, there will be no forgiveness for you coming from me."

"We've been through this already," I said. "I didn't lie to you before, and I'm not lying to you now. Someday you will understand why I'm doing this, and I promise you will thank me for it."

"Then I will return to Halhaven immediately," Malo said as he put his helmet back on. "If you have need of me, you know where to find me."

Silence filled the tent after Malo left, until finally, Jebido cleared his throat. "You may have gotten rid of Malo, Hadrack, but Baine and I aren't House Agents. We're not leaving here until you tell us what is going on."

I saw Baine nod his agreement, his face set in that determined way of his. I shared a look with Fitz. Jebido was right, of course. After what they had already heard, I needed to tell them the rest of it. I knew I could trust my friends to keep it a secret. I cracked open the ancient tome and began to read. Baine and Jebido reacted like Fitz had at the words inside, and as I had before him, and it was almost an hour later before I finally closed the codex again.

"You were right not to tell anyone," Baine was the first to say, his face still white from shock.

"Definitely," Jebido agreed. He shook his head in wonder. "How did Einhard take the news?"

I shrugged. "About as well as you might expect."

"What if the Piths tell someone about this?" Baine asked.

"Who would they tell?" Fitz responded. "They're not likely to talk to any Ganders on the way home, and even if they do, who is going to believe such a wild tale coming from heathens?"

"Good point," Baine muttered.

"So, what do we do now?" Fitz asked me.

"That part is easy," I replied. "We go north, find Pernissy and Lord Boudin, and crush the bastards once and for all."

24: The March North

It took almost three weeks to march the remainder of my army northward. We had lost men against the Piths—many of them. But despite that, we were still a force to be reckoned with, one which was now reasonably battle-hardened and in good spirits. We had seen no sign of either King Tyden's army nor Pernissy's as we progressed, and now that we were less than twenty miles from Gandertown, it appeared more and more likely that the city was not under siege as I had feared. I would have to wait a little while longer for my scouts to return from Gandertown, though, before I would have definite confirmation of that fact. Had the king managed to intercept Pernissy at Silver Valley to the west like we'd discussed? I could only hope that was the case, though it would mean a long march for us to get there if it was.

I led my army along a dirt road that cut through a thick woodland and then out onto a grassy plain. Blankets of thick clouds had filled the sky to begin the day, but now they were slowly breaking up, allowing the full strength of the sun to beat down on my marching soldiers. A series of rounded hills choked with purple lavender rose in the distance, with the road we traveled curving around them. That road would either lead us north to Gandertown or westward toward the valley, depending on the news my scouts would be bringing with them.

I kicked Angry into a canter as Jebido joined me, the two of us climbing to the top of the closest hill to get a better view. I paused to look back the way that we had come. My forces marched five abreast along the road below me before disappearing back into the woods more than a mile away. The wide-open grasslands here would make a good place to halt and wait until we got word where the king was.

"Hadrack," Jebido grunted. He pointed to a cloud of dust rising along the road to the west. "Looks like riders coming this way."

I shielded my eyes from the sun, waiting long minutes until the mounted men drew closer before I was sure which banner they flew. Then I urged Angry down the slope as Jebido followed. We reached the road, waiting to one side of it as the riders approached. I counted twenty soldiers on horseback, every one of them grim-faced as they surrounded a carriage pulled by a set of sweat-streaked black horses. Many of the soldiers were wounded in some way, and they slowed suspiciously when they saw us. I lifted a hand in greeting as they came to a dusty halt thirty feet away. A man of about forty guided his horse toward me. His hair was grey and cropped close to his scalp, and he was dressed in blood-stained mail. The man's right arm hung limply in a sling and I realized that I knew him.

"Lord Hamit, is it not?" I said. I had met him briefly at the king's coronation, and I knew that he was a close confidant of Tyden's.

"Lord Hadrack?" Lord Hamit said in surprise, his eyebrows rising as he recognized me. "I thought you were supposed to be defending the south from the Piths?"

"I was," I said with a curt nod. "They agreed to a peace settlement and have returned to their homeland." I gestured to the hills. "I have thirteen thousand men with me in the fields yonder."

Lord Hamit sagged with relief in his saddle. "Well, thank The Mother for that."

I studied the wounded men behind him critically. "What happened?"

Lord Hamit's face clouded. "We met the Cardian army six days ago near Mount Taril," he said. He lowered his eyes. "We were outnumbered and they held the high ground. I advised King Tyden to withdraw, but he chose to attack their position anyway."

I frowned. Mount Taril was many miles west of the Silver Valley where Tyden had intended to trap Pernissy. I flicked my gaze to the carriage and the eagle banners flying there. "Is the king inside?" I asked, feeling suddenly anxious. "Is he hurt?"

Lord Hamit shook his head. "No, the king is fine. It's his advisor, Clamon Krael. We're taking him back to Gandertown." The lord shrugged. "Not that it will do him much good. It's doubtful the man will live much longer, by the looks of things."

"Where is the king now?" I asked.

"Encamped at the mouth of the Silver Valley," Lord Hamit explained. "He plans on holding the Cardians there while I gather more conscripts."

"He was supposed to hold the Silver Valley all along," I said, my voice thick with bitterness. "Not go after Pernissy like that."

Lord Hamit nodded his agreement. "That was his original intent, Lord Hadrack. But the Cardians refused to enter the valley and the king finally became impatient." He shook his head. "We tried to get to the bastards, but we had to cross a stream and climb a hill to reach them, and with all the rains lately, we became bogged down in the mire along the banks."

"And his archers decimated your men while you crossed," I said, secretly cursing Tyden for being such a reckless fool.

"Yes," Lord Hamit said. He grimaced, his face turning angry now. "We pushed through the muck anyway and made our way up the hill. The fighting was fierce, but it seemed like we were making headway and that we were going to triumph. Tyden brought up our archers to drive the Cardians from the ridge, but then a second force hiding in some woodlands swept down on us from the north." He shrugged, looking like a beaten man. "You know as well as I do what happens to archers caught in the open by horsemen."

I nodded. I did know. "So, Pernissy held back his reserves to draw you in," I said with grudging respect.

"Yes," the older man said. "But they weren't Cardians. They belonged to the lords Hendry and Ralice." Lord Hamit spat on the road with distaste. "Those bastards have hated the king ever since he confiscated some of their lands after the Pair War. I guess they saw this as a chance to get even with him."

I grunted, not in the least bit surprised. Tyden had made many enemies during the civil war, and it stood to reason that some of them might have joined with Pernissy. I pictured the former Lord of

Corwick laughing at the king's humiliating defeat. The bastard probably thought he had already won the fight, but he didn't know about me yet. I was looking forward to reuniting with him and turning that arrogant laughter into screams of agony. The trick would be getting my men to that valley in time to do it.

Lord Hamit and I talked for a few minutes more, and then he continued toward Gandertown with the dying advisor.

"If the Cardians get past the king with that many men, we are going to be in trouble," Jebido said, riding beside me on my right as I led my army west. Wiflem, Baine, and Fitz rode to my left, with the steady clump of thousands of boots crunching along behind us.

I nodded my agreement. Tyden had brought an army of twenty thousand men to face Pernissy, but he had lost more than half of them in his foolish attack. If Lord Hamit was correct, then the Cardians and their Gander allies numbered close to forty thousand soldiers. I had thirteen thousand, including Malo and his fellow House Agents, who I had brought along with me. Would they be enough coupled with the king's men? Cardians were not the fighters Piths were, of course, but defeating an army of that size would be no easy task regardless of their skill, especially if the king had failed to contain them in the valley.

I glanced behind me at the men filling the road, then at Wiflem. "How long before we get to Silver Valley at this speed?"

Wiflem looked up at the sky as he thought. "I would guess we're moving at a little less than three miles per hour. The valley is roughly eighty miles from here, and we can make fifteen miles per day, perhaps twenty or twenty-five if we take shorter breaks and extend the march."

"That depends a lot on the terrain and weather, though," Jebido pointed out.

Wiflem bowed his head in acknowledgment. "That's true."

"So, assuming all goes well, then we are looking at four days at best," I said, not happy in the least.

"Yes, my lord," Wiflem said. "That sounds right."

I cursed. "Tyden could be long dead by then."

"We could send the cavalry ahead," Baine suggested. "If nothing else, it would help shore up the king's defenses until the rest of the troops arrive."

I nodded, having already considered that option. The problem was Tyden had lost most of his archers during the battle and a good portion of his infantry as well. His remaining force consisted mainly of mounted men-at-arms now, perhaps as many as seven thousand. But, without the support of archers, that mounted force would be vulnerable to the Cardian pikemen that I knew Pernissy would be sure to throw against them. Adding my men-at-arms would help, of course, but not enough to chance risking them if Pernissy had as many foot soldiers as Lord Hamit had told me. I also wasn't keen on separating my forces, which would leave me just as vulnerable as it had Einhard. I didn't have siege engines along like the Piths had, but I did have a long baggage train filled with food, grain, fodder, and water that I couldn't chance risking. An army lives and breathes on its supplies. Take them away and that army quickly withers and dies.

"Very well," I said, coming to a decision. "We increase the pace to four miles per hour and shorten the breaks from ten minutes to five every hour." I glanced around. "That should save us a day."

"But what do we look like when we get there?" Jebido muttered.

"Like an army of tired but angry Ganders thirsty for blood," Fitz said with a chuckle. He shook his head and gestured over his shoulder with a thumb. "I wouldn't want to be the Cardians when these boys arrive."

The rest of that day remained clear and bright, though the heat intensified just before midday. There was no breeze to speak of, either, yet my men marched along in surprisingly high spirits, laughing and joking with each other as drummers pounded out the increased walking beat. Every hour we would take a five-minute break, with hundreds of boys from the baggage train running down the lines of sitting men doling out rations of tepid water. We made twenty-eight miles that first day, and I couldn't have been prouder of my men, positive now that The Mother was watching over us and all would be well.

Things changed for the worst on the second day, however, as the oppressive heat somehow increased even more. Men who had laughed and joked yesterday now stared at their feet in dismal silence, trudging to the unrelenting beat of the drums. Several soldiers had already been lost to the unforgiving sun, with no sign that the heat planned on showing us mercy anytime soon. Perhaps The Mother wasn't watching over us after all, I thought bitterly as I sat Angry along the road and studied my men. I called out encouragement through cracked lips to them on occasion, though few if any of the weary soldiers bothered to look up or even acknowledge my words. A tall, thin man suddenly fell in front of me, collapsing without warning to the dusty road as exhausted soldiers stepped over or around him. I jumped off Angry and made my way forward to help, but it quickly became apparent that he was dead. I instructed two red-faced men to drag the body to the side of the road as indifferent soldiers continued onward with barely a glance at the corpse as they passed.

"That won't be the last one to drop," Fitz said with a sigh as I returned to Angry and swung myself onto his back. Beside him, Jebido and Baine nodded their agreement.

"I expect not," I said, trying not to sound as dispirited as I felt.

"How far do you think we've come today?" Baine asked. He removed his helmet and wiped sweat from his brow.

I shielded my eyes as I looked up at the sun. It was already past midday, I realized with dismay. "Maybe eight miles," I said, tasting the bitterness in my voice. "Maybe less." I glanced toward a vast forest standing to the north that seemed to shimmer and dance in the distance from the heat. "We're falling way behind." I looked at my friends. "Should I increase the beat, do you think?"

"I don't think it matters how fast those drummers bang their drums, Hadrack," Jebido said. "I'm a lot older than any of you, and I don't recall it ever being this hot. Those poor bastards can only move so fast in this. If you try to increase the pace now, we might not make it to Silver Valley at all."

I cursed, knowing that he was right as I closed my eyes, trying to ignore the heat, fatigue, and buzzing insects. I had sent scouts on fast horses to the valley, of course, but I didn't know when I might be hearing back from them about what the situation was there. I felt like a blind man trying to feel his way through an unfamiliar room. Where was Pernissy? What had happened to Tyden? Was he already lying in a field somewhere, rotting as scavengers feasted on his flesh? It was maddening beyond belief to not know what was happening.

I opened my eyes just in time to see Tyris riding past us as he led five hundred of my Wolf's Teeth. The tall archer bowed his head to us, his eyes shaded by his leather helmet as his horse plodded onward, while the men behind him on foot labored to keep the pace.

"All right," I said, coming to a decision after seeing the archers. I turned to Baine. "Go get Tyris and tell him I want to see him." My friend rode off immediately as I glanced at Jebido. "I want you to take over command of the army here, Jebido. I'll take three thousand men on horseback and forge ahead. Maybe we can reach the king in time."

"You wished to see me, my lord?" Tyris said as he and Baine approached.

I nodded. "How many of your men can ride?"

Tyris blinked in surprise. "Why, I don't know, my lord. I never asked them."

"Then I guess we are about to find out," I grunted. I glanced at Jebido and Baine. "I need horses for the Wolf's Teeth. Packhorses, mules, whatever you can find with four legs and a heartbeat."

"But what about the supplies they're carrying?" Jebido asked.

"Do whatever you can," I said. "You can distribute the packs among the men if you have to. Just get me those mounts. We leave in an hour."

Just over an hour later, we set out with almost three thousand men-at-arms, followed by the Wolf's Teeth. Jebido and Baine had confiscated every animal possible, including mules, aged horses, and rickety wagons pulled by oxen. Some of those animals and wagons belonged to the many camp followers that always trailed an army like vultures, waiting to rob the corpses of the fallen combatants. Those camp followers had not been pleased with Baine's and Jebido's demands. But given a choice between cold steel and giving up their animals and possessions, the decision had ultimately proved to be an easy one for them to make.

Many of the Wolf's Teeth were riding for the first time in their lives, though almost half their number were relegated to the wagons, where they could at least sit in relative comfort. Some of the archers riding mules and the older horses quickly fell behind my main force, even farther than the wagons, but I pressed onward anyway, not willing to wait for the stragglers. Those men would just have to do the best they could to keep up.

We made thirty miles that day, riding well into the night, with the coolness of the evening a welcome relief from the heat. We finally halted to pitch camp in a wide hollow, and the next day my force was on the move again well before dawn. A persistent drizzle began to fall at daybreak, leaving men wet, cold, and miserable, and no doubt wishing for a return to the heat from the day before. That persistent drizzle turned into sheeting rain by midday, turning the road beneath our horses' hooves into a river of muck and ooze that clung stubbornly to everything it touched. I wondered what effect the weather was having on Jebido and the main body of my army coming behind us, guessing that things were probably not going well for my friend.

Finally, as dusk was approaching, the rain began to ease up, then it ended abruptly just as we came to a series of rock-strewn hills. We followed a winding canyon through those hills, with the rocky floor almost ankle-deep in water until we found ourselves breaking out onto a barren plateau. A well-worn trail led down to a lush valley ringed by mountains, with the tall, white-capped peak of Mount Halas dominating everything else below it. We had reached Silver Valley.

"Hadrack," Baine said, pointing west across the valley floor.

Flickering campfires were burning briskly almost a mile away where two of the mountains pinched together, helping to illuminate the vague outlines of hundreds of shadowy tents. I grinned at my friend as I urged Angry down the steep trail. We had found the king.

The incline proved surprisingly treacherous, slick, and unstable from all the rain, and once I reached the valley floor, I waited for Baine, Wiflem, and Fitz to join me.

"Wait here with the men until I send for you," I told Wiflem. I was afraid that with such a large, unexpected force like ours bearing down on their camp, that the king's men might not realize who we were and think they were under attack. "Fitz," I said to the young lord. "Come with me."

Fitz and I rode to within a hundred yards of the king's camp before a sentry challenged us.

"Who rides there?" the man called out.

It was dark now, and I could see little of him other than the brief wink of his mail and the glint of the bare sword he held. "Lord Hadrack and Lord Fitzery to see the king," I said.

The sentry spat on the ground as he took several steps closer, peering up at us. "I have it on good authority that Lord Hadrack is in the south fighting the Piths," he said suspiciously.

"Listen, you dim-witted fellow," Fitz said in annoyance. "We have just marched for three solid weeks to get here. If my ass wasn't being baked by the sun or rubbed raw by my saddle, it was developing rot from all the damn rain that's fallen. I'm tired, I'm hungry, and I need a drink. So, unless you want me to get down off this horse and unleash my frustrations on you, I strongly recommend that you let us pass."

The sentry hesitated, then he sheathed his sword and gestured behind him. "Of course, my lord. Please forgive me. These are trying times."

"Indeed they are," Fitz said with a sniff as he and I rode into King Tyden's camp.

Several boys dressed in filthy grooms' clothes ran to take our horses while a tall, grey-haired soldier made his way toward us. Men sat in silence around campfires, studying us wordlessly, with an almost overwhelming mood of dejection emanating outward from them.

"Lord Hadrack," I said, introducing myself to the grey-haired man. I indicated Fitz. "This is Lord Fitzery."

"Please tell me you have men with you, lords," the man said, looking weary and anxious at the same time.

"I have," I said. "An entire army is just days away. But for now, I've brought three thousand men-at-arms and five hundred archers."

"Then perhaps we are saved after all," the man said, sudden hope rising in his eyes.

"And who might you be?" Fitz asked.

"Forgive my manners, lords," the man said, coloring. "My name is Fignam Ree. I am in command here."

I raised an eyebrow. "What of the king?"

Fignam's face clouded. "He has fallen ill, lord, and has delegated responsibility to me until he recovers."

"What's wrong with him?" I asked, my heart racing as we headed toward a large tent.

"We fought the Cardians days ago," Fignam explained. "During the battle, the king took a wound to his leg. It seemed like nothing to worry about at first, but then it began to fester yesterday. Now a fever has taken hold. We have done what we can for him, but we have no healers here."

"Where are the king's physicians?" I asked, knowing no king went on a campaign without at least two of them by his side.

"One is dead, lord," Fignam announced with a shrug. "Killed yesterday morning when the Cardians attacked our position here. The other went back to Gandertown three days ago with Advisor Krael, who was grievously injured."

I cursed, realizing the physician had been in the wagon Lord Hamit was protecting. "Is there no one else here with medical knowledge?" I asked as we paused at the entrance to the king's tent.

Fignam shook his head as he pulled aside the tent flap and we stepped inside. "No, lord. None left alive, anyway."

The tent was lit by several lanterns hanging from pole rafters, and the king lay swathed in furs on a makeshift bed of straw and grass. His eyes were closed, and a boy knelt on the floor beside him, using a wet cloth to dab at the sheen of sweat on Tyden's face.

"My lord," the boy said, jumping to his feet in surprise when he saw me. I recognized him immediately. It was Kacy, the half-wit cook's helper who had been with us at Gasterny.

"How is he?" I grunted at the boy as I knelt by the bed. I felt the king's forehead. Despite the cold cloth Kacy had been using, the king's flesh still burned against my palm.

"I think sick, lord," Kacy said, looking at the ground as he shifted from one foot to the other.

"Yes," I grunted. "I think you are right." I pushed aside the furs, wrinkling my nose at the sudden smell of rot. Tyden was dressed in a long white tunic and I pulled it up, grimacing. The king's right leg just below the knee was swathed in bloody bandages. I carefully unwound them to reveal a long gash running along the inside of his leg. Green and yellow pus mixed with watery pink blood oozed from the wound. I glanced over my shoulder. "Fitz, go back to the hills and find Malo. Tell him what's happened and that we need Goldenseal right away."

"What's Goldenseal?" Fitz asked.

"Something that will hopefully save me from having to cut off our king's leg," I said in irritation. "Now go!"

Fitz blanched, then spun on his heels and dashed out of the tent.

"You no cut leg off, lord," Kacy said as giant tears started to roll down his cheeks. "Please."

"Is that really necessary?" Fignam asked, looking worried now. "Won't the fever just pass on its own?"

"Maybe," I said. "But if it doesn't, I would rather have a one-legged king than a dead one."

"Hadrack?"

I looked up to see Tyden's eyes were open. He was staring at me, his forehead furrowed. "Is that really you? Am I dreaming?"

I moved closer and took his hand in mine. "You're not dreaming, Highness," I said gently. "It's me, and I've brought an army from the south along with me."

Tyden coughed, trying to sit up. I helped him, waiting as more coughs wracked his body. I glanced at Kacy. "Water?" The boy hurried to hand me a waterskin and I placed the tip to the king's lips. "Easy there," I admonished as Tyden took in great gulps, most of it splashing down his chin. "Take it slow."

Finally, Tyden nodded that it was enough. "The Piths?" he gasped. "What happened?"

"They have returned to their homeland, Highness," I said, adding no other details than that.

Tyden lay back then, sighing as he clutched at my hand. "I imagine I have you to thank somehow for that miracle, Lord Hadrack."

"Not just me," I said with a tired grin. "All of your men. They're the ones who deserve your praise the most, Highness."

"Modest as usual," Tyden said with a weak chuckle. He shook his head. "You are forever my protector, aren't you?"

"I do what I can, Highness," I said. I looked up as Malo arrived with Fitz. The House Agent took in the situation at a glance as he motioned me aside. "I will return shortly, Highness," I told the king. "I want to get my men settled. Malo will make you well again, I promise."

"Lord Hadrack," Tyden called out as Fitz and I turned to go. I paused. "Pernissy will have had enough of this playing around by now. He is going to be coming in the morning with everything he has." I glanced at Fignam, who nodded his agreement. The king pointed weakly at me. "You will take command here. Crush the bastard for me, Lord Hadrack. Do you hear me? I want my cousin's head on a pike. Will you do that for me?"

I smiled. "With pleasure, Highness," I said. "With pleasure."

25: The Battle of Silver Valley

The next morning brought with it a return to the heat the moment the sun broke over the hills in the east. I had gotten very little sleep the previous night, spending much of it talking with Tyden, who was barely lucid at times, while Malo cleaned and then packed his wound with Goldenseal. The House Agent was more reserved than normal, which was saying a lot. I knew he was distracted with thoughts of the codex and what it might reveal once we had finally dealt with Pernissy. To his credit, though, Malo never once broached the subject to me, even when we were alone together.

I could feel the ancient tome with its startling secret pressing into the small of my back with every move that I made. I had tied it snugly against my skin with strips of cloth, afraid to let it out of my sight. Jebido, Baine, and Fitz were all made aware of the codex's location, and if I fell in battle, the burden of what lay inside its pages would then fall to one of them.

I had managed to deflect Tyden's questions aside about why the Piths had returned home, citing my friendship with Einhard as the main reason. Malo had looked up sharply at that, but he had wisely remained silent. I could tell the king wasn't fully satisfied with my answer, either, but in the end, he had let it go. I think his fever had a lot to do with that. The Goldenseal mixture helped lessen that fever after several hours, though the king's persistent cough continued. Once I was confident that Tyden could be moved safely, I sent him in a wagon back to Gandertown with Malo and three other House Agents to watch over him. The king's life now lay in Malo's hands, just as once Jebido's and Baine's had after the fall of Gasterny. I could only hope that this time things would turn out just as successfully as they had the last.

I had spent the rest of the night after Tyden's departure getting briefed by Fignam about the strength of his men. I was delighted to learn that Putt and the soldiers that I'd sent with him to escort the king to Gandertown weeks ago were all in camp and were in reasonably good health. Putt had suffered an injury to his sword arm during the failed attack on Pernissy, but he insisted it was nothing that would keep him from standing in a shield wall. Tyden had erred in making that attack, but at least the king had chosen an ideal spot to make his final stand. I only wish he had stuck with it the first time and had never left.

Silver Valley was almost thirty miles long and a mile across at its widest point, curving in a wide arc to the south before sweeping east. It then narrowed down to a quarter-mile where rocky outcrops from both Mount Hajal and Mount Lespin jutted toward each other like outstretched hands, creating a natural bottleneck. That is where King Tyden had placed his men, and it was there that I was determined to be rid of Pernissy Raybold once and for all.

The Cardians had thrown themselves at the king's lines several times the previous day. Fignam assured me neither of the attacks had been serious though. The enemy had come with less than five thousand infantry and archers on both occasions, retreating in disarray after engaging our forces for only a short time. Fignam believed Pernissy was trying to draw his men away from the bottleneck and around the bend, where the main Cardian forces could then overwhelm them with as little loss of life to their side as possible. I agreed with him. Taking our position would not be easy, and the Cardians would lose many men in the attempt. Men that they would need if they hoped to take Gandertown afterward. Pernissy might not value the lives of the soldiers he commanded, but clearly someone else on the Cardian side did. Our only chance lay in staying patient and holding our position until Jebido and the rest of my army arrived to reinforce us in the next day or two.

Four hundred and seventy-seven of my Wolf's Teeth managed to make it to camp, though many of them didn't arrive until well into the evening. I never did learn what became of the others, guessing that most had lost heart at some point during the journey and had fled. Fignam still had three hundred archers to call upon, as well as close to a thousand infantry and six thousand mounted men-at-arms. There were also almost six hundred cooks, servants, carpenters, and blacksmiths, as well as many other trades in camp. All of whom I intended to throw into our lines. They might matter little in the end, I knew, but if we fell to Pernissy, they would all be slaughtered anyway, so a Gander victory here remained their only hope.

    The sun was almost completely over the hills now as I walked our lines, with Baine, Fitz, Wiflem, and Fignam all joining me. I had dismounted all but five hundred of the men-at-arms, giving every man a spear to go along with their shields and swords. I now had almost ten thousand infantry—most of them battle-hardened—broken up into four squares of twenty-five hundred men each. Wiflem was to lead my left wing, Fitz my right, with me taking command of the center where I'd placed the remaining House Agents. Fignam would command the final block of infantry, which I would hold in reserve behind my center line along with the five hundred horse. Those infantry reserves would also be used to spell tired units in the front ranks as the battle wore on. Fignam's remaining three hundred archers would shoot from between the two ranks in the center with their lighter bows.

    I heard a shout as the mounted rider I had sent down the valley turned and raced back our way, his hand waving urgently over his head. The Cardians were coming.

    "You better get going," I said, turning to Baine. "They'll be around that bend in a few minutes."

    My friend glanced south toward the jutting outcrop that towered over the valley. Archers were ascending a network of hastily-made rope ladders hanging down the rock face that led up to a flat section almost three hundred feet above us. The same was happening along the outcrop to the north, where I could see Tyris' tall form looking down over a ridge as he shouted at the few stragglers still on the ground to hurry. The right side did not have as convenient a shooting platform as the left, however, so Tyris' men were perched wherever they could gain a decent foothold.

"You sure I shouldn't start with their infantry?" Baine asked.

I shook my head. "No, let them pass. I want those first few volleys to catch their archers by surprise. You leave the infantry to us."

"All right, Hadrack," Baine said, looking unconvinced. He started to go, then paused to point at me. "Take care of yourself."

I grinned and nodded. "You too."

Baine hurried to the south and grabbed one of the ladders. I marveled at how nimbly and efficiently he climbed upward just as faint horns began to sound from down the valley. Fitz was beside me and I gave him a shove. "Go," I commanded. "All of you to your posts and may The Mother watch over you."

I ran to the center wedge's front line, placing myself between Niko and a stocky soldier that I didn't know who held two spears. The man grinned at me, revealing two missing front teeth as he handed me one of the spears. "It's an honor to fight by your side, lord," the man said, each word whistling oddly. He gestured to a one-handed battle-axe with a sharpened point jammed into his belt. "I'm Pax, and I've been itching to cut up some Cardians all morning with this thing."

"Well, Pax," I said as a shadowy line of men appeared around the bend almost half a mile away. "I think you are about to get your wish."

The Cardians came on at least ten ranks deep, the crunch of their boots loud in the stillness of the morning air as the steady beat of drums echoed off the valley walls. A flock of starlings startled by the approaching infantry took off in a dark cloud from a stand of hickory trees, swooping up and over the rocks, heading south. I glanced nervously toward my Wolf's Teeth, worried that they would be seen, but the last of the ladders were even now being drawn up as my men crouched low, hidden from sight from the valley floor. I breathed a sigh of relief.

"Damn, that's a lot of the bastards," Pax said with an eager grin as more Cardians on foot and horseback appeared behind the marching infantry.

The mass of riders held raised lances in their right hands with the butts balanced easily on their stirrups. The iron tips gleamed like a thousand suns in the morning light, with either bright yellow, pale blue, green, or orange pennants tied just below the sharpened points snapping in the wind. Four standard-bearers rode in front of the main body of horsemen, each one carrying a massive flowing banner on a long pole. The banners coiled and rippled like living things over the heads of the men coming up behind. I could see Pernissy's golden dragon clearly, along with a charging boar on a blue background that I was certain belonged to Lord Boudin. A green banner depicted a roaring lion, and an orange one a strange black, cat-like creature with long fangs and gleaming claws. Those would belong to the two traitorous Gander lords, I guessed.

A horn sounded three times from somewhere behind the massed horses, the shrill notes rebounding against the rock walls. The Cardian pikemen cheered the horn and locked shields without losing a step. Thousands of archers wearing the familiar bright red capes that I had learned to despise marched in tight formation between the mounted lancers and the infantry. Those archers were going to be a problem unless I could silence their longbows.

I glanced again to where my Wolf's Teeth waited. My pikemen would be vulnerable to the Cardian arrows soon, but my archers would be difficult to target as high up and as well-protected among the rocks as they were. The Cardian longbowmen would be lightly armored, if at all, believing that they were safe from our few archers and their smaller bows. But they didn't know about the Wolf's Teeth yet, and once my men started shooting, those vulnerable archers would be caught between the advancing infantry and the massed horsemen behind. Cardians were all cowards at heart, and I hoped if enough of those archers fell in the first few volleys, that the rest would break and try to flee, causing mayhem and confusion among the mounted ranks. If the archers stood their ground, and the infantry managed to breach us, allowing the lancers through, then we were finished.

"Shield wall!" I shouted as the Cardians drew closer. I jammed my shield into the ground as Niko and Pax overlapped their shields with mine. The second rank behind us raised their shields, covering the heads and torsos of the first rank. "Spears!" I cried. Nine-foot pikes with leaf-shaped iron heads lined with steel lowered all along our lines in the first three ranks, clattering into position. The back two ranks would be using the lighter and thinner throwing spears, hurtling them and axes over our front ranks into the faces of the Cardian infantry.

Many of my men were yelling taunts toward the oncoming Cardians, and then they began to cheer as a soldier from Fitz's right wing suddenly broke out of formation and ran toward the enemy. I realized that it was Berwin. The thin youth went twenty yards, then paused to shove a spear with my wolf's banner tied to it into the ground before he raced back to our lines. A roar of approval that shook the valley erupted from my men, then they started to chant, "Wolf! Wolf! Wolf!" as they banged the shafts of their spears against the tops of their heavy, steel-rimmed shields.

I grinned as I focused on Pernissy's great yellow banner, certain that I could see the bastard wearing gold-plated armor and mounted on a brown horse behind the first rank of lancers. What was going through his mind as he listened to the chanting of my men? I hoped that it was surprise and fear as he realized that I was here. "I'm coming for you, you bastard," I growled.

The bottleneck where we awaited the Cardian army was a quarter of a mile wide, which was roughly thirteen hundred feet. I had calculated that each man with his shield and weapons occupied a little over three feet of space, so once our wedges all locked together, we would have five solid ranks of fifteen hundred men per rank stretching from one side of the valley to the other. Would it be enough to hold back the Cardians? Only time would tell.

"Stand firm!" I shouted to my men, looking left and right. "We hold this line no matter what, or those bastards will be raping your wives and selling your children into slavery by tomorrow!"

The Cardian front rank was approaching the lance Berwin had shoved into the ground, and despite myself, I was impressed with their discipline. Only a few overeager fools had broken to charge our lines so far, and those men had died quickly on our spears. I knew their wasted blood was just a taste of what was to come. I wished there had been more of them as undisciplined troops in a shield wall usually meant easy pickings.

A sharp horn blast sounded from the west, and the advancing Cardians abruptly halted just as spinning black shafts began to fall among my lines. A volley of deadly spears and twirling throwing axes followed the arrows from the Cardian middle, turning the sky black before whistling downward into our masses.

"Hold your positions!" I shouted. My men were dropping all along the front ranks as steel-tipped arrows, spears, and axes found vulnerable flesh or clattered off shields, helmets, and armor like deadly hailstones. "Keep your shields tight and work together!" I screamed, cursing as many of my men ignored their orders and threw spears back at the Cardians, breaking the shield wall. The man next to Pax was one of them, and he tossed his spear high into the air, then sagged and fell with an arrow lodged in his face above his cheek guard. I heard Pax curse at the man standing behind in the second rank, then he grabbed the reluctant soldier and dragged him forward to take the place of the dead man.

I chanced a quick look past my shield, wondering what my Wolf's Teeth were waiting for just as I heard Baine's voice echoing from above. My archers suddenly appeared among the rocks on either side, shooting vengeful shafts down into the midst of the unsuspecting Cardian longbowmen. The waves of arrows coming our way started to falter, though they did not cease entirely as black shafts continued to clang off shields and armor all along our line. I could hear the terrified screams of the Cardian archers echoing off the valley walls and I smiled, while around me, my men shouted their encouragement to the Wolf's Teeth.

But then another series of horns sounded over the cries of the wounded and the dying, signaling the enemy infantry forward. The cheering from my men quickly ceased, and our lines suddenly became silent and grim as the very ground we stood upon started to shake beneath the weight of the advancing Cardians. The dark, featureless wall of men advanced in unison step by step toward us, banging their weapons on their shields, while heavy pointed boots raised a cloud of dust that hung over the battlefield. The odd thrown spear or axe was still being sent our way, but my men had regained their composure by now and had tightened up, so little damage was being done. Then, less than thirty feet from our position, a roar erupted from the Cardians' throats as they charged.

"Brace yourselves!" I screamed, turning my shoulder into my shield and planting my feet.

The Cardian front rank of at least two thousand strong crashed into us in a wave of pure hatred, fear, cold steel, and spurting blood. Men collapsed along both front ranks in droves, with Ganders and Cardians spitting curses back and forth at each other as they pushed, hacked, lunged, and stabbed at the opposing lines of shields. The initial charge had snapped many of the pikes on both sides, or they had simply been lost, and now men fought ferociously with secondary weapons like battle-axes, long and short swords, lead-weighted mauls, spiked clubs, and flails. We had initially fallen back several paces beneath the fury of the Cardian onslaught, but despite their superior numbers, our lines held firm. Now it was time to teach these Cardian scum a lesson.

"Kill them! I cried, tossing my broken spear into the midst of the enemy as I rammed my shield into the opposing shield directly in front of me. I drew Wolf's Head. "Kill every last one of the bastards!"

I could see my opponent's bearded face above his shield contorted into a soundless scream as he swung a mace for my head. I twisted aside, though not fast enough, as his weapon caromed off my helmet with a clang. The blow dazed me, but it didn't slow my sword arm as I hacked savagely at his exposed face. The Cardian's eyes widened and he fell back into the mass of his companions as dark blood shot out from his neck, drenching me in its foul warmth. Another man immediately took his place, this one young with odd protruding eyes and a bushy mustache wet with gore. The Cardian stabbed tentatively at me with the spike of a poleaxe, his strange eyes filled with indecision and fear. I snorted in contempt and grabbed the poleaxe below the head and yanked, drawing the man forward onto the point of my sword.

Cardian after Cardian came at me then, and I hacked them down one by one, moving without thinking as I cut and stabbed. Warm, sticky droplets of blood fell like rain all along the line of struggling combatants from one end of the valley to the other, drenching both sides in a sea of red madness. Pax chortled as he slaughtered men to my right, while Niko remained silent and focused on my left, cutting down one enemy after another with his short sword. The heat became oppressive, with clouds of dust continuing to rise from the thousands of churning boots, clogging airways and mixing with dripping sweat that stung the eyes mercilessly.

We fought and cursed each other beneath the unforgiving sun for long minutes, the dust finally settling as the ground became wet and slick beneath our feet with piss, shit, vomit, and bloody entrails. My men didn't give an inch, fighting with the kind of ferociousness that can only come from desperation. We all knew that if the Cardians managed to get behind us, then Ganderland was doomed. We held our position stubbornly as the Cardians threw everything they had at us, then slowly, we began pushing them back into the ranks pressing from behind. The Cardians became entangled with each other in a mass of confused arms, legs, and shields as men cursed and hammered away at friend and foe alike, trying to break free.

I sensed the Cardian first and second rank was close to breaking, and I raised Wolf's Head. "Forward!" I shouted. "No mercy! Kill them all!"

My men cheered as they advanced, tearing into the Cardians as we cut a wide swathe deep into their middle. The Cardians scattered or fell writhing beneath our fury, and for a moment, it seemed as though we were going to carve a hole right through them all the way to the other side. We smashed past the second rank, then the third as well. But then we reached the men waiting in the fourth and fifth ranks, those who had not been fighting for the last half an hour without let-up. Many of those men still had spears, and suddenly we faced a wall of bristling points. Our forward momentum slowed, then stopped altogether. We were stuck and could go no further.

I realized with dismay that we had come too far too fast, leaving our right and left wings behind in our eagerness to kill the enemy. I glanced over my shoulder, but couldn't make out what was happening behind me. Had Fignam filled the hole we'd left with the reserves? I cursed myself for allowing my bloodlust to overcome common sense as I glanced to my left, where even now, I could see hundreds of Cardians hammering away at my men like hungry wolves as they tried to break through on my flank. If they got behind us, I knew we would be cut off and eventually overwhelmed.

I saw a huge man battling twenty feet from me, his square helmet gone as he laid about him with a monstrous maul. It was Guthris, the House Agent who had taken over command from Malo. Blood poured in a stream from a cut along the big man's temple, but he seemed unaware of the wound as he smashed a Cardian's shield to ribbons, then grabbed the man by the throat, throttling him one-handed.

"Guthris!" I shouted over the heads of battling men. The House Agent glanced my way, his eyes bright with the killing-blood. I pointed urgently. "Shift your men to the flank and hold it. We need to pull back."

The big man turned to glower at the wall of attacking Cardians as he tossed the corpse aside, then he nodded. He paused to bring his maul down on the back of a Cardian's head, and then I lost sight of him in the swirling press of fighters. I could only hope his Agents would give us the time we needed.

"Fall back!" I shouted, turning to Niko and shoving him back the way that we had come.

The youth immediately began to retreat, but Pax carried on, hacking into the face of a Cardian with his battle-axe, oblivious to my command. Pax finally left the dead man lying in a pool of blood, searching for more prey just as I reached him and grabbed the back of his mail. The stocky soldier hissed in anger, turning on me with his blood-stained axe raised before his enraged brain finally registered that it was me.

"We have to retreat," I shouted at him over the wails of dying men and clash of weapons. "We've gone too far! We need to go back."

Pax just shook off my hand, his face covered in blood. "The fight hasn't even started yet, lord," he shouted with a laugh. And then he was gone, throwing himself with a howl against the waiting lines of Cardians.

I cursed as Pax died almost immediately with a spearpoint in his belly and one in his neck. I backed slowly away, pausing to slash a Cardian's leg just above the ankle as he struggled with one of my men. The soldier screamed and dropped to one knee while the man he had been fighting skewered him with his spear. Then a Cardian appeared behind the triumphant spear-wielding Gander, and before I could do anything, his sword flashed. The Gander fell even as I lunged with Wolf's Head, taking the Cardian in the belly. I twisted my sword and yanked as the dying man's stomach muscles and leather armor clung stubbornly to my blade.

"Fall back, you bastards!" I cried again to my men, putting a boot to the corpse as I pulled in frustration at Wolf's Head. Another Cardian rushed at me with the head of a broken poleaxe held low just as my weapon came free. I twisted aside in desperation, too slow, and the sharpened steel spike cut through my mail and deep into my side. I bellowed in pain even as I cracked the man on the helmet with the hilt of my sword as he swept past me, the poleaxe ripping from my flesh. My adversary's helmet shattered and he collapsed to the ground, only to be trampled underfoot by the combatants swarming above him. "Get back!" I roared, trying to ignore the pain in my side as I gestured with Wolf's Head toward a small knot of my men who seemed frozen in place. I kicked the closest one, setting him into motion. "Get your asses back to our lines!"

Our retreat became a slow, disorganized affair then, with so many Cardians pressing us from in front and our own men from behind that it was getting hard to move. Soldiers from both sides were pushing and shoving at each other, not able to tell friend from foe in the panicked, bewildering carnage of the battle. A Cardian and Gander were locked in a death embrace in front of me, fighting over a mace. I used my elbow on the Cardian's face and he gasped and fell back, letting go of the mace. The Gander soldier whirled with the mace, deflecting another Cardian's sword coming for my head as I skewered the man he'd been fighting, then shifted to cut down the second man. The Gander with the mace smiled wearily at me. "Keep moving," I growled at him. "We're almost there."

I could see Guthris and his House Agents had shored up our left flank, making quick work of the Cardians who had tried to breach us. A wall of House Agents is an intimidating sight at any time, and the eagerness that the Cardians had displayed trying to flank us quickly waned as they saw their companions being slaughtered by the fearsome warriors. Guthris was in the forefront, creating a wide swathe as he shattered shields, pulverized armor, cracked open heads, and snapped bones with his gigantic maul.

My men finally made it back to our original position, with the House Agents shifting from the flank to take over the first rank, causing instant mayhem as the Cardian center hesitated and then drew back from the ferociousness of the Agents.

"Lord!" I turned as Fignam pushed his way toward me. An arrow with bright white feathers struck his shield, quivering in the wood several inches from the metal boss, but the older man didn't even acknowledge it. He leaned close to me. "My men are ready, lord. You need to give yours a break."

I nodded, knowing that he was right. I didn't know how long the battle had been raging so far, but if we didn't switch out our exhausted men for the fresh reserves soon, we would eventually lose this fight. "Do it," I ordered. I turned, calling my men back as Fignam's forces hurried to fill the gap they had left while the House Agents held the Cardians at bay. I led my men away from the battle and around Fignam's archers, halting in a rough formation fifty yards back from them. The archers were shooting arrows into the middle of the Cardian infantry as fast as they could, but as far as I could tell, their shafts were having little effect. Answering arrows came our way occasionally, but for the most part, we were relatively safe where we were for the first time since the fighting began.

I glanced around. We had lost almost a third of our number, I realized, with the rest looking bone-weary, bloodied and battered, but satisfied with what they had done so far. "You beautiful bastards!" I said to them with a wide grin. "If you weren't so damn ugly, I'd kiss every one of you!" Laughter and cheers erupted at that, and I turned away, smiling as young boys came running with wineskins. I drank sparingly, then rinsed my mouth and spat it on the ground.

I motioned to the two closest men. "Up," I said, gesturing with a thumb toward the sky.

The soldiers moved forward, each grabbing a leg and hoisting me into the air so that I could see better. I suppressed a groan at the stabbing ache in my side as I rose, then cursed softly at the sight that awaited me. Despite our best efforts, the sea of enemy infantry seemed just as numerous as before. I looked past the thousands of battling footmen, then grunted in satisfaction. At least there was some good news. The Cardian archers were in complete disarray, with my Wolf's Teeth continuing to pour wave after wave of shafts down into their confused midst. It looked as though many of the enemy archers had tried to run, only to find themselves cut down by their own lancers. Bodies of red-caped men lay piled all along the front rank of mounted men. I chuckled, knowing that Pernissy was to blame for the slaughter.

"Stupid," I muttered. The Cardian archers were essential to Pernissy's plans, I knew, yet the former lord was too blind to see past the moment at hand. Just because a man runs today does not mean that he won't fight tomorrow—unless, of course, he is dead.

I could see Baine clearly where he stood with one foot braced on a rocky formation, sending arrow after arrow down at the Cardians. My friend must have sensed my eyes on him, for he paused to glance my way. I thought I saw him nod when he saw me and then he focused back on the task at hand.

Wiflem's left wing had fared better than my center, and I could see the captain fighting gamely in the front ranks with a blood-spattered Putt battling by his side. I decided I would give my men several more minutes to catch their breath before we went to relieve them. I turned to look north, then cursed. Fitz's lines were in trouble, with his right flank pressed against the outcrop of Mount Lespin slowly giving ground beneath sustained pressure from the Cardians.

"Put me down!" I snapped at the soldiers holding me. I started to run north the moment my feet touched the ground, waving at my men to follow. "To me!" I shouted.

I drew Wolf's Head, my heart in my throat as I raced north with my tired men streaming out behind me. I prayed out loud that we would make it in time, but even as I spoke the words, Fitz's right flank collapsed entirely. The Cardians poured through the breach, screaming in triumph. We were too late. I turned and glanced back to my lancers, who sat waiting two hundred yards from the battle near our camp. Lord Stegar led them, and I could see him sitting astride his horse, though he was looking away to the south and hadn't noticed the crumpling of our right wing yet. I stopped running and put two fingers in my mouth and whistled shrilly, surprised when the lord actually turned his head. He saw me, and I pointed urgently northward. Lord Stegar looked that way, and even from that distance, I could see the look of dismay on his face. The lord swung his horse about, shouting to his men to follow as he led five hundred lancers and men-at-arms toward our ruptured line at a gallop.

I started running again, cursing as every second the Cardians widened the breach even more. Fitz's men were now in complete disarray, falling back as the fresh, rear ranks of the Cardians surged forward into the hole, expanding it as they roared in triumph. Niko caught up to me as I ran and I glanced sideways at him. The youth's lips were pulled back from his teeth with exertion, his eyes straining as his chest heaved. We shared a worried look, neither one of us bothering to waste a breath to say anything. It was obvious what was about to happen if we couldn't stem the tide of Cardians.

I heard urgent trumpets blaring from somewhere to the northwest, knowing what they meant as I tried to run faster. I had taken numerous small wounds during the battle, but the one along my side was causing me the most problems, and it seemed only to be getting worse. Every step I took now brought a sharp stabbing pain with it that left me hissing and gasping for air. I started to slow reluctantly, unable to run any faster as Niko pulled ahead of me, then more of my men, until I was left to bring up the rear with the other stragglers. I clutched at my side and pressed onward as Lord Stegar's men swept past me, the shod hooves of their horses throwing dirt and grass in my face. I wanted to cheer them on, but I couldn't waste the much-needed air.

I could see the tops of hundreds of lances flying Pernissy's yellow banner and Lord Boudin's blue one moving above the heads of the opposing infantries as they pushed their way toward the breach. It was a race now to see which side could get there first. Cardians on foot were spilling out from the gap in our line like angry fire-ants, throwing themselves at Fitz's rear ranks. I saw Tyris gesturing urgently with his bow to his men as the Wolf's Teeth shifted their attention from the Cardian archers to the approaching lancers.

"Good boy, Tyris," I gasped as I stumbled along. "Good boy."

But despite the withering barrage of arrows that I knew were raining down from above, the banners came on, until finally the first of the great horses appeared in the breach, battering both Cardian and Ganders fighting there aside. Lord Stegar was still two hundred yards away, and I almost sobbed in frustration as the Cardian horsemen burst out onto open ground on our side of the line.

"Damn! Damn! Damn!" I grunted over and over again as I stumbled along with my shield arm pressed tightly to my side.

Lord Stegar finally reached the northern flank, but the Cardian lancers had seen him coming long before and were ready for him, having formed into a tight mass with lowered spears. Enemy infantry continued to pour through the breach around the protective cordon of Cardian lancers as Lord Stegar's men crashed into the mounted defenders. A horrific shriek arose then as metal spearheads impacted shields, sounding as though a thousand tormented souls burning at The Father's feet were all screaming at once. Men were instantly flung lifeless from their saddles by shattered lances or were tossed aside like dolls as their mounts collapsed beneath them, only to be crushed moments later into unrecognizable pulp by the milling hooves of the combatants' warhorses.

Lord Stegar's desperate charge had managed to punch a hole in the Cardian defenders' line. But even as I watched helplessly, more enemy horsemen were passing through the breach to reinforce it, forcing the Ganders back with the sheer weight of their numbers. Some of the mounted Cardians fighting along both sides broke off, sweeping around the two battling forces into the open. Those riders then joined with their comrades on foot who were wreaking havoc against the back ranks of Fitz's infantry. I could hear the young lord screaming at his men to shift around to face the new threat, but it seemed in all the confusion that no one knew what to do and the slaughter continued.

I was still a hundred yards away from the fighting, with only a moaning youth running beside me with dark blood pouring from where his right eye had been. I fought to draw air into my aching lungs, but with every breath I took, pain ripped like fire along my side. I kept running anyway and ignored the discomfort, tasting blood in my mouth as I stumbled and bit through my lower lip. The battle in front of the breach had changed after the initial charge. Most of the mounted combatants had tossed aside their lances in the confined space now to hack at each other with swords, maces, and flails in a wild, free-for-all melee of swirling death.

Niko was running well ahead of the rest of us, and I saw him change directions toward an enemy lancer who had just run down one of Fitz's men with his horse. Niko shouted in anger and the lancer turned his head, his features hidden by a full-faced helm. The lancer swung his horse around to face Niko, urging the beast into a gallop with his heels as he headed directly toward the oncoming youth with his lance held low. The warhorse's dark flanks were glistening with white foam as it bore down on Niko, and just when I thought it was too late, the youth twisted aside, with the fearsome spearpoint of the lance narrowly missing his torso. The Cardian hauled on his horse's reins savagely, cursing as he fought to slow and turn his mount to try again. But Niko hadn't been idle during that time, and he ran at the Cardian, ducking nimbly under the belly of the horse before rolling across the ground to the other side. I shouted in admiration at the move. Niko bounded to his feet and dragged the startled lancer from his saddle, then I saw his short sword rise and fall twice. After that, I lost sight of him as the rest of my men swarmed over the mounted lancers and infantry attacking Fitz's rear.

I paused, grabbing hold of the youth with one eye and stopping him as I shouted at my men. We needed to seal the breach first, and then we could mop up the remaining Cardians. But my men had thrown themselves into the thick of the fight and were so overcome with battle lust that they didn't hear me or just didn't care. Guthris rose up suddenly like a giant in the midst of the struggling combatants. The huge House Agent held a howling Cardian high above his head, and he tossed the man contemptuously into the sea of battling, cursing men.

"Guthris!" I shouted.

The House Agent turned to kick a Cardian pikeman in the teeth. The man fell to the ground as Guthris slammed the edge of a steel-rimmed shield down on his throat, sending blood spraying skyward before he tossed the shield aside.

"Guthris!" I cried again with the one-eyed youth adding his voice to mine. This time the House Agent heard, and he straightened and looked over at me. I pointed north with my sword. "We have to seal the breach now! Bring your men!"

Guthris looked toward the outcrop where Lord Stegar's men were fighting gamely to contain the enemy lancers, and then he nodded to me. I turned away just as a howling Cardian appeared out of the fray nearby. The man's eyes were fixated on me as he charged, his sword held in front of him like a spear. I easily evaded his clumsy attack, then slashed down with Wolf's Head as the man screamed and fell, his sword arm now a crimson mess. The youth with one eye whirled on the wailing Cardian, crunching the spiked metal ball of a flail into his face, silencing the man as blood sprayed. I looked up. Guthris was sprinting toward me, clutching his maul, with more House Agents following. "Keep running!" my brain shouted at me. "Don't stop! Run!" And so I did, trying not to think about the suffocating heat, the weariness turning my limbs leaden, the fear that we might be on the brink of losing this fight, and the throbbing pain in my left side that just would not go away.

I heard a raven cawing harshly somewhere above my head and I glanced up as I ran while the bird slowly soared over the battlefield. Was the raven's presence an omen of victory? And if so, for which side? I glanced to my left as the great bulk of Guthris fell into step beside me, the two of us leaping over the bodies of dead and dying men as we ran. More Agents caught up to us, and soon there were a hundred men in square helmets streaming toward the breach. Guthris and I were less than fifty feet from the battling lancers when I suddenly stumbled and then fell as I tripped over the leg of a dead Cardian. I landed hard, crying out as my wounded side scraped across the edge of my shield.

Guthris stopped and came back, then pulled me roughly to my feet as I hissed through my teeth. "Are you all right, lord?" the House Agent asked.

"Just go," I managed to gasp out as I gestured ahead with my sword. "Don't wait for me. Get over there and kill those bastards!"

Guthris began to run again with blood-splattered Agents following him, each man carrying a white painted shield embossed with the Blazing Sun. I took a moment to catch my breath, taking in the situation at the outcrop. Lord Stegar and his men had managed to hem the Cardian lancers in at the breach, pushing them backward with sheer determination and ferocity, which was now making it difficult for more of the enemy riders to get through. At the same time, Fitz had wisely shifted a part of his center to the right, attempting to pinch off the hole. The strategy was working, it seemed, as the flow of Cardians on foot had slowed, though there were still enough of them getting through to form a formidable shield wall in front of the battling horsemen. The House Agents descended on that wall without slowing, and any semblance of an organized defense by the Cardians quickly disintegrated beneath that unstoppable charge.

I finally reached the battle, winded, but growling with fury as I stalked toward a Cardian sitting on a Gander's chest as he slammed a knife over and over into the dead man's eye. The Cardian looked up just as I reached him, his face twisting comically in surprise as I swung my sword, tearing out the man's windpipe. Another Cardian rushed out at me from the press of battling men, his shield in tatters as it barely clung to his arm, his left shoulder a pulped mess of twisted leather, blood, and bone. The man was sobbing as he thrust at my belly with the six-inch stub of a shattered short sword. I twisted away awkwardly, crying out as my wound tore even more. The Cardian's jagged sword blade punctured my shield, jamming there as he continued to sob, yanking on it desperately. I drove Wolf's Head savagely up into the man's midsection, slicing through mail, cartilage, and vital organs before the tip burst out the back between his shoulder blades. The Cardian sagged against me as the light began to fade from his eyes, though he still managed to cling to his sword with both hands in a fanatical grip. I attempted to push him away, then frustrated, I swung my shield arm around, flinging the dying Cardian to the ground. I cursed as my shield went with him.

Two Cardians broke from the battle and began to stalk me, one to either side as they sensed that I was injured and might be easy prey. I sheathed Wolf's Head, then drew my father's axe, holding it firmly in both my hands. The two men hesitated, looking unsure of themselves just as I saw the Cardian to my right glance over my shoulder, his eyes widening in surprise. I whirled around, with barely time to register that a horse and rider were bearing down on me before the beast's shoulder struck my left side, sending me spinning to the ground. I landed heavily on my back, losing my grip on the axe as the breath was knocked from me. I lay where I was for a moment, stunned as I sucked in great gulps of air. Then I painfully forced myself to my hands and knees, knowing that the Cardians would be on me at any moment. I felt dizzy and light-headed as I groped around for my axe, while to my left, I heard one of the approaching Cardians whooping in anticipation as they came for me.

"Back off!" I heard a gruff voice command, though the words were garbled, as though spoken underwater. "This one is mine." I shook my head, trying to clear the ringing in my ears as I scanned the ground, my mind still fixated on locating my fallen axe. "Is this what you're looking for, Hadrack?" the same voice said, though this time it sounded much clearer.

Even with the pain in my side and the vicious pounding in my head, I couldn't help but smile. "Thank you, Mother," I whispered.

I slowly stood, glaring at the two Cardians who waited ten feet away, watching me warily. I drew my sword, but the attention of the two was suddenly taken away by Guthris, who threw himself between us, his maul whirling, sending the Cardians recoiling away in sudden fear. Confident now that my rear was secure, I slowly turned around to face Pernissy Raybold. The former Lord of Corwick had dismounted from the horse he had used to run me down. He stood now with his booted foot on the haft of my axe, a mocking grin on his face. He held a longsword stained red with blood in his right hand, with a triangular shield strapped to his left arm. I flexed my shoulder and arm where the horse had struck me, wincing. There would be an impressive bruise there later, I knew, but the arm still worked reasonably well. Something felt wrong with my left knee, though, and I bent it back and forth, frowning at the sharp pain that erupted there.

"You don't look that happy to see me, Hadrack," Pernissy said. His blond, sweat-streaked hair hung from his golden helmet almost to his shoulders, but his beard, which was long and spattered with gore, looked mainly grey and white beneath all the red stains.

I realized with a start that Pernissy had grown old this past year. I chuckled as I searched the ground, then hobbled over to pick up a discarded shield. "On the contrary," I said, shaking my head to clear the last of the cobwebs from my eyes. I limped back until I was fifteen feet away from Pernissy. "I have never been happier to see anyone in my life."

The fight for control of the breach had spilled out all around the two of us, with House Agents and Cardians locked in deadly combat, but I barely noticed it now. All I could focus on was

Pernissy, who just laughed at my words, looking at ease as he swatted his horse on the rump with the flat of his sword. The horse jumped with a startled snort, then galloped away to the east where my camp lay, its silky mane and tail streaming in the wind.

"I'm surprised you didn't just trample me when you had the chance," I said, not hiding my contempt as I watched the fleeing horse skirt around Fignam's busy archers. "Or at least had your men kill me. You've always been good at letting others handle your dirty work for you, as I recall."

"Sometimes it's just easier that way, Hadrack," Pernissy said with a shrug. His face turned hard and cold. "But not this time. I've been dreaming about this moment ever since your treachery at the coronation. The Sons promised me that I would get my revenge on you, and here you are, just as they foretold."

"Since when do you care what the Sons have to say?"

"When it suits my purpose," Pernissy replied gruffly. He gave me a grudging look. "I thought I had you in Thidswitch, but I guess that fool Grindin was dumber than even I thought." He sighed. "All the man had to do was die at your hands. It wasn't all that complicated."

"Don't worry. Grindin will still die," I promised. "He'll be joining you soon enough in the firepits Below, mark my words."

Pernissy snorted as he jammed his sword point into the ground, looking unimpressed. "We'll see about that," he said. He glanced down at my father's axe. "But first things first," he added as he used the toe of his boot to flick the weapon into the air before catching it with both hands. He sneered at me, pausing for just a moment before he smashed the carved shaft down hard on his uplifted knee, snapping the handle in two. "There," Pernissy grunted as he tossed the shattered parts aside. "That feels much better." He grinned at the look of dismay on my face, then drew his sword from the ground and wiped it clean on his trousers.

I stared at the broken pieces of my father's axe as two men so smeared with dirt and blood that I couldn't tell which was a Cardian and which a Gander rolled back and forth over it as they wrestled desperately for control of a sword. I growled low in my chest, focusing back on Pernissy, feeding on the hatred that I felt for him. I started to advance, walking hunched over to help ease the pain in my side. I could feel a sharp pinch at the back of my knee as I moved as well, but I thrust it from my mind.

"That's right," Pernissy said, encouraging me. "Come on, little wolf. It's time to finish this. I have a kingdom to rule."

I snorted, Wolf's Head held low as Pernissy moved nimbly toward me. We were less than four feet apart when he suddenly twirled to his right, bringing his sword around hard and fast. I had expected the move, and his blade ricocheted against my raised shield. I lunged forward with the tip of Wolf's Head to counter, but Pernissy was faster than I had expected, and he danced away easily.

"Looks like you're sporting a wound or two there, little wolf," Pernissy said, grinning. He glanced toward my left side, where blood was seeping steadily through my padded tunic and mail coat as it rolled down my leg. He crouched, drawing his shield close to his body. "You're slower than I thought you would be. I'm actually a little disappointed. I thought this was going to be harder."

I said nothing as I advanced step by step across the battlefield littered with discarded weapons and corpses, my mind free of any thoughts other than the task at hand. Pernissy could talk all he wanted, but nothing he said was going to stop me from taking his head.

"How is that little half-sister of mine doing?" Pernissy asked as we began to circle each other. I was having trouble matching his movements, with my left leg feeling odd and unresponsive, tingling all along the length as though it had fallen asleep. Pernissy turned to spit on the ground, though his eyes never left mine. "Did she ever tell you why I married her to Lord Demay?"

I didn't bother to respond, my anger well contained, burning in a tight ball in my chest where I stoked it for use later. "Don't let your opponent goad you, ever," Jebido had warned me many times down in Father's Arse. "Pick your moment, don't let him pick it for you." I knew with my injuries that I would probably only get one chance at Pernissy, so I had to be ready when that moment came. Then, and only then, would I unleash the buildup of thirteen long years of seething hatred that I felt for the man in front of me who had caused so much misery to so many people.

Pernissy smiled as he slapped his sword tip against mine, the metallic clang loud even among the screams and ringing of other weapons around us. He shrugged. "I didn't really have a choice, you know. I had to marry her off. The little slut was rutting with every man in Corwick and it was becoming downright embarrassing." Pernissy looked disappointed when I didn't react, and then he shook his head in mock outrage. "She even had the nerve to try and lay with me. As if I would allow a skinny whore like that into my bed. She's probably humped more men by now than even those stupid Pith bitches you used to rut with."

"Is that so?" I grunted, my voice even and calm.

Pernissy frowned at me, and then he raised an eyebrow. "Didn't she tell you all this when you married? You really are naïve, Hadrack."

"And you talk too much," I replied.

"Sadly, that can sometimes be true," Pernissy agreed. Then he attacked.

I was expecting it, but even so, the former lord caught me by surprise, dropping to one knee with his shield held high to protect his head as he swept his sword low along the ground. I tried to leap over his blade, but my bad knee had no spring to it at all, and his sword cracked sharply against the metal greave protecting my shin and ankle. I felt something crack as my leg went numb, and I staggered backward, forced to drag the suddenly useless leg along as my attacker came on, sensing victory. Pernissy's face showed a mixture of fury and triumph as he rushed me, hammering away at my shield as I fought desperately to maintain my balance. I could do nothing but retreat from his savage attack, my weak counters with Wolf's Head easily slapped aside as I gave ground. Then something rolled out from beneath my good foot and I cried out, waving my arms wildly as I fell, landing heavily on my back.

Pernissy was on me in a flash like a striking rock snake, his sword at my throat as he dropped heavily onto my chest. I cried out from his weight pressing down on my wound. "You can't believe how good this moment feels right now, Hadrack," Pernissy hissed as he took Wolf's Head from my numb fingers and tossed the weapon away.

I closed my eyes in defeat, my chest heaving as I felt cold steel drawing blood at my throat. "I'm sorry," I whispered to my father and Jeanna. "Forgive me."

"There will be no forgiveness for you, you little peasant bastard," Pernissy growled. He pricked my flesh with his blade. "Now open those grey eyes of yours. I want to watch the light go out of them as you die."

I slowly did as he asked, staring up at Pernissy's leering face as a shadow suddenly crossed over our bodies. Pernissy glanced up in surprise just as Guthris' great maul slammed into his metal breastplate with a screech, snatching the former Lord of Corwick off me and sending him flying backward through the air.

Guthris strode forward then with determination, raising the maul to strike the fallen man a second time where he lay stunned on the ground, surrounded by blood, gore, and corpses.

"No!" I shouted, lifting a hand to stop him. "Don't do it!" Guthris hesitated, glaring down at Pernissy, who was wheezing and spitting up blood with every shuddering breath. "The bastard is mine," I said, groaning as I slowly sat up. Several coughs wracked my chest when I moved, feeling like daggers tearing away at my insides. Finally, once they had subsided, I braced my hands to push myself to my feet. But then I paused as my fingers contacted something hard and round on the ground beneath me. I looked down in surprise, realizing that it was the broken shaft and gore-smeared head of my father's axe. That's what I had tripped over. I started to laugh at the irony of it, though my laughter sounded more like the tortured shriek of a pig at slaughter to me. I grabbed the shattered axe at the base of the head, and then I slowly forced myself to stand.

"Are you sure about this, lord?" Guthris asked, looking worried. He glanced down at Pernissy. "The bastard is half dead now anyway."

"I'm sure," I said, wobbling. I began to move forward, dragging my bad leg behind me like my father had done so many years before. It seemed fitting, somehow. I finally reached Pernissy and stood over him, motioning Guthris away just as a roar of triumph erupted from the northern battlefield. I looked toward the cheering, expecting bad news, then I sagged with relief. Our forces had managed to push the last of the Cardians back through the breach. And even as I watched, they were massing to seal it off again. I raised my gaze to the sky and said a prayer of thanks, startled to see that the sun now hung low in the west, casting dark shadows all across the valley.

I turned my focus back to Pernissy. The former lord's breastplate was shattered in three places, barely clinging together from the incredible force of Guthris' blow. I could see the man was fighting just to breathe, with pink frothing bubbles oozing out of his mouth as he struggled to speak. Pernissy saw my eyes on him and he weakly lifted a hand, motioning me closer.

I knelt painfully beside him, putting the head of my father's axe to his throat as I removed my helmet and threw it aside. "What do you want?" I asked, my voice cold and hard.

"You're—" Pernissy started to gasp out. He gagged as dark blood filled his mouth. I thought the bastard was going to drown in his own blood then, which would have brought no tears to my eyes, but somehow he managed to turn his head sideways to spit wet redness on the ground in a fine spray. Pernissy's shattered chest quivered as he focused back on me. For some reason, I thought he was going to beg me for forgiveness. I don't know why. I really should have known better. "You're just a damn, stinking peasant," Pernissy rasped, the words wet and garbled. He clutched at my mail, ignoring the blade at his throat. "You are nothing, Hadrack. Do you hear me? You have always been nothing, and you will always be nothing!"

"No, Pernissy Raybold," I said, gripping my father's axe tighter. "You're wrong about that. You have always been wrong about that." I leaned forward and pressed my lips to his ear. "My father, Alwin, was the son of Coltin Corwick, you bastard." I saw Pernissy's eyes widen in disbelief. "That's right," I hissed. "I am the true Lord of Corwick, and you are on your way to spend all of eternity burning. Which is where a stinking whoreson like you belongs."

"No," Pernissy said, slowly shaking his head.

"Yes," I replied, enjoying the horrified look on his face. Finally, I sat back, holding Pernissy Raybold's eyes with mine as I lifted the axe. The former lord started to say something—I'll never know what—because I had heard more than enough from the bastard over the years to last me a lifetime. I slammed my father's axe down, cutting deep into his throat as dark warm blood cascaded all over me. Then I struck again, then again, until his head was clinging to his body by only a few strands of meat and tough, stringy sinew. I hesitated, feeling suddenly dizzy as I looked down at the remains of the man who had brought so much misery to my life.

"Here, let me help you, lord," Guthris said, stooping as he gently started to lift me to my feet.

"Not yet," I grunted, pushing him away. I glanced around, surprised to see a cordon of ten House Agents surrounding us protectively. I focused back on Guthris. "I'm not done," I said as I lifted the axe again and turned to Pernissy. "This is for everyone in Corwick, you bastard," I said as I chopped once, then a second and a third time, until Pernissy's severed head finally rolled away from his body. "Guthris," I gasped, not turning as my head swam nauseatingly. "Get me a spear and a horse."

The giant House Agent hesitated. "Yes, lord," he said, his voice grave. Within moments he was back by my side, a long spear in one hand, the reins of a blood-splattered and trembling white mare in the other.

"Help me up," I ordered, taking the spear from the House Agent. I stood with Guthris' help, then twirled the spear in my hands before jabbing the sharpened point savagely into the gapping, bloody rip where Pernissy's neck had been. The steel-tipped spear sliced easily through bone and brain matter before the gore-covered tip burst out the other side. I lifted the former Lord of Corwick's head into the air, then with the help of Guthris and another House Agent, I carefully mounted the white mare. Then I started to ride along the back of our lines while men on both sides continued to fight and die in the waning light.

"Behold!" I roared, shaking the spear and gruesome head at the skies. "Behold the traitor, Pernissy Raybold!" I galloped at full speed along our lines from one end of the valley to the other, shouting at the top of my lungs while Ganders cheered and Cardians cried out in dismay. I could see the Wolf's Teeth standing along the outcrops starting to raise their bows over their heads in celebration, and I looked for Baine. Finally, I saw a dark outline standing among the darker rocks, knowing with certainty that it was him. I yanked hard on the mare's reins and she reared back, her front legs pawing the air as I saluted my friend with Pernissy's grisly remains. Then we were on the move again.

Finally, after several more trips racing back and forth across the valley, I saw Fitz, bloodied and limping, coming toward me from the press of bodies to the north. The young lord was smiling as I slowed in front of him and he reached for the mare's bridle. Fitz said something to me then, though I don't know what, for suddenly I felt weak and light-headed again. The spear I held and its burden suddenly dropped from my numb fingers as I slid sideways off the mare to the ground.

I knew nothing more after that.

26: The Gamble

I awoke to find Baine sitting beside me on a stool, with a single candle burned down almost to the nub flickering beside him on the floor. My friend's arms were crossed and his eyes were closed, with his chin pressed tightly to his chest. I could hear air whistling through his nose with every breath that he took. I blinked in confusion, my eyelids feeling heavy and unresponsive as I looked around. I was in the king's tent, I realized, lying on the straw bed where Tyden had lain the day before. I could smell the heady reek left behind by his infection coming from the straw beneath me, and I unconsciously wrinkled my nose. Several thick furs were draped over me, yet despite them, I still felt a chill. I shivered, then shifted my upper torso, groaning as pain shot through my body. I felt around beneath the covers, my hand eventually coming into contact with thick bandages along my left side. Baine mumbled to himself in his sleep, then he lifted his head, staring bleary-eyed at me.

"You're awake," Baine said, obvious relief on his face.

I nodded, trying to form words with my dry mouth. Baine jumped to his feet and brought me a waterskin. I drank greedily. "What happened?" I croaked once I had sated my thirst.

"You fell off your horse and hit your head," Baine said. He grinned. "Though a bump on that thick skull of yours is the least of your problems right about now."

I felt sudden alarm. "The codex?"

"Fitz has it," Baine replied. "He thought it would be safer with him until you are on your feet."

I relaxed in relief. "What about the Cardians?"

"They withdrew to their camp," Baine explained. "After what you did with Pernissy's head, they lost their appetite for the fight."

"But they will be back," I grunted, closing my eyes for a moment as my head swam.

"Yes," Baine agreed.

I cried out then, caught by surprise as I shifted my left leg and sharp pain screamed along its length. I lifted the furs to see the lower half of my leg wrapped in a bulky felt cloth tied together with hemp bowstrings. I looked up at Baine, a question on my face.

"Your shin bone is broken," Baine said, his face grim. "We found a carpenter in the ranks who was able to fashion some splints out of ash and carve a leg tray for you from a broken shield. We also located a man who has some experience setting bones, though it was probably a good thing you weren't awake for any of it. Now, all we can do is hope that your leg knits properly."

I closed my eyes for a moment, trying not to imagine spending the rest of my life hobbling if the setting had been done poorly. I knew there was nothing I could do about it now, so I focused my thoughts elsewhere. "What time is it?" I asked.

Baine went to the entrance and peered up at the sky. "Judging by the moon I'd say around eleven o'clock," he said, returning to my side. His face brightened. "I have a bit of good news for you, Hadrack. A rider arrived a few hours ago from Jebido. The rest of our army is camped less than a day's march from here."

"That is good news," I agreed. Then my enthusiasm started to wane. "But it might be too late by the time they get here. I doubt Lord Boudin and those pet lords of his will wait long before they attack again."

"Probably not," Baine said. He sat down on the stool once more. "But we won't have to worry about those bastard lords, at least. They both fell trying to break through the breach." Baine ran his fingers through his hair, suddenly looking dejected. "But even without them and Pernissy by his side anymore, Lord Boudin still has an awful lot of men. We lost almost half our number in that fight, which means those lines of ours are going to be awfully thin come morning."

"What about the Cardians?" I asked. "I know we hurt them badly."

"We did," Baine said. "They must have lost double the amount we did. But that still leaves them with five or six times as many men as us."

I lay there for a moment, thinking. Even if we managed to survive until Jebido arrived with his ten thousand men, we would still be vastly outnumbered. I didn't know if Lord Hamit had succeeded in conscripting a second army as he'd intended. But even if he had, I had no idea how close that force might be, nor the quality of it. The entire fate of the kingdom hinged on the battle coming only a few short hours away. I glanced at Baine. "Is that man Jebido sent still here?" I asked. My friend nodded. "Good," I said. "Find him and tell him he is to ride back to Jebido right now."

"To say what?" Baine asked, already standing.

"I want Jebido to break camp immediately," I said, my mind whirling. I pointed at Baine. "Tell him he has to be here by dawn, no later. I don't care if the men have to run all night to do it."

"But, they'll be exhausted, Hadrack," Baine protested. "You can't ask men to fight after that kind of ordeal."

"I'm hoping we won't have to," I said. Baine started to go and I called him back. "And find Fitz. Tell him I need to see him."

Ten minutes later, Fitz pushed his way into the tent, a smile on his face. "So, you decided to rejoin the living, my friend."

I frowned, in no mood for jokes. I held out my hand, my expression cold. "Give me the codex."

Fitz stared at me, his smile fading. "I wasn't going to keep it, Hadrack," he finally said, his voice turning sulky as he handed the book to me. "I didn't know how long you would be asleep, that's all. I didn't want to risk someone else seeing it."

"I know that," I said, my agitation easing now that I had the codex pressed to my chest. I looked up at my friend. "I'm sorry. I didn't mean it the way that it sounded."

Fitz studied me carefully, then he nodded. "That's fair enough," he said, the tension on his face easing as the familiar grin returned. "So, is that all you wanted?"

I shook my head. "No," I said. "I'm going to need you to reprise your role as the king again."

Fitz blinked in surprise. "For what purpose?"

"You're going to convince Lord Boudin that he has to surrender to us."

Fitz gaped at me. "How exactly am I supposed to do that?" he asked.

So I told him.

I sent scouts to the east well before dawn broke the next morning, watching for any signs of Jebido. So far, I had heard nothing back. If my friend failed and didn't arrive with his men before the sun rose, then there was a good chance that the gamble I was setting into motion would likely fail as well. The night had been a busy one, with my men working feverishly in the darkness to prepare everything before the skies lightened. I lay in my bed with less than an hour to go before sunrise, feeling frustrated with my helplessness as Fitz sat with me, his cheerful banter filling the tent.

"Don't you ever get tired of talking?" I finally asked in exasperation. My friend was dressed in the finest armor we could find that would fit him, with an elegant Cardian cape draped over his shoulders. A golden helm taken from a fallen enemy lancer sat on the stool beside my bed, a hastily fashioned crown fixed around the crest.

"Communication is good for the soul, Hadrack," Fitz said as he paced back and forth at the foot of my bed. "Without the gift of the spoken word, we would be nothing but rutting, grunting beasts."

"Uh-huh," I muttered, not really listening. I could tell Fitz was about to go into another one of his long-winded dialogues, and I looked up with relief when a squat man with silver hair poked his head inside the tent.

"May I come in, lord?" he asked tentatively.

I waved him inside, glad for the distraction. "Certainly, Quill," I said. Quill was the carpenter who had made the splints for my leg. I glanced in surprise at the set of crutches that he held in his hands.

"You're done already?" I asked. I hadn't expected the crutches until much later in the day.

"Yes, lord," Quill said. He lowered his eyes. "My apologies for the crudeness of the design, lord. I thought you could use them as soon as possible. Had I more time, I would have properly smoothed and oiled them for you."

"No need," I said, not hiding my pleasure as I carefully pushed the furs off me. I lifted a hand to Fitz, who helped me to my feet. I clamped my teeth together to keep myself from crying out as my broken leg dragged along the floor.

"Here, lord," Quill said, hurrying over and propping one of the crutches under my left armpit. "Just lean on it until you get a feel for things."

I bent my broken leg at an angle off the floor, then lowered my weight onto the crutch.

"Now the other one," Fitz said, still supporting me. He took the second crutch from Quill and guided it under my right arm. He studied me critically. "So, what do you think?"

I nodded to him that I was all right, and my friend stepped back a pace, his arms spread to catch me if I fell. I took a tentative step forward, the rough oak board beneath each armpit digging painfully into me. Then another step, quickly learning to support myself with my good leg first before I swung my body forward on the crutches. It took almost five minutes of going back and forth across the tent before I finally got the rhythm down correctly, though by then, I'd broken out into a cold sweat. I glanced at Quill and grinned, delighted. "They work better than I thought they would. Thank you."

"A pleasure, lord. When there is more time, I will make you a much better pair with padded armrests." Quill turned to go, and then he hesitated as he saw my father's shattered axe where the two pieces lay near my bed. He whistled softly between his teeth. "May I, lord?" he asked, gesturing to the weapon. I nodded as Quill picked up both sections reverently. "Incredible workmanship, lord," he said, studying the carvings with intensity. "It's been a long time since I have seen such a fine example of Vander Lane's work."

"Who?" I said, not recognizing the name.

"Vander Lane, lord," Quill said. "He was a master woodcarver, famous for his works. He died many years ago, but his son, Versin, is said to almost rival his skills."

I shared a look with Fitz and we both couldn't help but smile. "Could he repair it?" I asked eagerly.

Quill shrugged. "I don't see why not, lord," he said as he carefully set the pieces down again. He moved to the tent's entrance. "The last I heard, Versin Lane was working out of Halhaven."

I thanked Quill as he left, just as Baine stepped into the tent around him. "The sky is brightening over the hills, Hadrack," he said. He grinned when he saw me standing up with the crutches. "Those look good."

"Any word from Jebido?" I asked.

Baine's smile quickly faded. "Nothing yet."

"We're going to look pretty stupid out there if he doesn't get here in time," Fitz muttered as he and Baine helped me to put on my armor.

"He'll make it," I said, trying to sound confident, though inside my stomach was churning with nervousness.

Baine slipped Wolf's Head into its familiar sheath on my hip once I was dressed. "Are you ready?" he asked.

"Ready," I nodded.

My friend parted the tent flap for me and I shuffled my way outside on the crutches. A cool wind was blowing from the west along the valley, pulling at my cloak. Angry stood waiting for me, his tail swishing with impatience, though he did snicker softly in greeting at my appearance. A stained and bulging canvas sack hung from the pommel of his saddle. I hobbled over to the big stallion, balancing on my crutches as I lifted a hand to stroke his muzzle. "This is going to hurt me a lot more than you," I said. Two burly soldiers were waiting close by, their faces cast in shadow in the dim light. I nodded to them that I was ready as Baine took the crutches from me while Fitz steadied my arm.

"Here," Fitz said, holding up a wooden tent peg. "Bite down on this."

I looked at the peg sourly, but opened my mouth regardless, clamping down hard on the wood as the soldiers bent and lifted me awkwardly into the air, both grunting from the effort. I felt an explosion of pain in both my leg and side at the same time, thankful for Fitz's tent peg now as I bit deep into it.

"Don't grab him there, you fool!" Fitz snapped at one of the men who had just braced a hand against my bad side. The soldier yanked his hand away as though it was on fire, gushing heartfelt apologies to me. I barely heard him as I fought the nausea rising in me.

"Try to throw your leg over now, Hadrack," I heard Baine saying, though the words seemed to be coming from very far away.

I focused on the dark saddle across Angry's broad back as the men holding me started breathing heavier, fighting to keep me steady. Finally, I swung my good leg over the big horse, screaming around the wood in my mouth before I dropped heavily into the saddle. I sat for a moment in silence, shuddering, my head bent as I absorbed the pain washing across my body. I sat that way for at least a minute with my eyes closed, my breath rattling in my chest, before finally I sat up straighter and opened my eyes. I removed the tent peg with a shaking hand, not surprised to see that I had bitten halfway through it. I tossed the peg aside as Fitz handed a shield up to me.

"Are you going to be all right?" Baine asked, worry heavy on his face.

I tried to laugh, but it came out as more of a painful grunt. "Never been better."

"I can still go in your place," Baine said. "Or if not me, then Wiflem or Fignam."

I just shook my head as Fitz mounted a delicate-looking brown mare with downy, gentle eyes. I knew I was in no shape to ride and that what I was doing was not only foolish, but stupid. I had every confidence in Baine, Wiflem, or Fignam to handle the task ahead, but the simple truth was that I am a stubborn man. In the end, my sitting astride Angry with fire breathing down my limbs and my eyes swimming in and out of focus, came down to just one thing. I wanted to look Lord Boudin in the face and let him see his death unless he did what I wanted. I needed to convince the bastard that we could destroy him at our whim, and one way to make that happen was for him to believe that the Wolf of Corwick Castle was not only alive and well, but spoiling for a fight.

I looked down at Baine and gestured to my long cloak. "Fix this, will you?" Baine carefully draped the cloak over my splint, hiding it, then he frowned as the heavy woolen cloth unwound and fell back. He tried again with the same result. "Lash something around it," I said impatiently. "I can't let him see my leg like this."

Baine nodded, producing a knife from his boot before cutting a strip of cloth from his own cloak. I looked around as I waited for my friend to finish his task. The sky was growing lighter by the moment, and I glanced over my shoulder to see a faint orange ball pushing its way slowly above the hills—hills that were still silent, dark, and empty of men. I cursed under my breath and turned away. My forces stood where they had the previous day, though this time, all the archers had joined with them. I stared at the ranks of shields, armor, and spears facing west as I said a silent prayer to The Mother. Please let Jebido arrive soon.

"Are you ready, Hadrack?" Fitz asked.

I nodded, and together we urged our horses toward the north where the breach had occurred yesterday. Men stood watching us silently in the half-light, pikes ready, banners flapping in the early morning breeze. The soldiers moved aside to let us pass, and I saw Berwin and Niko standing together staring at us. I nodded confidently to the two young men as we passed. Dead horses and soldiers littered the ground all across the valley here, and both Angry and Fitz's mount shied away from the stinking corpses, carefully picking their way through the maze.

Fitz turned and looked back as we progressed west, whistling, but I resisted the urge to follow his example. "They look better than I expected," he said, facing ahead again. He grinned at me. "I can't vouch for their ability to wield a spear, of course, but they look good nonetheless."

"Just as long as they do their jobs," I grunted. "That's all I care about."

"What makes you so convinced this Lord Boudin fellow will even come?" Fitz asked. "The rider you sent said he would only consider it."

"He'll come," I promised. I glanced sideways at my friend. "My message said that the king wanted to discuss terms of surrender."

Fitz chuckled. "But Lord Boudin thinks you meant our surrender, doesn't he?"

I bowed my head in acknowledgment. "Well, you did say earlier that communication was important." I allowed myself a small grin. "Perhaps I should have been clearer about what I meant, now that I think about it."

Fitz laughed, the hearty sounds echoing off the walls surrounding us as we headed west along the valley. I could see a faint orange glow reflecting off the back of Fitz's helmet now, but I steadfastly refused to look behind me. We stopped our horses fifty feet from the bend, waiting in uncomfortable silence until finally several riders appeared. One of the riders held Lord Boudin's boar banner on a long pike that was braced against his saddle. The other man sat astride a brown stallion that was almost as big as Angry. I studied the man, knowing he would be Lord Boudin, surprised by how young he appeared. The Cardian lord had massive shoulders, with long black hair spilling out from his helm. His beard was black as well, though it was cropped close to his skin in the same way King Tyden preferred. His nose was long and thin, with a cruel slash for a mouth and hard eyes that bored into mine. I sat up straighter as we halted ten feet apart, turning Angry casually to my left, hiding my injured leg.

"You would be Lord Hadrack," Lord Boudin said to me, his voice low and even, almost bored sounding.

I nodded. "And you would be the turd-sucking Cardian who tried and failed to have me killed."

"It's still early," Lord Boudin said with a sniff. He focused on Fitz. "So, Your Highness, you wish to surrender?"

Fitz snorted. "What gave you that preposterous idea?"

Lord Boudin blinked twice, the only sign of surprise on his face, though I could see twin circles of red rising on his cheeks. "You do not wish to surrender?" he said in a flat voice, his eyes turning cold and calculating.

"Of course not," Fitz said, allowing himself a smug grin. "Why would I?"

"Then you have wasted my time here," Lord Boudin said curtly as he began to swing his horse around.

"On the contrary," Fitz said, raising a hand to stop him. "I am here to offer you terms for your surrender, Lord Boudin."

The young lord paused, this time unable to hide his surprise. "Why would I want to do that?" he finally asked, regaining his composure. "Your army is in tatters. You have lost."

"Have we?" Fitz said smugly. He turned and gestured behind him. "Does that look like an army in tatters to you?"

Lord Boudin shifted his gaze to the east, and I saw his eyes widen at what he saw. I finally turned to look back, unable to stop myself from grinning. Fitz had been right—they did look good. I'd had my men working all night to strip the dead of clothing, armor, shields, and weapons. We'd then stuffed the clothing with straw, grass, dirt, and even dung, whatever we could find that would help form the outlines of armored soldiers. Ten ranks of pikemen were waiting to the east now, stretching from one end of the bottleneck to the other. Only the first two ranks were actually living, breathing men, though, with the back eight rows of stuffed figures leaning precariously against thin pole fences. But Lord Boudin didn't know that.

The ruse wouldn't stand up to scrutiny for long, I knew, but from where we sat our horses with the sun in our eyes as it broke over the hills, it looked very convincing. Fitz had told me not long ago that men see what they expect to see, and I could only hope that my gamble here would work just as well as it had with Einhard.

"I could just kill you right now," Lord Boudin threatened with a growl as he stared at Fitz.

My friend chuckled condescendingly. "You could certainly try to do that," he agreed. "But before you make the attempt, please keep in mind who my companion is. Lord Hadrack's reputation as a fearsome fighter is, I assure you, well deserved. I have told him to be nice during this meeting of ours, which I am well aware is a hardship for him. You see, a wolf is by its very nature a bloodthirsty beast, and I'm quite sure this one would be delighted if I let him off his leash, should you choose to attack me. Just don't blame me if you don't care for the results."

Lord Boudin glanced at me, assessing me silently before he looked over my shoulder, studying our defenses with shrewd eyes.

"This rat turd isn't going to accept your terms, Highness," I snarled in contempt, trying to regain the young lord's attention. I was afraid that if he looked too hard, he might eventually see through my deceit. "We're wasting our time with this man. He's too stupid to realize he's facing the total destruction of his army." I smiled as I untied the canvas sack, holding the smile while white fire rippled down my left side. "And I am glad of it," I added, tipping the sack over. My voice was thick from pain, which I could only hope Lord Boudin would mistake for passionate anger. The severed heads of the two Gander lords, as well as Pernissy's gruesome remains, spilled out and landed on the ground, grinning grotesquely.

I pointed at Lord Boudin. "Your head is the only one my sword has yet to take, you bastard. Let's change that right now." I grinned as the color slowly drained from the young lord's face. "Send your men to die on our spears," I taunted. "I dare you. Forget about all this talk of surrender. You're so close to the throne you covet, so why stop now? Don't worry that without Pernissy Raybold, any chance you had of keeping that throne is effectively gone. Just give in and let your arrogance, greed, and stupidity be the end of you." I smiled my best wolfish grin. "Or are you just another Cardian bastard who runs the moment things get difficult?"

Fitz looked at me crossly. "What did I tell you about this, Lord Hadrack?" he snapped. "You are not the one doing the negotiating here. I am. So please keep your mouth shut about matters that do not concern you."

I breathed out angrily, glaring at Lord Boudin, then I finally nodded. "Forgive me, Highness. My emotions got the better of me."

"See that it doesn't happen again," Fitz said. "Or it will be your head on the ground next." He turned to Lord Boudin. "Now then, where were we? Ah yes, your surrender. I have forty thousand men at my disposal, and every one of them is very eager to spill Cardian blood. You couldn't defeat me yesterday when I could only muster ten thousand, so I would say that your position today has clearly declined. Lay down your weapons and you have my word that your forces will be allowed safe passage back to Cardia."

"That's not forty thousand men over there," Lord Boudin said, snorting as he pointed behind us.

Fitz smiled. "Of course it's not. You are very perceptive." He glanced over his shoulder, then waved a hand dismissively. "That is only half of my force. The rest will be coming through those hills to the east at any moment."

Lord Boudin opened his mouth to reply, and then he spat out a low curse as faint horns sounded to the east. We waited and watched in silence as hundreds of colorful banners appeared on the plateau leading down into the valley. Jebido had made it in time.

"Ah," Fitz said with a satisfied smile. "Right on time." He focused on Lord Boudin, his eyes hard now. "Here are my terms. They are not negotiable. Lay down your sword and consent to being a guest of mine in Gandertown until every last man in your army leaves Gander soil. Do this, and you have my word as a king, and as a gentleman, that not a hair on your head will be harmed. Once your army has left my shores, then you will be returned safely to Cardia. Try to fight me and you have my solemn oath that not one Cardian, including you, will be drawing breath by midday."

Lord Boudin sat his horse for long minutes, his expression unreadable. Finally, he seemed to come to a decision and he nodded. "I will withdraw my forces to Calban, Your Highness," the young lord said. "But no farther than that. If you can assure me that I have safe passage to return to my castle, then we have a bargain."

Fitz started to laugh. "Your castle?" he said. He looked at the young lord in mock surprise. "Have you not heard, Lord Boudin? My forces retook Calban weeks ago. You have no fortress to fall back to."

Lord Boudin stared at the king for a moment, then he shifted his gaze to me, neither one of us hiding our hatred for the other.

Finally, the young lord drew his sword in a smooth motion and threw it at the feet of Fitz's horse. "I accept your terms as stated, Your Highness."

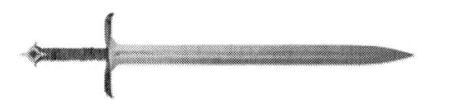

27: Malo

One of the most enjoyable moments in my life occurred when Fitz, Lord Boudin and I, finally rode back to our camp after the young lord had made arrangements for his forces to withdraw. The fury on Lord Boudin's face when he saw our silent army of straw and muck—not to mention the explosive curses flying from his lips that would have shamed even Nedo—gladdened my heart to no end. I sent Wiflem with two thousand men on horseback to follow after the defeated Cardian army as they marched weaponless to the west. They still had no idea that we had deceived them, and I expected little trouble from them despite their numbers. Even the most ferocious of beasts cannot function without a head to give it direction.

Ships would be waiting along the coast to take the Cardians home, though the problem of Calban still remained an issue. Despite Fitz's claim that we had retaken the castle weeks ago, we had not, in fact, done so. That problem, I hoped, would be quickly rectified once the Cardian army and the threat they posed were safely gone from our shores. Lord Boudin would be angered once again when he learned he'd been deceived about Calban, but in the end, he would have little choice but to order his men behind the walls to surrender.

I sent a rider to Gandertown with the news of our victory, and he returned days later to say that the king was alive and well and that he wished me to travel to the city so that he could thank me personally. I had no wish to be paraded around the king's court while fussy men and women in perfumed clothing offered me false praise and admiration, all the while secretly looking down their noses at me. I was tired, riddled with injuries, and sick of war. But more than any of that, the simple truth was that I missed my wife. So, whether Tyden liked it or not, my time in the north was over.

I sent Fitz and Fignam back to Gandertown with Lord Boudin and the bulk of the Gander army while my men and I headed south. Fitz still hadn't told the young lord that he really wasn't the king yet—mainly, I think, because he was thoroughly enjoying the role. I chuckled every time I imagined the moment when Lord Boudin learned the truth.

It took us more than three weeks to return to Corwick, which I mostly spent laid up in a wagon. My side had healed fairly well, but unfortunately, my leg was another matter. Mind-numbing pain wracked the limb constantly, and even walking with the new, padded clutches Quill had fashioned for me was nothing short of agony.

It was almost dusk when we finally reached the castle, and I insisted that Jebido stop the wagon as we entered the barbican. "Help me down," I growled.

"Are you sure that's a good idea?" Baine asked doubtfully.

I glared at him. "This is my castle," I said. "And I'm walking into it on my own. Do you have a problem with that?"

"No, of course not, Hadrack," Baine replied, though I didn't fail to see him roll his eyes at Jebido.

My two friends helped me from the wagon, and then Jebido hurried to get the crutches under my arms. I made my way slowly through the barbican into the outer bailey lit by torches as men on the walls looked down at me and cheered. I paused just inside the gate, my crutches braced on the cobblestones as I was suddenly surrounded by Ubeth, Parcival and his three sons, as well as many others who had gathered to welcome us home.

"My lord!" Shana cried, running toward me down an alley as panicked chickens and geese scattered out of her way. My wife pushed her way through the crowd, failing to notice the crutches beneath my arms in her haste to embrace me. I couldn't help but let out a moan as her leg brushed against my bent knee. Shana recoiled backward in alarm, finally becoming aware of the crutches. "What happened?"

I tried to grin, though I think it came out as more of a grimace than anything else. "I broke my leg," I said. I shrugged it off. "It bothers me now and then. Nothing to worry about, my love."

"How long ago was that?" Shana asked, her brows furrowed as she dropped to her knees to examine me. "Straighten your leg for me, but don't put weight on it," she commanded. I did so as Shana gently pushed aside the cloth to look at my exposed toes, wrinkling her nose at the smell.

"Three weeks," Jebido answered for me.

"And you didn't do anything other than wrap this filthy rag and a few sticks around it?" Shana snapped, looking up at him.

Jebido flushed. "We did the best we could for him, lady. A broken leg is painful. It needs time to heal."

"Not like this, it won't," Shana muttered. She nodded decisively as she stood. "Get my husband back in that wagon right now. We're taking him to see Haverty."

"Hold on, there," I protested as Jebido turned to obey. "I just arrived home. I didn't travel all this way to have Haverty fussing over me for no reason. The pain will pass and my leg will be fine."

"No, it won't, Hadrack," Shana said, her face filled with concern. "Your toes are blue and I can smell infection. Something is wrong. So, you either get in that wagon right now, or I'll have someone carry you like a sack of barley over to the Academy." Shana's eyes flashed in challenge. "Which would you prefer?"

I shared a look with Jebido, then sighed and motioned for him and Baine to bring the wagon up. There was no arguing with Shana when she was like this.

The Academy was situated in a wing of the Holy House that sat in the inner bailey. The school had begun modestly enough—with Shana the only student—in a small room near the nave. But it had expanded to encompass three rooms as more and more students came to study in Corwick. Soon, I knew I would have to give Haverty a building of his own if it continued to grow like it was. The aged apothecary was not pleased to see me when we arrived—or, to be more precise, he was not pleased to see my leg once he had gingerly removed the splints.

"Who is responsible for this abomination?" Haverty demanded in outrage as he stared down at the swollen, mottled skin covering my lower leg. "Was it that bumbling fool, Jevar?"

I just shook my head. I had no idea who Jevar was. I could see a shiny bump pushing outward where the break had occurred, as well as yellow, purple, and black bruising from my knee to my ankle. That ankle was almost black as well, with all my toes turned a fine hue of blue, just as Shana had said.

"Then, if not that imbecile, it must have been a blind half-wit with only one hand," Haverty grumbled, still fuming as he shook his head in disbelief. He had Jebido and Baine help me to lie on my back on a table, then he started going around and around me, muttering to himself and pulling at his shaggy white hair.

"You're making me dizzy," I finally muttered, tired of trying to keep my eyes on him. Baine and Jebido moved back near the doorway, both looking uncomfortable and out of place. "You two," I grunted at them. "Go help get everyone settled. I'll be fine once Haverty gets over his little fit."

Both Baine and Jebido nodded together, looking relieved as they hurried out the door.

"How bad is it?" Shana asked Haverty.

The apothecary stopped, staring down at my leg before he eventually sighed and looked at Shana. "Bad enough, my lady. Bad enough."

"Can you fix it?"

Haverty snapped his head sideways back and forth, his eyes bulging from his sockets. I would have thought he was having an attack of some kind had I not seen it many times before. The apothecary was thinking. Finally, he slammed his hand down on the table, startling both me and Shana. He turned to my wife. "I can fix it, my lady," he said before shifting his gaze to me. "But it will not be an enjoyable experience for you, my lord."

I wet my lips, looking down at my leg. "What's wrong with it?"

"The bones have knitted incorrectly," Haverty said, squatting down until he was eye level with the break. He clenched his fists and put them together. "The two ends of the broken bone have fused in the wrong place, my lord. That is why we have this bump here and why you are in so much pain." He offset his fists and ground them together. "Every time you move, those bones grate together. Because they are misaligned like this, the tissues around them swell and tear with every motion. That is what has allowed an infection to take hold. We will need to get that infection under control first before we do anything else."

"And then what?" I asked.

Haverty sighed a second time and stood, looking down at me. "We start over from the very beginning, my lord."

Shana gasped. "You mean break his leg again?" she asked.

Haverty nodded sadly. "Much as I wish it were not so, that is the only way."

"What happens if we just get rid of the infection and leave the leg as it is?" I asked, not relishing the apothecary's solution.

Haverty shrugged. "Then it will heal this way, my lord, and your left leg will be shorter than the other. You will spend the rest of your life as a cripple, limping and in pain. There will be great pain if I rebreak the bone as well, of course, but that will go away eventually. In time, with a strict regimen of exercise, you should be able to walk normally again." He raised his bushy eyebrows. "So, do you have a preference for treatment, my lord?"

I shifted my eyes to Shana, and she nodded, her face deathly pale. "Break it," I grunted.

One week later, Malo came to see me. I wondered what had taken him so long. I met the House Agent alone in my solar, sending all the servants away so we could talk freely. My leg was feeling much better, with only a steady throb to remind me of the horrors Haverty had put me through. The apothecary had promised me that the bones were set properly this time and that my leg would be as good as new. I dearly hoped he was right about that, because I would rather limp the rest of my life than have to go through what he had done to me a second time.

"I heard you were grievously injured," Malo said as he entered the solar. "But you don't look that bad." The House Agent appeared tired, I thought—tired and haunted by what he hoped to learn today.

I glanced down at my leg. Gone now were the crude splints and rough cloth, replaced by a tight leather sleeve with metal rods along the sides and laces drawn tight. It looked very much like a woman's corset, I thought. I was to wear the contraption for at least six weeks, Haverty had insisted, and not put any weight on my leg. A task easier said than done, I quickly found out.

"I'll heal," I grunted. I had been waiting for Malo near the table, standing for long minutes with the help of my crutches. It was silly, I know, but I didn't want Malo to see me sitting down when he arrived. Logic and male pride do not always go hand in hand. Now that Malo was here, I hopped over to a bench and sat down awkwardly, relieved to take the weight off as I leaned my crutches against the bench. "Close the door," I ordered with a wave of my hand.

The House Agent did as I asked, then moved to stand over me. "You know why I've come, Hadrack," he said, his eyes burning with intensity.

"I do," I agreed with a nod, meeting his steely gaze with one of my own. "I'm just surprised you didn't come sooner."

"I was occupied with other matters," Malo said.

I took a deep breath and let it out. I had been expecting this conversation for weeks and not looking forward to it. "I'm not giving you the codex, Malo," I said firmly. "The time still isn't right."

Malo just stared down at me, his face hardening. "The Piths have returned to their lands, and the Cardians are defeated," he finally said. "The king is healthy and secure. So, what better time could there be?"

I couldn't tell Malo that the Piths might be coming back soon, for if I did that, then I would have to explain why they had left in the first place. "I gave you my word you would have the codex when the kingdom is safe," I said. I folded my arms over my chest. "I do not believe that is the case yet."

The House Agent started to tremble with anger, and I didn't fail to notice that his hand had drifted down to his sword hilt. "You lied to me, Hadrack," Malo growled.

"I did no such thing," I said calmly. "You will have the codex when I am ready to give it to you, and not before. Nothing has changed." I gestured to his sword. "Unless you plan on murdering me for it."

Malo looked down at his hand in surprise; then, he slowly let it slide off the hilt of his sword. He looked back at me and I could see resolve burning in his eyes. "I had a feeling you were going to go back on your word," he said. I waited, not bothering to respond. Malo was up to something, I could tell. His features slowly smoothed and his body relaxed. "Would you please come with me, Lord Hadrack?" he said, gesturing to the door.

I blinked in surprise. Lord? Malo never called me that. "Why?" I asked suspiciously.

"Let's just say it's a surprise," the House Agent said. He even grinned—a rare sight. Something was definitely wrong.

I gestured to my leg. "I'm not exactly mobile here, Malo."

"Then call for some servants," Malo snapped impatiently, his voice rising. I looked up sharply at that and Malo smoothed his features again. "Forgive me, lord," he said in a lower tone. "The past few weeks have been taxing." He raised an eyebrow. "Should I go find someone to help carry you? I imagine all those stairs must be exhausting for a man in your weakened condition."

I knew what Malo was doing, of course, but knowing it and being able to resist it didn't necessarily go together. I snatched up my crutches with a snort and forced myself to my feet. "Let's go," I grunted.

Malo led me out into the hallway and down the stairs to Corwick Hall, never once offering a helping hand. I think he sensed I would likely bite it off if he tried. He was right. More than one servant, not to mention Finol and Hanley, wanted to help me navigate the stairs down to the main floor, but I waved each of them off with a growl. We finally made it outside, where a wagon pulled by a pair of fine-looking horses awaited. Six House Agents on horseback surrounded the wagon, which I thought looked suspiciously like Carspen Tuft's wagon, though this one was much newer. Curious onlookers were milling about, muttering to themselves in expectation as they tried to guess who might be inside. I noticed Baine and Jebido making their way forward through the crowd. "What is all this?" I grunted at Malo in irritation.

"If you will please come with me, Lord Hadrack," Malo said, ignoring my question as he urged me forward.

I frowned at his politeness, but hobbled along anyway, intrigued despite myself.

"What's going on?" Baine asked as he and Jebido met us at the base of the ramp. My friend glared at Malo with little love. "What are you doing here?"

"All will be revealed momentarily," Malo said, his features giving nothing away. He moved to the back of the wagon, where a single door stood just as it had on Tuft's wagon. There was even a small window with bars. The House Agent waited patiently for me to make my way to him, then he put his hand on the handle. He paused to look at me while Baine and Jebido peered over my shoulders curiously. "You have something I want, Lord Hadrack," he said as he twisted the handle. The House Agent pulled open the door, which squeaked loudly on rusted hinges. "And I have something that you want."

I stared into the wagon, anger exploding inside me as two men peered back at me sullenly. One was Grindin, dressed in dirt-covered apprentice robes. The other was a big man, with a bull-like neck, bald, gleaming head, and eyes the color of coal. The big man glowered at me in defiance while Grindin shrank away from the light pouring into the wagon, stopping when the chains around his wrists snapped taut. I barely glanced at Grindin, focusing on the bigger man as my mind traveled backward in time. I had never been able to remember what Luper Nash had looked like that day in Corwick, no matter how hard I tried, but as our eyes met, I knew without a doubt that it was him. There was no fear in the big man's eyes, just acceptance, maybe even a trace of contempt as he stared at me. I was just that scared peasant from years ago to him, and I could tell by his expression that others calling me lord would never change his opinion of me. I heard a growl of hatred coming from deep in my chest, and I started to push my way into the wagon without even realizing it.

"No, you don't," Malo said, grabbing my shoulder roughly and pulling me back.

I heard both Jebido and Baine protest, with my older friend already starting to draw his sword. I brushed off Malo's hand, stumbling on my crutches as I shook my head at Jebido. "Not this way," I said. Jebido reluctantly shoved his sword back in its scabbard as I faced Malo. "Why have you brought them here?" I demanded, though I knew what his answer would be.

"Are you not pleased?" Malo asked, gesturing inside the wagon. "I've brought you the last two living members of the nine. Shouldn't you be thanking me?"

"I won't trade them for the codex," I said firmly. "So you can forget it."

"Are you certain of that?" Malo replied, a hint of mockery in his voice. "Would you prefer I just ride away with them right now? Is that what you want? Because if I do, I swear you will never see them again."

I glanced into the wagon as the two prisoners listened warily to our conversation. "I'll find them again," I promised. "Even if it takes me fifty years, I will find them. Men like these won't get far."

"That is where you are wrong, Hadrack," Malo said. I noticed he had dropped the 'lord', now. He nodded to the wagon. "If you don't give me what is rightfully mine, those two cow turds in there will be on a ship first thing in the morning. They will be given new names, enough gold to last a lifetime, and plenty of incentive never to set foot in Ganderland again. You will spend the rest of your life searching for them, and in the end, I guarantee that you will fail."

"You bastard," I hissed under my breath, understanding now.

Malo shrugged, his eyes cold and hard. "This was not my first choice, Hadrack. But you have always been a stubborn man. Sometimes men like you need to feel the full weight of a hammer before realizing they are only a nail just like everyone else."

"What is that supposed to mean?"

"It means," Malo said, leaning toward me, his eyes flashing. "That it is not your place to decide things in this world. There are others better suited to that purpose."

"Like you, I suppose," I said, not hiding my contempt.

"Yes," Malo agreed. He held out his hand. "Now give me the codex."

"You're not getting out of here alive, you bastard," Baine growled behind me. He started to step forward, a knife in his hand and death in his eyes.

"Stop!" I commanded. "Killing each other won't solve anything."

"But, Hadrack, he—" Baine started to protest.

"I said no!" I shouted, turning on my friend. "And that means you too," I said, recognizing the dangerous glint in Jebido's eyes. The House Agents had all turned their horses to face us, only their eyes visible behind their helms as they put hands to swords and waited. We were moments away from bloodshed and I wanted no part of it. "No one draws a sword," I growled. "Or they answer to me."

"I am sorry for this, Hadrack," Malo finally said, breaking the tension. I saw his men slowly relax on their horses. "If there was another way, I would have taken it." The House Agent held out his hand again. "Now give me the codex and let's end this thing." I hesitated, looking once again into the wagon. "Think of your vow," Malo said, his voice soft, almost soothing now. "What does the codex matter when weighed against that? These men killed your family and your friends. I'm offering you an end to what happened at Corwick. Take it. You have done so much for this kingdom and the House. Now it's time you were rewarded for your service. Accept their lives as that reward."

I stood bent over on my crutches, wrenched by indecision as I weighed Malo's words.

"Hadrack?" Jebido said gently from behind me. I turned to my friend, the anger gone from his eyes now, with only love and compassion left there, laid bare for me to see. "Malo is right. Despite how the bastard has gone about this, he is right. You have done so much, sacrificed so much for everyone else." Jebido waved a hand toward the silent crowd, who were listening to us in confusion. "We all owe a debt to you that can never be repaid." He pointed his finger at the men in the wagon. "But inside there lies the end to a journey that started when you were only eight years old." He glanced briefly at Baine. "A journey that we both have been lucky enough to ride along on." Jebido shook his head, and I was startled to see tears threatening in his eyes. "My blood does not run through your veins, Hadrack, but I don't care." He tapped his chest. "You are my son in here, and I have watched you grow and become so much more than even I could have hoped for." Jebido thrust his shoulders back. "So, I say you have done enough, my son. This is your time now. Malo and the House can worry about the codex—it's not your problem anymore. Take his deal, Hadrack, and end this thing once and for all."

I could feel the codex pressing against me inside my clothing, sweat forming where the leather touched my skin. Did I dare do as Jebido said and give it to Malo now? What of Einhard and the Piths? What if they came back to find Ganderland embroiled in war again as the Sons and Daughters tried to come to grips with the codex's revelations? I closed my eyes, trying to ignore the searing pain in my skull as I wrestled with the decision. Then, a vision appeared to me.

I saw my father and Jeanna walking together, hand and hand. They were smiling, my sister beautiful and innocent, my father large and bent over as he dragged his ruined leg through the dirt. I couldn't help but smile at the sight, feeling love explode in my breast as the two chatted happily together. But then I felt a lurch rip aside the love, for behind them, nine men on horseback had suddenly appeared. I saw Crooked Nose, Hape, Calen, Heavy Beard, Quant Ranes, and Ragna the Elder with his son. Grindin was there as well, riding beside the massive bulk of Luper Nash.

The nine men were shouting, waving swords in the air as they descended on my father and sister. I cried out a warning, but my father and Jeanna seemed oblivious to their danger. Then, less than twenty feet away, Calen suddenly burst into flames, disintegrating along with his horse into a charred, smoking mass. One by one, each of the nine burst into flames in the same manner until only Grindin and Luper Nash remained. I waited for the fires to take them too, but they came on steadily, faces twisted with hatred. I screamed in helpless rage, praying for the flames to save my family, but they did not, and my prayers turned into a shriek of despair. I moaned and closed my eyes as the horses finally reached my father and sister, shutting away the flashing swords and spraying blood as great tears of misery seeped past my eyelids. I didn't need to look to know that my family was dead, cursing myself for being helpless to save them all over again. Finally, the vision began to clear, and I slowly opened my eyes, swaying on my crutches.

Malo was staring at me with a strange look on his face. "Are you ill, Hadrack?" he asked.

I could feel the tears still sliding down my cheeks unchecked, yet I felt no shame. I slowly reached inside my clothing and drew out the codex, and then I handed it without a word to Malo.

There really was no other choice for me to make.

28: A Vow Completed

One week after Malo left with the codex, I sat in the sun near the kitchens, enjoying the smells wafting from inside and the servants' cheerful banter. I spent every day in the same spot, staring up at the White Tower and watching the hours go by as I bided my time until I was whole again. Occasionally, I would see a face peering down at me through one of the tower's many open windows—just a flash of white before darting from sight again. I always chuckled softly to myself when that happened, fingering the golden hilt of Wolf's Head where it lay across my lap.

"What are you grinning about?" Shana asked as she stepped through the open doorway of the kitchen. She had a basket on her hip, and I knew she was heading out to feed the chickens. There were servants whose duty it was to handle that chore, of course, but Shana always preferred to do it herself. She said she found it soothing. I looked forward to watching her every morning, marveling at how her black hair shimmered in the sunlight and her musical laughter rang off the walls. Seeing Shana with chickens all around her, pecking and clucking, never failed to remind me of my sister, Jeanna.

"I wasn't aware that I was," I said, my eyes half-closed as the sun warmed my skin.

"Uh-huh," Shana replied. She set the basket down on the stone walkway, then moved to stand over me, her hands on her hips. "Sitting here every day isn't healthy, you know, my lord."

I saw movement in one of the tower windows behind her and I shifted my gaze there, briefly meeting the eyes of Luper Nash before he quickly stepped back into the shadows.

Shana followed my gaze and she sighed, turning to pull a stool close to me before she sat down. "It's going to be weeks before you can take that thing off, my lord," she said, gesturing to the leather cinched around my shin. "Do you intend to wait here all that time obsessing over those two?"

I was sitting in a cart-like contraption that Haverty had designed. Two wheels were attached to a high-backed chair, with long, heavily padded planks extending outward horizontally from the seat, keeping my legs elevated. It was awkward to move and damned uncomfortable most of the time, but Haverty was insistent that it was the only way that he would let me go outside. I might be the Lord of Corwick, but between Shana and Haverty, it seemed that I had no say in anything when it came to my health.

"What would you have me do?" I asked, turning to look at her. "I'm all but useless these days." I gestured to the tower where Grindin and Luper Nash were locked up. "At least imagining the deaths of those bastards up there helps to pass the time."

Shana took my hand in hers and she squeezed, not saying anything. Grindin and Luper Nash were alive only because I wasn't ready to kill them yet. But soon, the gods willing, my leg would be strong enough, and when it was, I would take them to my farm, where I would send their souls to join the rest of the nine in the firepits Below.

We sat for a long time, both of us enjoying just being together. Shana's hand was warm and strong, and I felt an almost overwhelming feeling of love and contentment come over me as I absently stroked her skin with my thumb. Movement appeared at another window in the tower, and I saw that this time it was Grindin. He looked out at me and I felt my contentment slide away. I glared upward and drew a finger across my neck, smiling at the sudden look of fear on the little man's face.

I felt Shana stiffen beside me before she drew her hand away. "What is it?" I asked.

Shana shook her head. "It's nothing, my lord." She began to stand. "I need to feed the chickens."

I put my hand on her arm, stalling her. "No, everything isn't fine. Sit back down." Shana's eyes flashed at my strong tone. "Please," I added, softening my voice. I motioned to the stool. "Sit and tell me what's bothering you."

Shana hesitated, then she slowly sat again, playing with her fingers. She did that when she was upset. "It's that awful man in there," Shana finally said. "He scares me."

"Who? Luper Nash?" I snorted, waving away her concerns. "I've fought men as big as he is before, and I'm still here to talk of it."

Shana shook her head. "No, the other one. The Son-In-Waiting."

I felt instant anger rise in me. "That bastard isn't a Son-In-Waiting."

"Yes, he is, my lord. And you know it." Shana breathed out of her nose noisily, her cheeks flushed. "You told me you didn't kill Grindin before because you couldn't bear to leave the baby and me alone to fend for ourselves. That you would be ostracized from the House and probably hung if you killed him."

"Yes, that's true," I said.

Shana lifted her chin in challenge. "So, what's changed between then and now? Tell me how the same thing won't happen this time." I opened my mouth to reply, then I shut it again, not sure how to answer. I hadn't actually considered that far ahead. Would the same rules still apply to Grindin once the secret in the codex came to light? "That's what I thought," Shana finally said as I remained silent, mulling it over.

I sat back in my chair. I had been so focused on Grindin and Luper Nash that I had somehow managed to push all thoughts of Malo and the codex into the background. Had anything actually changed now? I wasn't sure. The Master might be the supreme god, but the First Pair were still gods as well, with essentially the same roles as we had always thought. Would that mean killing a Son-In-Waiting was still the same sin as before, too? I couldn't see why it wouldn't, feeling disappointment rise in me as I realized there would be no solution to the problem coming from that direction. Shana was right. Nothing had changed, and I was just as stuck now as I had been months ago when I had first found Grindin.

I closed my eyes and rubbed them with my knuckles, suddenly tired. Malo would have reached Halhaven by now, I guessed, which meant Daughter Gernet already knew the truth. I wondered how she had taken it. We had heard nothing in Corwick yet, but it was only a matter of time before that would change. I couldn't see any way around being ostracized and probably executed for killing Grindin, but even so, there was no chance I would allow him to live once I was on my feet again. I hadn't told Shana about the codex yet, waiting for the right moment. My wife had a keen mind and might have a different take on things than I did, so if ever there was a time to tell her, this seemed to be it.

"I haven't been completely honest with you," I said, watching Shana from the corner of my eye.

"About what, my lord?" Shana said, looking at me warily.

"About why Malo came here."

Shana frowned. "He came to reward you for your service to the king and the House," she said. She gestured to the tower. "That's why those two are here, is it not?"

"Yes, it is," I nodded. "But that's not the entire story. Malo also came here to get something from me." Shana waited patiently for me to continue. "Do you remember why I went on the Walk?" I asked.

Shana rolled her eyes. "Of course, my lord. It was less than a year ago. My memory still serves me quite well, thank you. You went to find the codex."

"I did," I agreed. I looked up as I saw either Hesther or Hamber near the stables, squatting and petting an orange and white cat lying on its back. I had no idea where the other sister was. "Hesther," I called out, taking a chance as I motioned for her to come to me. The girl immediately stood and lifted her skirts as she hurried around the gardens and made her way along the cobblestone pathway.

"Yes, my lord?" she said out of breath when she reached us.

I pointed to the basket of chicken feed. "Your mistress will be delayed. See to the chickens."

"Yes, my lord," Hesther said with a curtsey before picking up the basket and heading away.

"We need to move from here," I grunted to Shana. I pointed toward the fish pond, where a tall maple towered over the water. "Do you think you can push me over there, or should I call for a servant?"

"Why must we move?" Shana asked. "What's wrong with right here?"

"Right here has ears," I said, gesturing to the kitchens behind us. "Over there does not."

"Very well," Shana said with a frown. She stood and went behind me, pushing on the handles at the back of the chair. It took Shana some time to maneuver me to the pond, but though I suggested that she ask for help more than once, she steadfastly refused. I wasn't the only stubborn one in this family.

We finally reached the pond and Shana placed my chair under the tree, far enough back from the bank that there was no chance of me rolling down into the water. "So," she said, sitting on the grass in front of me with her knees pulled up to her chest. "Now, what's all this secrecy about?"

I told her everything then—all about Rorian and the codex and the terrible secret that lay inside. Shana became deathly still as I spoke, and I could tell by the glint in her eyes that she was upset at what I was saying. But, as I would quickly learn, it seemed that she was more troubled by the fact that I had withheld this from her for so long rather than the knowledge that we had been lied to for generations. I never will understand women. It took quite a few repeated apologies on my part, along with my promise that it would never happen again before Shana was ready to hear more. I explained then about how I had ridden to the Piths with the ancient tome, gambling that Einhard would listen to me about the Master and the First Pair.

"Those savages could have killed you, my lord," Shana said with a gasp.

"It was a risk," I conceded. "But a worthwhile one if it could stop a war."

I told her then about how Malo had seen Rorian in Halhaven and that he'd cornered me into telling him about the codex. I explained that he had ridden here not to reward me with Grindin and Luper Nash as she had thought, but to coerce me into giving up the codex, using them as bait. When I was finished, we sat in silence for a time, watching the fish swimming lazily in the pond.

"You still can't kill Grindin, my lord," Shana finally said. She stood, one hand on her hip, her face flushed with intensity. "Nothing you have told me changes that." I opened my mouth to reply, but Shana raised a hand before I could speak. "Don't get me wrong, my love," she added. "No man deserves killing more than that one does. But I will not lose you to a hangman's noose for him. We will just have to find another way."

"There isn't one," I said with a hopeless shrug. "Son Oriell sits in the First Son's chair, and he would like nothing better than to see me dead. The moment Grindin dies, that bastard will get his wish."

"The House will be distracted by the codex," Shana said, her eyes calculating. "As will the First Son. Perhaps Grindin can just disappear forever and no one will care or be the wiser."

"It's an idea," I said without much enthusiasm, having already considered it. "But sneaking around doesn't sit well with me." I ran my fingers through my hair and sighed. "Besides, Son Oriell may be a fool, but he's not entirely stupid. He will know I had something to do with the man's disappearance. I don't want to skulk around like a thief in the night, Shana. The dead of Corwick deserve better than that. They need to witness Grindin's death properly."

Shana moved behind me, putting her hands on my shoulders as she kneaded the stiff flesh there. "Let me think on it, my lord. There's still plenty of time to come up with a solution before you are healthy again."

I looked back and smiled at her, patting her hand affectionately. Shana had taken the news about the codex better than any of us had. Once again, I was struck by how strong and resilient she was. If my wife had been born a man, I knew she could have ruled the world. "Thank you, my love," I said. "I couldn't have done any of this without you."

"Of course you couldn't have," Shana agreed with a chuckle. She bent and kissed my neck, then stood. "Shall we head back, then? By the sounds of things, it's already past midday."

I nodded my agreement, my mind already turning back to Grindin and the dilemma of his death as Shana worked to propel my chair through the grass. But, try as I might, I couldn't think of a solution that would satisfy both my vow as well as keep me safe from Son Oriell's vengeance.

Luckily for me, Shana already had.

I received two visitors the following week. The first was Saldor, dressed in Gander clothing. I barely recognized him as we met in my customary place by the kitchens.

"You are well, I take it, Chieftain?" Saldor asked once we had greeted each other warmly.

I nodded, indicating a stool for him to sit. "The healing process is slow," I said. "But I'm told I will recover completely."

"This is good," Saldor said. He saw me studying his clothing and he smiled sheepishly. "Piths are not exactly welcome here, Chieftain," he said. "It seemed prudent to try to blend in."

"A sound plan," I said with a laugh. I shifted on my chair. "So, how are things with the Amenti?"

"All is well," Saldor said. "I have taken the liberty of picking the rest of your Blood Guard. We are moving further south for the summer hunt soon, and I was not certain when you would be returning."

I frowned. "I told you when we parted last that I would not be returning to rule the Amenti."

"Yes, you did say that," Saldor acknowledged. He looked around him with distaste. "I had hoped that after living within these walls again that you might have changed your mind. Men such as we are meant to live free, not penned up like animals."

I laughed. "Walls have their advantages, my friend."

"Perhaps," Saldor said, looking unconvinced. He leaned forward. "The Amenti cannot go indefinitely without a chieftain, brother, so if you will not return, then you must choose another to take your place. Three candidates have an interest in leading the tribe."

"Only three?" I asked with a grin. I waved a hand. "There could be fifty for all it matters. We both know who I will pick." Saldor just stared at me steadily, his face expressionless. I realized that this was some kind of Pith formality that needed to be addressed, so I smoothed my features, trying to look disinterested. "So tell me then, Saldor. Who are these three men that I must choose from?"

"Stig the Crow, Shar the Moody, and myself."

I nodded, pretending that I was thinking. "All sound choices," I said. I glanced at my companion. "But Stig is old and his bones ache all the time as I recall."

"That is true," Saldor agreed.

"And Shar is a mean bastard who drinks too much," I added.

"We all drink too much, Chieftain," Saldor replied. "That should not be held against him."

"Perhaps," I said. "But Shar was rude to me once. I think he called me fat and slow with a sword."

"Shar can be impudent at times, brother," Saldor conceded, the ghost of a smile on his lips now. "It was wrong for him to say that, for clearly you are not fat."

I glared at him in mock annoyance. "And the other thing?"

Saldor smiled. "Your swordcraft does have holes, but there is hope for you."

"Thank you for your honesty, brother," I said sarcastically. I scowled as I stroked my beard. "An old man like Stig, so close to walking the Path to the Master, cannot be asked to lead the Amenti," I finally said. "Nor do I think someone like Shar would be the best choice to serve the tribe." I sighed and then shrugged. "So, it would seem you are the best qualified of the three to take my place, Saldor."

"If that is your wish, Chieftain, then I have little choice but to accept."

"It is," I said, fighting to keep the smile from my lips. "Just promise me you will try to teach those bastards some decency when you get back."

Saldor allowed himself a low chuckle. "Consider it done, brother."

'Good," I said, relieved that was over. "Was leadership of the tribe the only reason you came to see me?" I asked, suspecting that it was not.

"No, brother," Saldor said with a quick shake of his head. "The Pathfinders have a clearer message now, and Einhard asked me to deliver it to you personally." I felt my heart skip a beat as I motioned the Pith to continue. "The words written in your Gander book appear valid, and the Piths will not be making war on Ganderland. There is much for us to consider and reflect upon in the coming days."

I hadn't realized I'd been holding my breath, and I let it out in relief. "That is good news, brother," I said. Whatever repercussions the codex would have on the House, at least we didn't have the Piths to worry about anymore. "So, what happens now?" I asked.

Saldor shrugged. "That is not for me to say." He stood then. "I must return to my people and tell them of your decision, brother. It was good to see you."

"It was good to see you too," I said, meaning it. "The Amenti are in good hands."

The Pith turned to go, then he paused and looked back, a grin on his face. "Einhard had another son. He says to tell you that he's already two ahead of you and you need to hurry if you want to catch up."

I laughed, waving a hand to Saldor as he strode away. Everything was a competition with Einhard, even babies.

My second visitor came the very next day, arriving at the castle in a wagon guarded by four House Agents. A Blazing Sun emblem was painted on each door. I waited with Shana in the sunlight, knowing who would be inside. One of the House Agents dismounted and he moved to the door and opened it. A sandaled foot appeared from the shadows with a bright yellow robe flowing above it.

I shared a look with Shana. "This should be fun," I whispered sarcastically, not relishing the coming conversation with Daughter Gernet.

"You have no idea," Shana said with a knowing smile.

I stared at her for a moment, perplexed, then turned back to the wagon as the Daughter finally stepped out into the sunlight. I gasped in surprise. It wasn't Daughter Gernet as I had initially thought—it was Jin.

"What is this?" I asked Shana as Jin strode toward us. Gone now was the child I remembered, replaced by a self-assured, elegant young woman elevated to the status of Daughter. I could only stare at her in shock, mesmerized by the glow of inner peace coming from her.

Jin stopped in front of us and she smiled, her teeth dazzling white. "Are you surprised, Hadrack?" I nodded as Jin bent to kiss me on both cheeks. She straightened, regarding me critically. "You don't look as bad as I had feared."

"That's because I'm being well taken care of," I said, shifting my gaze to Shana.

"I can see that," Jin said as she embraced Shana. I heard her whisper something in my wife's ear, but I couldn't make out the words. The two women broke the embrace, holding hands as they shared a look.

"Would someone care to tell me what this is all about?" I demanded, getting angry now.

Shana smiled down at me. "I have errands to attend to, my lord. I trust you and Daughter Jin will have much to talk about while I am gone."

Shana turned then and headed into the kitchens, with me staring after her in confusion.

"May I sit with you, Lord Hadrack?" Jin asked. I nodded and gestured to the stool. Jin sat, smoothing her robes, while the horses attached to the wagon stamped their feet and the House Agents sat their mounts in stoic silence.

"So, you're a Daughter now," I said for want of anything else to say. The girl had matured greatly since I had seen her last, looking relaxed and confident in her yellow robes with her hair piled high in the traditional Daughter fashion. I realized the last time we'd seen each other had been just a few months ago in King Tyden's camp during my trial. It felt to me as though a year or more had passed since that day.

"Yes," Jin said in a calm voice. For just a moment, her eyes flashed with pride and I saw the excitable girl that I had known before shimmering in their depths. "I'm the youngest apprentice ever to don the yellow robes."

"And well deserved, I have no doubt," I said. "Your grandmother must be very proud."

"She is," Jin replied, composing herself again. She met my gaze. "The First Daughter has died, Hadrack, and my grandmother has been elected to take her place."

"I see," I said, nodding, not that surprised. The First Daughter had been ill well before Tyden's coronation. It was a wonder she had lasted this long. "Your grandmother will make an excellent First Daughter," I said. We sat there for a time, not saying anything as the sun slid behind several clouds, then reappeared, the rays gleaming off the White Tower. "Is this about Malo?" I finally asked, wondering why the subject had not been broached yet.

Jin blinked at me in surprise. "Malo? Do you know where he is?"

Now it was my turn to be surprised. "Don't you?" I asked.

Jin shook her head. "He hasn't been seen in weeks. Grandmother is beside herself with worry. There are six other House Agents who were with him that have gone missing, too."

I sat back in my chair, realizing that Jin didn't know anything about the codex, which meant neither did the House. "What did you do, Malo?" I muttered under my breath.

"What was that, Hadrack?" Jin asked.

I waved a hand. "Nothing. Nothing at all." Worrying about Malo and what he had done with the codex would have to wait. I had other issues at the moment. "So, Jin," I said. "Why have you come here?"

Jin folded her hands in her lap. "Your wife contacted me about your plans."

I felt my face tighten. "I'm not letting that little bastard live, Jin," I said. "I don't care what the House, you, or my wife have to say about it."

"I know that," Jin said, lifting a hand to soothe me. "I'm not asking you to let him live. But there is a complication."

"What complication?" I growled.

"The First Son is three days ride from here. He has learned that you hold Grindin, and from what I have been told, he is furious."

I cursed as I glanced up at the White Tower. Someone was watching us from the top window, though I couldn't tell which of the bastards it was. "Then I guess my plans have just been accelerated," I said.

"You can't fight them in your condition," Jin pointed out. "And even if you do and manage to win, your soul will be lost the moment you take Grindin's life."

"What am I supposed to do?" I raged, my anger spilling out from me. I put my hand on Jin's arm and shook it. "You were there in Corwick, too, Jinny! Grindin helped to kill your mother as well as my family. Every day he gets to breathe is an abomination. You of all people should see that."

Jin nodded solemnly as she put her hand over mine. "I do see that, Hadrack," she said gently. "That is the reason why I am here. I have a plan that will satisfy your vow of vengeance, as well as protect your soul. We will have to move fast before Son Oriell arrives, but it can be done."

I stared at Jin for a moment, overcome by the poise and determination on her face. "Tell me," I said.

The open wagon I rode in slowed, following the bumpy, barely-seen path that had once led to my farm. An elegant carriage with spoked wheels followed directly behind my wagon, then three more just like it, with men on horseback bringing up the rear. A man wearing a battered hat sat on a high bench high above me, and he turned to look down at me where I sat in my chair.

"Is this far enough, my lord?" he asked.

I shook my head. "A little farther," I said, searching the swaying grass with my eyes. Nothing was left to show a farmhouse had once stood here, not that I had expected there to be. It was almost a year ago the last time that I'd been in this place, and I could tell that little had changed since then. I had planned on returning once I became the Lord of Corwick, of course, but there always seemed to be something else to do that took my attention away. Maybe the truth was that I hadn't wanted to come back until I had something to offer Corwick's ghosts. I wasn't sure.

The sky above me was a startling blue, with no clouds to be seen for miles. A good day for death, I thought. I glanced to the west as the wagon shook and rattled beneath me, staring up at Patter's Bog while sunlight glinted off the white stones surrounding it. The bog looked just as dour and menacing as ever, I thought, and I couldn't help but smile, feeling strangely happy to see the dark, silent trees. We trundled along for a little while longer, then I grunted, satisfied as I instructed the driver to stop.

"It feels like we were just here," Baine said softly, as though afraid to break the stillness with his voice. He stood and stretched, then jumped from the wagon and dropped the rear gate.

"Are you sure you're going to be able to control yourself?" Jebido asked doubtfully as he started to untie the leather thongs holding my chair in place.

"Why wouldn't I?" I asked, staring at the spot where I believed my home had once stood. I thought I saw a gleam of white for just a moment as the grass danced and swayed. Perhaps I had only imagined it.

"Because you have a look on your face I don't like," Jebido grunted. He finished untying the lines keeping me secure, and then he jumped down to the ground before carefully rolling my chair backward to the edge of the wagon. Tyris and Putt approached, and together, they, along with Baine and Jebido, gingerly lifted me and lowered me to the ground. "Well?" Jebido said, pausing in front of me.

"I'll be fine, Jebido," I assured him.

"You better be," Jebido grumbled. He gestured to my leg. "Because Haverty will have my balls if anything happens to that."

"You're too old to need those balls, anyway," I said with a chuckle.

Jebido just glared at me, clearly not amused. I shifted my gaze away, gesturing to Niko, who held my crutches. The youth brought the crutches to me as Baine and Tyris yanked pins from beneath the planks of my chair, allowing the end pieces to swing downward on hinges. The two men helped me stand until I was secure on the crutches, then they stepped back.

I nodded to Jebido. "Find the bastard," I said. I lifted a finger off my crutch, pointing northwest. "I think he's over there."

Jebido, Baine, Tyris, and Niko spread out, searching the grass until Niko shouted in discovery. I grunted and began to move cautiously over the uneven ground as Putt walked ahead of me, beating back the grass for me the best that he could with his sword. I could hear people talking in hushed tones behind me as they exited the carriages, but I ignored them as I kept my focus on the ground and forged deeper into the field. Finally, sweating and out of breath, I reached Niko, where he stood over the remains of a man's body. There was little left to see other than a grinning skull, some scraps of cloth, and a gleaming ribcage burnt white from the sun. I guessed most of the other bones had been dragged off by scavengers. I could see teeth marks on several of the ribs and I smiled. Hervi Desh's last moments had not been pleasant.

I finally turned as my men spread out in a wide circle. The hushed whisperings had finally stopped as six priests, and six priestesses approached through the grass, with none daring to meet my eyes. They were not happy about being asked to witness this, I knew, but I was the Lord of Corwick and they lived on my lands, so they didn't have much choice in the matter. Berwin followed the priests and priestesses, and he herded them into a tight group fifty feet away to the south, where they would be safe. I took a deep breath, savoring the moment before finally I nodded to Jebido that I was ready. Niko and Putt went back to the carriages, drawing swords before opening the door to the third one in line. I heard Putt bark harshly into the interior, then watched as first the tiny form of Grindin stepped out, then the imposing bulk of Luper Nash.

"Move along," Putt said gruffly, giving Grindin a shove. The little man sobbed and almost fell, mumbling to himself. Niko started to shove Luper Nash as well, but the huge man just glowered back until Niko lowered his hand.

"It's not fair!" Grindin sobbed as Putt shoved him forward a second time. He was shirtless, wearing only thin trousers and black boots. The little man's torso was almost as white as Hervi Desh's bones, hairless and sickly looking. This won't last long, I thought. Luper Nash strode behind Grindin, his head held high, his massive arms and shoulders rippling with muscle. "Lord Hadrack, please!" Grindin cried, lifting his hands to me. "I swear to you, I'm a changed man." I just stared at him with hard eyes until Grindin sobbed in despair and looked away, snot dripping from his nose. He saw the priests and priestesses silently watching and he dropped to his knees, arms raised to them. "Please, you cannot allow this! You are of the House, the same as me! You cannot let them get away with this!"

Not one priest or priestess moved or said a word.

"Put the little bastard over there," I told Putt, pointing to a spot twenty feet west of the bones.

Putt grabbed Grindin by the back of his neck, ignoring the whines of protest as he forced the little man toward the place that I wanted. I glanced at Niko. "Over there," I said, gesturing twenty feet away to the east.

Luper Nash headed to the spot on his own, a contemptuous smile on his face, with Niko following warily behind him. Nash paused six feet from me as Baine and Tyris removed their bows and notched arrows.

"I have your word as a lord about this?" Luper Nash asked, looking calm and relaxed. He had good reason to feel that way, I knew.

I nodded. "You have it," I promised. I glanced at Grindin, who had fallen to his knees again. The apprentice was staring down at the grass, moaning softly to himself. "But I want him to suffer first."

Nash grunted his understanding, his face expressionless as I motioned for him to take his place to the east.

When Luper Nash was in position, I drew my sword, pausing to lift it hilt first so that the ruby eyes of Wolf's Head gleamed in the sunlight. "The sins committed here by these men will never be forgotten, nor can they be forgiven," I said, my voice flat and steady, though inside I could feel my emotions swirling. "The ghosts of Corwick demand retribution and blood, and that is what we are here today to give them." I motioned to the kneeling man, then to the glowering bulk of Nash. "One of these men will die at the hands of the other, paying for his crimes with his life. The victor will not be harmed by me or any of my men." I paused to stare at Luper Nash. "I swear this on my word as a lord, a husband, the son of a murdered father, and the brother of a murdered sister."

I put both hands on Wolf's Head and thrust the blade down between the gleaming ribs of Hervi Desh's remains, while to the west, Grindin muttered over and over, "It's not fair! It's not fair!" He was right. It wasn't. And I didn't feel a morsel of pity for the little bastard.

"On your feet," I growled in disgust at Grindin. "Stop your sniveling and act like a man." Grindin slowly stood, wiping the snot from his face with the back of his hand as he fixated his eyes on my sword thrust into the ground. "Remember," I said as I made my way toward where the priests and priestesses waited. "Only one of you will survive this. Wait for the horn before you move. Not a moment before."

Jebido, Niko, and Putt followed me, walking with drawn weapons as they watched the two men with pitiless eyes. Baine and Tyris moved twenty yards to the north and south with their bows. If the survivor tried to attack us with my sword, those two would cut him down before he got anywhere close.

I reached the priests and priestesses, ignoring their stern looks of disapproval as I turned to face the last two living members of the nine. "Prepare yourselves," I called out. "For soon, one of you will be a guest of The Father!" I closed my eyes then, saying a prayer of thanks to the gods—all three of them—before finally I nodded to Niko that I was ready.

The youth lifted a horn and blew on it once, the note sharp and strident in the silence of the fields. Grindin instantly burst forward, moving fast and with purpose, his tears forgotten now. The decisiveness and speed of the other man had clearly caught Luper Nash by surprise, and he cursed, dashing toward the sword, his great arms outstretched. I felt my heart leap in my throat, all my careful planning seeming for nothing as Grindin cried out in triumph, ripping the sword from the ground. Luper Nash bellowed, not pausing as Grindin swung Wolf's Head in a vicious arc. I heard the priests and priestesses gasping behind me as the big man dropped to the grass, rolling beneath Grindin's blade before he bounded to his feet and wrapped a great hand around the smaller man's throat. Nash started to shake Grindin like a doll until the sword finally slipped to the ground from the apprentice's numb fingers.

"Thank The Mother," I heard Jebido whisper beside me.

I felt relief wash over me, unconsciously leaning forward on my crutches as the men struggled, wishing it could be me over there. Grindin repeatedly struck at Luper Nash's chest with his fists, trying to break his hold, but the big man seemed like iron—implacable, merciless, and unyielding. I could hear Grindin choking, desperately trying to force air into his tortured lungs. I knew he would be dead in another moment.

"Nash!" I shouted in warning. The big man turned, his eyes burning. "Not yet," I said firmly.

Luper Nash grimaced, then he reluctantly released his grip as Grindin fell to his knees, gasping and coughing. Nash stooped to pick up Wolf's Head, and then he flung it end over end toward me, following it with a curse. The priests and priestess all shouted in alarm, scurrying aside, but I remained where I was as my sword landed point down in the ground three feet from me. I smiled. Even better.

Luper Nash held my gaze for a moment, and then he spat on the ground before focusing back on Grindin. He grabbed the little man by the stubby hair that had grown out since Malo had captured him. Grindin squealed as he was dragged to his feet, then Nash crashed a fist into his face, crushing his nose. Blood sprayed and Grindin staggered backward, both hands held to his shattered face. Nash came on, growling and slapping aside Grindin's frantic swings at his head. The big man grabbed Grindin by the neck again and held him as he pounded his fist into his stomach. Grindin bent over, clutching at himself as Nash grabbed one of his arms and twisted it behind his back. The little man howled, dropping to his knees as Luper Nash locked eyes with me a second time. I saw a question there and I nodded, not reacting to the sharp snap of bone or the screams of agony coming from Grindin.

It went on like that for long minutes, with the apprentice's howls echoing across the fields in waves of agony. I almost stopped Nash at one point, thinking that it was enough, but then I looked up at Patter's Bog and remembered sitting by the water huddled on a stone and weeping as similar howls filled the night. No one had said it was enough then, including Grindin Tasker, so I held my tongue and watched as Luper Nash tortured the little man to death.

Finally, when it was done, Nash dropped to his knees, panting in the grass. I moved to pick up my sword while Jebido and Putt ran forward and drew Nash's arms behind his back before slapping manacles on his wrists.

I turned to the horrified priests and priestesses. "You all witnessed what happened here today," I said. I pointed behind me. "Luper Nash killed Grindin Tasker, who was a Son-In-Waiting. His soul is now lost and he will burn for all eternity." I heard Nash snort behind me, knowing with the sins already on his conscience that he was hardly concerned about one more.

"But, you are responsible for this, Lord Hadrack," one of the Sons said to me timidly. "You forced those men to fight each other."

"I did no such thing," I said. I turned to Nash. "Did I force you to do this?"

The big man shook his head. "No, lord. Grindin and I have had a blood feud for many years. You were gracious enough to accommodate it."

"So you see," I said, turning back to the timid priest. "I was only mediating a dispute between enemies like any proper lord should."

"Well," the priest said doubtfully. "I'm not sure the First Son will see it that way."

I felt my features harden at the mention of Son Oriell and I fought to smooth them. "We can always take the matter to the king's court if it becomes an issue," I said. I gestured to the carriages. "For now, my men will escort you back to your villages. If the First Son has questions, I will summon you to offer your testimony as to what you witnessed here today."

Berwin and Niko led the grumbling priests and priestesses back to their carriages, and I waited impatiently for them to get settled inside. Finally, two of the carriages swung about, bumping along the trail of trampled grass that we had made on our way here. I waited until I was sure they were out of sight, then I slowly hobbled over to Luper Nash. The big man was on his feet by now, and Jebido kicked out one of his legs without warning, knocking him back to his knees.

"What is this?" Luper Nash growled. He looked at Jebido, who put a sword to his throat. Nash focused back on me. "You lying bastard!" he spat up at me. "You treacherous, lying shit. You promised you wouldn't kill me."

"I did," I said, nodding. I heard the door to the last carriage open, then close with a slam again. I smiled as a figure dressed in a hooded black robe quickly approached through the swaying grasses. "And I will keep my word to you."

"So, you're not just a bastard," Nash said in contempt. "You're a coward, too. A made-up lord who has to get one of his men to do his dirty work for him."

I grinned. "Wrong again," I said. I leaned down as far as I could on my crutches. "I promised you that neither I nor any of my men would kill you," I said. "And I will not break that promise." I slowly shifted to the right as the black-robed figure stepped in front of Nash. "But, I never said anything about her doing it," I whispered as Jin slowly removed the hood from her face.

Nash stared up at the girl in surprise, the look quickly turning to confusion. "I don't understand," he said.

"My mother's name was Meanda," Jin said, her voice thick with emotion. "She drew a knife from her robe and pressed the tip to Luper Nash's throat. "Hadrack wasn't the only one in Corwick that day, you bastard. I was only three years old, scared and frightened. But none of you cared."

"The little girl," Nash said in wonder. "The little girl in the white dress."

"That's right, you raping, murdering bastard!" Jin hissed as she shoved forward with the knife. Dark red blood shot outward in a spray, drenching the Daughter's hand, but she seemed oblivious to it. Her eyes were hard and cold as she watched Luper Nash gag, his tongue jutting out grotesquely. "The villagers called me Little Jinny," Jin whispered, her lips mere inches from Nash's face. "Tell that to the others down Below when you see them." Then Jin ripped the knife sideways, tearing out Nash's throat with a savage motion.

The big man fell then, flopping over on his side as Jebido and Tyris released him. Jin looked up at me, tears in her eyes as she dropped the knife into the grass.

"You did good," I said, feeling tears of my own start to flow as the girl hugged me and started to sob. "You did really good."

I stood over the graves of my father and sister, listening to the stream gurgling pleasantly as it wound its way through the forest. Birds sang from within the trees, and somewhere a squirrel scolded, its cries harsh and agitated before abruptly falling silent. The vow that I had pledged in this very spot so long ago had finally been fulfilled, and for the first time since I was a child, I was free to live my life without the need for vengeance. It was an invigorating thought. One that gave me overwhelming joy, coupled with a deep sadness that the connection I'd had to my father and Jeanna for all these years was now broken. The vow that I had sworn as a scared eight-year-old boy had been the link between the three of us, transcending everything, even the realms of life and death that bound the cosmos together. But now that it was complete, I knew the souls of my father and Jeanna were finally free of this world. And though I was saddened to lose that connection, I closed my eyes as I wept with joy for them, knowing even as I did that someday I would see them both again.

"Are you all right, Hadrack?" Shana asked.

I slowly opened my eyes, returning my gaze to the stream and the graves. My crutches lay discarded on the bank, unneeded at the moment, for I had Jin supporting me on my right side, while Shana did the same on my left. Shana had been in the carriage with Jin, though she had chosen not to get out with her. Not due to any faintness of heart, but more out of respect for the dead of Corwick. Shana felt the moment was for them, as well as Jin and me, and that her presence wasn't needed.

I pulled Shana close to me and kissed her gently on the head. "I have never been better, my love," I told her.

"I wish I could picture their faces," Jin said sadly from my other side as she stared downward at the two faint grass mounds where the graves sat. "But I don't remember much about that time in Corwick."

"How could you?" Shana asked. "You were only a small child."

"Just the same, from everything Hadrack has told me, they were people I wish that I had known."

"Thank you, Jin," I said. I kissed her as I had Shana. "They would have loved you just as much as I do."

We stood for a long time together, saying nothing, until finally Jin looked up at me. "I have to go, Hadrack. Son Oriell will arrive in the morning. I want to be rested and ready for him when he gets here."

I saw determination in her eyes and I smiled, knowing that Son Oriell had met his match in this fierce young woman. Jin had insisted on killing Luper Nash herself, despite her oath of purity to the House and my initial objections, resolving herself to spending time with The Father in penance for what she planned on doing. Luper Nash had been one of the men who had raped and killed her mother, she had told me, and justice for a life taken too soon needed to be served. I couldn't exactly argue with that statement, considering what I had done to the other members of the nine. As for how the gods might view things, well, I wasn't so certain now that Jin would ever see the flames. To me, if the gods Above, Below, and Beyond judged Jin harshly for ending a man like Nash's life today then, in my opinion, they were not only blind gods, they were fools as well.

"Are you two going to be all right on your own?" Jin asked, cutting into my thoughts. "Or should I send Jebido and Baine to help you get back?"

"We'll be fine," Shana and I said at the same moment.

We both laughed, and Jin smiled, bracing herself on my arm as she stood on her toes to kiss my cheek. "Then, I'll see you back at the castle."

Jin reached across and clasped Shana's arm affectionately, then she turned and walked away through the trees.

"She's going to make a fine First Daughter someday," Shana said. I looked at my wife, my eyebrows raised. "And why not?" Shana asked. She smiled playfully. "If they can make you a lord, why not her a First Daughter?"

I chuckled, then I grew serious as I realized there was still one thing left unsaid. "There is something else that I haven't told you," I said. "I don't know why I haven't yet."

"You promised me that it would never happen again," Shana said, her face clouding.

"This was long before I knew anything about the codex," I hurried to say. "So I haven't really broken that promise."

"What is it, Hadrack?" Shana asked with a sigh.

She put her head against my shoulder and I relaxed, knowing she wasn't actually upset with me. I stared down at where I knew my father's head lay, closing my eyes as I pictured him the last time that I had seen him alive. He had been so shattered then, so overcome with grief, believing that his children were dead. If only he had known that I was hiding safely in the bog, I thought with regret as I hugged my wife to me. I gestured to the grave. "My father was the son of Coltin Corwick," I said.

"What?" Shana gasped, lifting her head to stare at me in shock. "Surely you must be joking?"

I just smiled sadly. "I am not, my love. My father knew he was the son of a lord, yet he gladly lived the life of a peasant for the sake of his family." I told her everything that Daughter Gernet had told me then, and Shana listened in rapt wonder. When I was finally done, she just shook her head and pulled me down to kiss my lips.

"You poor man," she said when we broke the embrace. "All this time you have been a lord, born to one of the greatest families in the history of the kingdom, and you had no idea. Not that I care one wit either way what your bloodline really is. I have loved you unconditionally from the moment that I laid eyes on you, Hadrack, whether your name be Corwick or not. That will never change."

"Then you're not mad because I kept it from you?" I asked.

"Of course not," Shana said. "I understand the reasons why now." Her face suddenly clouded. "But you do realize what this means, don't you?" I just shook my head dumbly. "My father was Terain Raybold, Hadrack. Which means I am a Raybold, too." Shana stared at me, her face suddenly grim and serious. "We're enemies now." I gaped at her, then I slowly grinned in relief as Shana started to chuckle, a twinkle of amusement in her blue eyes. "Don't you want to be my enemy, my lord?" she asked coyly.

I felt a sudden desire come over me. "I would rather be something else," I said huskily, nuzzling at the exquisite lobe of her left ear.

"Then let's go home," Shana said, her eyes filled with promise. "Where we can work out our differences properly."

"A fine plan, my lady," I whispered into her ear. "We're well behind, after all. Einhard is already two ahead of me, and I am not going to lose to that smug bastard."

Shana drew back, looking up at me in confusion. "Ahead of you, how, my lord?"

"I'll show you tonight," I said with a wide grin.

And I did.

Epilogue

My grandfather is dying. Three of the kingdom's greatest physicians all agree on that. Each is widely respected and renowned for their skills, and each studied right here in Corwick at the famous Haverty Academy. But despite their assurances that Lord Hadrack will surely die within days, I do not believe this to be true. I am no physician, of course, nor do I pretend to be one. I am just a simple girl blessed to have been born into the Corwick family, with the beloved head of that family fighting now for every breath that he takes as I write this. And though I am aware that these great physicians look down their noses at me whenever I voice my doubts, I am utterly convinced that they are wrong and that I am right. But my certainty does not stem from any form of expertise or worldly knowledge such as those esteemed physicians possess, of course. No, nothing as impressive as that. It comes from somewhere deep inside me, where simple, blind faith in one of the greatest men this kingdom will ever know burns fiercely and refuses to be extinguished.

My grandfather will not die now, simply because he promised me that he would not. Not yet, anyway. That might not be sufficient for anyone else, but it is more than enough for me. He will live because he must live, as the last conversation we had three days ago before he fell unconscious proves.

"You look distraught, child," my grandfather had said to me.

I was sitting by his bed, tears rolling down my cheeks, his story of the final moments of the nine finally finished. It was a lovely day for a change, with the snows finally beginning their reluctant retreat beneath a warm spring sun. I could hear birds singing and children laughing outside, yet I wanted to be nowhere else but in this room with my grandfather. I'd had little knowledge of the story he had told me these past months, and I could only weep for the grandmother that I had never known and for the heart-broken man lying beside me. The pain and anguish, so evident in his eyes whenever he spoke of Lady Shana, never failed to grip my heart with sorrow. Few of us are lucky enough to feel such love for another person the way that I knew my grandfather still did for Shana Corwick.

"Do not cry, so, child," Lord Hadrack said to me gently. He reached to take my hand, his own shaking, thin and white. "This all happened many, many years ago to people who have been long dead. Do not weep for them, my sweet Lillia. Rejoice in who they were and all the great things that they accomplished. Some people in this world just exist, child. Simply happy to eat, shit and sleep their way through life." My grandfather released my hand, settling back into the bedclothes as he stared upward, his eyes far away. "But not them." He sighed then and I could see tears in his eyes now, despite his words about my own. "Jebido, Baine, Fitz, Einhard, and Alesia, and even that bastard Malo—they were all so alive!" He looked at me, pain and loss etched on his face. "And of course, my darling wife," he said, so low I almost missed it. "She was life itself, wrapped in warmth and love, so beautiful, kind, and good. The gods must have rejoiced on the day they made her, child, for surely they must have known that perfection had been achieved." He choked then, fighting to breathe as I stood up in alarm. "It's nothing," my grandfather gasped. He closed his eyes for a long time and I thought that he had fallen asleep. But then he reopened them, fixing his gaze unwaveringly on me. "But enough of all that. I imagine you have some questions for me?"

"Yes, lord," I replied. "Many of them. But they can wait. You need your rest."

"Nonsense," Lord Hadrack snorted, waving a hand. "I've never felt better in my life." He grinned at me then, both of us accepting the lie. My grandfather glanced behind me toward the window. "But I think you need to go outside for a while first. The day looks welcoming after such a harsh winter. You have been cooped up in this stuffy room with me for far too long, child. A little sunlight will do you good."

"Very well, my lord," I reluctantly agreed, knowing by the familiar, set look on my grandfather's face that refusing was not an option. "Just answer two questions for me, and then I promise I will go. And when I return, I'll bring some of that spiced custard with me that you like so much. Is it a bargain?"

"You are a shrewd one," Lord Hadrack said, smiling at me. "You know I can't resist a pretty girl, much less custard." He waved a hand. "I will give you your two questions, child, and then you go and get some fresh air for at least an hour."

"Agreed," I said. I sat back down then, composing my thoughts. Finally, I asked, "What happened to Malo and the codex, my lord?"

My grandfather shrugged as he looked down at his hands. "The revelations inside turned out to be too much for him to bear. Malo might have been a strong man on the outside, but inside it seemed he was less so. He and the House Agents with him renounced their vow of service to the House and disappeared with the codex." My grandfather grimaced and motioned toward the fireplace and the weapons hanging above it. "I received Malo's short sword, Boar's Tooth, by messenger several weeks after Grindin and Luper Nash died."

"Why, my lord?" I asked, not understanding.

"I thought at first that it was Malo's way of thanking me for not telling Daughter Gernet about the codex," Lord Hadrack said. He glanced sideways at me. "Malo foolishly believed that the House would stay as it was if he disappeared with the codex. But it wasn't long before I realized the sword wasn't a thank you at all. It was actually Malo's way of telling me to remain silent, or else." My grandfather chuckled. "I've kept it all these years to remind me what a bastard he was."

"But the House did not stay the way that it was anyway," I said, knowing that it was true.

"No," Lord Hadrack replied with a sigh. "Sadly, it did not. Though it would be some years later before anyone other than a select few finally learned the truth."

"Did you have something to do with that, my lord?" I asked. My grandfather merely nodded his head, his eyelids drooping as his chin slowly lowered to his chest. I waited for a time, then I stood once more and started to make my way carefully and quietly across the room.

"You still have one more question, child," Lord Hadrack called drowsily from behind me.

I turned. "It can wait, my lord."

"Don't be silly," my grandfather said, blinking his eyes as he tried to focus on me. "Ask your question so that I can sleep." I stepped closer to the bed, desperate to know yet reluctant to ask. "Out with it, child," Lord Hadrack finally scolded. "Whatever it is, it can't be worth scrunching your face up like that."

I took a deep breath, then hurried to say the words before I lost my courage. "How did my grandmother die?" My grandfather lay still for a moment, his grey-blue eyes ringed by red fixed on mine as I saw sudden pain crease his features. "I am so sorry, my lord," I said, my heart racing. "It's just that you have never spoken of it, ever. Not even to Uncle Hughe or anyone else. No one seems to know, or if they do, they won't tell me." I hung my head, regretting speaking my thoughts now. "I should not have asked you."

"It's all right, child," my grandfather said kindly. He took a deep breath, pausing to cough twice before he nodded to me. "But it is a question that deserves a proper response, one that will take many days. Go outside now and feel the sun on your skin. I will tell you all that you wish to know on your return." My grandfather must have seen the look of indecision on my face, for he held out his hand as I hurried around the bed to take it. "Do not fear, my child," he said, gently patting my hand. "I have planned on telling you this part of my life all along. You and every other Corwick deserve to know the truth before I die." Lord Hadrack chuckled when he saw my expression. "Do not worry so much. I promise I have no plans on leaving this world before you know the truth. So go now and enjoy yourself." He smiled then, a look of mischief crossing his features that gave me a glimpse of the handsome, charming man he must have once been. "And don't forget my custard, or I'll tan your backside."

"I won't," I promised as I gently lowered his hand to the bed. I leaned forward and kissed his forehead. "I will be back in an hour, Grandfather, and then we can talk some more."

"An hour," Lord Hadrack agreed, his eyelids drooping once again.

I had paused in the doorway on my way out, staring back at the silent figure on the bed, marveling at the life he had lived and the wondrous things that he had accomplished in that life. Then I had left to enjoy the sunshine, expecting that in an hour, I would finally learn the mystery of Shana Corwick's death. But of course, by the time I returned with his custard, Lord Hadrack lay unconscious, with the truth about my grandmother still locked out of reach inside his head.

I sit now over this paper brooding, with nothing left to write. All I can do is stare at Lord Hadrack's still form and pray that he will awaken to continue his story. Would his pledge to me be enough to keep him in this world for a time longer, or were the three physicians right and he really was going to die?

Only the gods Above, Below, and Beyond knew for certain, and they weren't saying.

Lillia Corwick

THE END

Author's Note

Thank you, once again, dear reader, for your overwhelming support of this series. Had someone told me two years ago when I first sat down to write The Nine that it would be this successful, I would have laughed and called them crazy. I owe a great deal of that success to my darling wife, who has supported me without hesitation from the first word I typed, though I know she is looking forward to getting a break from tiptoeing around the house all day while I pluck away at my laptop. It took me seven months to write The Wolf on the Run, and I freely admit I struggled with the plot at times. This final book flowed almost effortlessly for some reason, and I completed it in just four months. I can only hope future books will be just as easy and fun to write as this one was.

Speaking of future books, I will be taking a break from this series for a while. I have other books I am eager to try, and I feel it's time to get out of Hadrack's head—or for him to get out of mine, I'm not sure which it is. I originally envisioned only four books in this series, but even though the nine are all dead, the truth is I have come to love these characters and cannot imagine never writing about them again. As you probably guessed by the epilogue, Hadrack's story and troubles are far from over. The Wolf of Corwick will ride again soon!

All the best

Terry Cloutier
March 2021

By Terry Cloutier

The Wolf of Corwick Castle Series

The Nine (2019)
The Wolf At Large (2020)
The Wolf On The Run (2020)
The Wolf At War (2021)

The Zone War Series

The Demon Inside (2008)
The Balance Of Power (2010)

Novella
Peter Pickler and the Cat That Talked Back

Printed in Great Britain
by Amazon